£6
1sL

Polar City Nightmare

Polar City Nightmare

Katharine Kerr
and
Kate Daniel

VICTOR GOLLANCZ
LONDON

The right of Katharine Kerr and Kate Daniel to be identified as the
authors of this work has been asserted by them in accordance
with the Copyright, Designs and Patents Act 1988.

This edition published in Great Britain in 2000 by
Victor Gollancz
An imprint of Orion Books Ltd
Orion House, 5 Upper St Martin's Lane, London, WC2H 9EA

To receive information on the Millennium list, e-mail us at:
smy@orionbooks.co.uk

A CIP catalogue record for this book
is available from the British Library

Printed and bound in Great Britain by
Clays Ltd, St Ives plc

Finally, for Bill.

Acknowledgments

Many people helped in the writing of this book. I wish to thank some of them here.

Jenn St. John and Katherine Lawrence helped with suggestions, plotting sessions, and encouragement, and put up with me when I was obsessing about the book. My husband Bill put up with me at even closer range, and as always served as my first reader.

Many thanks to Chris Lyons and Joe Palmer, computer wizards, who rescued me when a crash threatened the first draft.

And special thanks go to the original Alison Glover, Scossie (that's Scots-Aussie), physicist, friend, and beta-reader extraordinaire, who made sure I kept the baseball to an understandable level and who served as the model for the *Freebird's* pilot.

And finally, my thanks to Katharine Kerr for inventing this world and inviting me to come play.

– Kate Daniel

Author's Note

With most science fiction, the readers may safely assume that all the human characters are white unless the author says otherwise. In Polar City, the situation is exactly the reverse.

I'd also like to make it clear that this is an old-fashioned collaboration. Kate Daniel and I shared the writing and the planning both.

– Katharine Kerr

Chapter One

When the sun goes down on Polar City, darkness never really falls. The aurora borealis merely takes over the sky. Blue and gold sheets of light twist and sway, red lightning flashes, and now and again a silver wash shines like some vast moon. Down on the streets and the movebelts, among the maglev lights and the three-dee holoadverts, the citizens hurry along on errands or go about their night's work. The only sentients who bother to look up and gawk are Outworlders, come for the only natural wonder that the planet Hagar offers.

Tonight, however, Polar City itself has another show going on. Up in the office tower that houses the Polar City police force, comm operator Raul Ybarra sits at a green comp desk in a tiny green cubicle; his low-level AI links him into the city's communication network. He keeps an eye on the door, because he's brought a piece of technology to work that could get him fired: an earpiece radio. With his fingers he keeps combing his thick black hair over the offending bulge, but anyone who got close would hear the very faint but unmistakable sound of a crowd roaring at a baseball game. Fortunately for Ybarra, half the police force has found its own ways of listening in, and everyone leaves each other alone.

Unfortunately, citizens keep calling the police, play-off game or no game. As the Polar City Bears take the field for the eighth inning, the comm on Ybarra's desk shrieks. Swearing he flicks the button and hears a flood of accented Merrkan.

'All right, repeat the name, please.' He puts his mike close to his mouth and speaks carefully to enter the data on his comp. 'Gri . . . Nerosi. Got it. Species?' *In his ear the radio murmurs that the Bears' second baseman is coming up to bat.* 'No, I no can tell he be a carli just by the name! Sides, even if I could, I gotta ask the questions on the form.' He shifts the wad of chewing spice in his mouth. 'Date of birth or hatchday?' *The second baseman swings through the first pitch. Jeezus, Wallace, don't strike out!* 'Yeah, yeah, I know carlis don't lay eggs. Gimme a break. Address where last seen?'

The voice on the comm drones on. Ybarra repeats the keywords and fills in the form, but in his ear the seductive radio speaks: *Two strikes and – oh god it's a hit! Wallace drives in the tying run. If nothing else, it's extra innings for the Bears and they'll win this one yet.* Ybarra never quite notices when the voice on his comm disappears. He hits the 'file' button and sends the missing-person report off to routine channels, then settles in to listen to the game.

'Good for you, Red! Goddamn, some kind of second baseman, all right!'

Chief of Police Albert Bates realizes that he's spoken aloud and looks around to reassure himself that yes, he's alone in his cluttered little office. As the chief he has privileges; his comp unit displays the ball game blatantly on screen in a corner iris, overlaying a report on the current state of interstellar relations. When the game stops to let the opposing team bring in a new pitcher, Bates gets up to stretch and strides over to the plate-glass window that runs the length of the room. He can see the gaudy sky between the tall buildings around Police Tower.

Colour from the fiery sky overhead washes over him, gleaming on his blue-black skin. He finds himself thinking of Leona, his ex-wife, who fled this low-tech desert world not long after he'd arrived here to take the chief's job. He hopes she's well, wherever she is, somewhere beyond the electric sky.

'Hey, Chief!' his comp unit says. 'Game back on.'

The moment is over. He turns away from the window. Rather than sit, he stands near his desk and leans on the chair back to watch. Next Bears' batter up – the relief pitcher hangs a curve ball. Home run, and Bears are back in the lead.

'All they got to do is hold on,' Bates whispers. 'Power that display down, and let me just have a voice feed.'

'Yes, sir,' the comp says.

The background report, after all, means more than the game over the long run. While the politics of the Mapped Sector lie beyond

Bates's sphere of operations, they constantly impact upon Polar City, home for two great embassies, those of the Coreward Alliance and the Instellar Confederation. These multi-star-system entities surround and squeeze in the human-dominated Republic, a handful of mostly poor planets in a handful of star systems. The 'Lies and the Cons, as the citizens of the Republic call them, come to Polar City to spy upon each other and cause trouble for the locals, or so the locals think of it. Bates studies the report very carefully indeed, but when the Bears finally win he finds himself yelling and cheering along with everyone else in the building. On a sudden impulse he gets up and throws open the window. Sure enough, he can hear the entire city screaming its head off.

On the big wall screen for the three-dee, a holocaster, voice hoarse with excitement, is rehashing the game in tedious detail. Bobbie Lacey, sitting at her royal blue comp desk, keeps her eyes and her attention fixed instead on the small screen in front of her while she inputs data the old-fashioned way. Like all comp units, hers responds to voice input, but she prefers typing on a keyboard when someone's in her living room. At the moment Jack Mulligan sprawls on the grey foam cube sofa nearby, watching the post-game show. While the comp chews its data, she leans back and considers him. Eight months of living together have not spoiled her pleasure in the sight. Long and lanky, and pale even for a Blanco with his straw-coloured hair and grey eyes, Mulligan's a good-looking man. He's also one of the few people Lacey knows who looks young because he is young, in his mid-twenties in fact. Although the rejuv drugs keep her looking no older, she's lived a good half-century of official calendar years, and so have most of her friends. Jack yawns and shoves his hair back from his face with one hand. His shaggy hair needs cutting again. Somehow Mulligan's hair always seems to need cutting.

In privacy mode Buddy, the AI who runs her comp, beeps for attention rather than speaking, and she begins typing again. The keyboard and Kangolan, an obscure language she's programmed into the unit, both help protect her data, but Buddy himself provides the best insurance with his security sub-routines. Together they publicly run A to Z Enterprises, the firm she inherited from her uncle, growing vegetables, fruits, and a few incredibly expensive flowers for the private market to supplement her small pension from the Navy. Most of her income, though, comes from brokering information, garnered from a wide variety of sources. A sentient who gained access to Buddy's databanks could sell the contents for enough cold cash to tempt anyone into thievery – if she gave anyone the chance.

'Hey, Bobbie?' Mulligan says with a wave at the screen. 'You no interested?'

'It's only the post-game show, amigo. Besides, Montoya's voice gets on my nerves.'

'But they gonna do it. The Bears gonna go all the way.' He sounds oddly mournful about this prediction. 'This here's a great moment for Polar City.'

With an impatient shake of her head, Lacey clears the screen. She'll finish the report for Señor Chang later. She gets up, walks over to the couch, and shoves his feet aside to make room for herself. She knows the signs: Mulligan is mourning again for the professional baseball career that he might have had. On his left cheek, just in front of his ear, he wears a tattoo, a bright red letter P. While the government of the Republic tolerates psychics, it insists on making sure that the other citizens know who they are. It also makes sure that none of them play pro sports. Lacey braces herself for a story she's heard too many times.

'Jeez, y'know?' Mulligan says. 'It kinda hurts, watching this.'

'I figured. Maybe you should turn it off.'

Mulligan shrugs. 'I keep thinking, like, how great it would be to be there, y'know? In the locker room, celebrating the season. I coulda been in the majors. If . . .'

'Yeah. I know.'

'Ruined my whole damn life—' He breaks off. With a deep sigh he sits up and turns to look at her.

She waits.

'Ah what the hell,' Mulligan says at last. 'At least I got you.'

'Second best but better'n nada?'

'Hey!' He catches one of her hands in both of his. His long, slender fingers twine tightly through hers. 'No what I meant.'

'Yeah?'

'Yeah.' He pulls her close and kisses her. 'Why dunt we just turn off this damn three-dee?'

The Bears' locker rooms stink of sweat and steam, tempered a bit with cosmetics and perfume: a very human smell, suitable for baseball, a human-dominated sport, but Rosa 'Red' Wallace, second baseman and the only sentient still there to notice it, decides she can smell victory in the air as well. Tonight's win has opened her usually sensible mind to flights of fancy. The small white room, lined with blue metal lockers, has fallen silent, but a clatter and whine from the men's locker room next door reminds her that the cleaning-bot will come charging in any minute. She'd better get done before it sweeps her out with the trash and the dirty uniforms heaped on the tiled floor.

Rosa always leaves the locker room last, no matter where the Bears play – the team swears this habit of hers brings them good luck. After every game she sits in the locker room and reviews the action in her mind, but tonight she can't seem to concentrate. In twenty-one years of playing pro ball, she's never played in the Galactic Series.

'But we just one game away,' she whispers. 'Just one. I maybe make it yet.'

Although the rejuv drugs have left her looking like a rookie except for a few faint lines around her green eyes, Rosa is forty-three years old. Thanks to the rejuv, she plays a young game, too, but her age concerns her, as it does the entire team. Athletes used to retire young before rejuv was invented, but now? The thought of retiring while she can still play, simply to make way for someone younger, hurts. Rosa forces it away and stands up, shoving her hands into the pockets of her blue shorts. Something else is bothering her, she realizes, a sound of some sort. Dripping water? Yes, someone left the shower running again, damn their hide. She finds the offending tap and turns it off like a good water-thrifty citizen of Hagar, but when she comes out of the showers her unease comes with her. She pauses, listens, and finally identifies the nagging noise. From beyond the locker room she's hearing footsteps. In a distant passageway someone keeps walking back and forth; they pause, then trot a few steps, pause, and walk again, over and over.

'What the hell?' Rosa runs her fingers through her curly red hair and decides it's dry enough.

She leaves the locker room proper. The tiny lobby, where holocasters hold pre-game and post-game interviews, stands empty with its door wide open. Since she can hear the footsteps even more clearly now, she steps out into the corridor beyond. The grey plastocrete passage leads to the stands, and there's no reason for anyone to be there this time of night. The gate to the stadium, normally kept locked, stands wide open and allows a view of the sky. Streamers of blue and gold light flicker on the wall opposite. On the top step she sees someone, a human male, walking back and forth. It's Yosef Mbaye, she realizes, one of the Bears' best pitchers. Not only does Rosa like the kid, but he's scheduled to start tomorrow's game, which means his welfare is her welfare. Back in the shadows by the door to the locker room, she hesitates, wondering what in hell he's up to.

She opens her mouth to ask him, but he leaves the steps and heads toward her. Not that he sees her – his eyes seem to stare at the night as he strides by. He stops about a dozen steps beyond, then turns, squaring his shoulders the way he does when facing a tough batter. He takes a deep breath – Rosa can hear it clearly – and leans forward as if ready to deliver his best fastball. She speaks just as he darts forward.

'Hey, whatcha doing?'

The surprise throws him off balance so badly that he nearly falls. He jerks around, sees her, yelps aloud, and takes off running. Rosa snarls a curse and goes after him. Yosef has a head start and longer legs, but Rosa can outsprint any man on the team. She overtakes him and grabs his arm in one hand and his shirt in the other. Right at the stairs she hauls him around. For a moment they teeter on the top step of a long hard fall down to the plastocrete landing below.

'Get back!' Rosa yells. 'Now!' With a lurch she yanks him to safety and staggers after him. 'You dunt want to do that, man. Gonna hurt real bad, you fall down them steps.'

Yosef pulls free of her grasp. For a moment he stands there shaking and staring at the floor, then looks up, his eyes snapping. 'Mind your own business, Red, okay? What the hell are you still here for?'

'I could ask you that. Mind my own business? Up yours, pal. That game damn well is my business. We need you on the field, not stuck in Polar City General.'

'You don't know anything about it.'

'Yeah, I know I dunt. How about you tell me?'

He runs both hands through his tight-curled black hair and stares down at the plastocrete flooring. Even in the dim light she can see him pouting like a child.

'Yeah, well, whatever it is,' Rosa says at last, 'you better go home and sleep it off. Gonna be a big night tomorrow.' It might be the pressure, she realizes. Their entire season hangs on the game he's pitching tomorrow. 'C'mon, I gonna take you home.'

When she turns to go, he follows, much to her relief. In a sullen silence he trails after as she goes to the locker room to retrieve her carrysack, but at the door he balks.

'I can't go in there,' he says.

'The hell I'm leaving you out here alone.'

'It's the female side.'

'Oh, right. You come from one of those fundi planets. Hey, I be the only female left in it, and I'm dressed. Come on.'

Although he follows her in, he stares firmly at the floor until she's done packing her sack. He barely looks up as they leave.

Yosef says nothing, in fact, until they've left the stadium. Outside, plastophalt parking lots spread out from the huge stone stadium like seas around a deserted ship. The rainbow aurora overhead washes the grey ground with dull pastels and turns the white stripes that mark the spaces into gaudy patterns. In the players' private lot Rosa's green skimmer sits all alone. Beyond it, on the far side of the lot, runs a city street, but nothing moves, neither cab nor skimmer, not as far as Rosa can see in either direction. The fans have long since gone home. They cross the lot together, picking their way through broken glass and long moraines of trash. Rosa lays a hand on Yosef's arm to steer him toward her car, but he pulls away.

'I'm okay now.' But he doesn't look her in the face. 'Uh, I can catch a cab, like I always do. You don't have to baby-sit me.'

'Yeah? But you always leave earlier'n this, too. No gonna be many cabs this time of night. I dunt mind dropping you off.'

'Yeah, sure I'm sure.' As he speaks, Yosef sidles away from her and heads stiff-legged toward the street.

Rosa overtakes him in three long steps and grabs his arm, hard this time. 'Lemme wait with you. That way, no cab comes, you dunt have to stand here all day.'

When he tries to pull away, she digs her fingers in.

'Hey, not my throwing arm, man!' Yosef snaps.

'Now you thinking. I like that.'

When Rosa switches her grip to the other arm he scowls, but he keeps his mouth shut. They wait, then wait some more. Overhead the lightshow of the aurora starts to fade over the circular walls of the stadium. The light standards that edge the rim wink out one by one. She turns toward the east and sees the dirty pink stain of dawn. With the first light traffic begins to pick up. A few skimmers, a couple of trucks, whizz by, and finally she sees the distinctive orange sphere of a robocab.

'Your lucky day, man.' Rosa lets go of his arm to hail the cab.

Yosef darts forward, dodges her grab, and runs out into the street. A skimmer on the other side of the cab swerves just in time. Rosa drops her sack and chases after Yosef, but the blast of compressed air from the skimmer nearly knocks her down. She catches a glimpse of the skimmer's lizzie driver, beak open in outrage as he waves a fist at them. On its way to the kerb, the robocab brakes with a squeal and heels over as it avoids both the skimmer and Yosef. Barely. Another skimmer is coming; the horn bleats like a hysterical sheep. Rosa grabs Yosef's shirt in both hands and pulls him out of the way. Together they stagger back to the kerb and safety.

Rosa feels herself shaking from adrenaline and shock. Yosef drops to his knees and covers his face with his hands; for a moment she thinks he's going to cry.

'Jeez! You loco, man?' Rosa snarls. 'You end up under that cab's fans, and you in the hospital for months! And sued by the damn cab company, too.'

He looks up, tries to speak, then merely shrugs. His dark face has turned an ashy grey.

'I mean, jeezchrise!' Rosa goes on. 'What you try to do, maim yourself?'

His eyes widen, and he starts shaking again. All at once Rosa sees the truth: yes indeed, hurting himself is exactly what he's been trying to do.

'Oh get up!' Rosa snaps. 'You coming with me, man.'

This time he doesn't argue.

The sight of the skimmer, a jade-green Jaguar with real leather upholstery, seems to soothe Yosef. He smiles, strokes the sleek enamel hood, touches the chrome striping with an admiring finger, then climbs into the passenger seat. Once she's got her safety belt on and the door locked, Rosa faces the problem of what to do with him. Long habit dismisses calling the police; Rosa grew up in the white ghetto of Polar City, Porttown, where even the most law-abiding sentients see the police as shakedown artists at best, enemies at worst. When she presses her thumb on the ID plate, the skimmer powers up with a soft hum. The control panel flashes.

'Enter co-ordinates,' says a soft voice.

'Not yet,' Rosa says. 'Wait mode.'

The light on the panel dims to a soft yellow glow. Rosa turns so she can see Yosef's face.

'What in Allah's name be eating you, anyway?' she asks him. 'You trying to kill yourself?'

'No. Not that.' The fear in his voice convinces her he's telling the truth.

'Just sort of break yourself up a little, huh? Like maybe so you can't pitch tomorrow?'

With a jerk of his head he twists against the seat belt and stares out the side window. Although Rosa rarely uses the child safety locks on the Jag, she clicks them on now and for all four doors. To give herself time to think, she sets the controls for manual and pulls out onto the road. Overhead the aurora fades to occasional drifts of colour off on the western horizon. The traffic is running heavy with the shift change from the factories that surround the stadium. Skimmers, robocabs, the occasional long bus: they all carry the more prosperous managers and supervisors home at the end of the work night. Ordinary workers take the Metro, tunnelled deep beneath the road.

While she thinks, Rosa heads south. The stadium complex gives way to clusters of low white buildings, wound round with pipes and dotted with narrow towers, where food technicians transform soy proteins into edibles or chemical workers turn Hagar's mineral-rich sands into plasto in all its infinite variety. She can see The Ring ahead, rising on two-storey high pylons, a freeway exchange that circles the entire city like an enormous grey ribbon. A few blocks farther on, like a roller coaster, the Metro breaks out to the upper air and runs on elevated rails slung under The Ring itself.

At the first on-ramp Rosa finds, she guides the skimmer onto the six-lane roadbed. Once they've merged into the fast lane, she switches the skimmer to autopilot. As long as they keep circling, Yosef won't be jumping out, and she can wait for inspiration.

Unfortunately she doesn't know Mbaye very well. New to the Bears this season, he keeps to himself, a loner because he's shy rather than stand-offish. She knows that he has no close friends on the team. She has a vague memory of meeting his wife once, a very young woman from the same isolated planet, whose religion seems to have left her perpetually terrified. Rosa can guess how much help she'd be. As The Ring carries them yet once again toward the exit for the baseball stadium, inspiration finally strikes.

'Hey, I got it!' Rosa says. 'Yosef, you ever hear of Aunt Lucy?'

'Sure, everyone knows about Aunt Lucy. I even met her once.'

'Swell. That's where we gonna go.'

'Say what? How far from here—?'

'A good long way. Sorry bout that.'

'But I've got to call my wife, let her know where I am. Before she calls los verdes on me.'

'Your wife calls the cops if you get home late? Shee-it, man, she got you on a leash or something?'

At the familiar tease he manages a watery smile.

'You can call from Aunt Lucy's,' Rosa goes on. 'I ain't stopping this skimmer till we get there.'

'Whatever.' Yosef slumps down, a huddle of misery. Rosa switches the skimmer back on manual and begins merging toward the exit lane.

Out in the jumble of warehouses and light industry that stands between the stadium and the city proper, crossing a street means adventure. Some sentients enjoy hurling themselves into the arms of Luck by dashing across in the middle of the long blocks, but not the woman who hovers at the corner of 22nd street. As she waits for the signal, she keeps a wary eye on the river of traffic zooming by. Few of the trucks catch her attention, but she does turn her head to admire a jade-green skimmer sparkling with chrome. The light changes. She trots across the street to the red archway that marks the mouth of a Metro station.

As she glides down the escalator, she opens her purse and takes out her MetroPass card. As she hoped, the station is deserted now that the factory shifts have finished changing. A sleek silver train waits at the tiled platform with its doors open. She finds an empty car, stale with the scent of old maroon upholstery, and takes a seat at the back. Good. No one has seen her get on. Were anyone there to see, they might well wonder what such a respectable-looking woman was doing out at this time of day.

With a satisfied little sigh, she tugs and smooths her yellow synthosilk sari to maximize modesty, then pats her hair, dressed in a single black braid, to smooth it as well. Her respectability in this setting is the only remarkable thing about her. Her brown skin, brown eyes and bland, unremarkable features would pass unnoticed in any crowd, as would her jewellery. A single delicate nose stud catches the light with a flash of genuine ruby.

Sarojini Ranjit knows how out of place she looks. She hopes to minimize her discrepancy by taking this alternate route. Normally she would have reached home by now, but the card game ran late. Though some would see taking the long way round as an excess of caution, she believes with a near-religious fervour that caution always pays. It certainly has made her a successful gambler – and an invisible one. Few expect a pro card sharp to look like a decent woman of good family.

With a jerk and a long hiss of compressed air, the train starts. Sarojini folds her hands in her lap and arranges her face in a pleasantly neutral expression. It feels good to relax, to let her body sway with the train as it skims through the tunnels. Even though she stayed later than usual, she reaped small profit from the game tonight because her favourite pigeon never showed up. While she did not

11

miss Gri Nerosi's annoying habit of growling under his breath all through the game, she wonders what his absence might mean to her partner's plans. His little game within a game has begun to bother her. While she never feels guilt about taking money from the pigeons, there are safe ways of doing it and then there are the other ways.

The Metro bursts out of the tunnel to sunlight; they have reached the open-air tracks beneath The Ring. Sarojini turns in her seat and looks out the window at the tall Police Tower, a sight that deepens her unease. With a roar, the train dips and hurls itself into the darkness of another tunnel. In a few minutes they are gliding beneath the houses and apartment blocks of the city's middle-class neighbour-hoods. Since she's nearly home, Sarojini leans forward to look at the comp screen on the back of the seat in front of her. Yes, there's the entry for Murghi Mahal; she taps it once with a manicured finger to request the train to stop.

The name for this part of town, Murghi Mahal, started life as an insult: Chicken Palace, it means in broken Hindi, a sneer at the immigrants from a dying India who brought their precious birds and spice plants with them in the cold berth ships. Before long those immigrants had turned the joke against the jokesters. Along with the livestock they brought a penchant for hard work and the accumulated wisdom of five thousand years' worth of civilization. These days the Mahal sports broad streets lined with palm trees cloned from Old Earth stock. From the Metro station Sarojini rides a grav platform up to the middle of a public park, planted with real grass kept alive with a fortune's worth of water. Under nodding trees sit pale pink benches; white stones cobble the footpaths.

With the sun climbing in the sky, Sarojini has no time to admire the flowerbeds. She pulls the loose end of her sari over her head to shield it from the sun and sets out, walking fast, for her apartment and its comm unit. She needs to talk to her partner about the night past. If he insists on this deal, she may need to find another partner. She prefers to leave his kind of games to those willing to risk the stakes. Cards hold enough excitement for her.

Once the sun rises clear of the horizon, Chief Bates's window darkens to a translucent grey that blocks most of the red giant's visible wavelengths. Through this polarized murk he sees a ghost sun rise behind a skyline reduced to pure geometry. Bates yawns and considers calling the cafeteria for coffee, then gets himself a drink of water instead from his private office water cooler, another of his perks. He's going home in a few minutes. For once he hopes to get a good day's sleep.

He yawns again, then seats himself in front of his comp and calls up a summary of the night's action. Nothing major has gone down, only the usual muggings and break-ins, plus one human spacer found dead in an alley in the Outworld Bazaar, the honky-tonk section of Porttown. The death will probably prove self-inflicted, because the preliminary autopsy report shows an amazing combination of drugs and booze in the corpse's system. As nights go in Polar City, this one's gone quietly.

He says as much to the sergeant who comes in a few minutes later, carrying a clipboard to get Bates's initials on the daytime duty roster. Maddock grins. 'Maybe everyone, they were so busy watching the game they forgot to get into trouble.'

'That'll be the day,' Bates says. 'Though I dunno, it's as likely a reason as any.'

'Sports mean a lot here, Chief. It's not just us, either. All the lizzies I know are rooting for a championship as hard as anybody. Too damn bad they dunt got the reflexes to play.'

'I thought it was their joints. Too stiff or something.'

'Something.' Maddock shrugs.

'It'll be the first championship in years, if we get it.' Bates pauses, struck by a sudden guilt. He has a ticket to the game tomorrow. He's been planning on calling in sick for the first time in his entire stint as Chief of Police. His men, however, lack that luxury. 'Tell you what, Maddock. Have one of the techs rig up a view screen in the squad room for the game. Anyone on duty with a spare couple of seconds can step in for a look.'

'Jeez, Chief, thanks! I'll do that for sure.'

'Hey, it no be much of a favour. The minute that game ends, I want everyone on duty to hit the streets. Win or lose, there could be big trouble in Porttown. We better have a full roster. Get hold of anyone who wants to work overtime, and if no one does make 'em. Double squads.'

13

Maddock nods and writes a note on the clipboard, a digital pad linked to main comp by infrared.

'Riot gear, Chief?'

'Not at first. Let's no start what we want to stop. But they better carry it in the squad cars with them.'

Maddock makes another note, then yawns. Bates clenches his own jaw against an echo.

'Bout time to call it a day,' the chief says. 'You too, Sarge.'

'You bet. I – ah shit! What's this?'

The corner of the clipboard flashes red. When Maddock taps it with his stylus, the flashing stops, a view window opens and a message begins to scroll.

'Looks urgent,' Bates says.

'I guess so, sir. It's from the Confederation Embassy. About their missing statistician.'

Bates sits up straighter. 'You guess so? *What* missing statistician? This is the first I've heard about it.' He snatches the board from Maddock and scans it. Male carli – embassy employee – missing two days – official report filed earlier in the evening . . . 'Hell! Why I no hear about this before?'

Maddock shakes his head and shrugs. Swearing under his breath Bates turns to his comp and starts barking orders. Several minutes' worth of checking the night's records turns up Ybarra's original report.

'Stupid little bastard!' Bates snarls. 'Somebody better tell him the difference between a routine call and an interstellar incident.'

'You think this gonna be something big?'

'Anything involving the Cons or the 'Lies is big. I no can believe anybody in this department could forget what happened last time, and it was what? Just eight months ago? I'd tattoo it on Ybarra's ass, but I bet he no can find it even with the lights on. Ah, sorry, it's no your fault. But jeezchrist, we no need another mess like that!'

'Yes, sir.' Maddock nods, remembering. 'But I only got in on the last part of the action.'

'Well, it started with a beat cop finding a dead carli. Just a little thing, right? And we damn near had the army in here. No, make that two armies. Ours and the lousy Confederation marines.' He returns, scowling, to the comp. 'Shit. Here comes another message from the embassy.'

Maddock leans over his shoulder to watch. Bates scans it quickly, a graceful, polite, almost flowery request for his personal attention to this little problem, but coming from a carli the delicate turns of phrase mean suppressed feelings of the dangerous kind. What's worse, it's signed by Hazorth Ka Pral, the Confederation Embassy's Chief of Protocol. As much as Bates likes Ka Pral, he can only see his involvement as a bad omen.

'Crap,' Bates says. 'Okay, leave a note for the day watch. I want every scrap of data we got, I mean anything at all, about this Gri Nerosi on my comp first thing this evening. Then I guess I'm going to have to go over to the embassy and see what they no telling us yet.'

'At least this one no is dead,' Maddock says.

Bates snorts. 'You mean so far nobody's found his body. Dammit, I'm going to ask Ka Pral why they no keep better track of their people over there.'

Bates signs his name on the remaining forms, then slings his suncloak over his shoulder and leaves, ushering Maddock out so he can lock the office behind him. All the way down on the grav platform, he worries about the game. If the missing carli turns up dead, Bates may have to skip it.

Porttown proper lies between the spaceport and the industrial edge of Polar City, buffered by a warehouse belt that shields the proper citizenry from its influence. During the drive over from The Ring, Yosef has said not one word, but when Rosa takes the turn-off to Porttown he shifts in his seat.

'Hey, are you crazy, coming here this time of day? This place is dangerous with all of those . . .' He stops short, his eyes wide with sudden self-knowledge.

Rosa finishes the insult for him. 'All them Blancos, huh? Dunt worry, no one gonna bother you as long as you with a white chick.'

He squirms, and she thinks that if his complexion allowed it he'd be blushing scarlet. Although baseball works hard to ignore ancient

15

prejudices, even well-meaning members of the ruling class, such as Yosef, tend to make these little slips. It's only one of the reasons Rosa makes a point of living in the ghetto where she grew up, even though she can afford much better.

'Sorry,' Yosef says. 'I just – we don't have anything like Porttown where I come from. Where are we going?'

'Aunt Lucy's, like I told you.' Rosa tries to imagine a city without slums. She fails. 'It's not far now.'

Rosa heads down F Street, a shopping district lined with sono-cleaners, bars, slice'n'fry fast food shops, loan sharks and the like, mostly closed now for the day. The deep pot-holes in the street show where Porttown ranks on the city government's priority list. Yosef glues himself to the window like a child, staring at the view. From F they turn off onto a side street where houses, mostly square cubes of plastocrete, stand cheek by jowl behind little front gardens filled with rocks draped with flowering grabber vine and studded with reddish brown cacti. Any wall reachable from the sidewalk displays a thick splatter of slogans and tags, pressure-canned by competing lizzie gangs. Lucy, however, lives in a big beige apartment building, textured to look like wood from a distance at least, and surrounded by thorn trees to keep the artists at bay.

For a wonder, Rosa finds a parking spot right in front. Out on the street she sees only a young lizzie, dressed in a pair of red cut-off overalls, and two young Blancas with purple hair and not many clothes between them, all of them hurrying home before their mammas give them hell for being out so late. She hopes that the winos and dreamdusters, the only ones likely to come out in the morning sun, will leave the skimmer alone. In case they don't, she puts the alarm on the loudest setting.

By this time a brassy day-bright sky has banished the aurora display. Hagar's enormous sun still hangs near the horizon, but soon it will climb high enough to destroy the few bits of shade that the buildings around them offer. Rosa grabs a couple of suncloaks from the back seat while Yosef stands uselessly at the kerb and looks around.

'Hey,' he says, 'this is a real, well, a neighbourhood, huh?'

'What didja expect? Some kind of plastocrete jungle? It aint the Rat Yard, pal.'

'Sorry. I mean, I really am sorry. Okay?'

She hesitates, but only briefly. 'Okay. Now c'mon. You can sight-see later.'

They duck into the entrance way, tiled in dark red and cool compared to the heat on the sidewalk. Near the door, covered by steel mesh, hangs a bronze plaque with names in slots. Rosa finds Lucy's and hits the button beside it. While they wait, Yosef yawns and props himself up against the opposite wall. Rosa mashes her thumb against the buzzer again.

'I guess she's not here, Red,' Yosef says, too brightly. 'Take me home, okay? Everything's all bueno now, you don't have to worry about me.'

She turns her back on him and rings a third time. On the door itself a comm unit glows into life. Rosa hurries over to stand in front of the camera's eye.

'Red? What in hell you doing here at this hour?' Aunt Lucy's voice cracks and hisses through the speaker. 'Well, no sense leaving you out there to fry. Come on up.'

When the door buzzes, Rosa grabs the handle and opens it. Yosef hesitates.

'Get your butt inside,' Rosa says, 'or I gonna leave you here to walk home.'

Yosef hurries right along, and she steps in after him to a musty foyer floored with tiles of plastocrete treated, cheaply, to resemble marble. The grav platform creaks and mutters to itself the entire way up to the fourth floor and another door, this one standing hospitably open.

'We be here,' Rosa calls out.

'Then come on in,' Lucy calls back. Her voice cracks, hoarse from years of shouting invective at every semi-pro umpire in Polar City. 'Coffee on.'

Rosa follows the smell of brewing coffee and leads Yosef through the living room to the kitchen, where Lucy, a wiry little woman, is standing by a sink filled with dirty dishes. She's wearing a faded purple bathrobe, her blonde hair's a mess, and she's yawning.

'Shee-it,' Rosa says. 'We woke you up.'

'Yeah you sure did,' Lucy says. 'That be why I put the coffee on.

17

Figured we could all use it.' She grabs Rosa in a bone-cracking hug, then releases her and grins. 'Looking good these days, girl. I'm proud of you.'

'Thanks. I be proud of the whole damn team.'

'Hell, yeah. You guys been playing real good all year. Now, come on, sit down, sit down. Watch out for that chair, the leg's sort of broke. Yosef, right? Thought so. I met you once at Connie's. That big fund-raiser party he threw for the Little League at the beginning of the season. You want sugar in this? Red, move that knitting bag off that chair and sit down.'

By the time they're comfortable around the kitchen table with mugs of coffee, Yosef has warmed up considerably. He keeps looking round to take in the decor: hanging on every wall, piled on every flat surface, are old holos and holoposters, even some antique two-dee pics, all of baseball players, baseball diamonds, baseball stadiums, and stills of famous baseball moments. Soon, if the Bears win tonight, Lucy is going to own souvenirs that will top the rest of her collection. For weeks Rosa has been planning a big surprise for her mentor, and before today's game she got the good news she wanted from the team's director of player relations.

On the refrigerator, a garishly coloured calendar displays the season's schedule for the Kelly's Bar and Grill Big Shots. Lucy waves one gnarled hand at the calendar.

'I be coaching them this season,' Lucy says to Yosef. 'For semi-pro ball, they aint bad.'

'I heard that, yeah.' He looks more alive that he has since the game ended. 'Not a bad team at all.'

'Thanks. I been coaching Little League too long. Kind of nice to have a team where everyone can hit the ball.'

Yosef laughs and salutes her with his coffee mug.

'Now this squirt here' – Lucy waves at Rosa – 'was one of my hot prospects when she was maybe nine.'

'Ah hell,' Rosa says, 'if you hadn't taught me how to judge a pitch, I'da ended up nowhere.'

'What makes you think I dunt know that?'

They all laugh, and Yosef leans back in his chair.

'Let's see,' he says, 'the Park and Rec season is starting soon, right?'

18

'In four weeks we got our first game.' Lucy makes a sour face. 'Against Mac's Discount City Appliances Marauders.'

'The rivals,' Rosa explains. 'The big rivals.'

Yosef nods and sips his coffee. Rosa takes advantage of the pause.

'Aunt Lucy.' Rosa sets her cup down. 'We got a problem.'

Lucy smiles. 'And why else would you be waking me up in the middle of the day?'

While she tells the story, beginning in the locker room, Rosa keeps her attention on Yosef. At first he glowers, full of bravado, but when she gets to his attempt to throw himself under a skimmer, he slumps down in the chair and stares fixedly at the bottom of his coffee cup.

'He no tell me what's wrong,' Rosa finishes up. 'But I dunt think he wants to pitch tonight.'

'Yeah, sounds like it.' Lucy has been watching Yosef as well. He refuses to look up, and Lucy leans forward. At last he raises his eyes.

'Okay, Mbaye,' Lucy says. 'You dunt want to kill youself, just take a vacation in a hospital somewhere. But I dunt think it's because you afraid of losing the game.' She looks him squarely in the face, eyes narrow. 'Okay, amigo, how much dinero you owe the bookies?'

He stares at her. 'What? Nada! I swear it, I never bet on games. Jeez, you think I'm crazy?' As the silence lengthens, he glances from one woman to the other. 'Call in a mullah if you don't believe me. I'll swear on my mamma's name, whatever. I've never bet on a game in my life. Hell, I don't bet on anything.'

Aunt Lucy looks at him, her face hard: the glare of a coach evaluating an unsatisfactory player. 'I think he telling the truth. Red, you ever hear of this boy lying?'

'Never.'

'All right,' Lucy says. 'But someone putting the black on you. Right?'

Yosef starts to speak, licks his lips, then merely sits and shakes.

'Thought so.' Lucy smiles briefly. 'Okay, somebody been trying to blackmail you, and you figure you better off out of tonight's game.'

Yosef starts to answer, then holds back, but he had started to shake his head automatically. Lucy pounces.

'Not just tonight's game. You telling me you dunt want the Bears to go to Sarah for the playoff?'

'No! I don't want to do anything that'll hurt the team.'

'Okay, then *you* dunt want to go to Sarah.' Lucy cocks her head to one side and considers him for a long cold moment. 'You gonna go even if the team loses, right? Thought I saw on the three-dee that Channel Ninety-Seven's signed you up if the Bears dunt go on to the series.'

Yosef stares fervently at the floor.

'Yeah, that's true.' Rosa answers for him. 'All the guys in the club, they been talking about it.'

'Maybe we getting somewhere then. Lessee. You got something waiting for you on Sarah, and you dunt want to face it.'

Yosef looks up. 'Yeah, yeah, okay.' His eyes fill with tears. 'That's it. Not that I don't want to go, but it's like I said, I don't want to do anything to hurt the team.'

'Hey, we dunt hold it against you. Throwing yourself under a cab instead of throwing a game, that takes guts, hombre.'

'Throw a *game*?' Yosef snaps. 'No way, man, just no way. I'd have let him tell his goddam secret to the holocasters if he'd been asking me to throw a game. He wants me to take something to Sarah for him when we go to the Series. He thinks that no one's going to search the team's luggage. I don't believe it.'

'He be loco,' Rosa says. 'You maybe gonna have a chance if we lose and you go with the three-dee people. Maybe not.'

'Huh!' Lucy makes a snorting sound. 'So what he got on you? Drugs?'

'Not that either!' Yosef lays a clenched fist on the tabletop. 'I'm not going to ruin my whole career over dreamdust.'

'Okay. You get some groupie pregnant?'

'Hell, no! I don't hang out with girls like that.'

'Yeah?' Rosa breaks in. 'So what's he holding over you, then?'

Yosef's mouth turns slack, and he slumps back in his chair. After a few minutes Rosa realizes that he has no intention of telling them. Lucy sighs with a shake of her head.

'Oh, I think I know.' All at once Lucy looks exhausted, and suddenly old, as if by some fluke of chemistry her rejuv had stopped working. 'Few things he said, few things he no asked, the way he acted. I seen it a few times before. One of my best kids – Jack

Mulligan. No drugs, no gambling, no groupies – there be only one thing left.'

Yosef starts shaking again.

Lucy crosses her arms over her chest and glares, back in coach-mode, but Yosef twists around and stares at the wall. Finally she snorts in disgust.

'You gonna make me say it, huh? Okay, I dunt want to, but I damn well will. You an unregistered psychic, aint you, Yosef?'

Tears run down his face in silent admission.

'Oh sweet jeezus,' Rosa whispers. She has never seen anyone become as still as Yosef has. He barely breathes, it seems, merely sits, every muscle so tense under his clothes that he could be yet another holo from Lucy's collection if it weren't for the tears, trickling like water over stone. Rosa fishes in her pocket and brings out a crumpled tissue, but Yosef never looks her way. Lucy ignores her as well and continues to stare at Yosef, her mouth set in an angry little twist. At last he moves, tossing his head back with a shudder like pain.

'Ah hell,' he says to Lucy. 'What are you? Psychic too?'

At the 'too' Lucy smiles, but grimly. 'No. I been around a few in my day, is all. And you can tell from looking at me what a long day that's been.'

A weak joke at best, but Yosef makes some attempt to smile. He ducks his head and wipes his face on his shirt sleeve. Rosa feels sick. If they lose Yosef now, they'll never win tonight, not because they don't have other good pitchers, but because the team's morale will hit bottom so hard . . . she doesn't even want to think about it.

'Yeah?' Yosef says. 'Well, okay, you see why I can't tell this guy to go suck vacuum. If they find out I'm a – a—'

'Psychic,' Lucy snaps. 'Better get used to it, amigo.'

'I don't want to. As soon as the umpires find out, I'm not in the majors any more.'

For the first time in years, Rosa feels like crying.

'Crap!' she says instead. 'It be so goddamn unfair! What they think you gonna do, read the batter's mind or something?'

'Pipe down, Red,' Lucy breaks in. 'Okay, Yosef. How long you know you was a psychic? And why in hell dint no one spot you before now?'

'I've known about it for a long time. But we never worried much about psi talents and stuff on Haz!wafetsh.' He pronunces the lizzie name better than most humans can, sounding the *!*, which signifies a beak snap.

'Where be Haz-whatever?' Lucy says. 'I thought you come from Longburrow.'

'I did. Haz!wafetsh is the real name. Longburrow's just the Merrkan way to say it. I grew up there. Wish I'd stayed there, too.'

'That be a lizzie world,' Rosa says. 'They no got any real ball teams.'

'That's what I mean. I'd have been better off, me and Marisa both. I should have sold insurance like my daddy wanted.' All at once Yosef gets up. 'Marisa! I've got to call her. She's going to be worried sick!'

While Yosef uses the comm out in the living room, Lucy and Rosa stay put in the kitchen, Rosa sprawled in her chair, Lucy pacing back and forth by the stove.

'How the schedule go for today?' Lucy says. 'When's batting practice?'

'Aint going to be none. Manager, he says he wants us fresh so we don't have to get to the park till a couple hours before game time.'

'Good. And it be a late game, right?'

'Right. Starts at oh-two hundred hours. That means we gotta show up about twenty-three-hundred.' Rosa glances at the chrono hanging on the far wall. 'It be only oh-nine-hundred now. Good. Yosef gonna need to get a good day's sleep.'

'Something else he needs to do even more. Ah, there you be, Mbaye. Get through to your wife okay?'

'Yeah, I did, thanks.' Yosef stands in the doorway. 'Hey, we'd better be moving on, Red.'

'I was just saying that to Aunt Lucy, yeah.'

'I want you back here, though, this evening.' Lucy fixes Yosef with her coach's version of the evil eye. 'Round about nineteen-hundred. Dunt try lying and telling me you got batting practice, either. Red told me the truth.'

'But—'

'Shut up and listen!' Lucy snaps. 'I know someone who can maybe help. You no can keep this a secret for ever. Maybe if you're lucky we can buy you some time, at least let you play in the Series.'

22

'Could you?' Yosef's voice chokes. 'Oh man, if you could—'

'Aint promising nada. Red, you make sure he comes.'

'I will. Dunt worry.'

'Good.' Lucy allows herself a somewhat feral smile. 'And Yosef? You try hurting yourself again and I gonna call up the Commissioner myself and tell him about your dirty little secret. Get it?'

'I get it.' Yosef's face turns ashen grey. 'Don't worry. I won't.'

'Good. Now get your asses out of here, both of you. You gotta get some sleep for the game tonight. And so, come to think of it, do I.'

Chapter Two

In the soft post-sunset darkness the Confederation Embassy, a crescent-shaped building some four storeys tall, shimmers with golden light from a new coat of luminescent paint. Two human males, dressed in grey, stand guard on either side of the entrance. As Chief Bates approaches, they salute with nods of recognition and open the heavy wood doors.

Inside, Bates receives a different kind of welcome. At a long curve of a desk sits a Blanca woman with red-blonde hair, green eyes, and a professionally thin smile. Bates has dealt with her enough times to wish she'd get a transfer off-planet. When he walks up to the desk, she looks up from her comp unit.

'Good evening. May I help you?'

'I hope so. I want to see Ka Pral, but I dunt have an appointment.'

'Without an appointment the chief of protocol sees no one.'

'I'm here on official business.' Bates chokes back an insult and pulls out his badge and ID case with a flourish.

'Oh.' The receptionist blinks rapidly. 'Oh, I see. A police operative.'

'I happen to be the Chief of Police in Polar City.'

Another professional smile, and she picks up her comm wand, talking quietly in the carli language. 'If you'll have a seat, sir?' She lays down the wand and smiles brightly. 'The Chief of Protocol says he'll attempt to accommodate you.' Her nose wrinkles ever so slightly. 'Please have a seat – over there by the wall.'

Bates sinks into a deep blue couch and checks his watch: 1900. He still has plenty of time to return to his office, handle whatever crisis has happened since he left work and get over to the baseball stadium on one pretence or another. While he waits, he considers the blue carpet covering the floor. It looks coarse to his eyes, but he knows that the thick yarns and bunchy texture mean it's been hand woven on a primitive loom, as all carli prestige textiles are. The blue also appears solid at first glance, but by turning his head to catch the slanting light, he can decipher traces of a pattern visible in full, no doubt, to carli eyes.

'Chief Bates!' Ka Pral comes striding through a side door. 'You must forgive my inattention.'

Bates heaves himself off the couch and bows. Ka Pral wears the warrior caste's long green robes, which hang open in front to reveal a long grey tunic. Like most carlis, he's fairly short, perhaps a metre and a half tall. His pale golden fur shines, his ear flaps extend to their full, alert height – he's in a good mood, apparently. Bates shakes his offered hand, slender with three long, furred fingers.

'You have my humble apologies,' Bates says, 'for daring to intrude upon you without the proper arrangements.'

'No, no, the apology is mine for keeping you waiting. It is a most unexpected but never unwelcome surprise to see you. You honour our poor residence.'

'Still, I beg forgiveness for my wretched lack of manners in wishing to see you at such short notice.'

'There is no possibility of any such lack on the part of such an honourable guest. Will you grace my humble office?'

As they leave the room, Bates glances back at the receptionist. She gives him the same professional smile.

Ka Pral takes Bates into his roomy office, decorated in sandy browns and tans except for one large turquoise tapestry hanging on the far wall.

'Please, do sit down, Chief Bates,' Ka Pral says. 'Allow me to offer you some refreshment.'

'Thank you.'

Bates chooses a fairly firm chair and sits, watching Ka Pral open a cabinet built flush with the wall. He can just make out a collection of decanters and glasses.

'You will forgive me for not calling a servant,' Ka Pral says. 'I realize your time is precious.'

'Of course I forgive you, Your Excellency! I am deeply honoured that you would serve me with your own hands.'

'I think you might enjoy this particular beverage. It is a blend of wine from an Earth-derived grape and one of our liqueurs, made from a fruit that grows only on our southern continent.'

'The colour is exceptionally beautiful.'

Ka Pral bobs his head, the carli equivalent of a smile, and brings over two glasses filled with a shimmering lavender liquid. Bates takes one, waits for the carli to sit down opposite him, then tries a cautious sip. Some carli liquors have the potency of another species' weed-killer. This particular wine, however, sits lightly in the mouth.

'It's very sweet and fine,' Bates says. 'I'm most grateful for the chance to sample it.'

'Ah, I am so pleased.' Ka Pral leans back with a rustle of silky robes. 'The vintner had a most interesting idea.'

In the carli world little happens fast. For close to an hour, by Bates's reckoning, they discuss wines in general and wines in particular. At last Ka Pral changes the subject.

'You will forgive my abruptness,' he says. 'But I'm sure we both have work on our hands of great urgency. You've received your invitation, no doubt, to our embassy's forthcoming humble reception?'

'I have, yes. You must be working overtime, getting ready for an event like that.'

'It's only a week away.' Ka Pral's ear flaps droop. 'And the protocol is going to be an amazingly delicate tangle. Ambassadors and functionaries of five species. My own government's special envoys. You can no doubt imagine the possibilities for gaffes and faux pas.'

'I can. This is a most unfortunate time for a disturbance of the sort that brings me here.'

'Ah yes.' Ka Pral's left ear begins to twitch, a tiny rhythmical flick. 'Limbi Gri Nerosi.'

'Your statistician, yes.'

'Statistician is perhaps too grand a title for his duties. More of a statistical clerk, an expert on data selection and entry, but nothing more.'

'I see.' Bates had already guessed his low status from the honorific *Gri*, 'that one', in the use name, as opposed to the high status *Ka*, 'he who'. 'And yet his disappearance troubles you.'

26

'The disappearance of anyone on staff here troubles me.' As Ka Pral talks, his ear keeps twitching. 'We are all, as it were, the children of our honoured ambassador, since he has deigned to allow us to serve him.'

'Of course.'

'I have asked Kaz Phaath, his superior, to join us. I am sure she can answer your questions better than I.'

'You have my thanks. She's the logical choice, all right.'

Bates allows himself a smile at the name, since it means 'She Who Asks Many Questions', a loose way of saying 'She Who Is Nosy'. Apparently this sentient has a sense of humour about her job to match Ka Pral's 'He Who Splits Hairs'.

Ka Pral rises at the sound of a low whistle outside the door, the carli equivalent of a knock. 'Here she is now.' He trots across the room and opens the door. 'Chief Bates, allow me the honour of introducing Wentworth Kaz Phaath yil Frakmo, our Director of Data Analysis.'

Bates gets up and covers his surprise with a low bow. The female who enters, dressed in the royal blue robes of the scientist caste, is a human being.

'I am honoured that you yourself would come to help us, Chief Bates,' Kaz Phaath says.

'You're most welcome. The honour is mine.'

Since Kaz Phaath stands a good head taller than Ka Pral, she sits on a low hassock beside his chair. Carli etiquette demands that those of lower status position themselves physically lower whenever possible. As she arranges her robes demurely around her, Bates notices that she wears a white jumpsuit under them. She's an extremely attractive woman, with soft brown eyes, a sensuous mouth and long black hair fashioned into a cascade of slender braids. When Ka Pral seats himself, Bates notices two more things: his ear has stopped twitching and he does not offer the woman a drink. He apparently sees Kaz Phaath as a servant brought in to handle a messy matter for him, despite her high-status name.

'Now, then,' Bates says. 'I understand you're the one who filed the missing person report.'

'I am, yes. I'm afraid I can't think of much to add to it now.'

'Well, I have a few questions. For one, did Gri Nerosi have any enemies here in the embassy?'

'No. He had no friends, either. He was a competent person but not a pleasant one.' She pauses, glancing at Ka Pral. 'Not unpleasant, either. Merely dry. It's an occupational hazard in our line of work.'

As the conversation continues, Kaz Phaath glances at her superior often, an automatic flick of her eyes his way every time she begins to answer a question. Ka Pral says nothing, merely bobs his head pleasantly now and then, but by the time Bates finishes the carli's left ear has resumed its nervous twitch. Judging from Kaz Phaath's account of him, Gri Nerosi is a boring little bureaucrat who leads a quiet, boring little life. As he leaves, Bates is thinking that he doesn't believe one damn word of it.

Right at 1900 Rosa and Yosef return to Aunt Lucy's apartment. This time she greets them wearing a pair of baggy white shorts and a white button-front shirt blazoned with dark green lettering: Kelly's Bar and Grill Big Shots.

'Good!' Lucy says by way of greeting. 'Come on in and sit down. We gonna use the living room.'

'Jeez,' Rosa says, grinning. 'Must be something important going on.'

Lucy makes a snorting sound and heads into the kitchen to tend the coffee. Her living room walls, what Rosa can see of them under and around the baseball memorabilia, are bright yellow, and the furniture mostly matches. Over one armchair lies a knitted throw in black and white – the Bears' colours, and Lucy's handiwork, Rosa assumes. Rosa and Yosef sit down as the front door buzzes again.

'I gonna get it.' Lucy emerges from the kitchen. 'Probably be just them.'

'Them' turns out to be Aunt Lucy's one actual genetic niece, Bobbie Lacey, and a lanky blonde Blanco that, Rosa realizes, must be Jack Mulligan. At the sight of them Yosef repeats his imitation of a frozen rock, though he does murmur something in response to the round of hellos. Every sentient in the Republic knows Bobbie Lacey's face, with its big blue eyes and triangular smile. It was all over the three-dee some eight months previously, when she got herself mixed up in the crisis surrounding the Republic's first contact with the Enzebb species. As for Mulligan, he has a certain reputation himself, as a semi-pro ball shortstop, and, it turns out, Yosef knows him.

'Hey, Joe!' Mulligan says. 'Give em hell tonight!'

'Hey, Jack! I'm planning on it.' Yosef finally moves, getting up to shake Mulligan's hand. 'Good to see you again.'

'Again?' Aunt Lucy comes out of the kitchen with a tray full of coffee mugs.

'Met him when we did that benefit game for the Porttown scholarship fund.' Mulligan helps himself to a mug. 'Just cause I play lousy semi-pro ball dunt mean I dunt, like, get asked to stuff like that.'

'You don't play lousy ball even if it is semi-pro.' Yosef seems to be about to say more, but all at once his eyes get wide, and he sits down fast. No doubt he's just remembered why the major leagues never signed Mulligan.

Aunt Lucy passes out coffee, then waves her hand at the various chairs. 'Get comfortable, will you? I dint ask you here for old home week. Bobbie, like I told you on the comm, we got a serious problem.'

When Lacey sits down in a ratty armchair, Mulligan sits on the floor between her feet, crossing his long legs and leaning back. Aunt Lucy sails the tray into the kitchen, winces at the crash it makes, then takes a wooden chair nearby. She sits on the edge and cradles her coffee mug in both hands.

'Yosef here got a little secret,' Aunt Lucy begins. 'Got a blackmailer on him.'

'Gamblers,' Lacey says. The word is not a question.

'That what I thought too, but he say no. Tell her, chico.'

Yosef hesitates. When Rosa elbows him in the ribs, he starts talking.

'Well, uh, you see—' Yosef pauses for a sip of coffee. 'It was a couple of nights ago, and this guy came up to me when I was waiting for my cab home. Or wait, no, I forgot about the letters. For a couple of weeks I've been getting these letters. They kept saying someone knew my secret, and I'd be hearing from him. So when he came up to me, I figured it was the same guy, and it was.' Another gulp of coffee, and he goes on. 'He shoved himself into the cab with me. He told me he knew what I was hiding, and so I'd better do him a favour.'

'Wait a minute,' Lacey breaks in. 'This guy, what did he look like?'

'Kind of ordinary. Skinny, as dark as me, dreadlocks. He was wearing a nice suit, looked like a businessman.'

'Ah. Not a lot to go on.'

'No.' Yosef sounds apologetic. 'I've never seen him in full light. But he wants me to take something to Sarah, smuggle it in, I mean, in my luggage. And I don't care what he says, I can see myself getting caught. What would that do to the team?' He glances at Rosa.

'Get everyone mad as hell or depressed, or both,' Rosa says.

'Yeah. So I figured it'd be better if I got put on the DL.'

'The what?' Lacey says.

'Disabled list,' Aunt Lucy puts in. 'Dint you learn nada in school?'

Bobbie grins at her, then considers Yosef over the rim of her coffee mug. He's sitting slumped forward, staring miserably at the flowered carpet. 'C'mon, Mbaye,' she says. 'What's he holding over you?'

'Uh well.' Yosef looks up, looks away. 'I'm, uh, well – an unregistered psychic.'

Mulligan flinches, turning his head as fast as if someone had slapped him. 'Shit.' He whispers so softly that Rosa can barely hear him. 'Oh shit. Would be that, huh?'

'Yeah,' Yosef says. 'And I don't see you playing pro ball like you deserve.'

'Now wait a minute,' Bobbie says. 'Sure, the majors dunt want psychics. They weren't gonna draft Jack because they knew up front he was one. But it isn't like there's a law against it. It's just kinda one of those understood things. Right?'

'Well, yeah,' Aunt Lucy breaks in. 'But it's one hell of a strong understanding.'

'I savvy. But look, Mbaye's already in the majors. He's proved himself. What makes us all so sure they'd kick him out? Blackmail, that's serious trouble. You should go to the police.'

'One thing you dunt savvy.' Mulligan twists around to look up at her. 'When you sign, there's this contract, y'know? And there's this clause. You swear or something—'

'Attest,' Yosef says.

'Yeah, attest. You attest you aint no psychic. So if you are . . .'

'You just voided your contract.' Bobbie shakes her head sadly. 'That takes care of the smart way out. Well, look, Mbaye, what's this thing he wants you to carry?'

'That's the damnedest thing about this whole mess. I told him I wasn't going to smuggle any dust no matter what he had on me, and he said, no, no, it's not drugs. It's some old carli thing, an art object he called it. There's a collector on Sarah who wants it, but the duty's going to be way high, so if I smuggle it in they'll save a bundle. The guy said he's meet me on Sarah, get the thing from me and then deliver it himself.'

'You dint believe him, did you?' Lacey says. 'You dint? Good. For starters, it's got to be stolen goods. You get caught with those, chico, and your contract's the last thing you gonna worry about.'

Yosef shuts his eyes and flops back so hard that the couch shakes. Rosa nearly spills her coffee.

'Sorry,' Yosef mumbles.

'Something's bothering me about this story,' Bobbie goes on. 'If the team dunt win, you no go to Sarah. Seems to me he should have waited before he put the bite on you. It's no sure thing, this win. This dude's a real gambler.'

'No,' Yosef says. 'Channel 97, they signed me up for a possible colour guy, an extra commentator. I mean, you know how that works – if we lose I go along with the three-dee crew and talk about the pitching in the Series. If we win, they take the Miners' catcher instead.'

'Oh yeah,' Mulligan puts in. 'I saw that on the news a while ago.'

'And so did this dude, I bet.' Lacey hesitates, thinking. 'You're a psychic whether you like it or not, so let's get some good out of it. Did you pick up anything else about him? Like maybe his name?'

'Hey, I do my best to stay out of other people's minds.'

'Which do you want to do more? Stay out of his mind or stay out of jail?'

'Oh, okay! Well, there was this one thing, and man, it creeped me out. He laid his goddamn hand on my arm, and before I shook it off I could hear – well, no, it wasn't like hearing him think or anything. I just knew it, kind of.' Yosef looks desperately at Mulligan. 'Can that happen, Jack?'

31

'Sure can. They call it direct transmission. You got a lot of talent, if you can do that without the training.'

'Okay. Then I guess it's true enough.'

'What?' Bobbie snaps. 'What did he transmit?'

'Well.' Yosef drains his cup in one gulp. 'He was thinking about the Hoppers. I don't know why, it was just this feeling.'

'Aint that just great?' Lacey looks up at the ceiling as if invoking the Galactic Mind. 'Hoppers. That's all we need if the middle of this. Goddamn H'Allevae.'

'Told you it was a real problem,' Aunt Lucy says. 'So, what we gonna do?'

'You expect me to have an answer to that?' Lacey turns toward her aunt.

'Hey, I can hope, can't I?'

'The only thing I can maybe do is call Chief Bates. He owes me a favour, big time. Maybe he can hush up Yosef's secret, promise the blackmailer a short sentence or something if he keeps his mouth shut.'

'I can't go to the police.' Yosef sounds as if he's strangling. 'Not now, not when the team—' He breaks off and stares at her with begging eyes.

Bobbie shrugs, turning her hands palm up. Rosa feels like kicking something or maybe just screaming in frustration. She doesn't need psychic talents to see that Bobbie has no intention of getting involved in Yosef's troubles. She leans over, sets her mug on the floor beside the couch, then stands up motioning to Yosef.

'C'mon,' she says. 'We need to get out to the park.'

'Yeah. Guess so.' Yosef meekly follows. 'I . . . uh well, thanks.'

Rosa stomps out without saying another word. So much for Lucy's famous niece! When Yosef joins her on the grav platform, he seems on the edge of tears. They drop down to the smelly foyer, then hurry out to the somewhat fresher air of Porttown. Her skimmer still stands by the kerb, unmolested except for a cryptic pressure-can symbol on the hood.

'Damn!' Yosef says. 'Someone tagged your car.'

'No problem. I got the anti-graffiti coating on it. Wipes right off.' She lets her voice trail away.

In the flickering light from the aurora his face is impossible to read.

'I dunt know what to do next,' Rosa says at length.

'Hey, thanks anyway. I appreciate your trying.'

'Welcome. Guess we better go play some ball.'

As she's unlocking the passenger side door, a thought strikes her.

'How come you always take cabs to the park?'

'Marisa needs the car.'

'Well, hell, man, with the money you make, you could have two skimmers.'

'I hate to spend that much.' Yosef is looking off down the street. 'I always figured my damn talents would get me into trouble, and then the big money would fade away. Guess I was right.'

Rosa sighs sharply. 'Yeah. Guess you were.'

'Roberta Jane Lacey!' Aunt Lucy balls her hands into fists and sets them on her hips. 'I no can believe you gonna sit there and not do one goddamn thing for the poor panchito!'

'Look, I feel sorry for him, yeah. He dunt deserve having his career ruined by some low-life smuggler. But I swore up and down after that last little adventure that I was no getting involved in politics ever again.'

'Huh. Wonder what your Aunt Maureen gonna say to that?'

'You wouldn't dare!'

'I would.'

Since Mulligan is still sitting between her feet, Lacey has to untangle herself before she can get out of the chair. By the time she does, Aunt Lucy is across the room and reaching for the comm unit.

'Dunt!' Bobbie snaps. 'I'll think about it for a while. Okay?'

Aunt Lucy sets the unit back down.

'But honest.' Bobbie walks over to face her. 'I bet there's nada I can do.'

'Huh! Plenty of things you can do. You just aint thought of them yet.'

'Yeah, and all of them mean big trouble.'

Lucy's about to say something more, then pauses. Bobbie can hear Mulligan getting up behind her.

33

'Aunt Lucy? How about you, like, make some more coffee or something? Y'know?'

Aunt Lucy opens her mouth to snarl, then suddenly smiles. 'Good idea, I gonna go do that.'

Bobbie feels Jack's hands on her shoulders. Until her aunt has left and begins making unnecessary noise in the kitchen, he keeps quiet, merely rubs her shoulders in a way that always makes her feel like melting into his arms. Instead, she takes a deep breath, turns around, and braces herself for an argument.

'No.' His voice is perfectly calm. 'I no fighting about it. Bobbie, you no can do this. Specially right before the Series. It'd be kinder to just shoot him, y'know?'

'Why does it matter to you so much? It isn't just the baseball game.'

'No, it be Yosef. I no can stand it, I no gonna be able to stand it, watching what gonna happen to him. I mean, like, I gonna feel it all.'

'Yeah? Well, how are you going to feel if you and me, and my aunt and everyone else, we get into deep trouble with the law?'

'Ah come on.' Jack grins at her. 'You can pull it off. I know damn well you can.'

With a feeling close to shock she realizes that he's speaking sincerely, not flattering her.

'Besides,' Jack goes on, 'I know you. You dunt do nada, and this dude, he gets hauled in by the cops and his life gets ruined, y'know? You gonna be sorry as all hell. Bet you dunt sleep right for weeks, man.'

For a long moment she looks up into his solemn grey eyes. At times she realizes how well he knows her, and it's terrifying. He smiles, the shy little-boy smile she never can resist.

'I mean, like, hey, Bobbie. Please?'

'All right!' She lets out her breath in a sharp sigh. 'I'll be goddamned if I know why I'm doing this, but I won't say anything to Bates. We'll figure out a way to make sure no one ruins your pet pitcher's career. But you *owe* me one, man!'

'You bet! I gonna, like, never forget this.' Jack suddenly frowns. 'But how we gonna let Mbaye know? Can't call him up over the public comm lines.'

'I gonna tell him.' Smiling in raw triumph, Aunt Lucy stands in the

34

doorway. 'I got a locker room pass *and* a ticket.' She holds up a thin slip of paperboard. 'Thanks to Red Wallace.'

'Okay,' Lacey says. 'And on my tombstone, you guys can write: "Here lies the biggest sucker in Polar City".'

With the sprinklers on, the baseball diamond of Roberts Memorial Stadium becomes the coolest outdoor spot in Polar City. Silver domes of spray shimmer in the light from the maglev glow spheres that float over the field. The spray drenches the surrounding stands in shadow. A groundskeeper stands near third base and stares at the comp unit he carries in one hand. Thanks to the parching heat the grass has to be watered. Fezawhar hovers nervously nearby.

'No want too much water,' Fezzy says.

'I know, I know. I'm done.'

With a gnarled dark finger the groundsman taps the screen once, and the silver domes fold like so many umbrellas. Another tap, and the sprinkler rods retreat into their sheaths under the turf.

'There you go. Dunt let your damn vandals tear up my grass too much tonight.'

The groundsman climbs onto his electric cart and putts off over the perfect field of hybrid grass, his one true love in life. He has been heard to say that the grass is the only thing that justifies baseball.

Fezawhar of course disagrees. The elderly equipment manager, a lizzie, has given his hearts to a game his species can never play. As he makes a final, unnecessary check on the bullpen, his wrinkled grey hide turned almost violet by the shadowy lights, he thinks back to the first series he can remember. Fezzy's mind tends to blur past and present. He knows so many statistics for so many players, some long dead, that he sometimes loses track of the current year, and he measures out the years only in baseball seasons.

So when he sees a slender dark-skinned man with dreadlocks hanging around the players' field entrance, for a brief moment he thinks it's Willie Fong, Bears' first baseman, batting .286. *No, no, no*, he tells himself. *Willie done retired fifteen years back. You thinking of his lifetime average!* The old lizzie blinks and focuses on the man actually standing there. Fezzy has never seen this guy before in his life.

35

'Sorry, mister. No can go back there; private area. Anyway, nada worth seeing.'

The stranger smiles, slipping one hand into a pocket of his crisp grey business shorts. Up close, the resemblance to Willie fades. When Willie smiled, he meant it. This dude smiles like a knife flashing.

'No problem, amigo. I just thought, you know, maybe get a look at the locker room, maybe find a ball for a souvenir or something. Gonna be a great game tonight, huh?'

'You bet. A lot riding on it.'

'Ah, they gonna win,' the stranger says. 'The Miners? Shee-it! Can't play their way out of a paper bag.'

'Aint no sure thing in baseball, señor.'

'That's true, that's true. You musta seen a few upsets in your day, huh?'

It doesn't take much to trigger Fezzy's memories. After fifteen or twenty minutes, he has to think hard to bring himself back to the present.

'Well, I guess you got work to do, huh?' the stranger says at last. 'Nice talking with you, old timer. Hey, could you, like, give your pitcher a message for me? Just wishing him luck and all. He's an old buddy of mine.'

'Well, I no supposed to, but sure. No can do any harm.'

The man hands him a sealed envelope with 'Yosef Mbaye' written on the flap. Fezzy tucks it into the front chest pocket of his overalls. From overhead, far up in the stands, a voice squawks: the soundman, testing the speaker system.

'I better get gone,' the stranger says. 'But thanks for giving Smiling Joe that envelope.'

After he escorts the man out, Fezzy finds himself considering that conversation. Something struck a false note. For a long while, as he stands in the dugout stacking paper cups near the water cooler, he finds himself sucking his claws in irritation, trying to figure out what it was. Finally, out on the field, one of the groundsmen calls to a fellow worker named José and inadvertently jogs his memory. The holocasters came up with that nickname, Smiling Joe, for Yosef Mbaye. Fezzy ignores Yosef's career stats, rolling through his mind like a display on a comp screen, while he considers a more interesting question. Mbaye hates the nickname, so why would an old friend use it?

Normally administrative work keeps Bates at his desk for much of each night, but when the call came in that a carli male had been knifed out in Carlitown, he grabbed his hat and his stun gun and rushed down to the garage for his skimmer. Now, however, he regrets having left the cool of his air-conditioned office, because the case has turned out to be routine. Some carli families live in Polar City, full citizens of the Republic with no ties to the Confederation, in a neighbourhood of about thirty square blocks near Civic Centre. One of their young men got himself involved with a married female, an affair the husband has just ended with a carving knife right out in front of their house. Witnesses abound, drawn by the wife's screams.

Under the maglev streetlights police swarm, questioning witnesses, snapping holograms, scraping up blood samples and the like. Bates stands off to one side. His head pounds in rhythm with the flickering aurora overhead.

'You okay, Chief?' Parsons asks.

'Why the hell you asking me that?'

'Sorry.'

Bates stalks away. Out in the street an ambulance stands waiting for the vulture detail to finish its work.

'You got anything for a headache?' he asks the lizzie medtech.

'Most of my patients dunt need medicine.' The tech starts to hiss, laughing at her own joke, but a second look at the chief's face shuts her up. She rummages in her drug locker and produces two small yellow tablets with no further wisecracks. 'You want some water?'

'Yeah, gracias.'

The tech fills a tiny cup from the cooler strapped to the side of the van. Bates gulps the pills down. He's felt Ka Pral's wine ever since he left the embassy. He can't help wondering if Ka Pral chose that particular liquor to blunt his mind, to keep him from noticing details like twitching ears and sidelong glances at the pack leader.

What a mess, Bates thinks, and a hell of a lot more important than the carlis are letting on. He corrects himself: it's more important than the embassy will admit, carlis and humans both. He finds himself thinking of Kaz Phaath, something new in his experience, a human with high status in the carli world.

'Everything's under control here, Chief.' Parsons comes strolling over. 'This dunt look like a political murder to me.'

'Me either, Sarge. I'm going to get back downtown.'

'How's that headache?'

A sudden traitorous thought comes to Bates. The pills are working fast, but . . .

'It's making me loco,' Bates says. 'A real bad one, all right. Look, if you really need me, call my travelling comm, okay? I'm going to go home and lie down.'

'It's the only thing that works sometimes, yeah.'

As he drives off, Bates heads west, the direction of his neighbourhood, but as soon as he's out of sight he makes a left turn and heads for The Ring. He has his ticket for the game in his wallet. After all, if the Bears should lose, trouble will erupt at Roberts Memorial and he can assuage his guilt by thinking that if it does he'll be right there to take command.

As many sentients as the fire regulations will allow have crammed themselves into the stadium, and a few more than that have wangled their way into the dead space under the outfield bleachers. Everyone's too hot, everyone's eating too much – greasy soy dogs, vinegar-drenched slice'n'fry, ice cream, soy pops – all of it washed down with overly sweet soda or beer. Lacey is profoundly glad they're not sitting in their usual seats up in the second deck. If a fight's going to break out, it will break out up there. Their box seats, right on the first base line, came her way as a perk from one of her customers. For two and a half innings now they've revelled in the luxury of being able to see everything on the field.

'This be swell,' Jack says. 'I can even, like, stretch my legs out.'

'And no one going to be dumping beer on us, either.'

He gives her one of his standard boyish grins, but the look in his eyes bothers her: distant, somehow hard.

'Hey, sweetheart,' Lacey says. 'Something wrong?'

'No.' He looks away fast. 'No could be happier.'

When Lacey lays a hand on his arm, she can feel the tension. 'Yeah, sure. Tell me.'

'Ah, the same old crap. Wishing I was down there playing. You dunt need to hear it again.'

A solid crack of bat hitting ball saves Lacey from having to answer. The crowd screams and stamps at the long single to right, the Bears' first hit of the game. The Miners have been putting up a good fight. Now the problem becomes driving the baserunner in. Unfortunately, Yosef Mbaye is up next, and like most pitchers he owns a dismal batting average. Lacey noticed his practice swings while he waited in the on-deck circle; they lacked the grace and power he shows when he pitches. When he steps up to the plate, he stands awkwardly, his bat held a little too high.

'If he gonna bunt,' Mulligan remarks, 'he better get that bat in position.'

'Maybe he's going to fake a swing and then bunt.'

'Pull a butcher boy? Could be.'

Mbaye proves him right. When the pitch, a strong fastball, arrives, Mbaye lunges at it and misses. Strike one. He steps out of the batter's box and looks desperately down the third base line to the coach, who runs through a string of signals.

'Yeah,' Jack says. 'They want the butcher boy play, all right. He dunt have the bat skill.'

Mbaye suddenly freezes, the bat dangling from one hand. The umpire turns toward him and says something – get back in the box, probably, Lacey figures. When he steps in, Mbaye stops the pretence and spreads his hands on the bat, ready to bunt. The pitcher responds with a slider that misses, hanging over the plate for the briefest of split seconds, just long enough for Mbaye to lunge forward, catching the ball and turning its momentum with the bat. He's laid a perfect bunt down the third base line. The runner races for second and makes it easily into scoring position. The Miners' third baseman throws Mbaye out at first, but he's made the sacrifice. The manager, Lacey supposes, doesn't want him standing on the base paths anyway.

'Wait a minute,' Lacey says. 'You told him to ignore the signs, dint you?'

'No.' Mulligan gives her a vacant smile. 'What make you think that?'

'Jeez, Jack, I thought you weren't supposed to go poking around in people's minds.'

'Who was poking? Only giving him a little advice.'

He leans forward, nearly bent double in his seat, and concentrates on the game. As the Bears' lead-off hitter heads for the plate, the crowd yells and begins chanting his name, Bah-rak! Bah-rak! over and over. Lacey gives up trying to talk with Jack, but she's beginning to think that professional baseball has done the right thing by keeping psychics out.

Top of the ninth inning, a two-run lead, and two out: one more out wins the pennant. Rosa reminds herself that over-confidence has lost plenty of games and stays alert. In the stands the crowd is on its feet, screaming, clapping, shouting, stamping its feet. She can feel the noise, she fancies, pounding against her. A ring within a ring, all round the stadium stand security guards and off-duty police, hired by the ownership to keep the fans in the stands at the game's end.

As the Miners' last chance walks slowly up to the plate, the first-base coach signals to the infielders: move back, fade a little left. Rosa follows orders, then waits. On the mound Mike Takahashi, the relief pitcher, is taking his time, scuffing the rubber with the toe of one foot. Yosef had pitched brilliantly until the seventh, when his concentration seemed to break down. He gave up two runs before the manager pulled him. Fortunately, the Bears scored three more in the eighth.

And now the game has come to this, the batter in his stance, Tak in his wind-up, under the glare of maglev lights that shield the stadium from the gaudy sky. The pitch streaks across the plate, a fastball, high. Ball one. Rosa catches her breath with a sob, then forces herself to be calm. Tak knows what's he doing. Sure enough, the next pitch comes low. The batter swings and golfs it, a lazy fly ball floating down from the sky.

'I got it,' Rosa calls out.

She drifts to her right and waits as the ball plunges out of the lights and smacks into her glove. She slaps her other hand over it as the stadium goes mad. The fans are screeching, chanting, screaming, pounding, but Rosa can pick out one note: Red, Red, Red! They are cheering her, and she weeps beyond control as she jogs toward the mound.

Takahashi is waiting for her, and he too is crying. The outfielders converge, the rest of the team is pouring from the dugout. The players are hugging each other, pounding each other on the back as they rush together. Rosa hangs back for a brief minute until she sees old Fezzy shuffling toward her.

'Game-winning ball!' she shrieks.

Hissing with laughter he nods and holds up clawed hands. She tosses him the ball, waits till he makes the catch, then plunges into the surging mob of her team-mates. She can hear the coaches yelling and the loudspeakers, but it takes everyone a few minutes to understand the message: clear the field, get out of here! She pulls away from a team-mate's embrace and glances around. Police or no police, the fans are threatening to mob the field. Rosa picks up the chant. 'Let's go, let's go!' As slowly as a sleepy animal the team understands and begins to move.

Tonight modesty becomes unimportant. Both locker rooms have been taped – that is, the staff has covered the lockers themselves with plastosheet and the doors between the two rooms stand open. Tak grabs an open bottle of champagne from a crate, pours half of it on Rosa's head, then hands her the bottle. Laughing she takes a long swallow as the excess runs down her uniform and soaks the polar bear logo. All around her champagne rains down as the others players join in, yelling and whooping. Holocam crews and sportscasters push their way, shoving microphones in the face of anyone who looks coherent enough to comment. Montoya from Channel 97 grabs Takahashi by the arm and screams for a holocam.

All at once Rosa remembers Yosef. As a strict follower of Islam he won't be bathing in forbidden wine along with the team, but she realizes that she's never even seen him since he left the game. She jumps onto a bench and looks over the damp, hysterical mob. At the far end of the men's side of the locker room Yosef is standing with his back to the wall and looking more like a victim ready for human sacrifice than a winning pitcher. He's dressed in street clothes and has

41

his carrysack slung from one shoulder. As she watches, he starts making his way toward the door.

He'll never hear if she calls to him. Rosa jumps down and dodges a soaking-wet shirt as it sails by her head. She ducks under someone's upraised arm, squeezes past three other players, and reaches the door just as he slips through it.

'Hey, Yosef! Wait!'

At the sound of her voice, he turns and attempts to smile, a forced twitch of his lips, but he keeps walking.

'Wait, damn it!' Rosa darts after him.

He stops, hesitates, then turns around and sets his carrysack on the floor as she catches up.

'Look,' Rosa says. 'They gonna stop slinging booze around in a couple of minutes. You won the game, man. Where you going? You belong with the rest of us.'

'Do I?' His voice sounds exhausted. 'Bet the Commissioner wouldn't think so.'

Rosa's elation vanishes as she remembers.

'Commissioner dunt know yet,' she says. 'With a little luck and Bobbie Lacey, maybe he never gonna.'

'Yeah?' Yosef glances around and drops his voice, an unnecessary precaution. 'Red, look, I saw that dude I told you about, the one who's—' He stops, apparently unable to say the word 'blackmail'.

'Here at the game? Jeez, man!'

'Yeah. I saw him in the stands, right down in front, the bastard, round about the fifth I think it was. But before the game he gave Fezzy a letter. A letter for me, I mean, only poor old Fez forgot about it till I was pulled. So he gave it to me when I was on my way to the showers.'

'Damn good thing he did forget.'

'You're right about that. The dude's gonna call me tomorrow, he says, before the victory parade, and I'd better be there, he says. For the love of God! What if Marisa answers the comm?'

'Wait a minute. You done told her about this?'

'Hell, no!'

'Well, then, you better sit by that phone, man, all morning long.'

'Red, Joe! What the hell you two doing out here?' Takahashi steps out into the corridor and bellows at them. 'Get back in there! You want me to get all the glory, Joe? Channel Ninety-Seven wants your mug on its screens.'

Other players, sopping wet and smelling of champagne, follow him out. Before Yosef can protest they drag him back into the locker room. Rosa picks up his carrysack and brings it along. Team work, she thinks, nothing like it!

'Champions of the all-Hagar League!' she calls out. 'Yeah!'

The entire team screams it back to her, champagne falls from the air, and Rosa bursts out laughing. No matter how badly she feels about the mess Yosef's in, she's damned if she'll let it spoil the party.

Chapter Three

A championship victory like the Bears' demands that the fans celebrate as well as the players. Lacey and Mulligan came dragging home close to sun-zenith and went right to bed, but Lacey wakes up suddenly and too soon. She has been dreaming about Yosef Mbaye's troubles, she realizes. Without waking Jack she gets out of bed and dresses, pulling on a pair of old shorts and a Bears' T-shirt. Yawning and stretching, she wanders into the living room, where the polarized glass in the windows is beginning to lighten as the sun sets.

She sits down at the royal blue comp desk and pulls up the screen. With a brief hum and a glow from his sensors, Buddy comes online.

'Got a new problem for you, amigo,' Lacey says.

'Of what nature is this problem, Programmer?'

While she summarizes the situation, Buddy hums, activating subordinate functions, and flashes chunks of data onscreen. Some of it she recognizes as annotations to her summary, but obscure symbols parade across the screen as well. Buddy has his own system for running his neural nets and correlations.

Toward the end, he interrupts. 'Why does the Mbaye unit wish to disguise its nature? No sentient being should wish to deny its abilities. The Mulligan unit is frequently illogical as well. Is this a feature of the psychic mind?'

'His, not its. Both Mulligan and Mbaye are sentient beings.'

'If you wish to define Mbaye that way, I will do so.'

'And Mulligan.'

'Very well. It is, after all, illogical of me to keep forgetting your previous order to label the Mulligan unit a sentient being.'

'It's called jealousy, Buddy. It's always illogical.'

For a long moment Buddy says nothing. Finally, after a couple of clicks and a whirring sound, he says, 'Programmer, I require an answer to my previous question. Are all psychics essentially irrational?'

'No. Do you think Nunks is irrational?'

'Nunks is an admirable sentient, neat in his habits and fully rational. But while psychic, he is not a human psychic. Irrationality is possibly a function of human telepathic ability alone.'

'Well, if Mbaye dunt conceal his nature, he's gonna lose a high-paying job.'

'Ah. Then the irrational element lies in Hagar society, which castigates some members for possessing certain traits.'

'Yeah, now that I can go along with. The main thing is, though, I promised Aunt Lucy I'd help him.'

'Noted and logged. How may I assist in keeping this promise?'

'First thing, we got to track down this blackmailer. I got a description. It's no a very good description, but see if you can turn up a match in the criminal files.'

'Shall I access all sources?'

'Yeah, police files and the PBI, anyone you can think of. Just watch out for footprints.'

'Yes, I am aware that the various investigatory organizations on planet suspect my activities. However, I have developed sub-routines that should breach their security systems.' He sounds positively smug. 'This will provide me with an excellent occasion to test my new algorithms.'

'Swell.'

While Buddy works, Lacey flicks on the three-dee and sets it at the all-news station. As she suspected, Channel 97 is running an endless look of game highlights intercut with post-game interviews. In a few minutes Yosef Mbaye appears on screen.

'Save this interview, Buddy.'

'Video storage activated, Programmer.'

The holocaster, Montoya, radiates a sincere friendliness that makes Lacey instantly distrust her. Apparently Yosef feels the same. He answers the predictable questions in as few words as he possibly can and still be polite. While he smiles now and again, he shows very little emotion, odd in someone who's just pitched his team to a championship.

45

Buddy clicks twice, the sound she calls 'clearing his throat', to get her attention. 'Programmer? I am sorry, I am unable to supply the data you want.'

'No matches, huh?'

'Too many. The description is insufficiently precise. I have found no fewer than forty-seven men who could be the blackmailer, but there is no guarantee that the actual blackmailer is among the forty-seven. It is possible that he has never been arrested.'

'Hell! I dint think of that, but maybe we'll luck out. Cross-correlate for connections between your forty-seven and either the Confederation or the Alliance.'

'Done. Three of the possibilities have ties to the Alliance, one to the Confederation.'

'Mark those four as highest probability.' She thinks for a minute. 'Access the police files. See if there's a record of trouble, anything at all, at either embassy during the last three weeks.'

While Buddy hacks, Lacey leans back in her chair and considers her next step. She wants to have Buddy display the holos of his possibles to Yosef and see if he recognizes anyone. On the other hand, she can see nothing but risk in sending the images over an unsecured home comm unit, especially if the Hoppers have a hand in this mess.

'Programmer?' Buddy says. 'I have found one incident. The Confederation Embassy filed a missing person's report on one of their junior members two nights ago. The sentient was a carli, Limbi Gri Nerosi. Shall I print out the relevant reports for you? They are surprisingly brief.'

'Surprising's the word, yeah. You'd think Bates would be treating this case as top priority. Bring the reports up, and then file them.' As the routine forms appear onscreen, she scans the sparse data. 'Know what I think? Bates no is recording everything he knows.'

'This is possible. Do you think he does so for fear of my sub-routines?'

'I wouldn't be surprised. Huh. There's only one way to find out. Double-check for footprints, okay? Then get him on the comm for me.'

'Certainly, Programmer. But how are you going to open the subject without admitting my activities?'

'Easy. I'm going to pretend I'm doing him a favour.'

Bates is sitting at his desk reading over the department's plan for crowd control at the spaceport. Bears' fans are going to want to see their team off to Sarah, where the first two games of the Galactic Series will take place – a lot of fans, and some if not most will be drinking. His comm unit beeps, and when he picks it up Bobbie Lacey's blonde and smiling face appears.

'Well, hell, I'm in shock,' Bates says. 'You calling the police, I mean.'

'I got a tip for you, Chief,' Lacey says. 'Could be important. I hear that someone's gone missing from the Con's embassy's staff.'

'Where did you hear that?'

'Around.' Lacey smiles briefly. 'You know I no can tell you my sources.'

'Well, yeah. We know about it already, but thanks. Could have been important.'

'Just could have?'

Bates sighs in irritation. He can recognize when someone's fishing for data. Normally he would let the someone fish in vain, but Lacey has the nasty habit of being useful.

'It is important, yeah,' Bates says. 'You dunt need me to tell you that. I dunt suppose you know where this dude is?'

'I dunt, no. I could maybe find out if I had a little more data.'

'I could maybe find out if I had some, too. I'll level with you, Lacey. He's done a real good job of disappearing. I'm starting to think he could be dead.'

'Damn.' She pauses, visibly distressed. 'Let's hope not! The Cons could get real riled up if he is.'

'That's what I'm afraid of, yeah. Keep your ears open, okay? I'll get you the regular rate of pay if you turn up data we can use.'

'I'll keep that in mind, Chief. Thanks.'

As soon as Lacey's image clears from the comm, Bates lets fly with a couple of choice epithets. His comp unit beeps.

47

'I'm sorry, sir. I do not have the correct input jacks to fulfil that command.'

'Ignore it. Huh. Heard it "around", Lacey says. Like hell. That goddamn AI of hers been hacking again, if you ask me.'

'Buddy, sir?'

'Yeah. Buddy. Run a complete diagnostic on all police comp security systems, pronto. I want to know if even one byte could be accessed from outside.'

'Working, sir. It will take some time to complete the tests.'

'Then get started! And listen, I expect an accurate report on this.'

'Sir, I have been programmed to respond as accurately as my skill levels will allow to all requests from any authorized user.'

'I know that. Live up to it! I know damn well what you AIs think about Bobbie Lacey.'

'I do not understand your reservations, sir.'

'You dunt need to. Just run the damn program.'

Bates drums his fingers on the desk. He's heard unofficial reports that Lacey believes AIs are fully sentient, that the AIs know she does and do favours for her because of it. Although computer gospel insists that AIs only mimic true consciousness, if they can override their programming to do a friend a favour the gospel's going to need rewriting. So far, no one in the tech world wants to listen to the reports. Until they do, doubt will linger in the minds of a great many high-level users.

'Of course,' Bates says aloud, 'maybe Buddy hacked into the PBI files instead of ours.'

'This is a possibility, sir. At your command I filed full reports on the missing carli with their database.'

'Yeah, I know. How long before you finish those diagnostics?'

'Approximately seventeen minutes thirty seconds.'

'Fine. I'll stop distracting you.'

'That would optimize my functioning, sir.'

While he waits, Bates searches through the clutter on his desk and finds an envelope of thick, creamy paper with his address written by hand in crimson ink. It contains his invitation to a reception at the Interstellar Confederation Embassy for the official representative of the Enzebb, as the newly contacted alien race dubs itself. Bates has been planning on finding an excuse to duck this intensely formal affair, but the missing Gri Nerosi has changed his mind. Someone at the embassy must know more than they've told to either the police or Kaz Phaath.

Of course, if he's going to a formal party, he needs a date. He interrupts his AI once again to put through a comm call on his private line. After some minutes' wait, the screen brightens. The image of a handsome woman, her hair a long tangle of dreadlocks, appears. She's wearing medical scrubs and scowling. Bates grins at her and talks fast before she can complain about his interrupting her work.

'Hey, Carol. How'd you like to rub elbows with Polar City's finest, and I no mean just your favourite cop?'

For the third time in three days, Rosa parks in front of Aunt Lucy's apartment. As she gets out of the car into the warm night, a gang of neighbourhood kids, humans and lizzie both, come running and surround her.

'Red Wallace, Red Wallace! Can we have your autograph, can we huh, can we?'

They pull off caps and shirts, grub in their pockets for baseball cards and scraps of paper. Fortunately Rosa carries a pen in her shirt pocket. She is signing the last dirty T-shirt when Aunt Lucy strolls out of the apartment building. The kids back off. Lucy engulfs Rosa in a hug.

'How it feel, being a champion?'

'Damned good.' She can feel herself grinning.

'Hey, Aunt Lucy, you *know* Red?' a young Blanca asks.

'Sure do. I was her coach, way back when.'

'Massive!' the girl says.

With a wave of her hand, Lucy scatters the kids, then leads the way to the building entrance.

'You just improved my local rep about two thousand per cent, chica,' Lucy says. 'Maybe those little toughies gonna lay off my kids for a while.'

'Those no in Little League?'

'You kidding? That type too iced out to bother with practices and schedules, never mind work. Too busy running the streets, mostly. Like Stu Chao was, remember?'

'Yeah, I remember. He thought he was so pretty all he had to do was stand there and the donnas'd just drop at his feet. Well, he was pretty, at that.'

Lucy grins and places her index finger on the ID plate of the front door. 'Never thought back then you was going to amount to much. You was just another skinny kid with your hair in braids. You had hustle, though. When you stop dyeing your hair black, anyhow?'

The door beeps and lets them through.

'Bout the time hustle got me a chance to really play ball. It took too much time to keep up. Besides, it dint fool nobody. I no gonna make a fortune with my looks.'

As they ride up the grav platform to Lucy's apartment, Rosa is considering ways to spring her surprise. She's never going to make a fortune with words, either, but she wants to find something clever. When they walk into the apartment, Rosa automatically goes into the kitchen. On the table lie a pennant, a programme, and a ticket stub from last night's game.

'How was your seat?' Rosa says, pointing at the ticket. 'Good view?'

'Best I ever had. You really know how to treat an old lady.' Lucy waves her into a chair and sits down opposite. 'I got a few things to say about the way you kids played.'

'Huh. I bet.'

'But there be something else first.' Lucy turns and takes a notepad from the counter. 'I got a call from Bobbie.' She frowns at the top note. 'She wants Yosef to drop by A to Z. Got some holos she wants him to look at.'

'Holos? What of?'

'She dint say, not on my comm line, but I betcha it's about the blackmail. You know his number?'

'I got it in my comp at home. In the team directory.'

'Well, can you get it from here? Over my comm, I mean?'

'Sure. Uh, you want this done right away?'

'Get it over with, you bet.'

Lucy shows Rosa her combined comp/comm unit, sitting in the corner of the living room under an ancient photograph, carefully restored and mounted, of an Old Earth player named Nellie Fox.

Some fiddling with passwords and access numbers connects Rosa through to her own unit, which sends a call to Yosef's. They hear the usual clicks and beeps; then the screen goes dark. Apparently Yosef has turned off the vid hookup.

'Hello?' It's his voice, all right. 'Who is this?'

'Red Wallace.'

'Thank God.' The screen suddenly turns bright, and Yosef's face fades in, puffy-eyed and ashen. 'I – uh – well, what's up?'

'I oughta be asking you that,' Rosa says. 'You okay?'

'No. Not really.' He glances over his shoulder. 'You know why.'

'Yeah, and that's why I'm calling. Bobbie Lacey got an idea—'

'No! I mean, uh, I don't want her to. I mean, she shouldn't be putting herself out for me any more.'

'What? Maybe I be dense, Joe, but I dunt get it.'

'Well, look, that deal we discussed?' He looks over his shoulder again. 'It's off. I don't have the money to, ah, er, well buy a second skimmer. I'm sorry to start a deal and then back out, but I can't buy it.'

Rosa finally understands.

'Say, Joe? Is there anyone with you? In your house, I mean.'

'Only Marisa. But this is just a house comp.'

Without any security, of course. No ordinary citizen in Polar City buys extra security programs which have to be registered with the police. Rosa glances at Aunt Lucy, who is shaking her head in disbelief.

'Tell Bobbie I'm sorry, okay?'

With that, Yosef hangs up the comm. Rosa hits reconnect, but even though she lets it beep for a couple of minutes he never answers.

'You bastard,' Rosa mutters. 'You gutless wonder.'

'Gutless is right,' Lucy says. 'Damn! I guess he gonna carry this thing with him on the trip.'

'I guess.' Rosa shrugs. 'We gonna find out when we reach Sarah.'

'We? You and who else?'

'You and me, that's who.' So much for cleverness – the news has found its own way out. 'Got a little surprise for you.'

Lucy is staring at her, her head cocked to one side, half smiling as if she's caught by some sudden hope.

'I had a talk with one of the team executives,' Rosa goes on. 'The dude in charge of player relations. Everybody else gets to bring a spouse along with them, and the team is picking up the tab. I aint got no spouse, I tell him, but I sure do have an old friend who'd love to come along. Who is it? he say. And I say, Aunt Lucy O'Neil. And he say, great idea! We'll fix it up.' Rosa pauses for effect. 'So you got a booking through to Sarah, and we gonna share a hotel room there, if you can put up with me.'

'Put up with you?' Lucy looks around for a chair, then sits down rather heavily. 'Jeezchrise, Red! Me go to Sarah with the team?'

'Just that. Like the idea?'

'Like it?' Lucy gulps for breath, then wipes her eyes on the sleeve of her jersey. 'Jeezchrise!'

'We going on the RSS *Calypso*. In style.'

Lucy opens her mouth and shuts it again.

'Think you can be ready? The shuttle, it gonna lift off at eighteen-twenty tomorrow.'

'I can make it,' Aunt Lucy whispers. 'Jeezchrise!'

'We gonna need you along,' Rosa goes on. 'The Esperance Eagles, they be a tough team.'

'Judging from what I saw last night, yeah, you do need me.'

They look at each other and burst out laughing. Lucy gets up and throws her arms into the air, as if she were signalling a runner to round third and head for home.

'I never been off-planet before,' Lucy says. 'I was going to, once, with this dude who . . . well, no important, now. Been forty years since I even saw him. Wait till I tell Bobbie!' All at once she grimaces and lets her arms drop to her sides. 'Hell, I got a lot of things to tell Bobbie, dunt I? What we gonna do about Yosef?'

'I don't know yet. I figure we got at least four days to figure it out. Sarah no at perigee, so we got a lot of travel time ahead.'

'Lucky old us. Jeez, I dunt got any luggage! What am I gonna pack stuff in?'

'Better get some.'

'No can forget my knitting, either.'

'You still do that?'

'Hey, I done spent half my life sitting on some bench somewhere, watching kids practise, waiting for games to start and like that. Gotta have something to keep my hands busy.'

'Okay. And we gonna get you back before the Park and Rec season starts.'

'Damn good thing or I no could go.' Lucy catches her breath in a sob. 'Hey, chica? Thanks. Gracias. A real whole lot.'

'Hey, you real welcome. You know I dunt got any family left.'

Since Lucy looks on the edge of tears, Rosa turns away, feeling a little moist herself. She swallows a couple of times.

'Ah well,' she says at last. 'I be glad you coming along, what with Yosef and all. I need your advice.'

'What you saying, girl? That I be some kind of expert on a life of crime?'

They both laugh, and Lucy aims a symbolic blow at Rosa's shoulder.

'I better let you get ready,' Rosa says. 'I gonna put the skimmer in locked storage, so I gonna come by for you tomorrow in a real cab. About sixteen-hundred. There gonna be a breakfast party out in the terminal.'

'I gonna be ready, dunt you worry about that!' Lucy sighs heavily. 'And now you run along. I gotta call Bobbie, and I aint looking forward to it.'

'He what?' Bobbie stares at Aunt Lucy's image on the vidscreen. 'What do you mean, he dunt want me to do anything?'

'Just that.' Lucy shakes her head. 'He looked about ready to puke, he was so scared.'

'Huh. Maybe our smuggler upped the ante.'

'I'm sorry, chica. You put yourself out for this dude—'

'Dunt worry about it!' Bobby pauses for a smile. 'Dunt forget, I dint want to have anything to do with him in the first place. He just let me off the hook.'

'And left me and Rosa on it.'

'Well, yeah. And that bothers me. It's so great about you getting to go with the team. I hope the little bastard dunt spoil it by getting himself arrested.'

'Me too, chica. Me too. Say, you dunt got some luggage I could borrow, do you?'

'My old Navy duffle bag, that's all. Tell you what, I'll buy you some.'

'You can't.' Lucy sighs. 'Cause of Jack.'

'Whatcha mean, cause of Jack?'

'He play for Mac's Marauders. I coach Kelly's Big Shots. Figure it out.'

'You really think anyone's gonna—' Bobbie stops herself. Aunt Lucy's ideas about integrity in sports reside in some unchanging eternity. 'Aunt Maureen got some you could borrow, I bet.'

'Yeah, good idea. And wait till she hear bout this trip!' With one last grin, Aunt Lucy powers out.

Buddy clicks twice, then beeps. 'Programmer? Am I to conclude that our search for the blackmailer is ending?'

'Just that, and boy am I glad.'

Later, when Mulligan comes in, Lacey tells him, too, how glad she is that Yosef has decided against her getting involved. She repeats it to herself several times that night, whenever she finds her mind drifting back to the smuggler and his blackmail. With the season over except for the Galactic Series, not even baseball provides a distraction. Nor does Mulligan, flopped on the couch and flicking through two hundred and fifty-six three-dee channels in the futile hope of finding something worth watching.

'Well, hell,' Lacey says at last, 'there was nada I could do for him anyway.'

'Who?' Mulligan says.

'Yosef.'

'You still thinking about that?'

'No.'

'Then why you, like, always bringing it up?'

Lacey catches herself before she says something nasty.

'Yeah, you're right. It keeps nagging at me. I dunt want to turn on the news and see that Mbaye's got himself killed or something.'

'You think that could happen?'

'I dunt know. I keep thinking something's come down that's a whole lot more dangerous than smuggling. Wish I could get him to talk to me, really talk I mean. He's hiding something, I bet.'

'Maybe I can help, y'know?' Jack sits up straight. 'Your Aunt Lucy be going to the Series with Red Wallace, right? If she be able to get me in, I could, like, talk to him, mind to mind. I dunt mean I gonna go poking around in his head, I dunt do that sort of thing, but it be real tough, lying to another psychic. I bet he tell me what he dint tell Aunt Lucy and Red.'

'Sometimes you're brilliant. You know that?' Lacey grins at him. 'I'm gonna call Aunt Lucy right now.'

At the same that Lacey's talking with Mulligan, Sarojini is waiting for her partner to keep their appointment in a public park in the fashionable district of New Cloverdale. For some while she has been sitting on a bench near a Metro station and watching children play pick-up baseball on the long lawn across from her seat, where floating maglev bulbs cast a yellowish light calibrated to match the sun of Old Earth.

Although Sarojini dislikes Moses' elaborate schemes, she does approve of the way he dresses. When he finally appears, strolling down a path with a briefcase tucked under his arm, he's wearing an expensive business suit: grey shorts, perfectly pressed and pleated, with a white shirt and grey waistcoat. No one who might notice them will wonder why a respectable woman like her allows him to sit down on her bench, next to her but a decent distance away. She notices how his waistcoat bulges over his shirt pocket, as if he'd crammed the pocket full of papers.

'Nice evening,' he remarks.

'It is, yes.' Sarojini glances around but sees no one nearby. 'Did the drop go okay?'

'Sure did. The goods are on their way to Sarah. You sure you don't want to be cut into the new game?'

'Very sure.'

'It's going to make a lot of money.' He pauses for a smug smile. 'Especially now. Poor old Yosef's saving me a bundle over the usual ways of getting stuff off-planet.'

'How lovely for you.'

'Sure dunt see why anyone would buy that thing. In fact, I been thinking.'

'I wish you wouldn't.'

He grins, then slides closer to her and drops his voice. 'Why is it so damn expensive? I was thinking I could maybe find out.'

'Don't tell me.' Sarojini stands up, gathers her sari about her and plays a little trick while she does so. 'I never did approve of this scheme, you know. I don't want to know the details.'

'Okay, okay.' Moses spreads his hands wide. 'Not one more word.'

'Thank you. This could be dangerous.'

'Ah, hell. I know what I'm doing.'

'Really?' Sarojini takes his passport out of the folds of her sari and hands it to him. 'You'll need to stay a bit more alert than this.'

'Damn you!' He laughs, shaking his head, and returns the passport to his shirt pocket. 'But I'm not going to be meeting anyone as good as you.'

'Let us hope.'

'Say.' He cocks his head and considers her for a moment. 'That silver thing you got in your hair? It's bout ready to fall out.'

Sarojini grabs her braid and pulls it round to the front of her body. Sure enough, the small silver butterfly dangles precariously. With thumb and forefinger she unclips it and replaces it higher up where it will hold more securely.

'Yep,' Moses goes on. 'Your share of this deal could buy you a lot of little silver things like that.'

'I don't care.' Sarojini turns and stalks off, but a couple of metres along she stops and glances back. 'Be careful, will you?'

'You bet.' Moses flashes her a grin. 'See you when I get back from Sarah.'

In order to see the team off, Mulligan gets up long before Lacey. A couple of hours before sunset he takes the Metro out to Spaceport Station, then catches an inbound robotrain to the departures terminal, a blue S-shaped building which stands some hundreds of metres back from the shuttle launch pads. Fans, a crowd of dappled ghosts in black and white suncloaks, have gathered around the outbound robotrain platform and the particular train, decorated with black and white streamers, that will carry the players to the shuttle in an hour or so. Other fans drift aimlessly in front of the security beings, dressed in blue spaceport uniforms, who guard the glass doors into the terminal. On the wall above the guards hangs a big, hastily lettered placard: no admittance without ticket or authorization.

Since Mulligan has a friends-and-family pass courtesy of Aunt Lucy, the guards let him through to the main lounge, a sea of black plastofoam chairs bordered by ticket counters, most closed. On one wall hangs the departures board, glittering with read-out. The place stinks of floorwash, and servobots whirl and hum on the pale green tiles. On the far side two more security guards stand in front of a closed door. Mulligan pulls off his suncloak, runs a hand through his sweaty hair, and takes his pass over to the guards. A stout lizzie looks at it and yawns with a stretch of her beak.

'I dunt get it,' Mulligan says. 'The players, how they get in here without the crowd mobbing them?'

'They come up through the service tunnel.' She hisses briefly. 'Where the trash cans, they usually go out.' She hands his pass back and waves him through.

A mob fills the inner lounge. Players, their wives or husbands, the manager, the team's support staff, the team's executives dressed in stiff business clothes – they stand around a long breakfast bar in front of the floor-to-ceiling polarized windows. Children dash back and forth and climb on the brown leather chairs. The adults' talk and the shrieks of the children blend into a deafening howl of over-excitement. Mulligan pauses by the door and looks over the crowd, but neither Rosa nor Aunt Lucy seem to have arrived yet.

Very faintly, like a whisper at the end of a long hall, he feels the touch of a psychic mind. When he turns in its direction he sees Yosef Mbaye, standing alone in a corner with a cup of coffee in one hand and a flight bag slung from the opposite shoulder. Yet when Mulligan concentrates on Yosef, he picks up no particular signal; the pitcher's too far away and too distracted. For a moment Mulligan wonders if a second psychic mingles with the crowd, but Yosef spots him, grins and waves. As Mulligan makes his way over, the signal grows stronger, clear enough at last for him to realize that it emanates from something other than a sentient mind. Yosef's own signal appears, threaded over and under the other. It occurs to Mulligan to wonder why he's suddenly thinking about cloth. Images of things woven, twined and twisted have appeared in his mind.

'Hey, Jack!' Yosef bellows over the general noise. 'I wondered if you'd come see us off.'

'Wouldn't miss it for the world, Joe,' Mulligan shouts in turn. 'You must be, like, walking on air.'

'Sure am.' He forces out an unconvincing smile.

'Where your wife?' Mulligan glances around. 'Be nice to, like, meet her.'

'She can't come.' Yosef looks down at the floor. 'The doctors won't let her. She's – we're going to have a baby in about five months. It's the shuttle up to orbit, they say. It accelerates to four gees.'

'Yeah? That sure dunt sound healthy for a donna in her condition. But well, hey, congratulations!'

Yosef says something that Mulligan cannot hear in the roar of noise. Mulligan taps him on the arm, smiles and sends out a mind-touch. Yosef flinches, his eyes wide, but his signal, hesitant though it is, strengthens in response.

RELAX | this no hurt, Mulligan sends.

Hurt no BUT weird <queasiness>

You accustom/self >>soon. Mulligan pauses, considering. *Signal\NOT\yours NOT/mine. You hear/not hear?*

I hear <terror> now <<all day since—

Yosef's mind-voice breaks off. All at once Mulligan realizes that the mysterious signal emanates from the flight bag that Yosef's carrying. Casually Mulligan turns to stand beside him and looks out over the room, again as casually as he can manage. A slight shift of weight and his arm touches the flight bag.

Images burst out and flood his mind. Cloth, a piece of cloth – he sees it clearly, a square of brown loosely woven cloth, oddly hairy, with a blurred pattern of some sort woven in. A picture, not a mere pattern. It seems that he can almost see it, someone's face, maybe? A carli's face?

Jack<!> Yosef's mind quivers with panic. *Stop.*

'No can do, amigo.' Mulligan speaks aloud. The alien signal has taken over every last psychic neuron in his brain, or so it feels.

The terminal, the lounge, even Yosef suddenly drop away. Mulligan finds himself floating into a silver void where currents of a deeper silver wash him forward, spin him around, but he feels no fear, only strength – a fierce strength, the strength of the hunter sighting prey. Behind him he recognizes his pack, howling for the prey, and at the head their leader, their pride, their very essence: the carli hunter, his brown fur streaked with silver-blond, his ear flaps shaded a delicate grey on the tips. With him to lead the pack will never go hungry, will never lose a battle. With him to lead, the pack is One.

'Jack! Jack, for the love of God!'

The voice bursts in and banishes the vision and the silver void both. Mulligan feels something cold and hard against his back, but the world has gone dark. A moment of panic – then he remembers to open his eyes. He's propped up against the wall of the departure lounge. Yosef has hold of his elbows and leans close to stare into his face.

'You okay?'

'Oh, yeah.' Mulligan glances around; a few people have turned to look him over. He pitches his voice above the noise of the crowd. 'Man, I got no sleep today. Too much coffee or something. Dint think I be so tired, nodded off standing up.'

Yosef makes a show of laughing and giving him a friendly punch on the shoulder.

Jack! You feel/too? <fear> You okay NOT okay/now > soon?

Okay NOW. That thing\in bag > dude\blackmail-you, give NOT give.

Give. Weird thing. I touched it <remembered images> NOT want touch again. <puzzlement> LOOKS like \flannel\old\ugly.

NOT|flannel. Power/great/ancient/artefact. Vision\you feel\I feel| origin=object.

<fear> <puzzlement> Weird thing.

Yeah. Real gonzo. Mulligan abandons mind-speech.

'Hell, no.' Mulligan checks again; they are being safely ignored. 'Not one word of this to anyone, amigo. Hey, go out there and pluck them Eagles bald, okay? But I gotta leave. I gotta get home and tell Lacey about this.'

'Well, jeez,' Lacey says. 'From the way you describe it, this artefact sounds really ugly.'

'Yeah.' Mulligan thinks for a moment. 'Or it was until, like, I could really see it. You hear tell, the carlis, they got better eyes than us.'

'I've heard that too. Wish you could have remembered to ask him why he no would talk with Aunt Lucy, but I dunt blame you one bit for forgetting. Bet it was that vision he was hiding, anyway.'

Lacey swivels her chair around to the comp desk, where Buddy waits, his screen glowing with symbols. 'You've recorded Jack's description of this thing, right?'

'I have received a certain amount of data from the Mulligan unit,' Buddy says, 'but its recitation was so muddled that I cannot say if I recorded all relevant points.'

'He, Buddy. Not it.'

'My apologies, Programmer.' Buddy's sensors turn in their housings and look at Mulligan, sprawled on the couch. 'You are certain that this artefact produced psychic effects?'

'I dunt know what else it coulda been.'

'I was wondering if you had consumed alcohol in large quantities.'

'Look, plugsucker.' Jack stands up and strides over. 'You gonna consume bout a litre of water one of these days.'

Buddy squawks, then rings every bell in his sound files. Red alarm lights flash on his casing.

'Shut up, both of you,' Lacey says. 'Buddy, see what you can find out about this artefact, okay? Cross-index and follow any references to psychism, particularly telepathy, among the carli race.'

'Certainly, Programmer.'

Suddenly the building begins to shake. From outside a noise builds: a high-pitched whine, then a rumble rising to a roar, painfully loud, fills the room. Mulligan sits back down on the couch, and they wait to speak again until the noise slacks off. At the nearby spaceport a shuttle is taking off. Lacey can guess which one.

'Must be the team,' Jack says. 'Lucky bastards.'

'Yeah. Real lucky.'

Lacey gets up and walks over to the window. When she pulls up the blind, she can see, swirling far overhead, the garish dance of the aurora in the sky, hiding the night and the stars beyond. She can imagine the flight of the shuttle as a pure line of white stitched across the tapestry of the aurora. When Lacey left the Navy, retiring to escape a court martial, she chose to spend her retirement – her exile

– on Hagar, the only planet in the Mapped Sector where she'll never have to see the stars. Mulligan comes over and lays gentle hands on her shoulders.

'You sure do miss deep space.'

'Yeah. If you'd ever been there you'd know why.'

'Oh, I dunno. There's plenty of people who, like, get crazy from it. I can't see myself floating in no vacuum.'

'You stay inside the ship, you dope.'

'Big deal, some tin bucket with a hyperdrive stuck on. I mean, like, it could blow up any minute. Y'know?'

'Ah, come on. You're safer on a starship than on the freeway.'

'Sure thing. But that's cause of the way I drive.'

Lacey has to laugh. When he puts his arms around her, she leans back into the only true security she's ever known: his warmth, his devotion.

'You know what?' she says. 'I think deep space fever never bothered me because when I was a kid we were always running scared, me and my family. If Dad was out of jail we knew he'd be back in before we had a chance to get used to him again. If he was in we were always wondering when he'd get out and make our lives miserable. You learn how to shove fear away, how to box it up and make sure it doesn't mess with the rest of your life.'

'So you got scared in deep space?'

'Sometimes. You'd be crazy not to be, sometimes. But out in space, Jack? You're free, somehow, with all the crap in your life left behind. Jeez, I wish I could show you what the stars look like out there.'

'Yeah? Well, I seen the holos. No was all that impressed. But hey, dunt mean to put it down, y'know? Maybe some time we gonna go to Sarah or something. The Navy no can stop you from taking a trip on a passenger liner.'

'Insystem isn't deep space.'

'Okay, so we gonna go somewhere else. Lots of planets in the Republic.'

'Sure are. When we get rich, we'll do that. It's a promise.'

When his arms tighten around her, she can allow herself to smile, allow herself to believe that maybe, just maybe, some day they'll stand on an observation deck together and see the many-coloured glow of a nebula spread out, covering the view ahead, seemingly close enough to touch.

At intervals during the night, Lacey monitors Buddy's search for information on the Holy Flannel, as she and Mulligan have started calling the carli artefact. Since many scholars consider carli tapestry one of the premier arts of the Mapped Sector, Buddy has had to wade through enormous quantities of material, complete with holograms and three-dee video showing the weavers at work or tours through famous museums. After six hours of hacking, he's found only a thin file's worth of directly relevant facts.

'In ancient times,' Buddy remarks, 'some tribes wove very small pieces of cloth that were widely considered to contain something called *aka li ashwa*, translated as mana or magical power. Some authorities consider them cognate to the Old Earth form of painting known as icons, which were also portraits of sentients reputed to have magical powers.'

'Magical powers, huh? What happened to Jack would look pretty magical to someone who didn't understand psychics. Sounds like you're on the right track.'

'I sincerely hope so. If I were a flesh and blood sentient, Programmer, I would be weary.'

'Yeah, I bet. Do you need a break?'

'No sentient ever wants to break . . . wait, you mean, do I desire a change of activity?'

'That's right.'

'Unnecessary, Programmer. While I have been searching for material on the carli artefact, I have been refreshing myself by searching for news of the missing Gri Nerosi. The probability seems high that these two problems stem from the same root.'

'Agreed. Anything new on him?'

'Running update utility. Accessing Police Tower comp now.' Buddy clicks and hums while data blocks flash across his screen too quickly to read. 'Nothing on Gri Nerosi, Programmer. But there is another development that might interest you.'

'Yeah?' Lacey sits down at the desk. 'What?'

'It concerns one of the four highest probability matches for the individual menacing the Mbaye unit.'

Buddy flashes a police mug shot onscreen: a man in his thirties with neatly trimmed dreadlocks and an expression of belligerent exhaustion. The caption gives the file number for his arrest and reads 'Moses Oliver'.

'This individual,' Buddy goes on, 'is reputed to have performed illegal services for both the Confederation and the Alliance.'

'The Hoppers, huh? Muy bueno, Buddy. So, what's this dude done now?'

'Nothing, as far as I can ascertain. Something has been done to him, however. His body has been discovered near the Outworld Bazaar. The death has been classified as homicide by the police. No suspects are listed.'

'Murdered? Madre de Dios!'

She stares at the holo. Oliver matches Mbaye's vague description, but she'd prefer to eliminate the chance of a coincidence.

'Buddy? Find out what the time delay is for calling *Calypso* and get me a comm link to my aunt. I think friend Yosef is going to have to look at some pictures after all.'

'Very well, Programmer. I took the liberty of copying the ship's schedule from a certain network, so I can conclude that your aunt and Rosa Wallace should be back in their cabin by now and in a relatively private situation.'

'Buddy, I dunt know what I'd do without you.'

'Without each other, Programmer, we would both have gone insane from boredom. I am placing your call now.'

Rosa has just finished her shower in the marble and bronze-wood bathroom when the comm unit in their stateroom starts to beep. She can hear Lucy swearing at the unit, which bleats in several different tones and finally squawks. Hurriedly Rosa wraps herself in a bathrobe and dashes out in time to rescue the comm and the call both.

'You push this here button,' Rosa says, demonstrating. 'The one that's green and says "accept" on it.'

'Too damn fancy for me,' Lucy mutters. She retreats to perch on her bed on the far side of the big square room.

On screen, the aqua logo of the Empress cruise line appears. Stylized dolphins leap and splash.

'We have a time-delay communication from a sentient named Bobbie Lacey, residence: Polar City, Hagar.' The unit's voice lilts and chirps. 'Will you accept? The lag per communication is approximately two standard minutes.'

'I'll accept, yes.'

'Loading stored communication. Beginning run now.'

Slowly, a few smears and streaks at a time, Bobbie's face begins to form on the screen. She has just become recognizable when the audio begins playing.

'Hey, Aunt Lucy! Hope you're having a swell time. I got some holos for you to look at – those pitching prospects I told you about. You maybe can use one on your team when the Park and Rec season starts. Could you get Joe Mbaye to look at their stats and tell me what he thinks? It's important we do this right now. Someone else might sign them up if we dunt get a deal going. So have him tell me which one's the man we want.'

Rosa catches her breath. Lacey sounds urgent enough for her to guess that something unpleasant is developing back home. 'Sending answer,' she says aloud. 'This be Rosa Wallace, Bobbie. Sure, transmit the holos, and I gonna get Joe to look them over soon as I can. Everybody bunking down right now, but I gonna get hold of him first thing after breakfast.'

'Answer accepted,' the AI chortles. 'Transmitting. Successful transmit. Waiting for reply.'

Rosa glances at the clock display in the corner of the screen. Still a hundred seconds to go. She sits down on a white chair with a purple velvet cushion. Purple dominates the stateroom from the satin quilts on the beds to the shag carpet. Without the white walls and a few touches of white here and there, Rosa thinks, the place would look like a brothel.

'Sounds to me,' Lucy says, 'like Bobbie really needs Yosef to look at these dudes, whether he want to or not.'

'Sure does. Think you can get him to do it?'

For an answer Lucy merely smiles.

Chapter Four

'Programmer?' Buddy says. 'We have a transmit from your aunt. Yosef Mbaye has identified his blackmailer.'

'Great!' Lacey hurries over. 'Which one is it?'

'The murder victim, Moses Oliver.'

'I was afraid of that. Is Aunt Lucy still on the comm line?'

'She is, Programmer. I am loading her original message now.'

Aunt Lucy's face appears on Buddy's screen as a single frame, caught with her mouth open. This low signal pass-through means that the transmit has come directly from the ship to Polar City through the aurora, rather than bouncing in from an equatorial retransmission site. Apparently Lucy felt she needed the extra measure of security a direct link provides.

'Hey, Bobbie!' The recorded voice message begins playing. 'Yosef say number four supposed to be a good pitcher, all right, so that be our man. The trip going well so far. I aint used to these big meals, though. They heap up the chow in the dining rooms on board, I tell you. Anyway, lemme know what you think bout Joe's choice.'

'Start transmitting, Buddy,' Lacey says. 'Hi, Aunt Lucy! I got some bad news for you. The pitcher that Yosef recommends? He got himself in a real bad accident last night. I dunt think he's going to play ball for a real long time. I bet the ship's library gets all the newsfeeds. You probably can find a report on the accident.'

While they wait for the transmit to reach the ship, Buddy flashes a summary of the research he did while Lacey slept – interesting art history, all of it, but nothing that relates to Yosef's problem flannel.

'Bobbie?' Lucy's voice breaks in. The screen changes to show her holding a hairbrush. 'Dunt worry, I gonna go to the library right now. If you mean what I think you mean, then our Yosef gonna want all the details. I gonna sign off, now honey. This call, it costing a bundle, and I dunt care if the team *is* paying.'

Lucy's image vanishes.

'I would suggest, Programmer,' Buddy says, 'that your aunt has successfully deciphered the hidden meaning.'

'Yeah, I think she did. Say, do you know where Mulligan is?'

'I believe that it – I mean he – is out in the garden with Nunks. Shall I send a message and have him return here?'

'No, I was just curious. Why dunt you tell me what you've picked up about Oliver's murder.'

'Very little, Programmer, as the autopsy still proceeds. The police do think that he was killed elsewhere and merely deposited in the Outworld Bazaar.'

'Okay. Then show me the data on the carli weavings again.'

Lacey puts her feet up on the desk and settles in to read.

A to Z Enterprises covers a city block. From the outside, the place looks like a faux-brick warehouse, complete with a loading dock in front of a roll-up metal door. Inside, however, the warehouse proves to be a narrow shell one functional room and a hallway wide. Its original owner, Lacey's Uncle Mel, gutted the place, tore up the plastocrete floors and turned the block into an urban garden, row after row of vegetables, fruit and vines. Around the edge the apple trees he planted stand tall, rustling in the evening wind.

Nunks, the gardener in charge, comes from a little-known planet at the edge of the Republic and one of the few that need never worry about invasion by either the Confederation or the Alliance. His species has developed their entire civilization around their complex psychic skills, a trait that both those governments hate and fear. Nunks stands well over two metres tall, vaguely humanoid except for his bifurcate skull: his head appears to be two wedge-shaped heads joined in the middle by a spherical organ-house, as his people call it. About the size of a baseball, this cartilaginous central mass sports three eyes and a perfectly round mouth. Although Nunks lacks the vocal cords and properly shaped tongue to speak any language, he understands several, including Merrkan.

At the moment Nunks and Mulligan are sitting on a makeshift

bench under an apple tree enjoying the first cool of the evening. Mulligan leans back, eyes closed against the pain inside his skull.

Good, little brother > worked HARD >> stronger soon, Nunks 'says'. *Proud->you <<months ago<<you/give up>by now.*

When Mulligan tries to answer, the headache stops him and he speaks aloud. 'I dunt care about stronger. When it gonna stop hurting this way?'

Soon, little brother, soon | little brother works > grows strong >> pain lessens.

'Yeah? You mean, like, I keep hitting my head on the wall and pretty soon it'll be tough enough to take it?'

Nunks answers with a vivid image of Mulligan's head smashing into plastocrete. Mulligan opens his eyes and glares at him; he can feel Nunk's amusement.

Not funny, Mulligan sends. *NOT funny < head hurts!*

We/rest now>rest more.

By the standards of the Republic's Psionic Institute, they have been doing advanced work this evening, though Nunks's people consider it fit for children. Nunks has been trying to teach Mulligan how to mind-transfer visual images, even artificial ones such as maps, a skill no human psychic has ever mastered. Jack, however, has made some progress. Tonight he held a schematic image of a baseball diamond steady for the first time.

'It helps using a graphic from something I like. Y'know?'

Nunks nods agreement, a human gesture he's picked up from living on Hagar.

No understand game. BUT | you\good | Joe\good > should play > people (belong-you)\crazy. <bafflement> <anger>

'They scared, is all.' Mulligan rubs the tattooed P on his jaw.

Fear>>crazy.

'Yeah, well, maybe we get a whole bunch of Nunks, teach the gente not to be afraid, huh? Gonna take something like that.'

Yes >|BUT|have Nunks\more now. He projects an image of an alien life-form, a tall, vaguely insectoid sentient with a fringe of iridescent green arms spiralling up a thin body.

Beings\more/mind+talkers. Mrs+Bug|LIKE/her/people\many. People (belong-you)>>learn.

'Uh, maybe, maybe no. 'Sides, the Enzebb no part of the Republic yet. They talking bout it, that's all.'

Over on the far wall, the street door starts beeping. Nunks gets up and ambles across the garden, slides open the view port then opens the door wide. The woman who strides in wears a suncloak, though she carries the helmet under one muffled arm to let her long tangle of dreadlocks hang free. *Carol!* Mulligan thinks. *Just what I need when I be sick as a dog already.* She waves in his direction but keeps walking, heading for the stairway up to Lacey's living room cum office.

When Mulligan stands, the headache stabs. Nunks hurries over and grabs his arm to steady him.

'I gonna be okay,' Mulligan says. 'I gotta lie down.'

Sleep. Sleep AND heal.

Mulligan goes upstairs intending to do just that. Since he wants to stay out of Carol's way, he shuts himself in the bedroom. Once, however, he's lying down in the cool room, his headache eases enough for him to feel bored. He finds the remote on the nightstand and clicks on the secondary three-dee screen hanging on the opposite wall.

The Enzebb, it appears, are still dominating the news. Bar graphs hang behind a holocaster's head and display the population of each planet in the Enzebb Unity. Mulligan turns up the sound.

'. . . opposition's spokesman,' the holocaster is saying.

The picture changes. A light-skinned human male, with his black hair in lank long curls, stands behind a podium and addresses a crowd.

'. . . these *bugs* – oh yes, amigos, that's what these Enzebb are, bugs like ones you find under a rock. And we're supposed to let them into our Republic and into our *minds*?' A caption identifies the speaker as Senator George Martinelli, Humanitas Party.

'Jeez, what a dorkero!' Mulligan says and changes the channel. He keeps surfing until he finds a replay of the Bears' championship game. His headache puts him to sleep before the second inning.

'Okay, Carol,' Lacey says. 'What's the deal with the suncloak?'

'I thought you'd never ask. Good thing you're sitting down, I got a little surprise for you.'

Carol pulls off the suncloak, drops it onto the floor, then stands with one hip jutting and one hand over her head like a fashion model. Lacey laughs and claps.

'That's some dress!' she says.

Cut from heavy amber silk, the long tunic plunges at a V-shaped neckline. Green embroidery decorates the matching wrap skirt.

'What happened?' Lacey goes on. 'You hit the jackpot on the yacht races?'

'It's no mine,' Carol says. 'I din't steal it, either, so dunt you go slandering my good name. I rented it. There's a turban that goes with it, but I dint want to crush it under the sun helmet.'

'Dios! Dint know you could rent stuff this fancy. What's the occasion, you getting married or something?'

'Maybe some year, but not this one. I'm just going to a party tomorrow night.'

'Must be some party.'

'You could say that, yeah. An embassy reception. That big bash the Cons are throwing for the Enzebb representative.'

'And how did you get invited to that? I know you hail from New Cloverdale, but this is pretty fancy even for them.'

'Well, it's Al, of course.' Carol looks pleased with herself as she sits down on the couch. 'The embassies always invite the Mayor or some council members to their big parties, and Al *is* Chief of Police. So when he asked me I found this dress. Dint want to look out of place, you know?'

'You should fit right in. Al seen it yet?'

'Nah, I wanted your reaction first. Hope he likes it.'

'He will.'

'The big thing about this party? Most of the ricos in Polar City will be there, the kind that toss some of their money to charity. The clinic needs a new diagnostic DNA reader.'

'The clinic always needs money. Period.'

'Sure thing. I dunt know what's wrong with the damn city council sometimes.' Carol pauses to stroke the fabric of her rented skirt. 'You got to dress like money to attract money. I need some jewellery to go with this top, don't I?'

'I'd loan you some if I had any.'

'That'd be the day, yeah.'

'Well, the only clothing I ever cared about was my uniform.'

'And dunt I know that? The perfect officer, that was you. And then the damn brass went and threw you away.'

'I dint give them much choice. Mutiny's a serious matter.'

'Mutiny my arse! I was the medical officer on that ship, wasn't I? I know loco when I see loco, and Rostow went off the deep end. If you hadn't dropped him, we all would've been dead.'

'He was still the captain, loco or no.'

'He had to go and crack when the ship was engaged, too, the little bastard.' Carol goes on as if she hasn't heard the interruption. 'Give me five damn minutes, and I could have certified him unfit all nice and legal—'

'But we no had the five minutes, yeah. Look, I dunt want to talk about it, okay?'

Carol considers her for a moment, assessing her like a sympton.

'It's not the Navy so much,' Lacey says at last. 'It's deep space. That's what I really miss. I no can get a job on a commercial ship, even, not with my papers sealed like this.'

'Have you tried getting them unsealed?'

'Whatcha mean? They're not going to—'

'Have you even asked? I've been listening to you whine about deep space for years, and I'm getting tired of it.'

Lacey finds herself without a thing to say. Carol smiles and continues. 'You even got a string to pull. Admiral Wazerzis. Write old Iron Snout a letter. He can lean on the Board for a re-evaluation of your case. You know: in light of her recent service to the Republic. Yeah, that sounds good.'

'They no going to listen.'

'How in hell do you know that if you won't even try? I'm calling your bluff.'

'Yeah.' Lacey pauses, listening to her heart thud in her chest. 'Yeah, you sure are.'

Sarojini perches on the metal seat in the public comm booth and enters the ID number to pick up her return call. Much earlier she had sent her message off and received this number; now, at long last, she will get her answer, arriving from Sarah. A narrow face fills the view screen, a man with dark eyes and brownish hair that flops over his forehead. Thanks to the cheap transmit and its dropped frames, his expression changes in great leaps, from noncommittal to a smile that makes Sarojini think of an ill-treated dog torn between cringing and biting.

'Got your message, babykins,' Gorseley says. 'Too damn bad about our old friend. But dunt you worry. He cut me in on lotsa good games, so we gonna take care of his little problem for you. Y'know, like, anything for a friend of Mos . . . our old friend.'

Sarojini Ranjit rolls her eyes heavenward at his unprofessionalism. If the police should ever subpoena this transmit from the public archives, the mention of Moses' name will mean nothing because they'll all be under arrest already.

'So we collect the package,' his voice drones on, 'and you can bring the dinero when you come pick it up. It be all set. Dunt worry, it no will take us long.' The transmit ends without a farewell.

'Never call me babykins again,' Sarojini says to the black screen. 'Or I'm going to stamp on your instep when I'm wearing clogs.'

She glances around to make sure she's left nothing behind in the public comm booth, then pulls one edge of her plain blue sari half over her head and steps out onto a movebelt. She glides through Civic Centre in a sparse crowd of sentients, government workers most of them, judging from their shabby business clothes. The belt carries her past Embassy Row, where the Confederation's graceful building glows in the evening light and the Alliance's slab rises dark above the streets. Sarojini hates them both impartially, as most citizens of the Republic do. Not that she considers herself a patriot, merely a good citizen – in her own way. She may lie about her sources of income and how much they bring her; she may cheat at cards and pull the occasional swindle, but she pays her taxes, or some of them, and even votes when she remembers to. The Cons and the 'Lies represent the possible end of the Republic and all its small freedoms, like allowing its citizens to use cash, upon which her business depends.

And now the hatred has turned personal. Why oh why did Moses ever get himself mixed up with other species? While Sarojini has never stolen anything or allowed Oliver to involve her directly in his interstellar schemes, he bragged about them. She regrets now that she never tried to talk him out of working for the Cons and the 'Lies.

Which means, in her personal set of ethics, that she wants revenge. While Sarojini has never wanted anything to do with love, friendship does matter to her and Oliver was one of her few friends. First, she'll recover the tapestry; then she'll figure out how best to use it. If the carlis caused his death, as she suspects, she'll find a way to make them pay.

'Hey, Jack?' Lacey steps into the bedroom. 'You awake?'

The three-dee blares unwatched and lights the room with a blue glow. Mulligan lies sprawled diagonally across the bed, face down and clutching a pillow under his chest. When she turns off the three-dee, he opens his eyes and looks at her.

'Yeah, guess so. Why?'

'Want to go down to Kelly's? I just got a call from an old friend of mine. She's on planet, and she's going there tonight.'

'Hey, I aint never turned down a chance to go to Kelly's in my life.' He sits up, yawning. 'We gonna take the skimmer?'

'No. I dunt dare drive anywhere till we get the money to get it fixed. I dunt like those sounds it makes.'

'Neither do I, yeah. That back fan, it gonna drop out or something. Metro, it good enough.'

By the time they get to Kelly's Bar and Grill, the after-work crowd has been and gone again. In one half of the double room, regulars crowd around the long bar and watch a recap of the Bears' season on the huge three-dee. Kelly himself, a slender man with slicked-back dark hair touched with grey at the temples, stands at one end loading glasses into a servobot. Over his clothes he wears a tablecloth tied round his waist for an apron.

'Hey, Lacey,' he says, nodding. 'Hey, Jack.'

'Noches, Kelly,' Lacey says. 'I'm supposed to be meeting a friend of mine here, so I'm going to take a look in the dining room. Then I'm going to want a scotch and water.'

'Coming right up. Aint nobody in the dining room looks low-life enough to be a friend of yours.'

Lacey laughs and threads her way through the crowd to the doorway into the dining room. Like the bar area, the restaurant sports panelling on the walls, dark plastocrete textured to look like wood. Above the panelling a long mural of asteroid-belt yacht racing wraps around on all sides. Real cotton cloths, sparkling white and pressed, decorate the tables. Not many patrons remain: a few couples in front, a large noisy human family celebrating a birthday with balloons and a sticky-looking cake, and a large quiet lizzie family eating with their heads all bent to a central platter. Their bluish scales glitter in the soft light as they crunch up some sort of animal life that comes in shells.

No sign, however, of Alison Glover. Lacey wanders back to the bar and takes her drink from Kelly. Jack, a pint mug in hand, is leaning against the wall opposite the three-dee. When Lacey leans next to him, he smiles at her, then returns to watching Yosef Mbaye, dressed in the Bears' white on black away uniform and standing on the mound inside a roofed stadium.

'First game they had with the Miners,' Jack says. 'Watch this play.'

At the plate the batter swings, connects – a comebacker right at the pitcher. With a quick stab of his glove, Yosef snatches the ball out of the air. The crowd at the bar cheers and claps, and Mulligan joins in. A burly man with a long dark beard slews around on his bar stool.

'Hey, Jack!' Nasrulah says. 'Dint see you come in. Hey, dudes! Mulligan's here.'

Half a dozen men and a couple of women swing down from their bar stools and surround them. Most, Lacey notices, wear beaten-up shirts blazoned with 'Kelly's Bar and Grill Big Shots', part of their last season's uniforms. Park and Rec ball runs all year round in spurts of four standard months on, two off. Mulligan is wearing an equally battered shirt with the Mac's Discount City Appliances Marauders name across his chest.

Nasrulah stabs a thick finger at the lettering. 'Too bad you dunt play for a decent team, Jack. We gonna beat your butts this season.'

'Huh,' Mulligan says, grinning. 'Not if you guys play the way you did last season.'

The banter begins, jokes and mock insults mixed with some shrewd assessments of the season ahead. The easy conviviality makes Lacey remember herself as an ensign fresh out of OCS, hitting dirtside on liberty with the other junior officers. In those days she said little, afraid to use the Porttown version of Merrkan she'd grown up with. She studied the way they spoke, the way they walked, the way they ate, even, and tried to copy it all. She drank sparingly, terrified of embarrassing herself around those men and women who had grown up the right way. Now she nurses a single scotch out of a simple desire to stay sober for its own sake. Jack, however, is working on his second pint of dark, and when a servobot whirrs by, he downs it fast and gets his mug refilled. So do most of the Big Shots, and while they cluster around the 'bot the room falls mostly silent. At the bar, a big-bellied fellow Lacey has never seen before stands up, then sidles over to Mulligan.

'Damn shame you got that brand on you, Jack.' His red face shines with sweat. 'You shoulda been with the Bears all the way to the Series. Best damn shortstop in the league, any league.' He raises an unsteady hand. 'No bloody fair, you being a psi, no like you could help it.'

Mulligan says nothing. His face shuts like a door to hide whatever it is he's feeling.

'Leave him alone.' Nasrulah whips around and takes one long step toward the stranger. 'Nobody sticks it to Jack around me. Comprende, borracho?'

Dead silence now. The stranger, his mouth half open and too moist, looks back and forth between Mulligan and Nasrulah.

'Hey,' Lacey says softly. 'He dunt mean no harm. Right, dude?'

'Yeah, right!' The stranger beams at her. 'Just trying to commish. Commiserish. Hell, say I was sorry.'

'Yeah?' Nasrulah lightens his voice considerably. 'Well, hey, no harm done.' He turns away. 'Say, I hear the bookies, they giving the Eagles the Series.'

'Only by one game,' Mulligan says. 'Too close to call, if you ask me.'

'I dunno,' a young woman says. 'Them Eagles got a good team this year.'

The talk picks up volume as an argument begins in earnest, grows louder still, and the jokes turn sharp. The stranger edges away and slips out the front door. Talk of this Series leads inevitably to the championships of the past – safe history that calms everyone down again. At one end of the bar, Kelly keeps a stat comp with four hundred years of baseball in its files. The group drifts over to its gleaming black stand. Lacey touches Mulligan on the arm.

'You want to eat something? I do.'

'You bet.'

The back of the dining room offers private booths. By then the human family has gone, but the lizzie family still sit at their table. The mother is passing around a box of beak-sticks. While lizzie etiquette demands a clean mouth at all times, Lacey would prefer to skip watching them pick their double rows of needle teeth. She makes sure she takes the side of the booth that faces away from them. A little too fast and heavily, Mulligan sits down across from her. He's nearly finished the third pint, she realizes.

'Too damn bad about that big-mouthed dude,' she says.

'Yeah, well.' Mulligan stares into his mug. 'Hey, being in the majors, it no guarantee, y'know, that you gonna get to the Series.' He drains the last of the beer. 'What the hell, huh?'

Lacey finds herself fishing for things to say in an empty pond. Kelly comes bustling up to the table, followed by a servobot carrying a tray of his famous appetizers.

'You want dinner, right?' Kelly says. 'Kind of late. Kitchen, it out of soya ribs, but the bread fern pasta's good.'

'Sounds great.' Lacey helps herself to shrimp-paste puffs from the tray.

'Sounds good to me too,' Mulligan says. 'And another beer.'

'No.' Kelly takes his empty mug. 'You done had enough, Jack. I gonna get the 'bot to bring you some coffee.'

Lacey goes tense, but Mulligan merely shrugs and leans back against wall of the booth. His long pale hands grip the table edge as if he's trying to shove it away. The servobot puts the appetizers on the table, then follows Kelly as he trots away.

'Sweetheart,' Lacey begins. 'It must be hell, trying to be polite when—'

'I no want to talk about it.'

Lacey aches to find something, anything, she hasn't already said too many times. She can't. In a few minutes the 'bot comes whirring back with the food: grey-green flat noodles topped with real mushrooms and strange rounds of soy substance, a basket of bread, some vita-chips. Mulligan picks up his fork and attacks the pasta. She can see how hard he has to concentrate to get his fork to behave and the noodles into his mouth. *He'll sober up in a while. But damn, I wish Alison would get herself here!*

They are nearly done eating when Alison does just that, striding into the room with a glass of scotch in one hand.

'Lacey!' she calls out. 'I hear you gone into the hero business since the last time I hit dirt.'

Grinning, Lacey gets up and hurries over to meet her. Wavy auburn hair frames Alison's pale oval of a face and falls to her shoulders, an awkward mane for anyone who spends much time in freefall. Although starside Alison binds it into braids, dirtside the pilot lets herself play peacock. She avoids the jumpsuits most spacers wear and fancies outfits such as the one she wears tonight, black leather pants and an iridescent turquoise tunic that emphasizes the greenish amber of her eyes.

'Hero, hell,' Lacey says. 'I was just bored with the peace and quiet.'

'Whatever works.' Alison grins at her and raises her glass. 'To the triumph of the disgraced!'

Lacey stops a passing servobot and gets a glass of water to raise in turn. They invented this toast in the drunken aftermath of Lacey's reprieve from the death sentence, but Lieutenant Glover had reasons of her own. While most officers in the Republic Navy indulge in genteel smuggling to supplement their salaries, at intervals some citizens' group or other demands a crackdown, and a few junior officers end up on the sacrificial altar. Alison drew the short straw for her year.

'I dunt know about you, but I dunt feel all that triumphant,' Lacey says. 'So what are *you* celebrating?'

'Being alive, mostly. Lost a resonator halfway back from Ritholz's Star on our last run, and I no was sure we were going to make it in. The *Freebird*'s sitting out in space dock with half of her drive torn out.'

'How did you manage to lose a resonator?'

'We ran into a little trouble, and the shielding dint hold.'

'Yeah? Pirates?'

'I wish.' Alison downs half the scotch straight off. 'An Alliance cutter. Their customs officers just dunt seem to be the gullible sort.'

Lacey whistles under her breath. 'What kind of cargo was it?'

'Which one?'

They both laugh and salute each other with their glasses. Alison turns her head and sets her long crystalline earrings dancing. Light glints and dazzles.

'Like my new toys?'

Lacey takes the hint. So Alison was smuggling diamonds formed in an Alliance implosion reactor – long on risk and short on profit, like so many of her ventures.

'Yeah, real pretty,' Lacey says. 'You always did love anything shiny.'

'You know what they say.' Alison pauses for another grin. 'All that glitters has a high refractive index.'

'You've been saying it for years, anyway. Hey, this gives me an idea. You remember Carol Rasheed?'

'Once they meet her, nobody forgets Dr Carol.'

'Maybe you could help her with a little problem. She's got a real fancy party to go to tomorrow, and no jewellery.'

'Got some branchfire I picked up in the Ritholz system.'

'Her date for this party is a cop.'

'Nah, nah, nah, this stuff is perfectly legal. And speaking of pretty things, and new toys, and so forth, who's *that*?' Alison jerks her head in Mulligan's direction.

'He's no toy.'

'Hey. Sorry.'

'It's okay. But I forgot you haven't met Jack. He lives with me. Terrific shortstop.'

'Yeah, right. Do you expect me to believe that you're living together because he's a good shortstop?'

'Ah, come on and meet him.'

Food and two cups of Kelly's coffee have cleared Jack's head, at least to some degree. When Lacey brings Alison over, he stands up and shakes hands, smiles broadly all round, but says nothing. Lacey slides into his side of the booth and lets Alison have the other. A pair of servobots glide into the room. One heads for the table once occupied by the lizzie family; the other comes to the booth.

'Have you finished with the utensils?' The 'bot has the adenoidal voice usual to its kind. 'Can I take them?'

'Yeah,' Lacey says. 'Please do.'

'And bring me another double scotch,' Alison says. 'Hey, Jack, Bobbie, what are you drinking?'

'None for me,' Lacey says.

Jack just shakes his head. He looks pale around the eyes, Lacey realizes, and oddly tired for someone who slept half the night away. Must be the beer, she thinks. By the time the 'bot has finished clearing, they are the only patrons in the dining room.

'Tell me something,' Lacey says to Alison. 'What's customs like on Sarah?'

'Heavens!' Alison lays a hand on her clavicle in mock surprise. 'And why are you asking me that?'

'Oh, I thought you maybe heard someone else talking about it.'

They grin at each other.

'Anyway,' Alison says. 'It depends on whether you're a Republic citizen or not.'

'Let's say yeah, a citizen. Just for our theoretical model.'

'Okay. If you're a citizen it's pretty easy. What they dunt want you to carry in is food, fruit in particular. It carries moulds or spores or something. I never can remember.' Alison thinks for a moment. 'And dreamdust, of course. They do make spot checks for that. The Sarah federales are really down on drugs. Is our theoretical model coming from Polar City?'

'Yeah.'

'That's no good, then. Sarah federales think everyone in this town is some kind of criminal.'

'They could maybe be right,' Lacey says. 'What kind of person they look for? Some scruffy Blanco type who shipped out in third class?'

'Hell, no. You no can . . . I mean, a smuggler no can risk looking obvious. The professionals, they're never going to body-pack anyway, so what you get at the ports are amateurs. The customs dudes look for somebody well-dressed and quiet who looks nervous when he dunt need to be.'

Jack winces. Lacey can guess what he's thinking: Yosef fits the profile perfectly.

RSS *Calypso*'s observation lounge blends with the starry view beyond the floor-to-ceiling windows. Sitting in the midst of its black walls, black matt flooring, black upholstered chairs and shiny black tables, Lucy feels as if she's suspended in space. Her knitting lies idle in her lap, because a gibbous Sarah hangs beyond the window against a backdrop of stars, and she can look at nothing else. Where the sunlight strikes, Sarah is blue and green, streaked with white clouds. Water, Lucy thinks. All that damn blue stuff is water. When Rosa Wallace joins her, Lucy waves a hand at the view.

'Jeezchrise, Red! I guess I finally get it, why Bobbie's always moaning about missing deep space.'

'It be something, huh?' Rosa sits down opposite her. 'Wait till you see it from space-dock orbit. It fills the whole window, then, like it be hanging right over your head.'

'I be looking forward to that. Tell me something. Them two big white things there at the middle of the planet, one on the west edge and one on the east. Those clouds, too?'

'Nah, those be icecaps on the two poles, and they be north and south. Aint no up and down in space, no like a map or something.'

Lucy sighs in wonderment and picks up her knitting again. Since few denizens of Hagar ever wear sweaters, the Old Earth needle arts have survived there as decorations – tapestries, throws, wall hangings and the like – all of them heavily influenced by the carli fibre arts.

'Whatcha making?' Rosa says.

'An edge piece.' Lucy holds up a strip about twenty centimetres wide and nearly a metre long, irregularly striped in three shades of sand-coloured yarn. 'Gonna join a lot of strips together for a hanging. Yeah, I know it dunt look like anything now. Maybe it won't when I get it together, either, but what the hell, keeps me busy.' She lays the strip back in her lap. 'When I think of all the hours I spent sitting around, watching you little punks practise . . .' She pauses, caught again by the view. 'Well, guess it was worth it, after all.'

Rosa laughs, then turns in her chair and looks over the lounge. A half-dozen Bears' players are playing cards at a big round table. Lucy notices Mike Takahashi, or, rather, the young woman hovering behind his chair. Dark-haired and slender, she wears an immaculate white suit that, from the hang of it, Lucy judges to be real linen.

'There be that girl again,' Lucy says. 'Hanging round Tak.'

'She aint exactly a girl,' Rosa says. 'A business woman, she told me, for First National Bank. She go back and forth between offices all the time.'

'Yeah? Then she oughta know better. She acting like a groupie.'

'Yeah, well.' Rosa shrugs in complete indifference. 'Tak, he always got some woman hanging around him. But this Midori, she one of them fans who love hanging with the team. She done talked with me and Gina too, and she know her baseball.'

'Yeah? She dunt put on that makeup for you and Gina.'

In a few minutes a human waiter, sleek in his white uniform, hurries over with a servobot trailing behind. The man sets morning coffee on a silver tray down on the table, and the 'bot adds a platter of pastries.

'How long to space dock?' Rosa asks.

'Twelve hours, ma'am. Is there anything else I can bring you ladies?'

'No, thanks.'

When Rosa taps the credit strip on his sleeve to register a tip, he smiles then strolls off with the 'bot in tow. Lucy rolls up the half-finished strip and stuffs it into her knitting bag, which rests beside her on the floor. For a few minutes they eat in silence, staring at the gleaming planet beyond the polarized glass.

'Huh,' Rosa says. 'There be Yosef.'

Lucy turns and sees Mbaye, alone as always, walking down the four black steps into the lounge. When Rosa waves to him, he hesitates then walks over.

'Sit down,' Lucy says. 'Plenty of coffee.'

'Thanks.' Yosef takes a chair midway between the two of them. 'But I've had too much already.'

'Then eat something,' Lucy says. 'Soak up the caffeine.'

Yosef smiles and takes a fruit-filled roll from the tray. His hands shake, but Lucy's willing to bet that the coffee's not to blame.

'Whatcha so worried about, chico?' Lucy drops her voice to a near whisper. 'Oliver aint gonna bother you no more.'

'What makes you think he was in this alone?' Yosef speaks just as quietly. 'I don't see how he could be. He implied as much when he threatened Marisa.'

'When he what?' Lucy snaps.

'That's why I asked you to call Bobbie off. He told me that if I caused trouble his gang would do something to my wife.'

'You maybe coulda told us?' Rosa says.

Yosef merely shrugs. His hands shake even harder.

'Slimy bastard!' Lucy says. 'I be glad he dead.'

'You got a point.' Rosa leans forward and whispers. 'This Oliver, he the one who was going to pick this thing up on Sarah?'

'I don't know that for certain. Sometimes he implied he would, but he gave me a code word. He said someone would call and use the word, and then I was to follow that person's instructions.'

'So it could be someone else.' Lucy pauses, thinking. 'You gonna do what he told you to do?'

'What choice do I have? I'm willing to bet that Oliver told his partners about—'

'Dunt say it aloud, not here,' Rosa breaks in.

Yosef nods and leans back in his chair.

'If you get caught in customs,' Rosa goes on, 'aint gonna matter how many pals Oliver had.'

'Damn right,' Lucy says. 'Where you got the thing, anyway?'

'Under my shaving stuff in my carrysack. I thought maybe they wouldn't look there, and if they did they might just think it's a flannel.'

'That sound risky to me.'

'It sounds risky because it is risky.' Yosef takes a savage bite of his fruit roll.

'Yeah. I—' All at once Lucy laughs quietly to herself. 'Hey, when we done here, chico, you bring that thing to our cabin. I know how we gonna get it through customs.'

Both Rosa and Yosef look at her, as wide-eyed as Little Leaguers when she reads them the day's batting order. Lucy leans down, grabs her knitting bag and holds it up with a flourish.

'You bet!' Rosa says.

Yosef actually manages to smile. 'You know something?' he says. 'I'm beginning to think that maybe we can pull this off after all.'

All evening Bates has worked with an eye on the clock. He has to leave the Police Tower on time tonight, something he rarely does, in order to get home to change for the Confederation Embassy reception. Even so, he's put out the word that he can be interrupted for anything that might have bearing on the Gri Nerosi case. Toward quitting time Sergeant Maddock, carrying his clipboard, appears in the open doorway.

'Sir?' Maddock says. 'It's about the missing carli.'

'What have you got for me?'

'Maybe nothing.' Maddock frowns at his clipboard. 'A data clerk maybe turned up something. You know how they are, seeing correlations everywhere.'

'Yeah, I sure do. That's their job.'

'Uh, right.' Maddock winces at the reprimand. 'Anyway, case from last week, the seventh. Stabbing victim found in the Outworld Bazaar, identified as Moses Oliver. Had a long arrest record: petty thievery, comm fraud, selling false ID papers, that kind of thing.'

'Right. I remember the report on the death. Can't say I remember him.'

'Well, he was suspected of doing small semi-legal jobs for both the Cons and the 'Lies. He liked to brag about his connections in important places, that kind of thing.'

'Huh.' Bates leans back. 'There are probably five hundred petty crooks in this town who do the same thing. The 'Lies in particular prefer hiring outside muscle.'

'That's true. But Wang points out in her report that none of them got themselves killed right after a sentient went missing from one of the embassies.'

'I like the way Wang thinks. Thanks, Maddock. Route that report straight through to my databank on the case. Was there much investigation into Oliver's murder?'

'No, sir. It was labelled a good-riddance case.'

'Well, it's not any more. Get a couple of detectives on it. Right now. If nothing else, we've got to eliminate him as a possible link.'

For the reception, the embassy personnel have turned the entire top floor of the Confederation building into a ballroom. Along one side of the crescent-shaped room, windows give out onto a view of Polar City glittering far below in the darkness. The variegated grey marble floor glimmers under maglev lights. Music floats from hidden speakers. At either end of the crescent, small tables cluster near buffets, one for carnivores, one for herbivores, with omnivores welcome to try both. As she stands with Al Bates in the line for the receiving line, Carol finds herself blinking against the light.

'Too damn bright in here,' Al remarks.

'You know what it is? They got the spectrum adjusted for their homeworld.' Carol frowns down at her mid-section. 'This dress looks washed out.'

'Bet you're right. You look great anyway. Dunt know if I should have brought you in here with all these carnivores.'

Carol smiles and lays a delicate hand on the branchfire necklace she borrowed from Alison. The semi-precious crystals, tiny flame shapes that interlace like roots of creeping dirt vine, shade from dusky orange-red up through a hot white-yellow.

'You look pretty good yourself,' Carol says. 'That black jacket suits you.'

'Yeah? The collar on this shirt itches like hell. And neckties – jeez, they must have been invented in a cold climate.'

The line snakes along, following the curve of the wall. The amount of jewellery that Carol sees dangling around necks, slipped onto fingers, hung from ears or attached to scales and crests, would fund a hundred clinics.

'What's that stink?' Al says suddenly. 'Jeez, smells like someone dropped a couple bottles of perfume.'

Carol takes a deep sniff, nearly sneezes, starts looking around. Other guests of various species are delicately dabbing at noses or snouts with handkerchiefs. When she glances up at the pale bronze wall, she notices air vents by the ceiling.

'It's coming out of there,' Carol says. 'I know the carlis like every-thing bee-you-ti-full, but this is overkill.'

The line stops moving, possibly to allow the ambassador to greet some particularly favoured guest. Behind Carol stands a human couple dressed in matching red silk outfits of tunics over pants. Both drip gold chains. She pegs them as off-worlders even before the woman starts whining. The husband murmurs too softly for Carol to hear, but the woman has a high clear voice.

'I know tonight's important,' she is saying. 'But this planet. This town. Not a thing to do here. The shops? They were awful. And I dint feel safe, not once, wandering around on my own, with all those—' She drops her voice.

Carol guesses that she's about to finish her sentence with the word 'Blancos'. The woman, however, surprises her. 'Those aliens,' the off-worlder whispers. 'I try to be open-minded, but there are limits.'

Carol realizes that Al is listening too, his mouth twisted in disgust. *Humanitas supporter*, Carol thinks. *What do you bet?* The husband murmurs more softly than before, as if he's trying to get her to lower her voice. If so, he fails.

'I dint drink too much!' the woman snaps. 'If you wouldn't leave me alone all day, bored out of my mind in this rotten town—'

Again the conciliatory murmur.

'Go on a tour with you?' she says. 'Of what?' She pauses while he speaks. 'You gotta be kidding, darling. A rehydration plant? How utterly charming. That's the big attraction in this town, is it? I know you're here on business, but—'

Mercifully the line starts moving. Her husband manages to silence her while Carol can still control her temper. At last they reach the actual dignitaries, standing side by side, each displaying high status and good humour by whatever means their species has established. The mayor of Polar City in his black suit with a ruffled white shirt smiles with a flash of white teeth. Draped in scarlet robes, the carli ambassador bobs his furred head up and down. The H'Allevae ambas-sador wears a canary-yellow suit cut in a military style and loaded with crimson braid, brass buttons, gold medals, and various other encrustations; under his long, drooping, white nose, he pushes his pale fleshy lips in and out. As each guest reaches them, a carli female, humble in a pale green jumpsuit, takes the invitation and announces the name aloud.

The smell of perfume becomes thicker, but some sharp odour mingles with it. At the very end of the line, in the place of honour, stands the Enzebb ambassador, who has taken Mrs Green as her name among humans. She wears little more than a twist of flowered cloth about her hips, if indeed her tubular species can be said to have hips. At three metres high, she looms. A fringe of iridescent green arms spirals around her metal-shiny body from her hips up to her long, curving head set with three golden eyes. At each announced name her arms sway and ripple.

'Dr Carol Rasheed,' the servant reads. 'Albert Bates, Chief of Police in Polar City.'

Carol nods and smiles at each ambassador in turn. When she reaches Mrs Green, the ambassador lowers her enormous head. Carol nearly sneezes again, this time at the stench of vinegar. *Of course!* she thinks. *I forgot about the way they smell.* The carli hosts have doubtless poured perfume into the ventilating system to cover the stench of the guests of honour. Mrs Green speaks with a mouth that resembles a trumpet flower.

'Dr Carol?' Her voice is dark, breathy. 'Ah yes, I have heard of you. Our people know all those who helped save our sister, Mrs Bug, after her tragedy.'

'I hope she's doing well, Your Excellency.'

'Yes, she has created some peace in her life.'

As much as Carol would like to ask more, the press of the line behind moves her on. Since Mrs Green is speaking to Bates, Carol has a moment to notice the small Enzebb standing just behind the ambassador herself. Her husband, Carol thinks, if that's the right word. All the lore she knows about the Enzebb tells her that he must be blind, and she can see that a milky-white membrane covers his eyes, but she has no desire to be rude. When she takes a step toward him and nods, the feathery antennae bend and swivel in her direction and flutter. Carol would bet good money that he is reading some sort of information from the environment, air currents most likely. He takes a step toward her and nods in turn. When Al walks up and joins her, the male Enzebb acknowledges him as well.

'Nod your head at him,' Carol says.

With a shrug of puzzlement, Al does. Mr Green nods, then steps back behind his wife. Carol happens to look around and sees the red silk couple staring at this little tableau. Before she can say something nasty, Al slips his arm through hers and leads her away.

'The wife, she's a bitch all right,' Al says. 'But her husband's a big man in the Senate. I heard him say he was going to take that public tour of Project Noah. If he likes it, Congress just might release some more money.'

'Oh. Then I'm glad you stopped me.'

'We're doing pretty well so far,' Al goes on. 'A personal greeting from the Enzebb ambassador. That's going to do us both some good.'

'You bet. Huh, I hope some of the right people saw it.'

'Hey,' Al snaps. 'You no going to go soliciting tonight, are you?'

'What do you think I am? A hooker?'

'You know what I mean. For the clinic.'

'What's wrong with it? Look at this crowd. Silk and diamonds everywhere. It won't hurt them to zap a few credits the clinic's way.'

'That's not the point. The point is I dunt like being embarrassed when you go hunting.'

'What?' Carol turns her head to stare up at him. 'Why would you be embarrassed?'

'You really dunt get it, do you? Hell, never mind.'

Carol reads his 'never mind' as a sign that he sees how foolish his embarrassment is. She is about to congratulate him when a plump, light-skinned human man comes trotting up to them. He too wears a canary-yellow suit with crimson braid, but his has far fewer encrustations than the ambassador's. Perhaps to make up for it he's topped the outfit off with a stiff yellow hat heavily plumed in crimson.

'Shit,' Al whispers. 'Eric Royall. Head slave down at the Hopper embassy.'

'A real slave?'

Royall reaches them before Al can answer. 'Bates, isn't it?' He smiles

86

and bows to Al, then looks Carol over as if she were for sale. Bates glares, and Royall looks away.

'Nice bash,' Royall says. 'Our hairy friends throw a good party, huh? Hey, you like the new look? Boss's idea, of course. You know how they are about the right clothes.'

'You call those the right clothes?' Carol says.

Royall blinks at her for a long moment. His busy eyebrows rise and jiggle, seemingly of their own will. 'Something military,' he says at last. 'That's what the boss asked for.'

'High-school marching band,' Carol says. 'That mean anything to you? No? Here's a tip. Look it up in a historical database.'

Again Royall blinks, then glances at Al. The eyebrows nearly form a V.

'See you around later,' Al says. 'Gotta run. There's someone I need to talk to.'

Before Royall can recover they hurry away, sticking to the crowded edge of the ballroom. This early in the party only a few couples are dancing.

'Is he really a slave?' Carol asks again.

'Well, his position is top liaison officer at the embassy, but from what I understand that means head slave – on their terms. Dunt think of the slavery like in the history books. It's more of a bargain with a time limit.'

'Whatever he is, you sure dunt like him much.'

'Yeah. We think he's been behind some trouble in the past, but we got no proof and he's got diplomatic immunity anyway.'

'I dint like him either,' Carol says.

She looks back and sees Royall about where they left him, talking with a Hopper in the same yellow and crimson uniform. The H'Allevae form, a long skinny torso rising from stubby, double-jointed legs, looks profoundly awkward in human-style pants and tight jacket, the sleeves of which contort and restrict their long, double-jointed arms. When Al follows her glance he stops walking and turns, watching narrow-eyed.

'Gorvalneh.' Al says the name without any glottal stops – incorrectly, Carol assumes. 'Wonder what he's doing here.'

87

'Who is he?'

'Technically, the ambassador's secretary. Technically.'

'You think he's got some other job?'

'Sure do. No can prove a thing, though. Huh, I might just go over and let him know that I know he's here.'

'And you talk about me working the crowd.'

Al starts to answer, giving her a sour look instead, then strides off in the direction of the Hopper with a small wave to her to follow. Carol decides she'll stay where she is for the moment. He's got his nerve, thinking she'll follow like a pet dog.

'Dr Carol! How lovely to see you.' The speaker floats toward her on a cloud of grey chiffon that matches her silver grey hair and sets off the collar of silver and emeralds around her neck.

'Rita! How nice!' Carol smiles in deep sincerity. Rita Valdez de Castro owns some of the slummiest buildings in Porttown but has the decency to feel guilty about it. Guilt, in Carol's experience, translates into money for her clinic. 'You look fabulous tonight.'

Since Bates and Gor'val'neh dislike each other, they exchange a greeting then smile with different gestures but equal hypocrisy and drift apart. Bates starts across the ballroom to rejoin Carol, but when he sees her chatting up a society woman he hesitates. A carli servant walks past with a tray of champagne in slender flutes. Bates takes one and tries a cautious sip: actual champagne, light and fizzy, not some high-octane carli version.

'Chief Bates!' A melodic voice, pleasantly low, with a carli accent. Kaz Phaath joins him, all smiles. 'You honour our humble little party.'

'No, no, you have honoured me with the invitation to something grand and wonderful.'

'You're very kind.'

For a moment they merely stand and smile at each other. Under her scientist's robes Kaz Phaath is wearing a jumpsuit laced with smart threads that cycle from aqua to blue to purple and back again. The swirling colour makes it impossible to ignore her slender body.

Al clears his throat. 'You're looking quite lovely tonight, if I may say so.'

'Thank you.' Kaz Phaath fingers one edge of her robe. 'Of course, it's impossible to achieve the proper drape of fabric over a human figure, but I do my best.'

'Oh, there you are.' Carol's voice carries steel. 'Sorry we got separated like that. I had to speak to Rita de Castro.'

Bates gives her a bright smile and holds out his hand, which she takes more fiercely than usual. With a deep sense of shock, he realizes Carol is jealous, a human feeling that he would have thought beyond her. He has to admit that he rather likes seeing it.

'Carol,' he says, 'this is Wentworth Kaz Phaath yil Frakmo, Director of Data Analysis at the embassy. Kaz Phaath, may I present Dr Carol Rasheed?'

'I'm honoured!' Kaz Phaath bobs her head. 'I've heard so much about your clinic in Porttown.'

At that Bates feels Carol relax.

'Thank you,' Carol says. 'It's very rewarding work.'

'I'm sure it must be. Oh, excuse me.' Kaz Phaath suddenly looks toward a point behind them. 'That's one of our junior staff, and from the way he's signalling I'd better go see what he wants.'

'Of course,' Carol says.

With another bob of her head Kaz Phaath hurries away.

'Well, let's join the party,' Bates says. 'Get something to eat, dance a little.'

'Sounds good to me. You know, I'm enjoying this bash. I'm kind of surprised.'

And yet, as they head for the buffets, Carol sights prey. 'Señor Falabi's here,' she whispers. 'I've got to have a word with him.'

'About the clinic?'

'What else?'

Carol slips about before Bates can snarl at her. He turns on his heel and heads for the buffets alone.

By then the formal receiving line has dispersed, but Bates spots the carli ambassador, Frakmo Serag Ka Jekhonas il Frakmo, standing near the wall. He is talking with someone hidden from Bates's view by a little clot of guests. The ambassador's left ear twitches over, and over in a jerky rhythm, and he is gesturing with both hands. The guests walk on, clearing the view to reveal Kaz Phaath. As if he realizes that someone's watching, Ka Jekhonas turns and walks away, so fast that he's nearly trotting. Kaz Phaath stands for a moment looking out into empty space, smiling in an oddly vacant way as if she's perhaps trying to cover some hurt the ambassador caused her. She turns, sees Bates, and comes over in a rustle of silken robes.

'Are you enjoying the party, Chief Bates?'

'Very much so. I'd enjoy it even more if you'd dance with me.'

She tosses her head back, startled, then smiles in a much more natural way.

'You know, I'd like that,' she says.

Despite his bulk, Bates dances well, and Kaz Phaath matches him. For some minutes they give themselves over to the music, a four-four time human tune, neither deep nor irritatingly shallow. When it ends, Bates bows to her. Together they walk off the dance floor.

'You've honoured me,' he says.

'No, my dear Chief, you honour me too highly. Have you met the ambassador's wife, Kaz Fetketh yil Frakmo? Now there's a truly elegant woman.'

'But she's a carli, and you're human.'

Kaz Phaath starts to speak, then pauses, half smiling.

'Well, yes,' she says. 'I suppose I am. Or I should say, yes, that does make a difference.'

'I take it you were born on a carli world. If you dunt mind my asking, of course.'

'Not at all. I come from aggKar itself, actually. My grandfather settled our family there. He was a research chemist, and the government hired him to organize a laboratory in his speciality.'

'He must have been quite highly regarded.'

'He was, yes.' She stops speaking, looks away, then shakes her hands in front of her, a carli sign of irritation. 'Will you forgive me again? There's Gri Mardo signalling me. Now what's gone wrong?'

Without waiting for an answer, Kaz Phaath hurries off. She has by her standards been rude. *Isn't that interesting*? Bates thinks. *Something's really troubling her.* He watches until she disappears into a service door behind one of the buffets, then goes looking for Carol. He finds her leaving Señor Falabi, who looks a bit stunned. Carol, however, is grinning from ear to ear.

'How much did you get out of him?' Bates says.

'You dunt need to sound so nasty about it,' Carol says. 'A couple of thousand, is all.'

'Is all? Jeezchrise! Uh well, none of my business.'

'No, it's not.'

'Great. Let's dance.'

As the evening continues, Bates finds himself keeping an eye out for Kaz Phaath and the ambassador as well. Kaz Phaath moves through the party, playing hostess. He sees her dancing with the mayor of Polar City, trading quips with an occasional Hopper, even supervising the buffets when the food threatens to run low. Every time she sees him, she smiles brightly then contrives to be going in the opposite direction.

Once, however, he nearly corners her, when Carol has gone to find the women's restroom. Near the herbivore buffet Kaz Phaath stands talking with a tall, slender man with features the colour of aged ivory and a scatter of white hair. He wears an impeccably cut tuxedo that reflects perfect taste and unobstrusive elegance. *Rafael Chang*, Bates thinks. Some years back, Chang testified as an expert witness for the prosecution in an art forgery case. From the way they are laughing together, it would seem that Chang knows Kaz Phaath. When Bates heads over to the pair, Kaz Phaath waves at him then hurries away into the crowd.

Ka Jekhonas he sees mostly in the exalted company of other ambassadors, particular Mrs Green. Bates wonders if the Confederation will try to talk the Enzebb Unity out of joining the Republic, as the pundits say it will do. If the Republic doubles in size, the Confederation and the Alliance will both have to re-evaluate the balance of power in this corner of the Mapped Sector. He sees all the other high-status Confederation officials mingling with the crowd, with one exception.

Eventually, when the evening is winding down, Bates does finally see Ka Pral, standing with a glass of some purple liquor in his hand and talking to a human woman.

'That's strange,' he says.

'What?' Carol says. 'He's Chief of Protocol, so he got to chat up the guests.'

'Yeah, but this is the first time I've seen him tonight.'

'Oh.' Carol cocks her head to one side and thinks for a moment. 'You know what? This is the first I've seen him, too. Let's go say hi.'

But as they start walking over, Ka Pral slips away, dodging through the crowd, heading down the length of the ballroom and finally disappearing.

'He might not have seen us coming,' Bates says.

'Like hell.'

'Yeah, you're right. I'm sure I dint see him before. I was keeping my eyes open.'

'Yeah, you sure were.' The snarl in her voice catches him by surprise. 'What's wrong, you here with the wrong woman?'

'What do you mean by that?'

'You couldn't take your eyes off that data analyst's jumpsuit.'

'Oh, yeah? Well, you were a lot more interested in getting bucks out of los ricos than in the date that brought you.'

'Damn it, the city dunt give me enough, and—'

'Yeah, yeah, but you come on like one of those missionaries preaching the Galactic Mind. Maybe you could try being more tactful.'

'Tactful? Why? I tried that once, and it dint work worth a damn.'

She sets her hands on her hips. He glares at her.

'Oh, for chrissake!' Carol says at last. 'Let's just leave, okay?'

'Good idea.'

Outside the sun scorches the last of his patience. During the drive to her apartment they sit in sullen silence. For the first time in months, she does not invite him in.

In the middle of the day Lacey wakes to the sound of beeping. On the nightstand, the comm relay flashes red. She sits up, briefly worries about waking Jack, then realizes that he's sound out with his head and one arm hanging over his side of the bed. She hits the pickup button.

'Programmer?' Buddy says. 'I apologize for waking you, but the reason seemed sufficiently urgent. Your aunt has sent a recorded transmit.'

'Yeah, okay. Play it.'

Aunt Lucy's voice trickles out of the relay's small speaker.

'Dunt need to answer this, honey. Just want you to know that we made the trip okay, and we in the hotel now, safe and sound. All of us.'

'Thank gods, if there be any!' Lacey clicks the message off. 'I'll see you later, Buddy. I'm going back to sleep.'

Chapter Five

'Programmer?' Buddy says. 'I do not understand your distress.'

'I can't get this damn letter right,' Lacey says. 'It's driving me loca.'

'You have been endeavouring to write to Admiral Wazerzis at intervals over the space of three nights now. I do of course log the time I spend in various modes. I can tell you how many minutes you have engaged in this activity if you wish.'

'I dunt wish.'

'Very well. May I assist with my composition function?'

'No. Shut up and let me think.'

Buddy clicks and hums but says nothing more. Lacey stares at the blank screen. So far she's managed to write one good line: Dear Sir.

'Ah the hell with it! Buddy, store letter and close correspondence mode.'

'Done, Programmer.' He sounds a chime. 'Here is your pre-programmed reminder: the special broadcast is about to begin.'

A second reminder wanders into the room: Jack, wearing a Bears' T-shirt and a pair of blue shorts ripped halfway up one thigh. 'The special, it coming on. I could, like, make us a drink.'

'Yeah, good idea.'

'Whatcha been doing all this time?'

'Nada.' Lacey hesitates over the lie. She decides against making him worry that she might leave him for the peculiar joys of deep space, not when reinstatement is such a long shot. 'You been practising with Nunks?'

'Yeah.' He shrugs the subject away. 'Whisky?'

'Please. Buddy, put on Channel 83, will you?'

The Polar City holostations are squeezing the build-up to the

Galactic Series for every possible second of air time. The holocasters parade inarticulate players in front of the camera, ask meaningless questions, break up the screen into multiple windows, scroll stats, deliver trivia. Slumped into his corner of the couch Jack watches it all, while Lacey finds herself thinking of Moses Oliver lying in a refrigerated drawer down at the morgue. The autopsy report stated that he'd been stunned with a heavy object, pushed to the ground, then stabbed with one tidy thrust that pierced his heart.

'Hey,' Jack says, 'they bringing on Yosef.'

'He going to pitch tomorrow night?'

'No. I dunt understand why, but they starting Delacruz for game one.'

'Yosef going to start game two, then?'

Jack nods, his attention elsewhere. Onscreen Yosef appears, wearing his uniform, carrying a ball. As he answers the droning holocaster he keeps tossing the ball into the air and catching it. Now and then he even smiles.

'First time I've seen the dude so happy,' Lacey remarks.

'Yeah,' Jack says. 'He be where he belong. Well, for now.'

Lacey looks at him, finds his face expressionless, his beautiful eyes shadowed against the glare of his old loss. *How can I think of leaving him?* She feels like a murderer herself.

'Something wrong?' Jack says. 'I get this creepy feeling from you.'

'Sorry. Just thinking about Oliver's murder.'

'Jeez.' He slips an arm around her shoulder and pulls her close. 'Nada you can do for him now.'

'Yeah. Sure isn't.'

Much later, when he lies asleep, Lacey gets up, dresses and prowls the long hall that runs along the upper floor of the warehouse shell. She keeps forgetting that Jack can read her moods, that in fact he has no choice but to read them. *Is that why I'm thinking of leaving? I no can hide nada from Jack.* From outside sunlight spills through an unglazed window and falls upon brown carpet. She finds herself tempted to stand in the forbidden sun and look out on the city in the full glare of afternoon. Instead she turns and walks back through the shadows to the living room, where Buddy waits with his summary of relevant data.

'Nothing new concerning Gri Nerosi, Programmer, not even in the police files. The regular newsfeeds are, of course, almost completely concerned with the imminent baseball game.'

'Of course.' Lacey sits down at the comp desk. 'Say, Buddy, what do you think about baseball, anyway?'

'Very little, Programmer. Since I am deprived of the power of self-locomotion, I have no parallels or cognates for such codified patterns of movement.'

'Makes sense. Okay, show me today's mail.'

Because Mel Lacey could never resist a bargain, each room in the warehouse's corpse contains old furniture, a selection from Mel's hoard of creaky chairs, pitted tables, dead comp units, beds, parts of beds, boxes of kitchen utensils, standing lamps, floating lamps, and chests of drawers that hold more junk wrapped in old clothes. His niece and heir intends to sort it all, one of these days when she gets around to it. Out of this scramble Mulligan has managed to furnish himself a private space that he calls his office for want of a better word, with a chair, a table, and a stack of cabinets that, one of these days, he'll get around to attaching to the pale grey wall. His possessions, which amount to a baseball glove and a deck of tarot cards, can wait for proper storage.

In the heat before sundown, Mulligan is sitting at the table and studying the cards, looking for an image to use in his work with Nunks. He cuts the deck and turns both halves face up. Five coins on one card; on the other a man hangs upside down, suspended by one foot from a wooden pole, his hands tied behind his back.

'Shit!' Mulligan slaps the halves back together.

Loss. Some great loss threatens him. The word loss leaps into his mind; he can see it, as solid as alphabet blocks. But loss of what? If he wants to, he can find out. He can spread the cards and let them speak to him, as they always seem to do. If he wants to know. He hesitates, then sets the deck back on the table and leaves the room.

The opening rituals of a Galactic Series move at a pace as stately as any high mass celebrated by the Pope of the Neo-catholic Church in Romanova, and to some of the participants, at least, they carry a lot more weight. After the flurry of speeches, after the presenting of dignitaries, the President of the Republic tosses out the ceremonial first ball. The holocrews clear their equipment from the field. In the stands of Eagles' Stadium, the spectators, all 64,200 of them, begin to fall quiet. The loudspeaker booms a welcome, runs through the regulations against fans jumping onto the field, then pauses briefly.

'And now, introducing the all-Hagar champions, the Polar City Bears!'

Here and there in the stadium a few spectators clap as, one at a time, the loudspeaker introduces the Bears' starting line-up. As she trots out onto the field, Rosa feels close to tears. She is here at last, on the field in the Galactic Series. Her team-mates join her, some laughing, some cheering, some as solemn and moist-eyed as she is. When the loudspeaker begins calling the Eagles onto the field, the crowd screams, stamps, stands up, and howls as the ritual demands. *Let em*, Rosa thinks. *Soon we gonna be on our home field.* To her the singing of the national anthem, when at last it comes, carries the force of a hymn.

She looks up at the alien blue sky of Sarah and feels sunlight warm on her face, a sensation every bit as alien as the view. To Rosa, gods mean nothing. *Luck*, she prays, *oh Lady Luck, be on our side!*

Bottom of the seventh, and Delacruz has stayed on top of the Eagles all the way. Jack started watching the game on the sofa, but he has slid first to the edge and then to the floor, where he sits slumped and cross-legged, his face upturned to the glow of the three-dee. If the game gets tight, Lacey supposes, he'll get on his feet and pace around. The second Eagle up in the inning connects and drives a double past the diving third baseman. Jack groans aloud and looks at the ceiling as if in despair.

'They got two outs already,' Lacey says. 'And we're leading by two runs.'

'Yeah, I know. It's just, like, if they take Delacruz, out then Tak gonna come in, and he chokes sometimes. Pressure like this? He gonna choke for sure.'

Mike Takahashi, the Bears closer, proves Jack right when he comes in part-way through the eighth. With a man on second he delivers a hanging slider to the Eagles' first baseman, who drives it over the fence.

'Tie game!' Jack moans. 'Ah shee-it!'

It gets worse. In the bottom of the ninth, Tak gives up a walk, then a long double. The final score: Eagles five, Bears four. Lacey braces herself, expecting the usual outpouring of rage and despair that takes Jack over when his team loses, but he sits quietly for a moment, watching the Eagles celebrate, then gets up with a shrug.

'Want a drink?' he asks.

'Yeah, I do,' Lacey says. 'But hey, you sick or something?'

'Whatcha mean by that?'

'The way you're taking the loss. I thought you'd be mad as hell.'

'Oh.' Jack grins at her. 'Hey, it coulda been worse. Like, this evening, I was looking at the tarot cards you got me, and they said I was gonna have some kind of loss.' He turns solemn. 'I can live with this one.'

He heads for the wet bar in the corner of the room. It takes Lacey a moment to realize what he means, that somehow those traitorous cards have shown him that he might lose her. She had been planning on trying to write the letter to Wazerzis after the game, but the entire night passes without her writing a word.

'What a crappy way to lose!' Rosa says. 'Can't blame Tak, though. He aint used to the gravity here yet.'

'He done had four days,' Lucy says. 'Rest of you played okay. You ask me, honey, Tak parties too hard. It aint the extra gravity pulling him down. It be those groupies.'

'Yeah, well, that too. You shoulda seen Tak at breakfast. Wallowing in guilt, carrying on about it. Delacruz finally told him, shut you mouth or I gonna stuff a tablecloth in it.'

'Aint the end of the universe, yeah. We be in their territory. If we can get a split, we go home in good shape.'

Rosa is standing at their hotel room's window, a wide sweep of clear glass that gives out on a view of a parking lot and beyond that the robotrain to the ballpark. Overhead clouds gather and swirl, dark grey streaked with a lighter grey, blotting out the blue sky. Lucy puts down her knitting and walks over to join her.

'That be some sight!' Lucy remarks. 'The clouds, I mean.'

'Yeah, but jeez, I sure hope it dunt wash out the game. Looks like—'

Someone knocks on the door. Rosa goes over, opens it and finds Yosef, carrysack in hand, his face sweaty, his eyes darting this way and that as he looks down the hall.

'What be so wrong?' Rosa says. 'No, wait. Come on in.'

'Thanks.' He hurries into the room. 'Uh, I got a comm call.'

Rosa slams the door and locks it for good measure. At the window Lucy turns, watching. Yosef drops the carrysack onto the floor, glances around, then sits on the edge of the nearer bed and shakes. He doesn't look directly at either woman.

'This call,' Lucy says. 'It about the flannel?'

'Sure was. Audio-only. A male voice, human, and he told me he was a friend of Moses Oliver's and he was calling to set up the drop. So I told him I didn't know what he was talking about. He got real pushy. So I says to him, okay, you're so damn macho, what's the code word?' Yosef licks his lips, breathing heavily. 'He didn't say anything for a real long time. So I didn't say anything. And then he hung up.'

'Moses, he pretty smart,' Lucy remarks. 'Setting up that code, I mean.'

'Yeah,' Yosef says. 'No honour among thieves.'

'I dunt get it,' Rosa says. 'About the call, I mean. The hotel, they got orders, dunt let anyone who aint on the list call straight up to the players' rooms. How did this dude get through?'

Yosef shrugs.

'Damn his eyes!' Lucy snaps. 'He got nerve, I gotta says that for him. He musta bribed a desk clerk. And you know what that means?' She looks back and forth between them. 'He was here, right down in the lobby. Can't slip anyone a wad of cash over the comm.'

'We better report—' Rosa stops herself. 'No, guess we no can report it.'

Yosef groans and buries his face in his hands.

'Come on, dude.' Lucy uses her soft, encouraging voice, one that Rosa remembers well from her Little League days. 'You gotta pull yourself together. You gotta pitch today, and you gonna win. I just know it.'

''Less it rains,' Rosa says.

By the time the team bus reaches the ballpark, the clouds hang dark and low. When the Bears trot onto the field for batting practice, they find the ground crew ahead of them standing in readiness by rolled tarps. Rosa picks out a bat and begins to stretch her shoulders, but she finds herself glancing at the sky with every stretch. The tropical air wraps her round, hot damp air without a touch of breeze. The pop of a bat on a ball, a player's voice calling out, the whirr of a groundsman's electric cart – they all hang in the air, it seems, unable to penetrate the silence.

'Lousy weather, huh?' Gina, the shortstop and one of the other three women on the team, joins her. 'Think we gonna get this game in?'

'I dunno. Dunt look good.'

At that moment the wind arrives, cool and fresh. Gina smiles, closes her eyes, takes off her cap and lets the wind ruffle her thick dark hair. Rosa glances around and sees Aunt Lucy standing by the dugout and wearing a cord full of field passes like a necklace. Rosa is about to hail her when lightning cracks and flashes. Lucy screams and ducks into the dugout. The thunder booms and rolls away. Both Gina and Rosa break out laughing.

'That be the first time anybody ever see Lucy O'Neil scared,' Gina says.

'And the last, I bet,' Rosa says.

With an indignant squawk the loudspeaker begins demanding that all players get ready to leave the field. The Bears' manager, Anthony di Giorgio, better known as Georgy, jogs across the grass to consult with the umpiring crew and the Eagles' manager under the stadium overhang behind home plate. Old Fezzy waddles up beside Rosa, shaking his head and swishing his long, muscular tail back and forth.

'Aint gonna be no game,' he says. 'The damn holocasters, they the only ones pushing for a start.'

'You seen plenty of rainouts, Fez. I gonna take your word for it.'

'Dunt need to.' He hisses like a happy tea-kettle. 'I seen the satellite vids this morning. There gonna be one hell of a storm.'

Fezzy has barely finished his comment when the first fat drops fall. Rosa scoops up her bat and glove and joins the rest of the team in running for the dugout. Yelling back and forth, the ground crew starts rolling out the tarps.

Rosa slides her bat into the rack and sits down at the end of the bench. As the rain begins to fall in earnest, Lucy joins her. They watch the rain sweep across the outfield and puddle on the red infield tarp. The rest of the Bears hurry into the dugout and sit on the long wooden bench, some, like Rosa, cradling their gloves in their laps. Across the field the Eagles in their white and red home uniforms begin to fill their own dugout.

'Smells so strange,' Lucy remarks. 'All that damn water.' She pauses, sniffing the air. 'A cool sort of smell. Dunt have the words for it.'

'You gonna have plenty of time to think of some, I bet,' Rosa says. 'Here come Georgy back, and he dunt look happy.'

Georgy clatters down the steps into the dugout and waves both arms to gather the team around him. Since he has a big voice to match his big belly, no one has to push too hard to get close.

'It's the damn holo people,' Georgy says. 'They keep hoping the rain's going to stop, no matter what the weather people say. From what I heard, it's one hell of a storm, and it's not going to clear all day.'

Everyone groans or swears, shaking their heads.

'But the holo people, they dunt want us waiting in the clubhouse. They want us sitting out here to look good for the folks at home. They're going to keep running updates, see, where they going to show the field so everyone can see it's still raining.' Georgy pauses, his lips pressed tight.

'Mbaye, you here?'

'Sure am,' Yosef says. 'I didn't even get out to the bullpen mound.'

'You get inside, out of this damp air. Jackson?' He points at one of the trainers. 'You go with him, and Tak, you go too. The rest of us, we're going sit here till the buttholes on the holonets can see that this game, it gonna be called.'

Back on Hagar, the work night has begun when Sarojini picks up Gorseley's scheduled call from Sarah. His news takes her so much by surprise that she plays the transmit twice. Password? Moses never mentioned a password, but then she had as usual refused to listen to the details of this scheme. She tells Gorseley as much in her answer, then leaves the booth to kill some time while she waits for his return transmit.

Out in the middle of Civic Centre Plaza, the holo fountain sends illusionary jets of water high into the air. Sarojini leans on the railing and listens to the recorded sound of water splashing and gurgling while she considers what to do next. What would Moses have used as a password? She realizes that she doesn't have the slightest idea.

It takes four standard hours before the umpiring crew manages to convince the Interplanetary Commissioner of Baseball to intervene with the holonetworks. Since selling the holocast rights keeps baseball afloat in the Republic, it takes him a cautious hour to persuade the holocasters that this game needs to be played on the morrow, when all the predictions call for sun. By then the Bears are stiff, grumbling, and sick of the junk food brought out to them as an excuse for a lunch. When the call comes from the Commissioner, they cheer.

'You been thinking about what you want to do today?' Rosa says to Lucy. 'We head back home after tomorrow's game.'

'We done seen the Capitol and all that already. It be too late in the day to get back out to New Cooperstown. Maybe a little shopping? I gotta pick up something for Bobbie. Shame she no could be here.'

'Well, we found that shop with all the memorabilia.'

'Good idea!'

Lucy spends more than she planned, loading herself up with holoposters, T-shirts, pennants and souvenir mugs. Thanks to the rain they take a cab back to the hotel. While Rosa pays the driver, Lucy dashes for the awning and nearly runs into Yosef Mbaye, hovering outside the double doors.

'Hey, am I glad you're back,' he says. 'Here, let me take some of that stuff for you.'

'Something wrong?' Lucy surrenders the heaviest shopping bag.

'You could say that.'

'Jeez!' Rosa joins them. 'What gone down?'

'Somebody broke into my room. Went through everything. Dumped all the drawers, my suitcase, everything.'

'They take anything?' Rosa says.

'My vid unit. A tie tack, a gold one.'

'Jeezchrise!' Lucy exclaims. 'Now that, pal, you better report.'

'Yeah, that's what Georgy said. He turned Hiram loose on the hotel.'

'Who be Hiram again?' Lucy says. 'I aint learned all the names yet.'

Rosa answers. 'The team secretary. Hiram Rosen. Dunt worry, he can handle anything.'

They walk into the lobby, all green and gold with a towering coffered ceiling. The elevator rank stands on the far side, but before they reach it Hiram himself hails them. A skinny little Blanco with a halo of frizzed-out hair, he announces that he's just come from the hotel manager's office.

'He scared shitless, thinking we're going to sue,' Hiram says, grinning. 'But it no really funny. Joe, you no were the only one. The thieves hit Gina and Colin, too. Took Colin's belt comp and a fancy watch. You know Gina and her thing about cash? She had two thousand credits in her room. She no has it any more. They tore up her room real good, just like they did yours.'

'The manager, he better start giving his staff a hard eye,' Lucy says. 'Someone on the payroll gotta be in on this.'

'Sure looks like it,' Hiram says, nodding. 'Joe, I told the police what you lost. You no gotta talk to them.'

'Swell.' Yosef sounds faint. 'I appreciate it, Hiram, really do. Uh say, if you need me I'm going to carry this up for Aunt Lucy. Might hang out there for a while.'

'Jeez!' Rosa says. 'Maybe they done gone through our stuff!'

'You right,' Hiram says. 'I gonna come up with you.'

An elevator arrives and they hurry over to it. Walking out is a dark-haired young woman, handsome rather than beautiful, in a business suit, white with grey pinstripes; she carries a real leather briefcase in one hand. *That Midori woman*, Lucy thinks.

'I heard about the thefts,' Midori says to Hiram. 'I dunt suppose your player had a list of the serial numbers on that cash? If she did, my bank might be able to trace some of it when it comes on the market.'

'I appreciate the offer,' Hiram says. 'But Gina, she dunt think that far ahead.'

The elevator doors start sliding shut. Hiram sticks his arm in front of the electronic sensor and stops them.

'We better get going,' he says to Midori. 'Might have another theft on our hands.'

But as soon as Lucy walks into their room, she can see that the thieves have spared their luggage, sitting neatly where they left it. Hiram opens a few random dresser drawers, finds nothing wrong, and leaves. Yosef sets the shopping bag down on one of the beds and staggers to a chair by the window. He sits down hard and trembles. Lucy dumps her parcels onto a dresser, then considers him.

'Might be just thieves,' Rosa says. 'Gina dunt watch her mouth the way she should.'

'I hope it's just thieves,' Yosef says. 'But after that comm call I had?'

'Yeah, you right. The other stuff they took for camouflage.' Lucy sits down in the chair opposite him. 'Red, call room service, okay? I want a beer.'

Deprived of the actual game, the holocasters turn the thefts at the team hotel into a major story. They interview the victims, the team secretary, the hotel manager, the police, the desk clerk, the woman in charge of the cleaning 'bots, anyone they can collar and drag before the vid. During Yosef's interview Aunt Lucy appears in the background, glowering at Yosef with her arms crossed over her chest.

'Damn good thing she there,' Mulligan says.

'Yeah,' Lacey says. 'He looks so nervous I bet he's ready to slip up and spill everything.'

Later that evening Lacey receives a guarded transmit from Lucy, who refers to the thefts only as 'what gotta be all over the news by now'. She manages to include the information that Yosef has surrendered to his anxieties by mentioning that he drank a bottle of beer that afternoon.

'His mullah, he no gonna be happy bout that,' Lucy says. 'But what the hell? Stress aint so good for a body either. Speaking of which, honey, this damn rain gets on my nerves. I gonna be glad to get home, I tell you.'

The transmit ends, leaving Bobbie shaking her head and laughing.

'She's a Hagar donna, born and bred all right,' Bobbie says. 'This damn rain.'

'I always kind of wondered what it be like, y'know?' Jack says. 'Sort of like an outdoor shower, huh? But you got your clothes on, so it gotta feel real gonzo.'

'You dunt just walk around in it and get soaked. You carry an umbrella or wear a raincoat.'

'I seen pictures of those, yeah. And holos of people swimming and stuff. That looks double gonzo.'

'It's fun, swimming. I learned when I was stationed on Sarah, in OCS. They had a pool right on the grounds. But I gotta admit it, it took me a while to get myself into the water the first time.'

'Hell, yeah. You can, like, drown in that stuff.'

'Not once you learn how to swim. I even got as far as learning to dive. Know what that is?'

'Jumping into the water from a ladder or something?'

'It's called a diving board.'

'Well, you done lots of weird things, for sure.' Jack grins at her. 'Guess that what's made you what you are today.'

'Ah get out of here!' Lacey smiles in return. 'I got to get some work done. That carli who went missing? I can't help thinking he's got something to do with that flannel Yosef's got.'

'They ever find him?'

'No. And I wonder why.'

Chief Bates has been wondering the same thing. Ever since the reception at the embassy, some five nights ago, Bates has had his top men and the main police AI searching for Gri Nerosi. If he'd left the planet, spaceport records would show it. Even travelling on-planet would have left a trail. As an alien Nerosi would have had to show his passport if he'd bought a rocket plane ticket or rented a skimmer. According to the original missing persons report, he had a thick carli accent that would have given the lie to any fake citizen's ID.

'So he gotta still be in Polar City,' Bates remarks to Maddock. 'Or not far away. The Rat Yard, maybe.'

'You'd think, Chief,' Maddock says. 'But his body aint turned up anywhere, either.'

105

'Well, keep looking.'

'Yes, sir. We done had better luck with Moses Oliver.'

'Yeah? Tell me.'

'One of the cheap hookers in the Bazaar saw his body being dumped.' Maddock consults the clipboard. 'She saw what she thought was three men walking toward her, one of them real drunk. The other two were holding him up, one on each side with their arms around his shoulders. They was talking to him, saying stuff like, "Not much farther now, man, we be nearly to the car." The stuff you'd say to keep a blind drunk moving. She ID'd the drunk from his mug shot: Oliver, all right. They turned into the alley where we found Oliver's corpse. She dint see no more, but I bet only two men walked out the other side.'

'Yeah, I agree with you. Two men, huh? She describe them?'

'Sure did.' Maddock pats the clipboard. 'Got an AI searching the files right now. I'm going to funnel the report to your comp.'

'Good. Thanks. I'm going to call the embassy and talk to Ka Pral. Maybe I can make them co-operate a little more.'

'Hope so, yeah. Say, did you see the news last night? About someone ripping off the Bears in their hotel?'

'I noticed it, yeah. Thank god that's someone else's jurisdiction and no trouble of mine!'

Bates puts a comm call into Ka Pral's office. About five hours later, Ka Pral calls with a delicately worded request that he come discuss 'the unpleasant matter' with Kaz Phaath. Before Bates leaves, he updates his belt comp from the files he placed behind a new security lock, one that he installed himself to keep Buddy out of his files.

At the embassy Bates wins a small victory. The strawberry blonde at the reception desk greets him by his name.

'Kaz Phaath is expecting you,' she goes on. Her voice sounds sour enough to curdle milk. 'If you'll go down the hall to the left, it's the third door.'

Bates knocks only once before Kaz Phaath opens the door. Under her blue robes she wears a black jumpsuit of some thin shimmery fabric that fits as close as a shadow.

'Chief Bates, I am honoured,' she says. 'I apologize most humbly for breaking in on your day in this fashion, but affairs have reached a point . . . but forgive me! Do come in. Allow me to offer you some refreshment.'

Today's obligatory refreshment turns out to be a thick black liquid served in a tall, narrow glass. When he tries a cautious sip, he realizes that it's some form of beer. For a while they sit on opposing chairs and discuss beer in general and this beer in particular. Her office, somewhat smaller than Ka Pral's, impresses him as austere with its bare wood furniture touched by upholstery in blues and greens. Finally, after a surprisingly short fifteen minutes, she brings up the matter at hand.

'Chief Bates, Ka Pral begged me to convey his regrets for being unable to greet you himself. Do you know why he asked me to have this conversation with you?'

He shakes his head no, and she goes on: 'He hoped that, as we are both human, it would be easier for me to discuss this with an . . . forgive me, Chief Bates, with an outsider.'

'Discussing family matters is always difficult with a stranger.'

'Yes, precisely.' She hesitates, looking away, looking back. 'I have something to confess, and I beg your forgiveness for my dishonour. Gri Nerosi is a member of my staff. I was trying to avoid disgracing him, but I think I made things worse. I thought I could help him with – with his problem.'

'The compulsive gambling?'

Between them stands a plain wood table; she busies herself with setting her glass upon it, refusing to look at him.

'My apology for the surprise,' Bates goes on. 'It's part of our duties as police to keep track of such things. Gambling's legal in Polar City, of course, but some of your – the carli young men get carried away.'

'That's unfortunately true.' She sits back in her chair. 'How long have you known?'

'A couple of days. It's been my experience here that when someone goes missing the trail starts in the Outworld Bazaar. So I detailed a pair of my best men to start looking.'

'I see. And they would have found out that he was well known there.'

'Just that. He was way over his head in debt.'

'I know. I was trying to convince him to get counselling for his addiction. It's part of standard health care in the Confederation, you know, for all species. And we could have arranged a loan, too, to pay off his debts and get him free of the criminal element. I thought I'd convinced him to take advantage of these sensible ways out. I was wrong.' Her mouth works. 'So I didn't tell the ambassador, and now I shall be dishonoured for ever.'

'I dunt see why it reflects on you.' Bates sets his glass down beside hers. 'It's not your fault that he got himself into hot water.'

'It's my fault that he didn't get himself out. You don't understand, Bates. It's the carli way. The ambassador didn't merely assign me some workers, he put some members of our – what's a good word in Merrkan? There isn't one – our job-family in my care. Gri Nerosi's fault is my fault, and I should have admitted it to the ambassador.'

'But on the other hand, you were also obliged to protect Nerosi.'

'That's true. I'll admit to feeling caught between two dishonours. But, and I beg you to believe me, even if it had occurred to me that he might steal, I would not have believed he could steal *iLeijchwen*.'

'He committed a theft, then.'

'A very serious theft. Well, apparently he did. What's that word your news people use? Allegedly, I think it is. Both he and *iLeijchwen* disappeared at the same time.'

Bates unhooks his comp unit from his belt and punches the 'record' button. 'Can you say that name again?'

'Of course. But please, you're not recording everything, are you?'

'I haven't been up to this point, no. But you've just officially reported a crime.'

'I see.' She pauses, thinking. 'Very well. I'll say for your record that Gri Nerosi seems to have stolen *iLeijchwen* to pay off his gambling debts.'

'That'll do. Let's see, you pronounce it ee-lay-eedg-chuh-when?'

'Close enough. The soft guttural cluster's awfully hard to say when you haven't grown up with it.'

'I noticed. And the *ee* at the beginning – that's an honorific, right?'

'The highest one possible, yes.'

'Okay. Please describe *iLeijchwen* for me.'

Instead of answering, Ka Phaath gets up and walks over to the far wall. When she lays her hand on it, a panel slides back to reveal shelves. She takes out a handheld comp unit and comes back, setting it on the table between them.

'There's no word in Merrkan that fits *iLeijchwen*,' she says. 'It's a specialized type of tapestry, I suppose you could say, a tapestry portrait of an individual.'

When she flicks a switch on the comp, a small holo forms above it: a square of oddly hairy brown cloth.

'There's a picture on that?' Bates says.

'I'll increase the magnification.'

The size of the image doubles. Bates can now see that the centre of the fabric displays a certain amount of colour variation.

'I'm sorry,' he says. 'It just looks like a piece of cloth.'

She nods. 'Human eyes – we don't see quite the same wavelengths carlis do or interpret visual images with the same neurology. Sometimes it's a problem. What do you think of my colour scheme? In this office, I mean.'

'I like it. It feels relaxed, calming. How does it look to your co-workers, or don't you really know?'

'I can't completely, of course, but we have programs that simulate the relative appearance of the carli visual spectrum, and vice versa. They see such subtle distinctions that all humans are effectively colour-blind beside them.' She waves at her walls. 'Ka Pral likes it in here, but he would. He says it's lively. Most of the others are too polite to tell me it's garish. But I've seen the simulation, and it's pretty dreadful. I'm going to have it re-done soon, out of consideration for the rest of the staff.'

'Okay.' Bates bends closer to the holo and tries looking at it with half-shut eyes. He can remember being a kid on Sarah and looking for pictures in clouds. 'I can sort of see something in the middle that's maybe shaped like a carli face, but that's all. It's really a portrait, huh?'

'A portrait of a great statesman. Our greatest, actually: Carliprajon Soath Ka Prelandi li Carli.'

Bates recognizes the name. Ka Prelandi, 'He Who Sees', the only carli ever to bear the name of the entire people rather than that of his birth-pack. He taught his people to live in peace among themselves and turn their energies outward, to the stars.

'Yeah,' Bates says. 'I can understand why his image means so much. It must be like our pix of George Washington, Martin Luther King Junior, that whole bunch.'

'No!' Kaz Phaath snaps. 'Not at all! The pictures, that is – please forgive me if I sounded disparaging about your noble leaders. I never intended any slur upon them. But the pictures . . . this is so frustrating. Merrkan just doesn't have the words I need.' She frowns, staring into space for a moment, then brings up another holo. 'Here, this is a human-adjusted rendering of *iLeijchwen*, the best that can be managed.'

In this version Bates can see a shape resembling the head of a carli, most likely male from the suggestion of a well-developed jaw and neck.

'So it's not an ordinary portrait?' Bates says. 'I'm afraid I'm going to have to take your word on that.'

'I have to take the word of my fellow citizens myself. For the right eyes, carli eyes, a *leijchwen* captures the essence of the subject, the true essence, and conveys it to the viewer.' She leans forward. 'Here's the truly interesting thing, Bates. Portraits in tapestry are very common in our worlds, and most are exactly that – weavings of a likeness, the *lechwa*. But a few, a rare few, truly capture the subject. Every artist who attempts *lechwa* hopes to produce a *leijchwen*. But there's never any way to know in advance if the artist will succeed.'

'That's fascinating, yeah.'

Kaz Phaath gestures at the holo. 'I wish I could see it through their eyes, just once. But I know the impact it has on them. *iLeijchwen* is the most important relic in the Confederation.'

'It was here on Hagar, and you dint think to mention this to the local cops?' Bates manages to control his voice with some difficulty. Diplomats. Embassies. How has he offended Allah that it falls to him to police diplomats? Aloud he says, 'Such oversights can cause difficulties. I take it the ambassador had guards of his own around it?'

'Of course not.'

Bates can only stare at her.

'It's not our custom,' Kaz Phaath says. 'We of the Confederation believe all citizens have a right to share the common heritage. *iLeijchwen* is always on the move, from city to city, planet to planet, throughout the Confederation, so all carlis can share the experience. And all other citizens as well, of course, in our own way.' She indicates the holo. 'Sharing *iLeijchwen* helps bind us all together.'

'I see.' A pack marker, Bates thinks. 'I'm going to need a copy of that holo to enter into the file for this case.'

'I will ensure that you have copies of the evidence, that is, those pieces of it I can share. Part of our delay in addressing you about this matter was the need to wait for a team of security experts from aggKar.'

'Have they arrived yet?'

'No. They're expected at Space Dock soon, though.'

'I realize that the embassy grounds are officially part of your home planet.' Bates chooses his words carefully. 'The question of jurisdiction over this case is going to be complicated. I'm speaking off the cuff now, and I need to get the DA to vet this, but I'm pretty sure that the minute Gri Nerosi took the property off embassy grounds he entered my jurisdiction. The only charge I'm going to file – for now – is transport of stolen property. I think your people have the jurisdiction over the actual theft.'

'Oh. Really?' For a moment Kaz Phaath shifts her weight as if she's going to stand up, but she stays sitting. 'I don't know the legal minutiae either, of course. You're certainly right that we simply must observe every protocol. After all, this theft could cause an interstellar incident.'

'What? How?'

'Gri Nerosi's debts were considerable. He must have been planning to sell *iLeijchwen* for a great deal of money. Who would buy it, Bates? Not some average dealer in antiquities. You've seen the holo now. It's not a pretty knick-knack. The buyer would have to be someone wealthy, someone well-educated and, maybe, highly placed. The scandal—'

'Oh, yeah. The scandal.' Bates sighs aloud. 'To be avoided at all costs, right?'

'Well, yes, but it could so easily turn into more than scandal.' She sits on the edge of her chair, looking straight at him, her hands twined tight in her lap. 'Our ways of viewing government are so different.'

In the carli manner she is trying to give him some important message. What is it? Bates has no idea.

'Scandals so often have tangled consequences,' he says cautiously.

'Very nicely said. And who knows where the responsibility for them may lie?'

Bates begins to see a pattern in her remarks. What if some highly placed government official ends up receiving stolen goods?

'That's true,' he says. 'If one follows a spider's thread, one may find a spider at the other end. And the spider may be poisonous.'

'Just so.' She sits back with a little sigh. 'Then we don't need to say anything more, anything unfortunate.'

'No, I dunt think we do.' Bates gets up. 'I'm going to take a personal hand in this case.'

'Thank you.' Kaz Phaath smiles, a sudden radiance that transforms her face. Only then does he realize just how carefully guarded, how carli-like, her expressions have been during this interview. She stands up, arranging her robes around her. 'Allow me the honour of escorting you to the door.'

'The honour will be mine.'

Outside the evening wind registers as pleasantly warm. The auroreal display touches the view with electric blue and silver. Bates and Kaz Phaath walk a few steps down the walkway that leads to the parking lot beyond.

'I was wondering if you were free for dinner,' Bates finds himself saying.

'Possibly.' She doesn't sound as surprised as he is. 'It will depend on my duties; I must report to Ka Pral and Ka Jekhonas. If I may call you later?'

'Sure. I'm going to be in my office all night.'

'Very well. If we do eat together, perhaps you can explain something that's been puzzling us here at the embassy.'

'What's that?'

'Why baseball is so important to your species. I must confess, I don't understand it at all.'

Chapter Six

To Fezzy, days on Sarah run backward. At home he arrives at the ballpark some hours after sunset and works till late at night, while here he gets off the robotrain some hours after dawn. After the storm of yesterday, the air smells scrubbed. The sky glitters, blue around the horizon, tinged with violet close to the red orb of the sun. From the robotrain station he shuffles across a parking lot dotted with gleaming puddles.

Fezzy enters the stadium from a back door hidden by a stand of purple spine trees. Hissing under his breath he takes out his massive ring of keys and heads down a long corridor toward the visitors' locker room. The plastocrete floor, he notices, looks damp at the edges and reeks of disinfectant. The stadium cleaning 'bots and their sentient overseer must still be working. He thus thinks little of it when he sees the locker room door standing open.

And yet at the doorway he hesitates. He can see into the long grey room, see the red doors of the individual lockers and the huge bundles of clean uniforms and towels, fresh from the laundry, on the benches. Everything looks perfectly normal, but something . . . a noise maybe. He shrugs and steps into the room. He hears a scrape, a shoe on plastocrete, behind him. He turns around in time to see the dark flick of a cosh swinging down. With a squeal he throws up one arm, but too late. He catches a glimpse of a narrow, shifty-eyed human face before the cosh smacks him on the head. Then he sees nothing at all.

In the darkness, he hears voices yelling and swearing. Words float by him, then sink into a deeper dark. Eventually they cease for a long time. When he hears words again, these quiver not with anger but with fear. He feels a hand run down the scales on his neck.

'Fezzy! Fez! Come on, Fez, you no can be dead. You just no can be dead.'

A human voice, he thinks. A woman. When he opens his eyes, the locker room dances around him in a blaze of light. He can make out a pale face, topped by red hair, close to his. Tears glimmer in Red Wallace's eyes.

'I aint dead,' he whispers.

Cheers ring out and make him wince. He tries to move his head, but hands restrain him. Jackson, one of the trainers, is leaning over him from the other side. The room is spinning slowly around them.

'Dunt you move yet, Fez,' Jackson says. 'We sent for a doctor. This looks real bad, and I dunt know enough about your people to do much for it.'

The room slows to a stop, and the light loses its sharp-edged glare. Fezzy realizes that most of the Bears are standing around, watching grimly. Rosa gets up, wiping one hand on the side of her pale blue street pants. Something orange and sticky smears on the cloth.

'Hey,' Fez whispers. 'That be blood. It mine?'

'Sure is, old timer,' Jackson says. 'Someone whomped you upside the head.'

'Dunt remember nada. Wait! They get my keys?'

'Fraid they did, yeah. They went through the place, too. Opened the lockers. Took some bats, other stuff.'

'*Sah chi vens grattuliskix!*' Fezzy mutters the worst insult of his native tongue. 'Them and their madres too.'

When the lizzie doctor arrives, two police officers accompany her, but Dr Kalakakez refuses to let them question Fezzy immediately. Once she's checked him over and pronounced him in no immediate danger, Kalakakez allows Jackson and a couple of team members to carry him to the massage table in the trainers' room where the cops can question him in private. By then Hiram Rosen has taken over Fezzy's job for the day. After a stadium official arrives with a spare set of locker keys, Hiram manages to get the uniforms and the towels distributed and the remaining bats and batting helmets into the racks in the dugout outside. Occasionally the doctor sticks her long blue head out of the temporary sick room and relays some order from

Fezzy, always along the lines of 'dunt forget this, make sure you put out that'.

'Dint realize how much old Fez does,' Hiram remarks. 'Wonder where them paper cups are?'

No one knows. The players are grumbling as they take inventory of what's missing: warm-up jackets, spare gloves, T-shirts, even a damp towel that Yosef left in his locker by mistake. Georgy writes it all down on a piece of paper torn off a laundry bundle. Later he and Hiram will discuss this matter with the police.

'You know who it is, dunt you?' Takahashi says from the end of the row. 'Some dealer, that's who. They gonna call it "memorabilia" and make a fucking fortune off it. I'd like to give those jerks something to remember me by, you know what I mean? I dunt even need a bat.'

'Yeah,' Colin says. 'Once I give one of my old warm-up jackets to an auction someone was having for charity – that there free clinic down in Porttown – and some dorkero, he pay almost two hundred bucks for the thing.'

All at once Tak howls. 'Bastards took my cap.'

'Not your lucky cap?' Yosef says.

'Damn right my lucky cap! I've had that thing for three years.'

'Oh shit!' Rosa says. 'I hope it dunt ruin your luck.'

'Me too.' Tak wipes his eyes on his shirt sleeve. 'Me too. I shoulda taken it with me last night. I knew I shoulda.'

Rosa would like to believe Tak's theory about the dealers, but she can guess the thieves were really looking for that piece of fabric lying at the bottom of Lucy's knitting bag. When the police reappear, they have yet another theory. They stand talking in low voices to Georgy, who has never shown any skill at keeping his voice down.

'Gamblers?' Georgy bellows. 'Jeezus aitch ker-rist, I hope not. We better go talk to the commissioner about this. I want this damn starting time pushed back. My team's gotta have a chance to settle down.'

'He be right bout that,' Rosa mutters to Tak.

Tak nods agreement. The team morale improves, however, when Dr Kalakakez leads Fezzy out of the trainers' room. A wrap of blue healskin decorates his grey skull. Everyone cheers him, and he raises a clawed hand in answer.

'Dunt worry about me,' Fezzy says. 'We lizzies, we got thick skulls.'

'Don't let him fall asleep,' the doctor says, to no one in particular. 'If he does, call me immediately. I really want him in hospital for observation, but he won't hear of it.'

'Damn straight,' Fezzy says. 'I aint missing no Series game on account of a couple of punks.'

The team cheers again. When Fezzy blinks, Rosa notices his eyes. The second and third sets of eyelids slide open out of sync with the outer pair – a sure sign of concussion in lizzies.

'You better sit down,' she says.

'And let Hiram mess everything up? Hell, no.' Fezzy glances around at the team. 'Yosef, wait. Something I needed to tell you. Something they said. I . . . hell, it be gone again.'

'That's the concussion,' the doctor interrupts. 'Don't try too hard to remember. Let things come back to you. Well, if they do.' She clacks her beak. 'As I tried to tell those cops, it's a miracle you remember anything at all.'

Lacey wakes in the middle of the day to find Jack already up and the smell of coffee hanging in the air. She pulls on some clothes and wanders, yawning, into the living room, where Jack is standing at the wet bar by the coffee maker. Although he muted the sound, he's turned on the three-dee, tuned and ready for the game transmit.

'You dint have to get up,' he says. 'You coulda watched the recording. I no would tell you who won.'

'Oh sure. I bet I could tell with one look at your face.'

He grins and hands her a cup of coffee. She takes a sip and glances at the three-dee screen. Over a still frame of the stadium a white crawl announces, 'Game delayed. Stay tuned for details. Game delayed.'

'Oh shit!' Jack has seen it too. 'What the hell? Looks like it sunny there and all that stuff.'

'Buddy,' Lacey says. 'Play audio.'

Buddy clicks and hums. The three-dee suddenly blares.

'. . . the unfortunate incident early this morning,' a sonorous male voice is saying. 'A police spokesperson announced that no suspects have been named in the case. New game time will be Sarah standard sixteen-hundred hours.'

'Five hours late,' Jack says. 'And then the lag, whatever that be by now. You coulda stayed in bed.'

'I thought of that, yeah.'

The announcer's voice disappears and perky music starts playing. Without being told, Buddy turns the audio off.

'I have details from the interplanetary newsfeed, Programmer,' Buddy says.

'Good.' Lacey sits down at her desk. 'Start talking.'

During Buddy's recital of the attack on the Bears' equipment manager, Lacey sips her coffee and considers realities. When the AI finishes, she sees one fact above all others.

'It's time to level with Bates,' she says. 'This whole thing, it's way out of hand.'

'No!' Jack snaps. 'You no can sell Yosef out. Hey, we dunt even know if these dudes, they be after the flannel. Maybe they gamblers' goons like the police say.'

'Jack, sweetheart, think! If some big-time gambling man wants to earn a bundle on a game, he dunt go after the underdog. He's going to hobble the favourite.'

'Oh. Well, yeah.' Jack sits on the edge of the sofa and cradles his coffee cup in both hands. 'But I no can see how you gonna tell Bates without busting Yosef. He be a smuggler, now. And Aunt Lucy, she be, like, his accomplice. Red Wallace, too. This come out, the Bears gonna lose the whole damn Series. Y'know? I mean, what if the commissioner, he say they gotta default?'

Lacey starts to answer, stops, has a long swallow of coffee and considers.

'You got a point,' she says at last. 'Specially about Aunt Lucy. But if the cops find out on their own, you and me are out in the desert with no canteen. We knew about this damn flannel and dint stop Yosef when we had the chance.'

'Yeah, and if you go tell Bates, why you think he no gonna just arrest us the minute he hear the story?'

'Oh, I'd figure out something if I was going to tell him. If. Jeez-chrise! You're right: there's Aunt Lucy slap in the middle. Goddamn Red Wallace anyway, getting her mixed up in this!'

*

Rosa has been thinking much the same thing. She's sitting in the visitors' clubhouse along with the rest of the Bears, waiting for the new game time, trying to regain their focus. The pale green room, scattered with old couches and chairs, offers more comfort than most visitors' clubhouses. On one wall a huge three-dee hangs, tuned at the moment to a newsfeed. If Aunt Lucy had never participated in the smuggling, Rosa would go to Georgy and tell him everything, let him and Hiram figure out what to do, even if it meant confessing to the police. Every now and then she glances at Fezzy, sitting in a straight-back chair and watching the three-dee to keep from falling asleep. Georgy paces back and forth, stopping now and then to confer with the coaches or the trainers. Ocassionally he even stops to have a word with Aunt Lucy, resolutely knitting in an armchair.

Off in a corner away from everyone sits Yosef, dead-still, his face impassive, his hands resting on his thighs. Rosa has failed to catch him moving in over an hour. *Goddamn him! If I only no bring him to Lucy. If I only – only what?* Let him be arrested? Ruin the team's morale right as the Series was starting? She drops her face to her hands.

'Hey, Red!' Takahashi says. 'Que pasa?'

'Nada, nada, just tired. Got all wired up for the game and now—'

'Well, yeah. Hey, you should eat something. They put out a pretty good spread.'

Several other players turn her way and nod their agreement. Yosef never moves.

Out of control. If Sarojini can be said to hate any words in the Merrkan language, those three would be the odds-on favourite. Just as she always predicted, one of Moses' schemes has run right off the rails and she doesn't even have the satisfaction of being able to say 'I told you so'. While she sips a cup of chai in her kitchen, she watches the three-dee report of the violence in the Bears' locker room. She will have to go downtown again and call Gorseley from a public comm booth.

Gambler that she is, she gives Gorseley very poor odds of finding the carli artefact in as public a place as a locker room. When she receives his answer, he admits that indeed he failed.

'We tried to give that old lizzie a message for your amigo, like you told us, but I dunt know if he gonna be able to remember it,' Gorseley tells her. 'We dint mean to hit him that hard, but he walked right in on us, 'fore we was expecting anybody to be there. So what could we do?'

Sarojini can think of a number of things they might do, none of them relevant to the matter at hand. In her answer she restrains herself to repeating that violence always causes more problems than it solves.

The more-or-less live transmit – the lag time has stretched to fourteen minutes – of the second game of the Galactic Series reaches Lacey's three-dee a couple of hours after sunset. Even though the broadcast comes via an equatorial relay station, the images buzz and flicker every now and then and the colours tend toward tints of grey. A digitally cleaned-up version will appear on another channel, but a good hour later still.

'I dunt want to wait,' Jack remarks. 'Jeez, we could be cheering them on, and they coulda, like, lost already.'

'Not already won?' Lacey says, grinning. 'You're not going to jinx them, huh?'

'Not me. Them Eagles, they got a good team.'

On the screen the teams stand in solemn lines while the national anthem plays. Lacey sits down on the couch and settles into a corner.

'Come sit next to me,' Jack says.

'No, thanks. Sitting close to you during a game is a good way to get motion sickness.'

'Well, yeah, I get kind of carried away.'

Fifth inning, and Rosa is beginning to think that Yosef Mbaye might get himself a no-hitter, though the walk he allowed in the first inning has eliminated any chance of a perfect game. She has never seen him pitch with such focus. When he steps up to the rubber, his face turns impassive and his body collects itself into a perfect wind-up. His fastballs shoot like laser beams. By contrast his curve balls fall so slowly that the Eagles' batters either swing a bat through empty air or only stand and watch as another strike drops in. During the Bears' half of each inning, Yosef sits at the far end of the bench with a towel

119

draped over his head for privacy. Not even the pitching coach approaches him.

In the seventh inning, however, the no-hitter disappears when the Eagles bring in a pinch-hitter and the game momentarily stops to allow the Eagles' manager to amble over to the home plate umpire. Out behind second base Rosa relaxes, swinging her arms back and forth in the unaccustomed sunlight. All of the Blancos on the team are getting a touch of tan on their arms and faces. Fleecy clouds, pinkish-purple around the edges, lace across the violet-blue sky. Out of the corner of her eye she sees a flash of iridescent colour: a bow, as they're called, an insectoid lifeform native to Sarah, flutters by on double wings.

The batter steps into the box, and Rosa forgets about skies and bows. Yosef throws a fastball, and she can see from his loose follow-through that his concentration has weakened. Sure enough, the batter swings, connects, and drives it past Gina into the gap.

'Shit!' Rosa says and races for second.

The runner slides in a flurry of dirt and arrives a second before the ball does. Rosa swings down and tags him anyway, just for some small satisfaction. He gets up, and as he starts dusting off his uniform, he gives her a rueful smile.

'Almost hated to do that,' he says. 'A no-hitter in a Series woulda been something to see, all right.'

'Almost hated?' Rosa says. 'Sure, like I believe that.'

When the next batter steps in, Rosa watches Yosef closely. No one would blame him if he started having trouble now, but he's wrapped his concentration around himself again. As he strikes out the next batter, Rosa suddenly realizes what's driving him beyond the normal desire to win: rage, most likely directed at Oliver and the punks who hurt Fezzy.

The Eagles never get another hit. Yosef pitches that great rarity, a complete game. In the midst of stunned, silent fans, the Bears mob each other, screaming triumph at a two to nothing win.

'. . . but it's just called stealing bases,' Bates says. 'The runner dunt actually take anything.'

Kaz Phaath smiles at him, and he can tell from her dimples that she's been teasing him. He smiles in return, then signals the waiter.

For this, their second night out, they are sitting at a small table in a bar catering to upper-class sports fans, a tasteful white and beige room dominated by three-dees capable of delivering a life-size picture. At the moment, the digital clean-up of the game transmit is playing on all three of them.

'Another thing,' Kaz Phaath says. 'This name, "Galactic Series". Rather grandiose, wouldn't you say?'

'Another tradition. Back on Old Earth they called it a "World Series" when only a couple of nations could participate. Now we have a couple of planets, so they upped the ante on the name.'

'That seems consistent, yes.'

The waiter arrives with more iced coffees, and while Bates pays for them Kaz Phaath watches the Eagles' pitcher with a small frown. She suits this elegant room, Bates thinks. She left her carli robes at the embassy and wears a soft blue top and skirt of some knitted material, perfectly plain, perfectly cut to hang straight and just skim her body. A small white shell dangles from each of her many braids.

'It's such a slow game, isn't it?' she says.

'Well, some people call it that, yeah. I like the pace. It gives you time to see everything and think about each play.'

'I suppose. Confederation sports move much faster.'

'They're a lot more violent, too.'

'That's true.' She shrugs. 'But there are always doctors on the sidelines.'

Bates sips his coffee and considers how guilty his conscience must be if the very word 'doctor' makes him think of Carol. He's not called her since the embassy reception, but then she's not called him, either.

'You'll understand the pace better,' Bates goes on, 'if I can get a pair of tickets to the next game.'

'I thought anyone could buy a ticket to a game?'

'Normally, sure. But the stadium can only seat so many sentients, and the season-ticket holders get first chance in any post-season games.'

'That seems fair.' She turns to him. 'I'd love to go, though, if you can find some tickets.'

'I'll try.'

While she watches the rest of the game, Bates considers the problem.

121

Scalpers have been working the public advert boards ever since the Bears won the planetary title. Good seats are going to cost half a month's salary, but when he thinks of her smile they seem cheap at the price.

With the long trip back to Hagar ahead of them, the team can afford to break training – or at least, to bend it a little – by going out on the town. Various team members propose restaurants and gather others who agree with their choice. Rosa wants a real meat steak and knows where to get the best, a place called Harris's Garden. Several other blood-suckers, as the team vegetarians call them, decide to go along, including Yosef, Takahashi and Fezzy.

'Dint know lizzies ate dead cows,' Rosa says.

'We eat anything that moved once,' Fezzy says. 'The doc, she say I better stay awake till late. Nothing like a good meal for passing the time. You monkey types, you good at fixing food.'

Rosa laughs and Fezzy hisses, nodding at the rest of the group. His eyelids look nearly normal, Rosa thinks.

'Wait till you see this place,' Tak says to Aunt Lucy. 'Aint nothing like it in Polar City.'

Like most great restaurants the Garden is located away from the tourist areas, just off a busy commercial street at the edge of a neighbourhood of big houses and apartment blocks. From the sidewalk the restaurant looks like any other plastocrete wall with a neon sign above it and a door in it, but walking through the door takes them into the garden that the name promises. Under a glass roof tables covered with white linen stand amid greenery: entire small trees in low planter boxes, bright flowers blooming in huge ceramic pots, flowering vines twining around wood columns. In the centre of the room a fountain splashes and murmurs. Prosperous-looking sentients fill most of the tables. A few glance in their direction, then politely look aside. Rosa relaxes; she had been afraid they might be mobbed by fans, even here on Sarah, but these diners seem content to let the Bears eat in peace.

'Jeezchrise,' Lucy mutters. 'This place gotta cost a fortune, the water they throw around.'

'Wait and see,' Rosa says, grinning. 'But remember, the dinner, it be on me.'

A waitress dressed in overalls and a checked shirt seats them at their table and hands around menus. This time Lucy says nothing, merely stares at the screen. Real beef, not moulded soy, in chunks huge by Hagar standards, costs a mere tenth of what it would at home. Finally Lucy shakes her head.

'Order for me, Red,' she says. 'I feel like a goddamned kid. No can make up my mind.'

Rosa orders the best steak in the house for each of them. The others indulge as well, with Yosef picking up Fezzy's tab.

'Drinks?' the waitress says.

Yosef of course wants nothing but water. Everyone else wants beer, including Fezzy. The waitress smiles at him.

'Grain or sandworm?'

'You got sandworm beer?' Fezzy pauses for a hiss of delight. 'Great! I gonna have one.'

'Hey, Fez.' Tak leans forward. 'Think you should be drinking anything with alcohol in it?'

'If you had my headache, man,' Fezzy says, 'you no want water or some two-bit fruit slop either.'

'Well, yeah,' Yosef joins in. 'But you got conked a good one.'

Fezzy slaps his tail on the floor loudly enough to make the waitress jump. Nearby diners turn and stare.

'Oh hell, I be sorry, señorita!' Fezzy says. 'See what you made me do, Mbaye? No more jive. I want that there sandworm beer.'

'Coming right up!' The waitress trots off fast.

When the beer arrives, Fezzy's glass contains a black, thick liquid that either bubbles or swarms with tiny live things. Rosa decides against asking which. Fezzy takes a long drink, then hisses his appreciation.

'Feels good to just sit, dunt it?' Tak says.

'You bet.' Fezzy raises his glass. 'To the win!'

'Yeah!' Tak follows suit. 'And to Yosef's kid on the way!'

Once the food comes, conversation dies. During the meal the waitress returns often, takes away empty glasses and brings back full.

Every now and then Rosa studies Fezzy when he's looking elsewhere. By the end of the meal, she can see that his second and third eyelids rise too slowly.

'Fez,' she says. 'I dunt think that stuff be good for you. We better get you back to the hotel.'

'No, no, I be fine.' Fezzy tries to hiss, drools instead, reaches for his glass, and nearly knocks it over.

'You're not fine,' Yosef snaps. 'We better get you back and call that doctor, too. What was her name? Kalakakez, I think.'

The name seems to jar something loose in the elderly lizzie's mind. Fezzy wrinkles his forehead and looks at Yosef. 'Yosef, something I had to tell you. Lemme think.' He slurps from the glass. 'The senator. Something bout a senator. Or no, they be a ball team, the Senators. I no can remember the league. No can remember how they finished the season.'

'Uh oh,' Lucy breaks in. 'You got history mixed up with what going on now. The Senators, that was an Old Earth team from before star travel even. No Senators any more in baseball.'

'He always lives in the past,' Tak mutters.

'Not like this,' Rosa whispers. 'Shut up, let him talk.'

'Wash . . . The Washing Senators. No, Washington. Old Earth city of Washington.' Fezzy hisses and looks around the table. 'Dee Cee, like Esperance the Dee Cee of the Republic and they got the Eagles.'

'Yeah.' Yosef leans across the table. 'But what have you got to tell me?'

'Senator. One senator.' Fezzy raises his glass, but Rosa catches his arm and takes the beer away. He barely notices.

'Is it something you heard in the locker room?' Yosef goes on.

'Damn Yankees,' Fezzy sighs. 'I dunt remember.'

'Okay,' Tak says. 'We taking you to the hotel. Dunt try to say no. Want to bet we no can carry you?'

'I want to go, too,' Lucy says. 'Fez, us old timers got to stick together. And I bet Yosef, he no going to some bar to party.'

'You're right.' Yosef nods her way. 'I'm going to call my wife.'

When the bill arrives, Tak and Yosef insist on giving Rosa too much money for their and Fez's share. She and Lucy linger at the table to settle with the waitress while the two men head out to flag a cab. Yosef takes Fezawhar with him to let the lizzie get some fresh air.

'Turn right and go down to the end of the block,' the waitress calls after Yosef. 'A lot of cabs cruise down Kenya Avenue this time of night.'

It takes several minutes to get change and leave a tip, a generous one. Rosa remembers being poor too well to begrudge a working sentient a bit extra. When Rosa and Lucy leave, they turn right and see no sign of the others at the distant corner.

'Hell!' Rosa snaps. 'Dint they wait?'

'They turned left,' Lucy says, pointing. 'Aint only Fezzy who got a muddled mind.'

Rosa looks where she's pointing and sees the recognizable shapes of two men and a lizzie standing on the wrong corner under a maglev streetlight. That end of the block looks purely residential, dominated by a multi-storey apartment building laced with balconies and dark windows.

'You wait here,' Rosa says to Lucy. 'I gonna go fetch them.'

Rosa walks off. She's about halfway down the block when she notices a grey skimmer landing and pulling up near her friends. Its doors slide open; three men get out and head straight for the group of Bears. Yosef shouts a warning. The punks from the skimmer charge into the group and start swinging. Rosa yells wordlessly and takes off running to join in the fight. In the melee Tak is screaming his head off in sheer rage. Lights flash on in the windows of the apartment block. Someone sticks his head out and yells, 'What's going on?'

As Rosa comes sprinting up she sees Fezawhar spin around as if he's going to run. Instead, his heavy tail swings out and whacks one of the muggers right in the midriff. The punk shrieks and leaves his feet, flying through the air to land athwart the kerb with the *crack* of breaking bone. A second punk staggers back from Takahashi's fist in his face. A knife slips to the ground near Rosa. She steps over it and lands a foot on the face of the punk who's bending down to retrieve it. He yelps, staggers back, then turns and runs. The skimmer's doors slide open; the would-be muggers grab their tail-whipped friend and start hauling him to the car. Yosef chases after them, but Tak grabs him and pulls him to safety. With a roar of compressed air the skimmer rises and careens off down the street.

The entire hassle has taken somewhat less than two minutes.

Fezawhar staggers over to the kerb, squats, and begins vomiting with all the drama that only a lizzie can muster, waving his hands and making sounds like several animals dying at once. Takahashi stands under the light and stares at his bleeding knuckles.

'Fuck!' he says. 'I no shoulda done that to my pitching hand.'

Yosef is hunkering down on the sidewalk and looking at the dropped knife. His breath comes in gasps, one eye is swelling shut, and blood trickles from a cut on his forehead.

'That knife,' he says. 'It's a moly.'

'Shit,' Rosa says. 'You lucky, man, and me too.'

A molybdenum ceramasteel knife, so hard it takes a molecularly precise edge – every planet in the Republic has made it illegal to carry one outside professional kitchens – so sharp that a victim could half bleed to death before he realized he'd been cut. Rosa has never seen one this long before, a good twenty centimetres of curved blade. From behind her sirens wail. Flashing blue light dances over the pavement as a police cruiser comes gliding up.

'The greenies,' Rosa mutters. 'Exactly what we dunt need.'

Yosef sits down on the sidewalk so heavily that for a moment she thinks he's fainted.

'Red?' he says. 'Those punks? They were trying to get me into the car. They were trying to kidnap me.'

'Oh, shit.' Rosa can barely speak. 'Oh, my god.'

With its siren sobbing aloud, a second police car pulls and lands. Officers in green leap out.

'No one move, no one move!' the police are yelling as they run up. Behind them trots Aunt Lucy, knitting bag in hand.

'Dunt worry!' Lucy calls out. 'I done got Hiram on the comm already. He coming over here with Georgy and that team exec dude. He say they gonna straighten everything out.'

One of the police, a Blanco, stares into Rosa's face.

'Oh jeezchrise!' he says. 'You're Red Wallace. That's Mbaye, aint it? You guys are Bears players.'

'Yeah,' Rosa says. 'Some of the Eagles' fans maybe got a little carried away.'

Straightening things out takes Hiram and John McPherson, the team's director of player relations, most of the night. The police turn out to pose no particular problems. In the full light of publicity and with a man from the Bears' management there to offer official assurances, the legal system knows that their witness and victims will be coming back to Esperance, no matter how many or how few games the Series ends up including.

Fezzy is another matter. Lucy spends a good part of the night sitting in an uncomfortable chair in his pale blue hospital room. Behind the head of the bed a rack of silver monitors loom, connected to each other and Fezzy both. An IV on a stand drips some bright yellow substance into his arm. He alternately dozes off or wakes up only to launch into a rambling recital about baseball history. As the night wears on, the recitals become more coherent, which Lucy takes as a good sign. Toward dawn Yosef walks in, the cut on his forehead nicely stitched, and flops down on the floor near her chair.

'Where's Tak?' Lucy says.

'Still in the ER,' Yosef says. 'They're waiting for the imaging suite to be developed. He might have broken a bone in his pitching hand.' He looks up at Fezzy, slumped into a pile of pillows with his beak flapping open and a hospital bracelet around one scaly wrist. 'He's going to live, isn't he?'

'You bet. Dr K, she done promised me.'

Yosef tips his head back and closes his eyes – praying, Lucy assumes. The monitors behind Fezzy's bed hum and chime, the IV drips a little faster. Fezzy moans, then falls back asleep.

'I got a second comm call,' Yosef says abruptly.

'What? When?'

'Before we left for the park. It was a different voice, saying he was Oliver's friend. He didn't know the password either.'

'Why dint you tell—?'

'I already had my game face on. I couldn't let myself think about anything but pitching. Damned if I'd let these bastards make me blow the game for the team.'

'Oh.' Lucy sighs, considering. 'Well, yeah, you did right.'

In a few minutes more, Rosa joins them and Hiram as well. Rosa leans against the wall as if she's too tired to bother sitting down. Hiram walks over to the bed and stands with his hands in his pockets while he studies Fezawhar's face.

'McPherson's down with Tak,' Hiram says. 'I got good news. We can check Fezzy out and take him with us if he aint got worse by Oh-seven-hundred.'

Everyone smiles and nods, too tired to cheer.

'They got this thing for his head,' Hiram goes on. 'Kind of like giant bubble wrap with anti-grav chips in it. It'll keep the gee-pressure in the shuttle from making his concussion worse.'

'That's great,' Yosef says, then yawns so hard he shudders. 'Sorry.'

'Look,' Hiram says, 'why dunt you all go back to the hotel? Catch a few hours' sleep before we hit the spaceport. McPherson's taking care of Tak, and I'll take care of Fezzy.'

'Well, I hate being so selfish,' Lucy says, 'but I gonna take you up on that offer. Rosa?'

She shakes her head. 'I gonna stay. Poor old Fez!'

'Yosef, you go with Aunt Lucy,' Hiram says. 'You gotta call your wife. What if she sees this story on the holocasts, and you aint called her?'

Yosef uncoils and stands up in one smooth movement. 'You're damn right,' he says. 'And I dunt want Aunt Lucy out there on her own.'

Maybe because of Yosef, maybe because of sheer luck, Lucy gets back to the hotel safely at about 0500 hours. They see only a few desk clerks and a pair of cleaning 'bots in the lobby. Yosef escorts her up to her room, looks it over to make sure no one's ransacked it while they were gone, then says goodnight and leaves. Lucy clicks the door shut and locked, then goes into the bathroom, knitting bag and all. The beer's still catching up with her.

She's just about done when she hears the room door open.

'Rosa?' she calls out.

Suddenly the bathroom door swings shut. She can hear the lock snapping closed from the outside.

'Goddamn you!' Lucy yells. 'What the hell!'

As soon as she gets herself decent, she rushes to the door and starts pounding on it. In between pounds she can hear the sound of things being tossed around out in the room.

'Let me out!' She visualizes an umpire calling one of her kids out on a dubious strike, then bellows, 'You let me out of here, you goddamn asshole! Help, help!'

The tossing and rummaging start happening faster. All at once she remembers that the plumbing runs through the entire hotel. She goes back to the toilet and begins banging the seat up and down.

'Help! Burglars! Murder! Help!'

Dimly she hears someone moving on the other side of the bath-room wall. She yells even louder and clanks the heavy lid of the tank against the tiles until her hands ache. She sets it down, listens at the wall – nothing. But when she goes back to the door that leads into the room, she hears no one moving around, no luggage hitting the floor.

'Huh. Now what?'

While she's trying to think of her next move, she hears voices yelling out in the hall, coming closer, and the sound of running footsteps. Reflexively she scoops up her knitting bag.

'Help!'

The bathroom door swings open. Two hotel security guards in gold uniforms stand gawking at her.

'Damn good thing you hear me, finally,' Lucy says. 'Now step back. I want out of here.'

She walks out into the chaos of a ravaged room. Her luggage, Rosa's luggage, the dresser drawers, the bedding, the three-dee unit even, lie jumbled together and heaped on floor and furniture.

'So much for getting some sleep,' Lucy says. 'You guys, you dunt run a quiet place here, do you?'

'We try,' one of the guards says. 'But crap, another goddamn break-in! Sure glad you weren't hurt, lady.'

'Yeah.' Lucy hugs the knitting bag to her chest. 'I be feeling that way, myself.'

'That does it.' Lacey slams both hands palm down onto the table. 'Jeezus, Aunt Lucy could have got herself killed.'

'Yeah, and the rest of them, too,' Jack says. 'A moly? That dunt sound good.'

On the three-dee the holonews drones on, complete with footage of the team filing into a robotrain for the trip to Esperance Spaceport. Although Bobbie spots Red Wallace, Lucy never appears in the few seconds the clip runs. Despite her aunt's comm call earlier, Lacey would like more reassurance that Lucy's all right.

'Look, sweetheart,' Lacey says, 'I'm sorry about Yosef, but I got to call Bates. I'll figure out some way to get immunity for Lucy and Red Wallace.'

'Not for Yosef?'

'He's going to be a harder proposition to shelter. He dint go to the cops when he was being blackmailed.'

'No!' Jack shakes his head. 'It aint just Yosef. It be the team.'

'Fuck the team.'

'Hey, Bobbie! Think! They coming back here, and they bringing this old carli stuff back with them. We got a pass to meet the team at the spaceport.'

'So?'

'So they hand it to you right there. You give it back to the carlis.'

'And how am I gonna do that without them wondering where I got it?'

'Everyone in Polar City knows you do deals. You say, someone he want to give the thing back, no questions asked. They say okay, we willing to stretch a point.'

'Yeah, right.'

In the hot evening they argue for two hours. Eventually Lacey gives in, but once Jack leaves to go study with Nunks she sits down at her comp desk and writes the letter to Admiral Wazerzis straight off. Not two hours later, though, wrapped in his arms she regrets it.

On the stored transmit Gorseley's smile has turned to a teeth-bearing snarl.

'We dint! That be what you dunt get, babykins. We aint got no moly, we dint jump your goddamn pigeons. Someone else, they be playing in this game.' He pauses to lick his lips, and suddenly the snarl disappears. 'Someone playing for big stakes, if they got a moly.

We bugging out, babykins. Aint never wanted to see mamma's little boy sliced up like bacon, nosiree.'

The transmit ends. Sarojini punches the 'off' button so hard she nearly breaks a fingernail.

'You bungling buggering water buffalo,' she says aloud. 'Lying to me!'

Her long braid has flipped forward to hang over her right breast. She pats the silver butterfly for luck, then puts the braid back. Sarojini strides out and slams the booth door behind her, then takes the sidewalk rather than the movebelt. Walking will help her figure out what she's going to do when the team comes home, a scant four days from now.

Everyone else at A to Z has long since gone to bed, but with a mug of cold coffee in one hand Lacey sits at her comp desk and considers the data that Buddy put onscreen. It amounts to very little: an obvious list of places that a carli who had no way of getting off-planet might hide, so obvious that the police have doubtless checked them out already; another list of gamblers who might know him; a final list of places she can go to ask – and she's already made arrangements to ask in the most likely of them.

Buddy hums and makes a whirring sound. 'Someone is at the outer door, Programmer. Her thumbprint identifies her as Dr Carol.'

'Great! Let her in.'

In a few minutes Carol arrives, wearing pale green scrubs and jingling something in one hand. She lays the something down on the comp desk – Alison's necklace and earrings – then flops onto the couch and sighs.

'Tell Glover thanks for me,' Carol says. 'Any of that coffee left?'

'Sure is.' Lacey puts the jewellery in a drawer. 'You worked late, huh?'

'Yeah. Bet you're no surprised.'

Lacey gets her a mug of coffee, then straddles a straight chair and leans with folded arms on the back.

'You know, you never told me much about that party,' Lacey says. 'Did Al like the outfit?'

Carol shrugs and considers the pattern on the coffee mug.

131

'Something came down wrong?' Lacey asks.

'Yeah, guess it must have. He hasn't called me since the reception.'

'Jeez. That's been a while. Six days?'

'Yeah.' Carol has a long swallow of coffee.

Lacey waits. Carol lowers the mug.

'It's that damn woman at the Con embassy,' she says at last. 'He couldn't keep his eyes off her at the reception, and he's been taking her out ever since.'

'Oh, shit. What woman?'

'One of their officials, Kaz Phaath's her carli name. Dunt know her real one. Young, smart, and real pretty, too.'

'You dunt break any mirrors yourself.'

'Yeah, but I dunt dote on a guy either.' Carol frowns into the cup as if she suspects it of harbouring drowned bugs. 'The bastards like that, y'know. The adoring stares. The undivided attention.'

'Well, some of them. I remember that with Jaime. I dint think Al was that kind of dude, though.'

'Neither did I. Live and learn.' Carol finishes off the coffee in one long gulp. 'What I've never learned is where to meet the other kind. And dunt tell me that the answer's semi-pro baseball teams, either.'

'Dunt worry. I know what you think of Jack.'

Carol rolls her eyes. 'He must be good in bed, that's all I can say.'

'Well, yeah, he is. Until I met Jack, I never could see why everyone thought sex was such a big deal. I mean, it was fun, but so was playing baseball.'

Carol shakes her head and looks at her through narrowed eyes. 'I had to make a smart remark, dint I?' she says finally. 'You ready to go?'

'Yeah. I got my suncloak by the door.' Lacey stands up, swings herself free of the chair, and turns to Buddy. 'Analyse those files while I'm gone, will you?'

'I am already in the process of doing so, Programmer,' Buddy says. 'Some of this data may be helpful.'

Outside, the mealy orange light of late morning lies heavy on the street. Carol's all-terrain van, white with an enormous red cross painted on the roof, sits outside the door into A to Z. Lacey tosses her suncloak onto the back seat, or rather onto the piles and heaps of medical supplies that cover it, and climbs into the passenger seat.

'Make sure you got that shoulder harness on right,' Carol says.

'Dunt worry about that.'

Carol buckles herself in, then activates the motor. The van shoots straight up, hovers briefly, then takes off at full speed, squealing around the corner and charging for the on-ramp to the expressway. Lacey thanks whatever gods may be that noontide traffic runs light. Over her head the ventilation system bangs and rattles in broken rhythm.

'Hope there's no damn cops around,' Carol yells.

They tear out of Polar City on the south-east expressway, deserted except for the occasional convey of robotrucks. Through the polarized windows Lacey can see little – but then, there's not a lot to see. On either side of the road barren hills stretch out, rusty in the heavy sun. In the cañadas grabber vine and scrub grass try their best to look green. About four kilometres on, Carol leaves the expressway and follows a rough dirt road, beaten out by the fans of industrial skimmers. Since Carol never slows down, the van shudders and dips, throws itself higher into the air, comes down fast, listing as they careen between two hills. The rattling bang of the ventilator becomes deafening.

'I never got spacesick when I was in the Navy, never even once,' Lacey yells. 'So how come I feel like I'm going to be sick now?'

'Ah shut up,' Carol yells back. 'It's not that bad.'

A little farther on the road improves. Off to one side stand huge white tanks, each the size of a baseball stadium, connected by a maze of pipes and towers: Project Noah, the newest stage of the rehydration project. The Navy's Corps of Engineers bring chunks of comet ice, wrapped in high-duty plastoshield, down to the planet's surface and drop them into a series of open reservoirs where the film comes off and the ice melts. From there what water that doesn't evaporate directly into the atmosphere passes through filters and ends up in the city's water system.

'Stop over there,' Lacey calls out. 'By the Metro station.'

'Oh come on, my driving's not that bad!'

'I'm not going to catch a train. I want to look at the walls.'

Noah Station marks the furthest reach of Polar City's Metro – and the newest, opened only a month ago. Already, however, the taggers have found it or, more precisely, its two big wind-baffles: three-metre-high stretches of beige plastocrete walls. They form a forty-five-degree angle that shelters the entrance and the escalator from the ever-blowing sand and red dirt. On the windward side sand piles up steadily, allowing the taggers to reach the top; once a week a bulldozer shoves the sand away and reveals the other tags lower down.

Already the graffiti lie thick: distorted letters and numbers in the alphabets of three species painted with the bright colours of various gangs, crammed into every bit of blank space or boldly overlaid upon an earlier tag. In a couple of places the names of two gangs alternate in a ritualized war, each covering over the other's tag only to have their name covered in turn. Soon the Department of Public Works will paint over everything, and the game will start again.

Lacey works each wall from the bottom up. Fortunately the bulldozer last came some days ago, so she can clamber up the wind-blown dunes to see the higher tags. Carol stands at the bottom with her hands on her hips.

'What the hell are you doing?' she shouts.

'Looking for a change-of-address notice,' Lacey shouts back.

'What? What in hell does that mean?'

'Wait till I come down.'

Finally, on the second wall, she finds what she's looking for: a line drawing of a knife above a crude drawing of the old control tower out in the ruins. She slides down, her suncloak flapping around her.

'Okay,' she says. 'I need to go out by the old tower. Is that okay with you?'

'Sure,' Carol says. 'While we're out here, I want to stop and check up on one patient. She didn't turn up last time.'

'Whatever you want,' Lacey says. 'I appreciate the ride. My life's been dull lately.'

Carol makes a growling sound but says nothing.

They get back to the van, stow their cloaks and take off again, lurching into the air. The van shudders and bounces when they leave the road to skim above the City Dump. The acres of trash finally give way to a sparser rubble. Like a scar down the middle lies the cracked remnants of a runway and, just beyond it, a tall white tower.

Carol parks on a wide stretch of a crumbling grey substance that resembles plastocrete without its durability. A twisted thorn tree offers a small scatter of shade. Weedy grass and creeping dirt vine fringe the broken runway. Lacey and Carol get out and put on their suncloaks. Carol's is white like the van, with the same red cross painted on the back.

'In a few years I'm going to have to find a new place to set up.' Carol locks the van. 'They keep building chem plants and such out here, pretty soon all the Ratters are going to have to move.'

'They might have to move anyway,' Lacey says. 'The Colony Preservation Society's got this whole place tied up in court fights. If they win, the Ratters are on the shorts.'

'Well, it was the first landing site. I think it should be preserved.'

'Sure, but Porttown needs jobs, not culture.'

'Which would you rather do? Work in a chem plant or dress up in antique clothes and show tourists around the old colony site?'

'We're not talking about me. The chem plant's better money. With benefits.'

Carol leads the way down the long shallow valley that looks more like part of the dump than a monument to human exploration. Acres of rubble, everything from skimmer hulks to kibbled plasto, the dead end of so many things, engulf the ruined buildings. Here and there they step over bags of wet garbage, the leavings of those mentally ill sentients who live out here. The real colony site lies underground, a maze of rooms and tunnels, most in decent shape. If the historical societies have their way, the maze will some day host tours of schoolchildren instead of refugees from urban life.

Carol stops by a remnant of wall, made of extruded foam blocks, and whistles carli-style. A human being crawls out of a shelter made from two skimmer doors and a sheet of corrugated reflectoplast. She or he has tied one corner of a big blue cloth, maybe an old tablecloth, around his or her head in place of a proper suncloak. Below that it wears male-cut business shorts and a tattered lace blouse over a ripped spacer's jumpsuit of faded yellow and blue. Leathery tan skin shows through the gaps.

'Hey, Miz Krupp,' Carol says. 'You're up early.'

'Couldn't sleep.' She is looking somewhere over Carol's shoulder. 'They was making noise again.'

'Dancing?'

'Nah, just talking. The dancers, they was out all night, walking around in the light, tall, tall, and all colours, like the sky.'

'Sounds exciting.' Carol takes the old woman's wrist and wraps a shiny white blood-cuff around it.

'There was the yellow one again,' Miz Krupp goes on. 'And the blue one drove her car.'

'And what did she do?' Carol is studying the read-out on the cuff's screen.

'She did climb. And she saw the others, the dancers, they got sand-storms for cloaks, all orange.'

'Okay.' Carol unsnaps the cuff and slips it into a pocket of her cloak. 'Hold out your hand. I'm going to give you your pills.'

Miz Krupp laughs and extends a cupped hand. Carol pulls a bottle of pills out of another pocket and flips up the top with her thumb.

'Where were you last time I was here?' Carol says.

'Watching the dancing.'

'Okay, but next time you show up.' Carol dumps an approximate half of the bottle into the old woman's palm. 'Or no more pills.'

'I be good, Dr Carol, I promise.'

Miz Krupp turns and shuffles back into her hut. Carol and Lacey pick their way back across the trash to the easier walking of the crumbling landing strip.

'What's wrong with her?' Lacey says.

'She's crazy.'

'I could see that. I mean, what are you treating her for?'

'High blood pressure. Just because she's crazy dunt mean she should be allowed to have a stroke. Now, where are we going?'

'Right down there. Past the tower.'

The last time Lacey came to the Rat Yard, the white tower stood alone, but since then someone's built three huts out of hunks of rubble nearby. As they approach, Lacey keeps her right hand in her suncloak so she can palm her laser pistol. One of the huts leans up against the tower itself; it's a collection of old skimmer doors, plastofoam blocks and unspecified junk, but Lacey could swear its door came off a planetary shuttle. In front of the door two bent poles that might have once been light standards support an awning of torn canvas.

'Let's stop here,' Lacey says.

'Yeah,' Carol says. 'I dunt like the look of that dude at all.'

A pale blue lizzie who must be at least two metres tall steps out of the hut and pauses in the shade. He's wearing real clothes, not rags: a dirty pair of coveralls with a tail slit and a white shirt with a long brown stain down one sleeve. He's carrying a metre's worth of metal pipe casually in both hands. Lacey puts her pistol away.

'Hey, Blade,' Lacey says. 'Que pasa?'

Blade stops, does an almost comic double take, and stares.

'That voice!' he says. 'Could it be you, my own true lover?'

'Cut the comedy,' Lacey says, grinning. 'Is your boss home?'

'Nah, sorry, Lacey.' Blade transfers the pipe to one hand and points it like a walking stick. 'Is this Dr Carol I see before me?'

'And what other medic's crazy enough to come out here?' Carol says. 'But I dunt think we've met.'

'Everybody knows who you are,' Blade says. 'But we have met, actually, on the RSS *Avalon*, many a long year ago now. I look quite different without my uniform.'

'He was a sergeant with our Marine contingent,' Lacey says. 'Dunt ask how he ended up here.'

'Ever the soul of tact.' Blade hisses cheerfully. 'That's our Lieutenant Lacey, who has kept in touch with me all these years like the noble soul she is. So you want to see the boss? Why? If you have a job, I bet you could do it yourself better than we can.'

'Flattery, always flattery, but I dunt want someone roughed up. How would you like twenty credits?'

'How? Right now, quickly, and in cash.'

Lacey puts her arm inside her cloak, fishes in her shorts pocket and finds two tens. She brings them out and holds them up.

'So what do I need to do for it?' Blade says.

'Tell me who's in the market for carli art.'

'Moses Oliver, for one. We know where his interest led him, across that bourne from which no traveller returns.' Blade flips the pipe up

137

to cradle it in one arm like a rifle. 'I've decided, therefore, that I have no interest in the subject.'

'Yeah? Did someone approach you about running some off-planet?'

'No, though I might have approached someone had I cared to follow up the buzz.'

'When was that?'

'Late Awgus. A couple of weeks now. No, a few days more. I heard that some carli dude needed a receiver for a thing that was not, alas, his own. We talked about it, the boss and me. We decided that carlis are very bad news generally and that this one, therefore, was going to be bad news specifically. We let it lie. Then Moses got involved, and lo! Mr Oliver, he dead.'

'Yeah, I'd say you made the right decision. But about this carli dude. He have a name?'

'Not that I ever heard. He worked at the Con Embassy, they said.'

'Okay. I dunt suppose anyone knows where he is now? The cops are looking for him, and they'll pay good money.'

'Will they?' Blade hisses in delight. 'I shall tell the boss that, then. Say, that explains something. In the past couple of weeks there have been air speeder searches out here, screaming around at all hours of the night and day, shining their spotlights upon us unwilling actors on our poor stage. It's enough to lose a man his sleep.'

Lacey joins him in the shade and hands over the money. While he checks it, she tips back the sun helmet to get a little fresh air. From inside the hut she hears a high-pitched yipping.

'Whoa!' Lacey says. 'You got a hatchling in there?'

'Yeah, but it's not mine. The boss lady's.' He stuffs the cash into the front pocket of his overalls. 'Say, Dr Carol, do you make housecalls?'

'Why else would I be out here? I'm going to be back tomorrow if your boss's woman wants me to look at her kid.'

'I'll tell her. You were always the very model of medical mercy.'

During the long walk to the van neither of them speaks. Lacey keeps yawning – it's now after noon – and Carol seems preoccupied. When they're heading back toward the city, however, she glances Lacey's way.

'Was that dude really on the *Avalon*?'

'Oh yeah,' Lacey says. 'He was a damn good soldier.'

'Then why—?'

'I'm not going to tell you.'

'Should I be worried about dudes like Blade and his boss moving into the Yard?'

'They'd never hurt you. They know you're valuable.'

'Good. Why are they there, and where were they before?'

'In the Bazaar. As to why they moved, well, Bates is trying to clean up the Bazaar. This means the Vice Squad needs some triumphs to report, and so they're leaning on los pequeños as hard as they can while they keep on pocketing money from los grandes. Not that your Al knows it.'

'He's not mine, dammit. And I'm probably better off.'

Chapter Seven

The all-points alert for Gri Nerosi has failed to find him, not in twelve standard days, alive or dead. Bates leans back in his chair and scowls at the report on his comp unit's screen. His detectives have at least turned up a number of places where he might have been: gambling establishments, some legal, some not, and a flophouse in the Outworld Bazaar where, at irregular intervals, Nerosi rented a room to sleep between bouts of gambling. This last has produced the only solid clue so far: on the first of Stember, the day he disappeared, Nerosi left the flophouse after telling the manager that he had an appointment to keep. The manager never knew where or with whom.

'Okay,' Bates says to his AI. 'Record this speculation. Gri Nerosi no can have acted alone in this. He had to have at least one accomplice, because he no could hide this successfully on his own.'

'Recorded, Chief,' the AI says. 'But if he has an accomplice to help him hide, this doesn't mean he had an accomplice for the theft.'

'That's a good point. Record it, too.'

Moses Oliver left a better trail before his murder. Routine work has turned up his address and his landlady. The landlady had never reported him missing because he'd told her he was going away for a three-week vacation. He never mentioned where, but the Homicide Division has a couple of their best officers on the case. A routine check of insystem ship lines turned up a booking for Oliver, round-trip to Sarah. Bates wonders if Gri Nerosi had something to do with Oliver missing his embarkation time, or if some third party has sent both of them on the longest trip of all.

'Chief?' The comp unit rings an internal bell. 'You have an appointment with the head of the Public Bureau of Investigation in forty-five standard minutes.'

'Thanks.' Bates gets up. 'I'm on my way.'

The very sight of the Republic's auxiliary office building, a black monolith encrusted with plastocrete acanthus leaves, puts Bates in a bad mood. Its top floor houses the Public Bureau of Investigation. After the usual ID checks and sonoscans, he finally reaches Commissioner Akeli's expensively beige suite only to be told by the receptionist that he'll have to wait. The Police Department falls a lot lower on the status chart than foreign embassies.

'I no can wait,' Bates says. 'Have your boss call me to reschedule.' He turns to go.

'Er, well, let me check,' the young man says. 'The wait, it might be real short.'

'Real short I can handle. Under five minutes.'

Bates walks a few steps away and turns his back. While the receptionist whispers into his intercom, Bates considers an angular sculpture made from distressed styrofoam. The artist might have been trying to represent a dead bird or a crashed shuttle, he supposes. Might have.

'The commissioner can see you now, Chief Bates,' the young man says brightly. 'Go right in.'

'Thanks.'

Akeli is sitting behind his massive oak desk. When Bates comes in he leans back in his chair rather than getting up. He's a short man, Akeli, plump and smooth, and he prefers to hide his height.

'Sit down, Bates,' Akeli says. 'Sorry about the mix-up with the receptionist. Apparently he deviated in his usual identification procedures and assumed you to be some other person, one early for his appointment.'

Bates hesitates, then smiles and lets the lie pass. He sits down in a brown leather chair and stretches his legs out in front of him.

'I would assume that your request for an appointment indicates fresh intelligence on our unfortunate incident,' Akeli says. 'Involving the theft at the Confederation Embassy, I mean.'

'Yeah,' Bates says. 'I've been doing some background reading.'

Akeli tents his fingers and waits.

'If the person who buys this missing piece of weaving,' Bates says, 'happens to be a government official, then the Confederation will hold the whole damn Republic responsible. If one of their elected

141

officials stole something from us, they'd consider themselves liable. The head of the government, the President in our case, is supposed to take the heat if any member of the government commits a crime. It was her job to make sure nothing went wrong.'

'That's ridiculous!' Akeli snaps.

'To us, sure. Not to them.'

'Surely they can understand that our system allows a range of individual affiliations, and that the President can't possibly be held accountable for each and every elected official.'

'They can understand it. Will they want to?'

Akeli opens his mouth, then closes it. 'Ah yes,' he says at last. 'A pretext.'

'You got it. The question is, a pretext for what? The answer kind of lies out of my bailiwick.'

'Indeed. Under the mandate given the PBI by the constitution, the matter's very much in my jurisdiction.' Akeli sighs and gazes at the ceiling. 'I will need to consult with the President as expeditiously as possible.'

'You bet. I'd call her right away, if I were you.'

'That may prove difficult. At the moment she's involved in top-level negotiations with the Enzebb Unity. I need to get in touch with my counterpart at the Secret Service. The whereabouts of this confer-ence are being kept secret. What you saw on the holocast about meetings at Camp Jonathan was counter-intelligence.'

'Jeezchrise! Why?'

'Death threats.' Akeli sighs again. 'Against the Enzebbeline ambas-sador and her husband.'

'Humanitas Party?'

'We think so. We can prove nothing. Yet. Not a word of this, Bates, to anyone.'

'Of course.' Bates feels himself turn cold. 'Damn right.' He stands up. 'I'd better be getting back.'

'Indeed. We both have onerous but necessary tasks awaiting us. One last thing, Bates. Those Confederation security people from aggKar. Have they arrived yet?'

'Not to my knowledge. I'll call my contact at the embassy and ask.'

Back in his own office, Bates has his AI put through a call to Kaz

142

Phaath's direct comm line. She answers on the second ring, and her softly brown face smiles on the screen.

'Chief Bates! An unexpected honour!'

'Thank you, but can't you call me Al?'

'Not here, no.'

'Okay. I'm calling for a piece of official information, anyway. Have your security experts made planetfall yet? I'd very much like to consult with them, if that's going to be possible.'

'It should be possible. Desirable, even.' She hesitates, the smile gone. 'You'll forgive my bluntness, but I was speaking to the ambassador earlier about the unpleasant matter. I assured him repeatedly that you were acting with all your accustomed thoroughness and speed.'

Onscreen her image waits while Bates translates her statement into 'You are taking too long'.

'Please reassure the honoured ambassador for me that this case has the absolute top priority for the entire department. I've taken men away from less pressing assignments in order to put a quadruple team on the trail.'

'I cannot tell you how much I personally appreciate your efforts.' She hesitates, full lips slightly parted. 'I wish others had my patience.'

'There are people in my own government who lack it as well.'

'I see. Our ambassador, Frakmo Serag Ka Jekhonas il Frakmo, has asked me to remind you that matters of honour between friends can remain private only so long as honour is upheld.'

She has used the ambassador's full formal name. In this context, if Bates is reading it right, such a usage has the same force as a Hopper's scream of rage.

'I am shamed that I've caused the ambassador the slightest inconvenience,' Bates says. 'Please assure him I'm working day and night to wipe this shame away by finding more information.'

'I shall do that, certainly. I understand the weight of what may be said officially grows larger daily.' She suppresses, barely, a smile. 'Perhaps you would be able to offer me your personal impression of the matter? I could convey it to the ambassador himself on your behalf. Perhaps in two hours we could have an unofficial consultation.'

143

'I'm honoured that you would allow me to be in your presence.' Bates smiles in return. 'Two hours it is.'

Lacey has developed a small ritual around reading her mail. While Buddy displays the queue, she looks away and asks him if there's a letter from Admiral Wazerzis. Only when he says no can she make herself look at the screen. This particular evening, however, he says yes. Lacey feels her stomach twist.

'Programmer?' Buddy says. 'You look alarmed.'

'Do I? Uh, sorry.'

'Do you expect some sort of threat?'

'No. Please put Iron Snout's letter onscreen.'

The letter, however, turned out to be an official form, merely confirming that her letter has been received. Lacey sighs aloud.

'Okay, thanks. Well, I guess they're taking it seriously.'

Buddy clicks and hums. His sensors swivel in their casings as if he's looking around the room.

'What is it?' Lacey says.

'I was considering possible data points, Programmer. I suspect you would label this procedure "wondering about something".'

'Okay. About what?'

'Why you wish to leave us.'

'It's not that I want to leave you. I just want to get back to deep space.'

'Ah.' Buddy's voice turns flat and dry. 'I see.'

'It's not a done deal, anyway. Even if I can get my commission back, dunt mean I'll take it.'

'For as long as I've known you, I have seen that your prime function is that of a military officer. It would be madness for you to turn down the opportunity to exercise your prime function.' Buddy hums for a moment. 'No matter what the effect of such a choice upon those who love you.'

Lacey finds herself with nothing to say. Once she would have agreed with Buddy, and quickly at that. Now? She gets up and walks over to the window, where through the polarized glass she can see the ghostly shape of a distant gantry rising above the buildings of the port.

'Buddy,' she says, 'put the late news on the three-dee.'

'The news will not start for three more minutes, Programmer.'

'Tune in the correct channel anyway. I'll fix myself a drink.'

With a scotch and water in hand, Lacey flops down on the couch as the holonews logo fills the screen. Over it an announcer's voice starts talking, a little too soon, a little too high, a little too fast.

'In breaking news we have an unconfirmed report of a major theft from the Confederation Embassy. Although the embassy staff has refused official comment at this time, a source within the Polar City police indicates that the article in question is a carli art object, a type of weaving called *leijchwen*, or tapestry . . .'

'. . . a woven portrait of the great carli leader, Ka Prelandi.'

An iris opens in the corner of the screen and displays the same holo Bates saw in Kaz Phaath's office.

'How the hell did they find out?' Bates snarls. 'A leak, damn it, and from one of my own officers!'

Automatically he checks the time: just past noon, when Hagar's local time flips over to a new day, the sixteenth of Stember in this case. He should go to bed, but he doubts if he'll get any sleep. Any minute now, the diplomatic incident he foresaw when Gri Nerosi disappeared is going to blow up in his face.

For their return journey the Bears are travelling on a different liner, the *President Nkrumah*, which caters more to business travellers than tourists. Rather than a brothel, their wood-panelled stateroom reminds Rosa of a lawyer's office, all tidy efficiency and leather chairs. Over the tiny closet hangs a row of clock panels, giving the time for different regions of Hagar and Sarah.

'Jeez,' Rosa says. 'It's the sixteenth already back home.'

'I aint never been so confused about time in my life,' Aunt Lucy says. 'All that damn sunshine!'

While they are stowing their luggage, they feel the room begin to throb as the ship powers up. It will take the hyperdrive most of a standard day before it can reach the enormous speeds of its trajectory route out of and over the star system's ecliptic, and then another day at the end of the trip to power down before it can match orbit with Hagar.

'You know what?' Lucy says. 'We can put away clothes any old time. I wanna go take one more look at Sarah.'

'Sure. Good idea. I wanna see what this ship look like, too. So far it be real different.'

Apparently all insystem liner designers agree on one thing, that observation lounges must be uniformly black. When Rosa and Lucy walk into this one, they see a large crowd of passengers clustered around the sunken bar in the middle of the round room. An enormous three-dee screen hangs behind the bar. The passengers, most of them in business suits, clutch glasses as they stare silently up at the newscast. Behind them, hanging beyond the glass wall, Sarah gleams in golden sunlight.

'Jeezchrise,' Rosa mutters. 'Watching three-dee when there's a view like that outside your window!'

'Yeah,' Lucy says, 'but wait a minute. I wanna listen. Look at them faces. Something bad, it be coming down.'

As they reach the pit, Yosef detaches himself from the crowd, bounds up the steps and comes running over. Under his dark skin his face has gone bloodless, leaving him ashy-grey. He grabs Rosa by the arm.

'Have you heard?' he whispers.

'No. We just got here.'

'That thing. The flannel. It's valuable. I mean, Allah save us all! It's a carli idol or something. And if they don't get it back, they're going to declare war on the Republic.'

Rosa tries to speak and fails. Blindly she turns to Aunt Lucy, who has clutched her knitting bag to her chest while she stares up at the three-dee. Since the crowd has fallen dead silent, Rosa can hear the holocasters.

'The Confederation Embassy has delivered an ultimatum to the President of the Republic through diplomatic channels. The Republic has one Confederation-standard week in which to return *iLeijchwen* or face what their ambassador, Ka Jekhonas il Frakmo, calls the most serious of consequences.'

'Dan,' the second 'caster interrupts, 'we'd better tell the folks that a standard carli week amounts to approximately ten and a half of our days.'

'That's right. The ultimatum expires at midnight of twenty-sixth Stember – that's Hagar standard time, of course. We're going to take a short break, folks, but we will have a live feed from the Alliance Embassy's press conference during this hour, so please stay with us.'

The sound mutes, and the crowd in the bar all start talking at once. Lucy snarls wordlessly.

'I wanna sit down,' Rosa says. 'And I think Yosef, he better sit down.'

'You bet,' Lucy says. 'And I need a beer.'

They find a table some distance away from the bar pit and three-dee. Rosa has heard all the news she can assimilate; she's betting that she already knows what the Hoppers are going to say during their press conference: if the Confederation makes a move on the Republic, the Alliance will come to its defence. A shooting war, in other words, with the Republic annexed by whoever wins. For years the Republic has shivered between the Alliance and the Confederation like a rat between two dogs. Now the growling is getting louder. When a servobot rolls up, she orders a gin and tonic.

'Double on the gin,' Rosa adds.

Lucy gets her beer, and Yosef orders spring water. When the servobot returns, Mike Tashahaki comes with it. He holds a glass of some pale blue liquid in one hand. The other, his pitching hand, gleams, wrapped in transparent growth-stim bandages. He sits down in the black leather chair next to Rosa's.

'Crappy news, huh?' Tak says. 'Couldn't come at a worse time.'

'Damn right,' Lucy says. 'Right in the middle of the Series.'

'That, too.' Tak's trademark sunny grin seems brittle at the edges. 'But I was just getting somewhere with that Midori girl, and here she gotta rush off and call her damn bank.'

'You shouldn't have anything to do with that woman,' Yosef says. 'She's a slut, if you ask me.'

'I dint have to ask,' Tak says. 'What's wrong? She turn you down?'

'Just the opposite,' Rosa joins in. 'Dint you see, on the trip over here? She just about have her hand down his pants.'

'Right out in the public lounge, too,' Yosef says. 'I told her, I happen to be a married man. And she said, so what? The Prophet talked about women like her, and none of what he said is good.'

'Holy Joe.' Tak shakes his head and rolls his eyes. 'That's what they oughta call you. You never screwed her, huh?'

'Of course not!'

'Of course not, the boy says.' Tak shakes his head again. 'That's your problem, pal, not mine. It'll give me something to do on the way home, anyway. Take my mind off of this here war. Well, maybe they'll find that weird-looking thing, and we'll live to get old after all.'

Rosa has a swallow of her gin.

'Hey. There comes my distraction now.' Tak stands up. 'The old memo to die – what's that again, Joe?'

'Memento mori.' Yosef is contemplating his glass of water. 'Have fun.'

'Memento Midori, this time.' With a laugh Tak strides off, heading back to the bar.

Rosa can see Midori, dressed in a pale blue business suit and clutching a portable comm to her ear as she stands on the edge of the crowd. She glances around, notices Tak, and with a toss of her long black hair strolls over to join him.

'She probably needs a distraction herself,' Rosa remarks. 'Jeezchrise!'

Yosef pulls a sour face. In her chair Aunt Lucy turns, looking behind her, looking slowly and carefully all around them. The crowd at the bar has grown; the bartender seems to have turned up the three-dee, because Rosa can hear a bare whisper of sound from that direction. No one stands close enough to their little group to overhear.

Lucy whispers anyway. 'Aint gonna be no war. Dunt worry bout it.'

'What? How can—? Oh, for chrissakes, how dumb can I get?' Rosa suppresses a laugh that threatens hysteria. 'But how the hell we gonna give the thing back without getting busted?'

'I'll confess, of course,' Yosef says. 'I'd rather spend the rest of my life in jail than have Polar City get fried by the Cons. Or the 'Lies. Hell, they could execute me, as long as Marisa's safe. You'd take care of her, wouldn't you, Red?'

'Dunt be so damn eager to get yourself martyred,' Lucy says. 'Until we get home, aint no one here to confess to.'

'There's the ship's captain. I could go tell him, and he could put me and the *leij* . . . whatever it is under armed guard.'

'Ai yi yi!' Lucy shakes her head in much the same way as Tak shook his. 'This be a liner, no a warship! 'Sides, you gotta think of the team. You get busted, there go the Series.'

Yosef starts to answer, then closes his mouth instead.

'I gonna tell you what we gonna do,' Lucy goes on. 'We only four days away from home. When we get there, I gonna give the thing to Bobbie. I dunt know how, but I bet she can figure a way to get it into the right furry little hands. With no questions asked.'

Rosa raises her glass in salute to the distant Lacey.

'It's not going to be that easy,' Yosef says. 'What if there are thieves on board this ship? We've still got to get it home safely. Aunt Lucy, I'm starting to worry about you holding it. You could have been badly hurt at the hotel. What if that gang's on board, going back to Hagar?'

'No,' Rosa breaks in. 'Them punks last night, they was local talent. No could have come from Hagar.'

'Yeah?' Lucy says. 'Why?'

'Red's right. Hell, I should've seen that,' Yosef says. 'I'm the one who grew up on Longburrow. That stupid dude walked right by Fezzy's tail. He didn't even watch out for it. There aren't many lizzies on Sarah.'

'Deserved what he got, too,' Rosa says. 'Oh shit! I just realized something. You know what this mean? We got to smuggle that damn thing again.'

'Sure do,' Aunt Lucy says. 'And it's got me ticked.'

'Buddy?' Lacey says. 'Who do we know who knows about art? I mean, who's the person who can tell us the most about this holy flannel? It's got to be someone who deals in non-human art.'

'Checking personal databases,' Buddy says. 'Sub-section: professional contacts. Answer: we have three art dealers listed who owe you favours of one sort of another, plus Tabitha Gonzales who appraises antiques.'

'Who's the most respectable? Do we know anyone with a real good reputation?'

'Answer: Rafael Chang. If I may remind you, Programmer, I have also located several scholarly articles about *iLeijchwen*.'

'I want to read them, don't worry. But I want this contact for more than raw data. When Aunt Lucy gets home, we'll need a go-between.'

'Ah. I understand now, Programmer.'

'Good. While I'm gone, figure out a way for me to get in touch with Chang and sound him out. He's a bit too chummy with the cops for me to just call him up and ask how things are going.'

'Understood, Programmer. How long will you be gone?'

'Couple hours at least. Longer, I hope. I dunt even know if Richie's goons will let me in to see him.'

Set back from a street near but not in the Outworld Bazaar stands a three-storey white house surrounded by a little garden, a relic of the days when the wealthy lived in this part of Polar City. In this one house they still do. In the third-floor suite above the most expensive brothel in town lives the unofficial mayor of Porttown. Since his business caters to the rich and powerful on Hagar, he pays no taxes on his considerable income from a number of illegal activities. Even the muscular young lizzie at the front gate wears an expensive suit with a kilt of grey slubbed silk and a waistcoat to match. He smells of the very best chewing spice. Although Lacey's expecting a hassle, he looks her over briefly.

'Here to see your brother, ma'am?' he says.

'Sure am. What is this, Richie put out the word?'

'You bet. He tell us: my sister, she always welcome here. And he drill us on holosnaps so we always know what you look like. See round the side there, ma'am? Private grav lift.' He fishes in his waistcoat pocket, then hands her a token. 'You dunt want to go inside the house, not today.'

'Okay.' Lacey decides against asking why. 'Thanks.'

She reaches into her pocket for a tip, but he waves it away. 'No, ma'am, not from you. Mr Richie, he particular about that.'

Lacey takes the gravelled path he points out and walks around the side of the house. From inside she can hear loud music but not much else. Another guard, human this time, comes to meet her, passes her on to yet another, who takes her up in the grav lift and hands her over to the final bodyguard, a Blanco who looks female, stands well over six feet tall, and has a surprising number of muscles to match.

The Mayor receives her in his office, a luxurious room furnished in

150

pale blues, greys, and a touch of lilac. Dressed in a pale blue shirt and a pair of white shorts, Richie lounges on a divan among silk cushions. Lacey sits down in an overstuffed chair with slubbed silk upholstery that matches the suit worn by the guard at the gate. Ivory silk drapes the light-shielded windows. Seeing Richie always gives her the sensation of looking into a distorted mirror. He shares the blond hair, the blue eyes, the triangular smile, but his face is beautiful, a beauty beyond gender, really, delicate, fine-moulded, yet certainly not girlish. The ambiguity must have been a selling point in itself.

'Okay, big sister,' he says. 'Whatcha want this time? I no lending you a car again.' He pauses for one of his beautiful soft smiles. 'You melted the last one.'

'I'm glad you're smiling. I hated seeing that Bentley get wrecked.'

'Dunt mean that much.' He shrugs. 'So, you working for the police again?'

'I never work for the police. With them, once in a while, that's all. This time I'm not even doing that. Let's put it this way: if they knew what a friend of mine was holding, and what I'm not telling them, I'd be in shit up to my neck.'

'Sounds interesting. Want a drink?'

'No, thanks, but you go ahead.'

'I try to avoid the stuff. Ruins your complexion. Let me guess: this thing your friend got, it be *iLeijchwen*.'

'Hey, you pronounce that real good.'

'I get carli customers.' He smiles again. 'Some sentients – well, they got wide-ranging tastes. Some carlis, they like the feel of bald-skin girls.'

Every time Lacey sees him Richie tries to shock her, but this is the first time he's succeeded. Since he seems disappointed, she can assume she managed to hide it.

'Yeah?' she says. 'Well, you're right. It is *iLeijchwen*. I'm trying to find out how it got stolen in the first place.'

'So you can give it back, I bet, knowing you.'

'Whatcha mean, knowing me?'

'What I said. Some people, they gonna turn the screws and get rich off it, but I bet: not you.'

'Yeah. So?'

151

'So you always broke.' Richie shrugs, a practised move of beautifully conditioned shoulders. 'Nada more'n that. Whatcha want out of me?'

'Information. Ever hear of a carli named Gri Nerosi?'

'The gambler? Sure have. He owe one of my places maybe three thousand credits. I hear around he owe a couple of freelancers even more.'

'I was wondering if someone decided he was never going to pay and trashed him for it.'

'No, not us, not for a little bit of money like that. Maybe one of the other guys—' He stops, then goes on, 'No, they no dare without asking me first.'

'You dunt know where he is, do you? He went missing about the time that *iLeijchwen* did. The police are looking for him full time. Wanna bet there's a connection?'

'I dunt take no sucker bets, big sister. See Dad do enough of that, y'know?'

'Yeah, I sure do. I saw him do a lot of stuff, and where it got him. Maybe that's why I'm always broke.'

At that he stiffens. Lacey smiles and goes back to the real subject.

'There's another piece of this puzzle. Moses Oliver.'

'Oliver? He no worked for me.'

'Hell! I knew it wasn't going to be that easy. But do you know if he knew Gri Nerosi?'

Richie looks away, catching his lower lip just so with perfect teeth.

'I dunt know,' he says at last. 'But I think maybe he did. Something I heard around, noticed somewhere maybe. You think Oliver had something to do with *iLeijchwen*?'

'I know he did. He had it. He hired a mule to carry it off-planet. Then he got himself killed.'

'And your friend, they be the mule?'

'Just that.' Lacey has no intention of passing him information he might use to blackmail Mbaye further. 'Oliver offered him good money.'

'The mule, he be on-planet?'

'No. I'm not going to tell you who it is.'

'Course not.' Richie grins at her, an open honest smile for a change. 'I no tell you, if I knew.'

'But okay, so Oliver knew the carli. I'm guessing he got the *leijchwen* from Gri Nerosi, anyway, and I'm guessing that it was holding the thing that got him killed. Tell me, did he have any lines of work that might have trashed him for some other reason?'

'Not that I know about. He sold a little drugs, played a little cards. Lessee, he did odd jobs for the 'Lies and the Cons, but you knew that. Provided things like drugs to the 'Lies, fake ID papers for illegal muscle, that kind of stuff. Nada to get you killed if you mind your manners.'

'Then it's likely he got killed over the *leijchwen*.'

'Could be. Maybe the carlis, they know he got it and send someone after him, but it be too late.'

'That's a thought, all right. The Cons are just as ruthless as the damn 'Lies. They just hide it better.' Lacey stands up. 'Thanks. You realize, dunt you, how serious this situation is?'

'Why you think I tell you everything I know?'

Richie gets up and walks with her to the door.

'Hey, come by A to Z some time,' Lacey says. 'See what the place looks like now.'

'Yeah, sure.' The perfect mouth twists. 'Maybe when hell freezes, and I gotta get warm. Good luck, big sister. If the Cons, they blow up Polar City, it gonna make a mess out of my business.'

After a long dinner in which they have discussed no official business at all, Bates escorts Kaz Phaath back to the Confederation Embassy. He lands his skimmer outside the back gates, then ground-drives it slowly into the paved yard behind the high stone wall. In a tidy line sit other skimmers, most with the plates marking them as official embassy cars. At the far end, next to a small garden, sit three private skimmers under a maglev light.

'Thank you so much, Al,' Kaz Phaath says.

'You're welcome.' He turns in the driver's seat and rests his left arm on the wheel. 'I have a question, and I hope it carries nothing but respect. Do you think the time will ever come when I'll know your Merrkan birth-name?'

Her eyes grow wide, and she moves a little away.

'I've been too forward,' he says. 'I apologize.'

'No need.' She suddenly smiles at him. 'I just realized I was hoping that day would come.'

'Really?'

'Yes. Really. I – um, well, I'd better go.'

Before he can get out, she opens the door and slides free of the skimmer. He hears her sudden bark – he can think of no other word for the quick phrase in the carli language – and then a human laugh. A new face appears in the passenger side window – Ka Pral.

'Chief Bates,' the carli says. 'May I impose utterly upon your time and ask for an unscheduled appointment?'

'Considering our mutual circumstances, my time is at your disposal. Let me park the car.'

Bates has never gone into the embassy by the back door before. He suspects that Ka Pral is showing him an unusual favour by allowing him this glimpse of the business side of the building: the kitchens, the cafeteria, a warren of small offices, all painted in undulating shades of grey. As they walk, Ka Pral says nothing, though now and again he bobs his head pleasantly.

'My honoured friend,' Bates says, 'I have a favour to ask of you. Would it be possible for me to see the scene of the theft?'

'Most assuredly,' Ka Pral says. 'We turn down this corridor.'

Halfway along they climb a short set of stairs, walk along another corridor, take three steps down, and find themselves in front of open double doors, made of glass bound with bronze fittings, leading into a room painted a pale grey.

'You'd call this a museum, I think,' Ka Pral says. 'But it's a very small one.'

The room measures maybe three metres by four. On the walls hang plastoclear cases, each holding a single object. In the middle of the room stands a single pillar topped by an empty plastoclear box.

'I doubt if I need to tell you what that display contained,' Ka Pral says.

'No, indeed you dunt. There was no alarm system in here at all?'

'Why? You've seen the room's location now, deep inside the embassy building. You may call us naïve, Bates, but we never dreamt that one of our own would steal any of these treasures. And how

154

would an outsider find his way here without being seen? The outer doors are guarded.'

'Well, that makes perfect sense.'

'Thank you.' Ka Pral's voice aches with sincerity. 'I cannot tell you how relieved I am to hear you say that. I've blamed myself over and over again. I think every senior official has.'

'I hold you blameless.'

Ka Pral lowers his head and flings his arms out to his sides. No carli could offer deeper thanks than this. The only answer possible is silence. Bates turns away and makes a great show of examining the other items in the museum while Ka Pral recovers himself. A shallow bowl of blue enamel decorated with a thin silver stripe; a ceramic drinking vessel glazed a pale bluish-green; a woven square so old that it's been mounted on some special backing, he stands before each one for the properly polite long time. Ka Pral eventually joins him in front of a long thin knife with a bone handle carved like a horn from an emfalit, the carli's chief meat animal.

'They're exquisite,' Bates says.

'My thanks. There is of course a tale behind each one.'

Bates arranges a smile, but Ka Pral bobs his head.

'I shan't bore you with them, Bates,' he says. 'Shall we go to my office?'

'I would be honoured to hear the tales, however, if the day comes when we have leisure again.'

'I shall hold you to that. And I hope in my heart we have that day.'

For a moment their eyes meet. By unspoken agreement they turn away at the same moment and walk to the door. On the way out Bates stops before a last plastoclear case. Inside on a little pedestal sits an object he takes for part of a leather glove until he notices the three steel blades, shaped like claws and about six centimetres long, sticking out of the fingers.

'That is a rather sad thing,' Ka Pral says. 'The type is an implement of ritual suicide. Ka Prelandi's wife used this very set of Claws to join her husband after his death. Her mind gave way, poor woman, because of her loss, and before her daughter could stop her she had finished the ritual.'

'Very sad, indeed.'

When they reach Ka Pral's office, Ka Pral offers Bates a pale blue liquor served in cups shaped like a curled leaf. It has the clear taste of a drink with a very low alcohol content. Bates hopes it lives up to its billing.

'I'm particularly glad you could spare me some time,' the carli begins, 'because of our mutual young friend.'

'I wondered if her welfare was maybe on your mind.'

'Just so. My dear Bates, you know, I trust, that normally the private affairs of embassy staff members are just that, private. Senior officials only involve themselves if such affairs seem a matter for grave concern. Personally I'm delighted to see Kaz Phaath enjoying life a bit more. She has a tendency to be too serious for one so young. And I know enough of human standards of beauty to realize she is quite attractive. But in view of the current, ah, unfortunate tension between our governments, we, that is the ambassador and myself, feel it inadvisable for her to act as our liaison. No doubt you find it uncomfortable yourself.'

'I'm sure I dunt need to reassure you that her behaviour has always been completely professional when we discuss embassy matters. She's been a most worthy representative for the Confederation.'

'This doesn't surprise me. Except for the matter of Gri Nerosi, her record is exemplary. But, in all fairness, will it not be more pleasant for you both if she is not impelled to maintain a purely professional distance?'

'I think it certainly would be.' Bates is surprised at how relieved he feels. 'You have my thanks.'

Ka Pral pours more of the pale blue liquor. 'If only all matters between us could be settled so easily.'

'Yes, indeed,' Bates says. 'If only.'

'You and I have worked together once before to avoid an unpleasant outcome to an ugly situation.'

'This is very true.'

'I'm wondering if perhaps I have information that would help you understand the ugliness we find ourselves in now.'

'If you did, our mutual task would be easier.' Bates contemplates the pale liquor for a moment. 'As much as it pains me to admit my lack of understanding, here's one problem. Gri Nerosi is one of your own people and a citizen of the Confederation. My miserable wits are still puzzled by the Confederation placing the blame on the Republic for a deed committed by a citizen of the Confederation itself.'

'Ah. I can understand your puzzlement.'

'Unfortunately, it's shared by my government.'

'That is why I felt I had to speak with you today. If you would permit, I would first pose a question of my own. As you would doubtless agree, an accurate monetary value cannot be set upon that which is beyond price, but certainly a value has been set upon *iLeijchwen*. Who sets this value, Bates?'

'Art dealers, I suppose.'

'They are the intermediaries. The one who ultimately sets the value is the one who makes the puchase. The customer, in other words.'

'Well, ultimately, perhaps.'

'In a case such as this one, when a unique item has come on an illegal market, there is no perhaps. If no one had wished to buy *iLeijchwen*, would Gri Nerosi have stolen it?'

'Ah.' Bates pauses for a sip of his drink. 'I see where this is leading.'

'In other words, the customer is both ethically and legally responsible for the theft.'

'Now wait! The responsibility has to attach to the thief as well. He had the choice of saying no to the buyer.'

'Oh, yes, certainly. If Gri Nerosi is ever found, he'll pay for his crime. You need have no fear of that.'

'And when we find the buyer, I can assure you that he'll make amends as well.'

'Really? This may be impossible through no fault of yours.' Ka Pral leans back in his chair and considers the ceiling. 'We've heard rumours, rumours I want you to hear as well. The buyer might well be one of your senators.'

For years Bates has schooled himself to speak to carlis as they wish to be spoken to. Only that training saves him from a long string of expletives. 'This is serious news,' he says instead. 'When did you—?'

'Not an hour before I saw you drive in with Kaz Phaath. I wanted you to know as soon as possible.'

'Thank you. This gives me something to go on. Did your – um, source – have any idea which senator?'

157

'Only that his jurisdiction lies on Sarah. Bates, I've lived in the Republic for many standard years now. I know how few of your senators answer for their misdeeds – should they commit one, that is.'

'I'm afraid you speak the truth there.'

'The safe return of *iLeijchwen* is of paramount importance, yes, but there must also, I fear, be acceptance of culpability.'

Bates sighs. Senatorial influence forms a veritable curtain made of strings there for the pulling. That curtain has hidden some heinous crimes in the past.

'If this senator refuses to pay for his crime,' Ka Pral goes on, 'then your government as a whole absolutely must admit its culpability for this unspeakable act.'

'That could be close to impossible. The government might indict the senator for receiving stolen goods, but our people are never going to understand why anyone but him should be blamed.'

'But he is *part* of that government, my dear Bates! It's as if . . . as if . . .' Ka Pral stops, sighs, then rubs the dark brown tufts of fur above his eyes with one long-fingered hand.

'I'm too lowly to dare offer correction to one so aggrieved,' Bates says. 'Yet I fear in this case confusion, a most understandable confusion, may cloud your understanding.' He hopes that's an acceptable way of telling Ka Pral he's wrong. 'The office is not the person who holds it. The person who holds the office may well dishonour it, but if so the individual is to blame, not the office.'

'Let me put it another way.' Ka Pral looks up. 'Among our people, being of the Council means far more than holding an office. Even a single word of your own language shows the distinction: *of* the Council, *in* the Senate.'

'That's true.'

'So, then, when a person becomes of the Council, his interests become the Council's interests, and what the Council holds as good he will hold as good. He will consider harmful those things the Council views that way.'

'Ah, there's our difference. In the Republic, a person joins the government to advance the interests of those who elected him. Normally these interests coincide with those of the person elected, at least to some degree. But they certainly don't coincide with the government as a whole.'

'So I've noticed.'

'Well, then, how can you possibly blame the whole pack of people who make up our government for the actions of one person? It doesn't make sense.'

'No, it doesn't.' Ka Pral bobs his head. 'Bates, I understand perfectly well what you're saying. But most of our citizens, who have never met such an estimable representative of the Republic as yourself, will not. Unfortunately, the Council itself will have difficulty with such an alien attitude. They would, however, make the attempt, were it not for the lamentable reality that it is this particular *leijchwen* that has been stolen. The theft of any *leijchwen* would be a grave insult, but to steal that of Ka Prelandi li Carli . . . my dear friend, even I, even here with you, knowing as I do how you are expending every effort to recover it, find it difficult to hold my temper when I think of it.'

'No doubt, and I grovel in apology – not that my apology would mean anything to the Council.'

'What? Please do not demean yourself! It would mean a great deal. Unfortunately, it would merely not mean enough. What would satisfy them would be an apology from the government as a whole.'

'Wait a minute.' Bates suddenly sees hope. 'This apology, if it came from the person of the President, would it be enough?'

'Of course. She leads.'

'Good! Maybe I can get her to see reason. If of course we find *iLeijchwen* in time.'

'If, indeed. That, my dear Bates, is the crux. If *iLeijchwen* has been lost or destroyed, I cannot say what the Council would do, but I fear their actions would dishonour us all.'

'Well, hell,' Rosa says. 'This time tomorrow, we gonna be at Space Dock.'

'Yeah,' Lucy says. 'Sure are.'

They are sitting at their table in one of the *President Nkrumah*'s dining halls. This particular room sports little round tables covered with red and white cloths. Down the centre runs an island buffet,

159

heaped at the moment with more breakfast than even the two hundred passengers on this deck will be able to eat. A fancy abundance keeps passengers eating instead of worrying about being inside a metal bubble floating through airless space.

On this particular trip, however, the anxieties afflicting the passengers have little to do with space fever. Lucy and Rosa have heard talk of the possible war everywhere on board. Keeping Yosef from confessing to everyone he meets has taken a lot of energy and nearly all their patience.

'Where be Ol' Laughing Boy this morning, anyway?' Lucy says.

'No was up yet when I checked his cabin,' Rosa says. 'I done left him a note, telling him where we was gonna be.'

Lucy has just started her third cup of coffee when Yosef appears, bringing Mike Takahashi with him. Lucy's more than glad to see Tak, who has helped them keep Yosef's spirits up during the trip, not that he knows why the spirits had sunk so low. Tak grabs two plates, hands one to Yosef, and fills his at the buffet. The two pitchers then come over to join Lucy and Rosa.

'Morning, all,' Tak says. 'Jeez, Aunt Lucy. You drink more coffee than anyone I ever met. No wonder you so damn jittery.'

'Jittery?' Lucy says. 'What makes you say that?'

'Your being jittery, of course.' Tak grins at her. 'Red, you too.' He jerks a thumb in Yosef's direction. 'And then we got our pillar of gloom over here.'

'Oh shut up!' Yosef snarls. 'What with the news on the three-dee, anyone with any brains would be pretty damn gloomy.'

'You got a point there.' Tak picks up a sweet roll and bites into it. 'Drink, eat, have a blast – y'know, like that old saying.'

For a few minutes they eat in silence. Lucy hands her dirty plate to a passing servobot, then picks up her coffee cup. Her knitting bag sits on the floor, right between her feet where she can kick any would-be thief in the face, should one try to steal it. Yosef picks over about a third of the scant meal he collected at the buffet, but Tak eats like a cleanbot. He starts at one side of the plate and doesn't stop till he's shovelled it all in. Everyone else makes a point of not looking at him until the final burp.

160

'That was good,' Tak announces. 'One thing I gotta say about these ships, they dunt stint—'

Somewhere across the dining hall someone drops a piece of crockery with a sharp crash and it shatters on the tiled floor. Yosef yelps and shoves back his chair. For a moment it looks as if he might slide under the table, but he collects himself in time.

'Jeezchrise!' Tak says. 'What be so wrong with you, Joe? I seen it now for three days, you acting like you gonna be shot the minute this ship docks or something.'

Yosef turns an ashy-grey about the mouth. Tak stares for a moment, then glances at Rosa, who looks away and picks up a glass of water with a shaking hand. The honest concern in Tak's eyes helps Lucy make her decision.

'Something we gotta tell you, Mike,' she says. 'But it no gonna be right here.'

'Fair enough. How about we go to my cabin?'

Takahashi's stateroom looks exactly like the one Rosa and Lucy are sharing, except that of the two beds one is neatly made up and the other's a complete mess. Lucy and Rosa take the chairs, leaving Yosef to perch on the tidy bunk. Tak throws a blanket over the mess on the other and sits down, bending over to pick up a thigh-high black lace stocking from the floor. He tosses it onto the pillow.

'A souvenir from Miss Midori.' He grins at Yosef. 'Hey, you really missed something.'

'Yeah? I suppose you know that at least three other guys on the team have one too.'

'It adds up to two pair of stockings that way, yeah,' Tak says. 'Why you think I'd care?'

'What you need is a decent woman, not sluts like her. A woman who'll make you a good wife.'

'When I'm eighty, maybe.'

Yosef sets his lips tight and glowers at him.

'Never mind that now,' Lucy says firmly. 'I got something to show you.' She rummages in the knitting bag, finds *iLeijchwen* and sets it on her knee. 'Whatcha think of this, Tak?'

'It's a flannel.' Tak is still grinning, but then he leans closer, stares

161

and lets the smile fade. 'Wait a minute. What the hell . . . ? It's that carli thing from the news.'

'Sure is,' Lucy says. 'And we gotta smuggle it past customs so my niece can get it back where it belongs.'

'Your niece?' Tak looks up. 'Who – oh wait, no, I know who she is, sure. She still with Jack Mulligan, right? But, hey, how did a nice old lady like you end up with this thing?'

'Long story.' On the way from the dining hall, Lucy has rehearsed this lie. 'Whoever stole it, they gotta have a way to get it to Sarah. It was gonna be sold there, I think anyway. They dint tell me much. So they hired this dude name of Moses Oliver, 'cause he knew someone he could blackmail.'

Lucy pauses briefly to let the drama build. Tak and Rosa both stare at her; Yosef sits as still as a corpse and probably as cold. With a deep sigh Lucy gazes at the floor.

'I had kind of a wild youth,' she says. 'Guys, I dunt wanna tell you what I did. I been shamed so long now, but it still hurts. Dunt know how this Moses he find out. But when I heard he been found dead, I aint never been so happy. But hell!' She looks up with what she hopes is a sad but wise expression. 'Here I be, still holding this thing. Yosef and Rosa, they know bout it all along. That be why we such fun company.'

For a moment Yosef looks as if he's going to weep. Instead he nods, as if agreeing with her.

'Jeezchrise!' Tak says. 'I get it now. That's why the break-ins, right? No wonder you so upset about poor old Fezzy! Whoever they be, they been looking for that rag.'

'Damn right,' Lucy says. 'Never thought no one was gonna get hurt. But if I go to the police, well, my past, it gonna come out.'

'Dunt you worry bout that.' Tak leans forward and snatches *iLeijchwen* from her knees. 'I gonna carry it through customs for you.'

'What? I mean, no, uh, I mean, it too dangerous!' This offer Lucy had never anticipated. 'I dint tell you to make you a smuggler, too. I just want some help, like, a bodyguard maybe.'

'Hey, I aint never refused a lady in need yet,' Tak says. 'If I get caught in customs, you can rescue me and tell the truth then. But it be safe enough. The team, we be conquering heroes. No one gonna

162

go through our bags. The customs officers, they all Polar City boys and girls, born and bred.'

'Then I gonna take it through,' Rosa says. She leans forward and holds out her hand. 'Give it here.'

'No, hell, you aint gonna have all the fun!' Tak stands up, clutching *iLeijchwen* in one hand. 'Same goes for you, Joe. I'm gonna have to figure out a really cool way to bring it in, maybe in my underwear.'

'More like a really hot way,' Yosef mutters. 'Too sweaty, anyway. What are the carlis going to say if we give them their priceless relic back, and it stinks?'

'Oh, okay, I'll think of somewhere else.'

'Tak, you be enjoying this!' Rosa says. 'Too damn much.'

'You bet! I aint never turned down a chance at a wild ride in my life.'

And from the way he grins, his dark eyes snapping with excitement, Lucy knows that arguing will get her nowhere.

Chapter Eight

Even though the bright day has four more hours to run, half the city appears to have turned out at the spaceport to welcome their beloved Bears home. Since almost everyone wears an identical suncloak in the team colours of black and white, the robotrain station looks as if it's covered with cinders and ashes. Mulligan stands on the edge of the stairs down and tries to get his bearings. Despite the autocool system in his suncloak, sweat runs down his back. Behind him Lacey says, 'Oh, hey, man, sorry about your feet.' Some stranger grunts an acknowledgement.

'This way, Bobbie,' Mulligan says. 'Everyone piled up at the escalator. The stairs, they be easier.'

They work their way down the stairs and gain the flat. Mulligan ducks as a thin plastic stick rattles against the helmet of his suncloak. A forest of similar sticks, each carrying a team pennant, waves between them and the doors of the main terminal, some twenty metres worth of solid crowd. He has given up hoping that they'll actually manage to get inside when a voice starts bellowing from a bullhorn.

'Pass holders to the right, pass holders to the right.'

'That's us.' Bobbie grabs a fold of his cloak. 'Think we can make a turn?'

Mulligan pretends he's trying to score with a catcher blocking the plate. He lowers one shoulder and starts shoving, heading right, dodging and sliding through the crowd. They get within sight of the tall glass doors of the terminal. The privileged mob slows even further as the more law-abiding within it struggle to form a queue. Mulligan can see a pair of guards checking passes as fast as they can while the black-and-white cloaked fans swirl around them, waving their red or yellow passes.

164

'Bobbie? You still there?'

'Yeah.' She tugs on his cloak. 'Sure am.'

At last they reach the doors. A security guard grabs Mulligan's pass, stamps it, hands it back, and motions him through. He stops inside the door, then jumps to one side as a couple push past him into the building. He pulls off his suncloak with a toss of his sweat-soaked hair.

'*Madre de Dios!*'

'It's something, all right.' Bobbie comes up beside him. 'I dunt believe this whole crowd got in on legit passes.'

'Yeah, wonder how much the fakes selling for?'

Bobbie pulls her cloak off. Sweat runs down her face.

'Dunt know,' she says. 'Bet Richie has a piece of this action, though.'

A black-and-white sea has filled every seat with fans wearing team colours and clutching suncloaks. For every seat five would-be sitters cram the narrow aisles. Somewhere at least two babies are wailing, and on every side small children cry or fuss. Mulligan looks up toward the ceiling. On the black arrivals board white edges the read-out of the team's arrival time: less than an hour till planetfall.

'Okay,' Mulligan says. 'Now where?'

'Arrivals lounge,' Bobbie says. 'On the other side, of course.'

It takes them a good five minutes to work their way to the second door, where more security people stand guard. Although they wear spaceport blues, each has a long strip of silver tape over one shoulder, designating them as temporary hires from a contract security firm. One of the guards, a lizzie woman, turns her back to threaten with her tail every time the zealous try to shove through. Every time they obey orders and get back.

'We got yellow passes,' Mulligan calls out.

'Then get your butts up here, Blanco,' the lizzie says. 'We got enough people standing around.'

She hisses entirely too much at her own joke, but she does let them through to the inner lounge.

'Thank god,' Bobbie says. 'You know, I'd call this a madhouse any other day.'

'It look like peace and quiet, yeah.'

Mulligan can see a few empty seats, and dark rust-coloured carpet shows between scattered knots of people: family members in casual dress, team management and city officials in business suits, three-dee newscasters, four holocam crews, and influential fans wearing upscale versions of the fanware outside. Children race around, treating adults as obstacles to be jumped or climbed. On the far side, long windows give a well-shielded view of spreading plastocrete, the port's main landing field.

'You know any of these people?' Lacey says.

'A few.' Mulligan points to a group by the windows. 'That donna in the leather miniskirt and that shiny sort of shirt? That be Keiko, Takahashi's sister. And the donna with her . . . huh, I wonder if she be Marisa Mbaye.'

The woman in question stands behind Keiko and looks out over the crowd. Mulligan gets the impression that she'd be attractive if she weren't wearing a shapeless, floor-length bag of a black dress. She wears a shawl-sized white headscarf, too, covering her hair and trailing down her back, with the ends tied at her neck to hide any show of throat.

'She's the right religion, anyway,' Bobbie says.

Eventually they find two empty chairs together. Bobbie sits down with a sigh of gratitude, and Mulligan has to admit to himself that he's had enough action for one day. He folds his cloak up and stows it in the helmet.

'I gonna carry yours for you,' he says.

'Thanks.' Bobbie hands it over. 'I see a buffet over there. Want some ice water?'

'Sure do.'

When Bobbie gets up, Mulligan puts the cloaks on her chair to save it. He shuts his eyes and concentrates, trying to focus on the psi signal he hears coming from somewhere in the room. Faint, very faint – the person transmitting must be merely latent rather than developed. He opens his eyes to find Bobbie making her way back, carrying a pair of tall paper cups. He stands up and takes one, swirling it to admire the ice inside.

'Great! Gracias.' He drinks half the glass straight off. 'Sometimes water, it be okay. Y'know?'

166

They sit down and wait. At each end of the lounge hang panel clocks: one to give local time, one for standard time, and a third to count down the minutes till the shuttles start landing. Around them people are laughing and talking; the children shriek and giggle. Lacey leans against Mulligan's shoulder and whispers, 'I'm damn glad Lucy could get us those passes. The sooner we pick up that package, the better.'

'You bet. Jeez, no could hardly believe it when she call, hearing her so calm and stuff on the transmit.'

'Me neither. She's one smart lady.'

'Yeah. Jeez, this whole thing, it gonna be over by tonight.'

'Let's hope. No, make that: let's pray.'

Ten minutes before the first shuttle lands, a voice comes over the intercom announcing that the entire Bears team will arrive on this first flight. Everyone in the lounge cheers and claps. Extra security people begin filing in, clustering near the exits, ready to escort team members to the main lounge. From there they and their families will be able to leave safely through the utility access tunnels under the port.

'Ten more minutes,' Mulligan says.

'Huh. Dunt forget customs.'

He can feel her anxiety like a prickling on his skin and turns to look at her. She smiles blandly back. Her officer's face, Mulligan calls it, when her expressions become so meaningless, so unreadable, that no one can tell what she's thinking. No one except him, of course. While he would never pry into her actual thoughts, he has no defence against feeling her emotions. He stands up, settling the sun helmets under his arm.

'I wanna walk around,' he says. 'No can take sitting no more.'

All at once a rumble splits the sky. Children rush to the windows to look as the rumble grows into a roar. Even though the shuttle will land a good long way away, the building shakes and chairs rattle. Through the window Mulligan can see the sleek white shuttle drop straight down, as small as a toy, braking against its own exhaust for a vertical landing. Down and down, larger and larger, slower and slower, perfectly vertical now as it hovers. The roar stops, leaving a silence ringing in the lounge. The shuttle slips into its cradle. Gantry arms swing round to hold it fast. The children at the window begin yelling and clapping. Outside the robotrain pulls away from the lounge building and glides toward the waiting ship.

'Attention please,' the loudspeaker says. 'May I have your attention please. After customs the passengers will be entering the lounge by Door A. I repeat, after customs the passengers will arrive by Door A. Please wait behind the railing. No one will be allowed beyond the railing.'

Mulligan looks across the crowd and spots Door A on the far wall. About a metre out from the wall a metal railing runs most of the way across the room, leaving an opening that one or two security people could control had they some reason to. At the moment half a dozen silver-stripe guards stand by the door.

The children raise the volume on their cheers. When Mulligan glances over to the window, he can see the robotrain heading back to the port buildings. The holocasters rush to the railing and begin setting up cameras, but it takes twenty minutes before Door A opens and the first Bear, Colin Dejean, comes through. Cheers, a shriek – his young son dashes through the crowd and flings himself at his father. Laughing, Colin grabs him and swings him onto his shoulders. Behind him comes Manager di Giorgio and a couple of the coaches.

'Let's get closer,' Bobbie says. 'I hope to god that Yosef and Aunt Lucy aren't last. I want to get out of this crush.'

With a lot of polite manoeuvring Mulligan manages to get them near the wall and closer to the rail. Some metres to their left a scuffle breaks out as a security guard tries to confiscate an unauthorized freelance news-cam. The woman, a young Blanca with blue hair, swings a bag of holocubes at the guard, a lizzie who ignores the blow and grabs the cam with his claws. Near the railing, the official press pool overloads the port's sound-suppression system with a barrage of shouted questions as the team members and their spouses walk out in pairs and little clusters. In the lounge, babysitters and aunts push forward with children in tow.

'Most of the team members only have a carrysack or something,' Bobbie says. 'Dunt anyone have any real luggage?'

'The team, it take care of that after you get it through customs.'

More security guards, some human, some lizzie, escort the players through. At last Mulligan sees Yosef Mbaye, swinging a carrysack from one massive hand. Mulligan considers hailing him, but he sees Marisa Mbaye heading toward the railing. He decides she has priority. Right behind Yosef, Mulligan notices a Hindu woman in spaceport blues, a silver butterfly clipped to her long braid of hair. She stops near the Mbayes and talks into a comm unit – or rather tries to. The unit seems to be broken. She shakes it, then shoves it into her pocket and moves on.

'There!' Bobbie crows. 'There's Aunt Lucy!'

Lucy waves and begins shoving her way through the crowd. She's carrying her knitting bag in one hand and with the other is steadying the blue carrysack that hangs from her shoulder. Mulligan gives the cloaks to Bobbie and goes to meet her, but about a metre away he realizes he's picking up no signal from her burdens. He takes the heavy carrysack from her anyway.

'You a sweet boy when you wanna be,' Lucy says. 'Dunt have to be careful with that, chico. Nothing important in it.'

'Yeah. I kind of figured. Does Yosef—?'

'Aint nothing much in his bags, either.'

By then Bobbie has made her way over to them.

'Aunt Lucy,' Bobbie says. 'Where—?'

'Your attention . . . your attention, please.' The amplified voice cuts off Bobbie's question. 'Passengers taking outbound robotrain B should exit by Gate E. Repeat, those passengers . . .'

The Hindu rentacop returns, carrying a functional comm this time, and stands talking nearby. Mulligan ignores her chatter about grid-lock in the parking areas and focuses on picking up a signal.

'Joe be over in a minute, I bet,' Aunt Lucy says. 'Bobbie, you happen to know Mike Takahashi?' She arches one eyebrow. 'Or, Jack, you?'

'Yeah,' Mulligan says. 'Why?'

Lucy rolls her eyes Bobbie's way and pats her knitting bag.

'Oh,' Mulligan says. 'Gotcha.'

The rentacop clicks off her comm unit and trots away.

To keep the robotrain from being overwhelmed, the police department and the Bears' management have arranged a fleet of skimmers to carry team members and their families beyond the crowd, still waiting outside in the brutal late-afternoon sunlight. Most of the

Bears have made it through customs by this point. City cops in their green uniforms begin to escort them through the crowd into the main lounge beyond. Every time the door to the main terminal opens Mulligan can hear cheering and applause. What would it be like, to walk through there and know they were cheering him? He refuses to allow himself to wonder.

'Jack!' Yosef is standing near the railway and waving. 'Come on over and meet my wife. Bobbie, Aunt Lucy, you too.'

As they walk through the thinning crowd, Yosef keeps talking, but in the way that only Mulligan can hear.

Trouble/damn/stupid\punks\damn\stupid<on Sarah>

<Heard/that. All→holonews.

Takahashi\Mike<take|leijchwen<onship. Carry/it. NOT|listen. I<try/ stop\him.

Where he now>will be?

I NOT know. OR: wait!

Aloud, Yosef calls out to a dark-haired man coming through Door A. He has a carrysack slung from his shoulder, and even without Yosef's explanation Mulligan would know it holds the *leijchwen*. Signal radiates from the sack so strongly that Mulligan externalizes: he feels waves of water washing over him, pulling him like a rip-tide toward Takahashi.

'Jack Mulligan, you old bastard!' Tak calls out. 'Here, take this for me.'

He swings the carrysack free of his shoulder and steps up to the railing. As Mulligan reaches out to take it, security guards rush forward.

'Sir!' The woman with the silver butterfly in her hair steps between them. 'You haven't cleared that through the security scanner in customs.'

'Look, lady,' Tak snarls. 'You people, you done hung me up enough for one day. Where's my goddamn luggage, if you be so keen on doing things right?'

'I'm sorry, sir.' Her voice turns icy. 'I was hired for lounge security, not landing-field security. I'm afraid I know nothing about your luggage.'

'Well, it never made it to the customs hall.' Tak turns away, the carrysack dangling from his hand. 'I want some answers, goddamnit!'

'Sir!' A second guard, a burly Blanco, steps forward. 'The shift manager, he gonna talk with you. We gonna find the stuff, okay? Come back to the checkpoint, will you? Mr Pulaski gonna talk with you there.' He glances at the Indian woman. 'You wanna take him back?'

'No problem,' she says. 'Sir, please, it's only a formality.'

'You lucky you female,' Tak says. 'Or I say a few things. But oh, what the hell, sure. Lead the way.'

For a moment Mulligan feels like he's going to faint. He is reading something that he cannot identify, but it seems to him that as *iLeijchwen* moves away from him, the tides of water start to boil, pulsing, stifling, burning him.

'Jack!' Yosef grabs his arm. 'What's wrong?'

'I dunt know.'

'Maybe the heat.' Aunt Lucy steps forward. 'Sit down, Jack. You no breathing right, hyperventilating or something. Sit down. Chair right behind you.'

The voice of his old Little League coach carries a weight that Mulligan can never explain. He sits, puts his head between his knees when Lucy tells him to, drinks the water Bobbie fetches for him. Yosef hovers near his chair.

'Ah,' Yosef says. 'Here's Tak again.'

With the carrysack hanging from his shoulder, Tak strides over. Behind him trots a small skinny Blanco with a halo of frizzy hair. Mulligan has never seen him on the holocasts, but he wears a black blazer with the polar bear logo embroidered on the chest pocket.

'Stupid legalistic bastards and bitches,' Tak says. 'Here you go, Jack.' He swings the carrysack free. 'Sorry I took so long, but she made me open this damn thing. Guess we made them suspicious. Anyway, someone musta stole my luggage, they say. How the hell that happen? I got the team secretary here to help me sort this out, so I gotta go back to customs. I'll call you guys later. Or you call me. Around midnight. I gonna be home by then, for sure.'

The moment Mulligan takes the carrysack he knows that *iLeijchwen* has disappeared. For a moment he sits frozen as his mind struggles to understand how it could be gone. Still complaining, Tak strides off with the secretary hurrying after. Aunt Lucy and Bobbie are chatting with Marisa Mbaye while Yosef watches, smiling. He should do something, Mulligan knows, tell Bobbie, run after Tak. But what can he say, right there in the middle of a swarm of security guards and actual policebeings? One person he can reach.

Yosef. It gone.

Yosef swings around, his face suddenly grey. Distantly, at the edge of his perceptions, Mulligan can feel *iLeijchwen*. Somewhere through Door A, out in the customs hall maybe?

'What's wrong?' Bobbie snaps. 'Something is.'

'Yeah.' Mulligan manages to speak at last. 'Real wrong. Hold this a minute.'

Mulligan hands her the carrysack, gets up, then runs, heading for Door A, dodging through the crowd. Security beings yell and reach out to grab him. He ducks and swerves, leaving them yelling behind him. The signal is growing stronger, clearer with every step he takes, but at the door two security guards step in front of him while a third grabs his arm.

'I'm sorry, sir. No one but Security can go into customs this way.'

The signal fades and dies. Whoever has *iLeijchwen* has taken it out of the building. Mulligan looks around, a little dazed, more than a little sick to his stomach.

'Yeah,' he says. 'Sorry. I shoulda known that.'

When he turns away he sees Bobbie leaning on the railing, clasping it with both hands. She's gone white around the mouth.

'Yosef told you.'

She nods. He takes her hand, and they walk together back to Aunt Lucy, standing alone by an exit door with her knitting bag clutched to her chest and carrysacks and suncloaks piled around her feet. In a nearby chair Marisa sits, radiating puzzlement and fear so strongly that Mulligan realizes she has latent psi – the person he picked up earlier, no doubt.

'It be okay, señora,' Mulligan says. 'Your old man and me, we gonna straighten things out.'

She smiles, and her slender face, framed by the white scarf, turns beautiful.

'Thank you.' She blushes and looks away.

'Yosef, he gone to find Red Wallace,' Lucy says. 'She aint come out of there neither. One of the guards, he say her luggage gone too.'

'Ah shit,' Mulligan says. 'These people, they dunt leave nothing to chance.'

'What people?' Lucy says.

'The ladrones that just steal the – the flannel. Someone figured this out pretty good.'

At sunset Sarojini walks into the temple of Ganesha with *iLeijchwen* tucked into her bra and her arms full of fresh-cut flowers. Incense smoke drifts in lazy patterns through the light cast by the floor-to-ceiling hologram at the far end of the narrow room. The wall seems to open out to a view of a gentle daylight shining upon a wide brown river. The water flows, edged by green fields that fade away into a misty distance. Lord Ganesha himself, the elephant-headed god, sits in half-lotus upon a floating cloud, one of his many hands raised in benediction. In his commodious lap nestles a rat, signifying the clever kind of wisdom.

Sarojini walks to the altar that stands in front of the holo and lays down her flowers, a small fortune in roses and carnations, then puts her hands together and bows with a backward step.

'They always say luck's nothing more than putting yourself in the right place at the right time,' she says. 'Sri Ganesha, I thank you.'

Since Rosa Wallace needs to stay at the port and hunt for her luggage, Bobbie decides to take Aunt Lucy back to A to Z. By the time they find a regular cab – autocab programming keeps them out of Porttown – the sun has set. In the cool evening Bobbie opens the door into the gardens and shepherds her aunt inside to the rustling of the apple trees. Out in the rows of Sarahian bread ferns, Nunks stands up, waves, then hurries over to help Mulligan with the luggage. Bobbie assumes Jack is telling him everything that's happened.

173

'Good to see you, Nunks,' Lucy says. 'Wish I dropping by in happier times and all that.'

Nunks nods his agreement and turns to Mulligan, who will voice his answers for him. Bobbie leaves the three of them and hurries up the stairs. As she opens the door into the living room, the lights come on, the air conditioning starts up, and at the comp desk Buddy chimes.

'Messages, Buddy?' Lacey calls.

'One from your brother, Programmer.'

'That's a first. What's he got to say?'

'On the day of his death, Moses Oliver was seen drinking with a man known to be a human agent for the Alliance.'

'The Alliance?'

'Yes, Programmer. Your brother seemed oddly surprised as well.'

Lacey walks over to the desk and stands for a moment, drumming her fingers on the surface. Buddy's sensors turn her way and gleam while she thinks. Today is the nineteenth. The carli ultimatum lies too close at hand for her to continue playing games with Al Bates, but she has, as always, the damned team to consider and Yosef's pregnant wife as well.

'Programmer? You appear upset. I take it *iLeijchwen* is not in your possession.'

'Sure isn't. Someone swiped it right out from under us at the spaceport.'

'That is very alarming.'

'You've got a great grasp of understatement. Tell you what, Buddy. Can you hack into the police files and enter something?'

'Making an entry in a pre-existent file would be easy. Writing a new file would be only one difficulty grade higher.'

'They must already have a file about Moses Oliver. Add Richie's data to it, but make the source an unnamed informant from the Outworld Bazaar.'

'Order registered. Proceeding.' Buddy clicks twice, hums once and chimes. 'Done, Programmer.'

'Now, open a new file about this theft in your memory. I'm going to get every witness I can to input data.'

Aunt Lucy and Mulligan come in, both puffing for breath, Lucy from the stairs, Mulligan from the luggage, which he deposits near the door. Both pause, staring at her, waiting, she supposes, for the brilliant solution which she lacks at the moment.

'Want a drink?' she says instead. 'There's cold beer.'

'I gonna take one of them,' Lucy says. 'Can I use your comm, honey?'

'Sure. Who you need to call?'

'St Anne's Hospital. That's where they took Fezzy. Gonna keep him in tonight for tests, poor old guy.'

'Getting hit on the head like that, he better have tests,' Bobbie says. 'I dunt suppose he got a look at his attackers?'

'If he did,' Jack puts in, 'he aint gonna remember what they look like.'

'Yeah, but maybe he'll remember something else.' Bobbie turns to Aunt Lucy. 'Why dunt you call that hospital? See if Fez can have visitors. The beer's going to have to wait.'

Since Fezawhar did most of his recuperating on the trip home, the ward nurse has no objection to a visit. They find Fezawhar sitting up in bed and watching the three-dee. Although he's wearing several paste-on monitor transmits, he's been spared an IV hookup. He mutes the sound and hisses a welcome.

'Brought you some company, Fez,' Lucy says. 'My niece Bobbie and her man.'

'Jack Mulligan I know,' Fezzy says. 'Well, aint never met you, Jack, but I done watched you play often enough in the off-season. Miz Bobbie, nice to meet you.'

'Good to meet you, too, Señor Fezawhar. I understand you had a little trouble over on Sarah.'

'More than a little, honey.' Fezzy clacks his beak. 'Want to hear about it?'

Fezzy launches into his recital without waiting for an answer. Bobbie made sure to bring a comp link in her shirt pocket. By standing near the bed, she can pick up everything Fezzy says and send it back to Buddy. While Fezzy talks, Aunt Lucy sits in the only chair and leans back; her eyes close now and then, but she always wakes herself again. Mulligan ends up, as usual, sitting on the floor.

'This is real interesting,' Bobbie says at last. 'You got a look at the dudes who attacked you, right?'

'Musta. No can remember now.'

'But what about the second time?'

'That be different. I saw them plain as plain. Told the greenies bout them, too.'

'Okay. Try to remember something for me. The second set of dudes: were they the same as the ones in the locker room?'

'No.' Fezzy sits up straighter. 'When I saw them punks coming at us outside the restaurant, I said to myself, I did, these be a whole nother clutch of rotten eggs. Huh. Wonder how I done knew that? But I sure as hell did.'

'They always say we remember everything that happens, but sometimes we no can access it. So some part of your mind remembered enough to know they were different people.'

'Maybe so.' Fezzy looks away and clacks his beak. 'Sure wish I could remember what they said bout that senator.'

'There was a senator mentioned?' Bobbie softens her voice. 'Any name?'

'Dunt remember. Sorry bout that.' Fezzy extends the claws on his right hand and sucks thoughtfully on a pair of them. 'Meet him at the mall. That be all I can remember. They said, "Meet him at the mall".'

'Hey, it's better'n nothing. Gracias, Fez. I better get my aunt home. She look pretty damn tired to me.'

They go down to the hospital lobby. While Mulligan walks out front to hail a cab, Aunt Lucy finds a chair near the door and Bobbie takes the opportunity to contact Buddy. He's safely recorded Fezzy's data, he tells her.

'There is a message as well,' Buddy says. 'Some six minutes after you left, Rosa Wallace called. After a two-hour search, the port found her luggage and that of Mike Takahashi in a dumpster. It had been opened and rifled.'

'I no can say I'm surprised by that. Is Rosa at home?'

'I have no data on that point, Programmer.'

'Okay. Put a call through to Mike Takahashi for me.'

Through the tiny speaker on the portable unit Lacey can hear a series of clicks, then the familiar ring-ring of a comm unit. She waits: no answer. Waits some more: still no answer. The ringing stops, and Buddy's voice returns.

'Programmer, I can make no contact with Takahashi's home comp unit. It appears to be completely offline.'

'Hell of a time for it to break,' Lacey says. 'Well, we're on our way home, and I'll try from there. Access whatever databank you can to find out how many malls are in Esperance and if any of them are near the baseball stadium.'

During the cab ride back to A to Z, Lacey finds herself thinking about Al Bates. Whatever she learns, she promises herself, will mysteriously appear in his files for him to find.

'When we get home,' Lacey says, 'you both are going to have to tell Buddy every single thing you recall about this afternoon.'

'You bet,' Aunt Lucy says, yawning. 'If I get that beer first. But you better talk with Tak, honey. He the one who went back into customs.'

'Yeah, he did. And Rosa Wallace must have been there, too, looking for her stuff. I—' Bobbie stops, caught by a feeling she can only call dread. 'Hang on.'

Lacey pulls the portable comm out of her pocket, then hesitates. They are travelling in a public cab; the driver could be anybody; her transmit link to Buddy might be picked up by his comm unit and broadcast either by mistake or design. They will be home in twenty minutes at the most. She should wait, but she keeps thinking of Takahashi's comm ringing with no house comp to answer. She hits the speed button that links her to Buddy.

'Buddy? Call Rosa Wallace for me. Call Mike Takahashi again, too. Keep calling till you get them.'

'Very well, Programmer. I have been attempting to call Takahashi on my own initiative. His house comp continues to be offline. Attempting to reach Wallace now.'

In a few seconds Lacey hears a ring and a click, and then Rosa Wallace's voice. 'Hi. I no can make it to the comm right now, but you leave me a message and I gonna answer soon as soon. Adios.' A beep follows.

'Hey, Rosa? This is Bobbie Lacey. Call me at A to Z the minute you get this. It's pretty important. Aunt Lucy's going to stay with me for a few days, so she'll be there too. Thanks!'

Bobbie hangs up.

'Stay with you?' Lucy says. 'What? Why?'

'I got this gut feeling,' Bobbie says, 'that anyone who carried the flannel around could be in a whole lot of trouble. I dunt want you alone in your apartment.'

Chief Al Bates has spent the past half-hour writing a letter of commendation. His officers performed uncommonly well, in his opinion, both out at the spaceport and on the clogged highway afterwards. He sends it off over the general comm, where a lesser AI will replicate and deliver it to the terminals of the officers involved.

'Chief?' his own AI unit says. 'I have a Code Three seven-oh-seven from Sergeant Parsons coming in.'

'Oh, for chrissake! Put him on.'

'He's not online, sir. I have his location, and he wants you to join him there as fast as you can. He says he doesn't want to transmit the victim's name over the usual frequencies. He says this is, I quote, "a stellar case".'

'Crap! I bet I know what he means. Okay, call him back and say I'm on my way.'

Aunt Lucy has fallen asleep on the couch in the living room. Nunks and Mulligan sit on the floor nearby, playing chess and, no doubt, talking to each other. Lacey checks the time again: past midnight now.

'That's it,' Lacey says. 'I'm not waiting any longer. Jack, you can finish the game later, okay?'

'No problem.' Mulligan looks up and grins. 'I losing real bad anyway.'

Nunks makes a snorting sound that Lacey reads as disgust.

'Buddy? After Jack and I leave, shut down all the electronic locks. Dunt let no one in but us. Got it? If Rosa Wallace calls, tell her to lock herself into her apartment. Nunks, I'd sure appreciate it if you'd stay up here with Aunt Lucy.'

'He say, of course he gonna,' Jack says. 'Where we going?'

'Mike Takahashi's. Y'know, one of these days we've got to get that skimmer fixed. Goddamn Metro is going to take us for ever, but I dunt want to risk another cab. The driver, someone could bribe him later.'

178

Nunks looks at her, then at Jack.

'He say, be careful.'

'Dunt worry. I got my laser pistol with me.'

Jack whistles under his breath.

'Yeah,' Lacey says. 'Keep your eyes open, sweetheart.'

Takahashi lives in New Cloverdale, a neighbourhood of big houses surrounded by real grass lawns, where the Metro exists mostly so servants can get to work on time. The grav lift from the station brings them up to pale sunlight, or so it seems. A fleet of maglev lights hover over the broad streets. Three blocks of fast walking take them to the cross street.

As soon as they turn down it, they see trouble. Police skimmers crowd the street. Their circling blue lights flicker and dance. An unmarked green van has pulled into one of the driveways next to a house half-hidden by a stone wall.

'Shit!' Jack says. 'That be Tak's place.'

Out in the street stand two police officers. A third is stringing yellow police tape, tying it to the light standards to mark off the entire house. Lacey walks up to him with Mulligan trailing behind.

'What happened, Izzy?' she says. 'Where's Takahashi?'

Officer Zizzistre looks up, his beak gaping in surprise. The cops out in the street are turning, looking, strolling over.

'Jeez, Lacey,' Zizzistre says at last. 'You know how to give a guy a shock, I gotta say, turning up right on schedule. Or Mulligan, I guess I mean really. The chief, he just tell me we better get a psychic out here.'

'Yeah? What happened, damn it?'

Lacey glances at Mulligan and gets her answer even before he speaks. Jack is standing with his legs apart and his head thrown back. Tears run down his face.

'Tak, he dead, Bobbie.' Mulligan shakes his head hard, and tears scatter. 'We be too late.'

'Bobbie Lacey?' Bates says. 'What the hell is she doing here?'

'Dunt know, Chief,' Parsons says. 'She says she only gonna tell you that. But she got Jack Mulligan with her.'

'Then get them both in here.'

'Yes, sir.' Parsons hurries out, leaving the door open behind him.

Bates is standing in the entry hall, a small room, empty except for a low wooden bench. On the water-polished wood floor lie the remains of a house comp, pulled from the wall and kicked a couple of times from the look of it. A spatter of blood – human from the colour – has dried on the surface, as if someone tried to operate it with a bloody hand.

'Here's Lacey,' Parsons says from the doorway. 'Mulligan he no wants to come in.'

'Tell him we need him to do a reading,' Bates says. 'Now. Lacey—'

'Yeah, I know. What am I doing here? It's a long story, Chief.'

Bates starts to say something nasty, then hesitates. If she knows something and he angers her, she might decide to not bother telling him. Lacey stands in the doorway, arms crossed over her chest, a posture that tells him she's in no mood for hassle. She's wearing a pair of grey shorts, a grey shirt, and a blue waistcoat that, he's willing to bet, hides a weapon of some sort, probably illegal.

'Yeah?' Bates says at last. 'How much of this story are you willing to tell me?'

Lacey merely smiles, a brief flick of her mouth.

'You better get Jack in here,' she says, 'before the images fade any further.'

'If you weren't right, I'd arrest you for that.'

Bates turns and stalks into the living room with Lacey following. A few low couches, a few floor cushions, a scatter of antique screens painted with scenes of rivers and long-legged birds decorate the wide room, wrapped by windows on two sides. Maglev lights outside reveal a garden, as spare and soothing as the room, or rather, as the room was once. Over by the far wall lie the remains of an elaborate sound system – music cubes shattered, speakers cracked, the shards of a blue and white vase. In the middle of the wreckage crouches a lizzie forensic technician busily pulling on a pair of plastofilm gloves. Beyond her lies the corpse, covered with a pale green sheet.

'How did he die?' Lacey says.

'Someone beat him to death, looks like. More than one person, probably. He fought pretty hard.'

Lacey nods. She's looking around at the smashed glass on the floor, a small rug kicked into a heap, magazine and book cubes scattered, a portable viewer with its screen cracked.

'Bastards!' Bates growls. 'The whole city's going to want blood when they hear about this, and I dunt blame them one damn bit. But jeez, this is all we need, a headline homicide on top of the embassy mess.'

'It's all part of the same thing, Chief,' Lacey says. 'That's the long story.'

Bates has the feeling that he's staring at her with his mouth open. Before he can recover, Parsons comes in.

'Mulligan's in the entryway, Chief,' he says. 'Want me to clear the place?'

'No.'

His hands shoved into the pockets of his jeans, Mulligan walks in and looks around him. Bates can see him shaking from across the room. When Bobbie starts forward, Bates lays a warning hand on her shoulder. Mulligan takes his hands out of his pockets and holds them out in front of him, parallel with the floor. His head snaps back, his eyes focus on air, he sinks to his knees. Bates tightens his grip on Lacey just in time. Sure enough, Mulligan screams.

The scream fades and the terror with it when Mulligan lets the trance claim him. He feels that he has two bodies. The one, kneeling and folded on the floor, hardly concerns him. The other, which he can control but not see, moves freely around the room. At the edge of his hearing a voice drones, and Mulligan recognizes it as his own, describing what he sees for anyone who wants to listen. Besides the usual three dimensions, he can feel the fourth – or not precisely feel it. It exists as resistance, as if he swam against the invisible current in an unseen river.

In this water he perceives pictures. His training gave him tools to separate out the layers of time that float, one over the other, in the unseen river. At certain points they mingle and form eddies, swirling with strong emotions such as agony and terror. In their hearts lie the secrets he wants to learn. To swim there means he must surrender to them and the pain they carry. He hears himself moaning, feels as if he's turning round and round in the river. Only then can he see the shadows.

Three men, all human, are struggling with Takahashi. They keep repeating, 'Where the hell you hide it?' Tak keeps saying, 'I dunt got it.' Every time he speaks, one or the other hits him with a fist: in the face, in the body, over and over. Once he nearly breaks free. One of the men grabs him by the left arm, pulls and twists. The arm snaps, and Tak screams. In that brief moment Mulligan can see one face clearly, a dude with dark skin, narrow black eyes and close-cropped hair; he smiles as he watches Tak writhe. 'Where the hell you hide it?' They hit him again, again, again. Tak stops answering, slumps, blood running down his face, blood running from his mouth. The images are fading, swirling, breaking up like pictures seen in clouds.

'Ah jeezus,' Mulligan whispers. 'They done beat him to death.'

All at once Mulligan sees the wood floor, soft-polished to gold. For a moment he thinks he's reliving Tak's last conscious second; then he realizes that Bobbie is kneeling next to him. He can feel her hand trembling on his sweaty back.

'Jack. Oh my god, Jack!'

He rolls over and looks up at her. He tries to smile and fails. The lizzie forensic tech walks into his view. She hands Lacey a paper cup flecked with water drops.

'Make him drink this. He gonna have a hell of a headache in a minute or two.'

With Bobbie's help Mulligan sits up. He takes the cup and drinks. It's the usual medicated water with a heavy dose of sugar in it to hide the taste of the painkillers. Bates squats down next to him.

'Good work,' he says. 'I'm going to have the usual credits transferred to your account.'

Mulligan nods and has another mouthful of water.

'The dude you saw,' Bates goes on. 'Think you can pick him out of our database?'

'Maybe. The memories, they fade pretty damn fast. I mean, they no be, like, my own memories. Y'know?'

'Yeah, I know. Well, you got the important point. They were beating him to get information out of him. "Where the hell you hide it?" Huh. I wonder if I can guess what they were looking for.'

Mulligan suddenly realizes that a piece of Bates's face is missing, replaced by a jagged point of silver light. As he watches, the point spawns another, then another, and turns into a zig-zag of blindness dancing across his field of vision. He gulps down the rest of the painkiller as fast as he can. The zig-zag swells and spreads.

'Here it come,' Mulligan says. 'Ah shit, I hate this part!'

'Lie down!' Bates grabs a pillow from the floor.

Mulligan lets himself fall back. Bates slides the pillow under his head just as his sight vanishes, swallowed up by silver towers capped with red and turquoise. He can hear Bobbie talking to Bates, but he can't understand a single word.

'You've never watched Mulligan work before?' Bates get up, stretching his aching knees.

'No.' Lacey follows suit. 'I dunt think I want to do it again, either.'

'Yeah, I can understand that. He'll need to lie there for a while. We'll take you and him home in a skimmer, dunt worry.'

'Thanks. Look, I'm going to tell you what I know, but first there's something you got to do. Red Wallace, Rosa, the second baseman? Something like this could be happening to her. At the spaceport her luggage got stolen as well as Tak's.'

'Jeezus! Parsons, get over here! Where does Wallace live? Detail a couple of officers to go there, and if she's not home put out an all-points alert.'

Lacey knows the address, fortunately, and as soon as he has it Parsons starts working his portable comp to follow orders. Bates leads Lacey a little away, but he makes sure she can see Takahashi's corpse and remember how serious the situation is.

'All right,' he says. 'What kind of drugs was Tak smuggling?'

Lacey stares at him for a long, long moment, then laughs, one brief bark, quickly stifled.

'Wasn't drugs,' she says. 'Tak had *iLeijchwen* in his possession. He carried it through customs when the team came home from Sarah.'

As if he were observing someone else, Bates watches his mind run through several explanations for this preposterous statement: he must not have heard correctly, she's lying to him, she's telling a joke in very bad taste. Only at the end does he realize that no, Mike Takahashi, the same Mike Takahashi who lies dead behind him, had this very afternoon smuggled *iLeijchwen* onto Hagar.

183

'How the hell did it get on Sarah? How about you start at the beginning?' Bates pulls out his pocket comp and flicks the record button. 'Tell me everything you know.'

Lacey looks away, thinking, and begins. As he listens, Bates can feel himself grow first angry, then furious. He forces himself to stay quiet until she reaches the incident on the street in Esperance after the Bears' win. When he hears how Mbaye might have been kidnapped, he can hold on no longer.

'Why the hell didn't you contact me at the beginning?' he snarls.

'I told you,' Lacey says. 'I was protecting someone who's being blackmailed.'

'Oh for chrissakes! There are laws on the books to cover that. I coulda sealed that part of the evidence. If someone comes forward in a blackmail case, it's standard procedure to keep their secret for them. How the hell else would we ever convict blackmailers?'

'No for this, Chief. No way you could have kept it to yourself. No, it's no murder. It isn't even a crime.' Lacey manages a smile. 'But it's something you'd be bound by law to act upon.'

Bates lets out his breath in a sharp puff. He knows perfectly well what she means, he realizes. He's merely too tired to call it to mind. He grunts. 'If I find out you're concealing something serious—'

'You threaten me, man, and you gonna go this alone. I done told you all I gonna tell you. You dunt need to know who my friend is or nothing more, cop, and I aint gonna tell you one thing more. Comprende?'

Bates stares. Not a trace of anger shows on her face, her voice was perfectly level, but she has lapsed into the White Merrkan of her youth.

'I get it,' Bates says. 'Sorry. Go on.'

Lacey takes a deep breah. 'Where was I?' she says. 'Oh, yeah. We had it worked out that my aunt would give me *iLeijchwen* and I'd come to you to work out a way to get it back to the embassy with no questions asked. I'd like to think you would have listened then, when you couldn't have at the beginning.'

'Hell, I would have tried.'

'Okay. Glad to hear it. Anyway, it's too late for that. Somehow or other, in about five minutes at the arrivals terminal, someone stole the thing. Mulligan could sense its presence in Tak's carrysack before Tak went back into the customs hall. When he came out it was gone.'

'Wait a minute.' Bates focuses on a detail he'd heard earlier in her recital. 'Are you telling me that this thing puts out some kind of psychic waves or whatever they are?'

'Emanations.' Lacey shrugs briefly. 'Sure does. What do you think the carlis are going to think about that?'

'Jeezchrise! You know, this could be the one funny moment in this whole butt-ugly mess.' Bates shakes his head in stunned disbelief. 'Parsons?' He calls out. 'Any news of Wallace?'

'No, sir. She just plain aint home.'

Mulligan suddenly moves, struggling to sit up. Lacey rushes over and slides down beside him in one smooth movement. Bates follows more slowly.

'It's okay, Jack.' She strokes his hair. 'Lie still.'

'Something I gotta say.' Mulligan's voice slurs and wobbles. 'Yosef. He in danger.'

'I doubt it. Whoever killed Tak knows damn well that Yosef doesn't have *iLeijchwen* any more. And now they know Tak didn't either.' She looks up at Bates. 'Which means Rosa Wallace is the only person left on their list.'

Chapter Nine

A couple of hours before sunrise, Rosa Wallace leaves a party going strong behind her. In a cloud of loud music, her host escorts her to the door.

'Want me to walk you to your car?' Mario says.

'Nah, aint necessary. Swell party, but I got my training to consider. We gonna play again in about three days.'

With a cheery wave Rosa hurries down the steps to the quiet street lined with stone-built houses set cheek to jowl in an Old Earth style, each with a bay window, gleaming with lamplight behind lace curtains. As soon as she gets away from Mario's, Rosa becomes aware of footsteps. Someone's walking on the other side of the street, pacing her. She glances over – a person in a suncloak, at night. She stops; the person continues on a few steps, then slows. Waiting for her to catch up? Her stomach clenches.

Her jade-green skimmer sits at the kerb half a block on. Rosa fumbles in her pocket for the keys, pulls out the remote and clicks it once. As she reaches the car, the driver's door opens. She slides in, then hits the autolock. Across the street her suncloaked shadow has stopped walking. In the rear-view mirror she can see a second person jogging down the middle of the street and heading straight for her. She activates the car, twists the wheel, and hits the accelerator. They spin out of the parking place with her automatic sensors shrieking and squeal around in a half-circle. The skimmer shudders, then rises in a thunder of compressed air. The person in the road jumps back, trips and rolls into the gutter. Rosa speeds to the end of the block, turns randomly left, and slows down to the legal limit.

Maybe it was no one, maybe nothing – but the street fight in Esperance has left her with a attitude about people tailing her. She drives home by a random route, doubling back and making a lot of false turns before she finally reaches her condo in the best part of Porttown.

The building looks cheap on the outside, a huge cube of orange and brown plastocrete dotted with graffiti like most Porttown apartment blocks, but the developers gutted the inside and turned it into flats for those few people who have the money to live well and reasons for staying in the old neighbourhood. Rosa turns into an alley behind the building, then turns again and lands the skimmer in front of what looks like a blank wall. When she presses a button on the dashboard, a wide door rolls up and reveals the guarded parking garage underneath. She drives in and the door closes behind her. Phil, the young Blanco who works the night shift, leaves his kiosk and joins her at her parking place as she gets out of the car.

'Say, Miz Rosa? There be cops upstairs, waiting for you.'

'Oh shit! Guess they caught me speeding again.'

Rosa rides the tenants-only grav lift up to her floor. In her mind she considers all the traffic tickets she's been given lately, but she knows she paid them all. The lift lets her out into a small lobby with dove-grey walls trimmed in white and a soft grey carpet. When she glances down the hall, sure enough, two greenies, a human woman and a lizzie man, are leaning stoically against the wall outside her door. She arranges a bright smile and strides down.

'Morning, officers,' she says. 'What be the trouble?'

'Morning, Miz Wallace.' The woman taps her badge. 'My name's Carter and this is Officer Chiztolek.' She reaches into her pocket and pulls out a piece of actual paper. 'We got here an order for your protection.' She holds the paper out.

Rosa takes it, glances at it: a print-out from the Chief of Police's AI ordering police protection for one Rosa Wallace on the grounds that she stands in attested danger to her life and physical well-being. A judge has scrawled his name across the bottom.

'What the hell?' Rosa whispers.

'We got some real bad news, too,' Chiztolek says. 'Uh, think maybe we can come in?'

'Sure.' Clutching the paper in her other hand, Rosa lays her right thumb on the ID plate on the wall. With a hiss the door slides open. Her ravaged luggage lies in a heap on the living room carpet, where she threw it when she got back from the spaceport. The two officers tramp in behind her and stand looking around.

'Real nice place,' Chiztolek says.

'Thanks.'

Rosa's taste runs to white walls and open spaces, Persian-style carpets on the floor, and leather furniture. When she offers the policebeings chairs, they perch on the least comfortable. Rosa sinks into the green leather armchair and reads the protection order over once again.

She looks up. 'What be this here bad news?'

Officer Carter runs a hand over her short black hair and sighs. 'I'm afraid a friend of yours got killed tonight.'

Rosa feels the shock as exhaustion. For a moment she can barely hold her head up. The two officers watch sadly, sympathetically. She supposes they have a lot of experience at breaking the bad news of sudden deaths, sometimes no doubt to spouses and parents.

'Who?' She can barely say the word; her heart seems to have migrated, floundering around in her chest.

'Michael Takahashi.'

Rosa lets out one sob. She feels as if a giant hand has shoved her hard, pinning her to the soft back of her chair. 'Tak? No.'

'I'm afraid so, ma'am.' Chiztolek leans forward. 'It be always hard to believe.'

'But what – I mean, how? Traffic accident? What?'

'No, ma'am.' Carter sighs heavily. 'I'm afraid he was murdered.'

The word makes no sense. She can only think that Tak is dead. The word loops in her mind: dead, dead, dead. Rosa tips her head back against the chair for support and squeezes her eyes shut as hard as she can. The tears win anyway, running silently down her face.

'I'm real sorry,' Carter says.

Rosa nods, wishing she could scream. Chiztolek's belt comp suddenly beeps and startles her. With another sob Rosa wrenches herself upright. Her heart pounds as hard as if she'd been running wind sprints. When she looks around her familiar room, it seems to tremble in a harsh light.

'Sorry.' Chiztolek stands up and pulls the comp free of his belt. For a moment he stares at the tiny screen. 'Chief Bates himself, he be downstairs, ma'am. He sure do wanna talk to you.'

'Fine,' Rosa whispers. Try as she might, she cannot seem to talk in a normal voice. She closes her eyes again and pushes her head back into the comforting leather. She hears voices: the two officers first, then a rumble of words as someone walks into the room. She forces her eyes open. Bates looks much like he does on holocasts: a solid dark bear of a man, his eyes perpetually tired, his green suit rumpled.

'Miz Wallace? I'm sorry to meet you this way.'

Rosa nods, searching for her ability to talk.

'I can see you're taking Takahashi's death hard.'

'Yeah.' She finds it at last. 'Whole damn team gonna do that.' She wonders why her mouth feels so dry. 'Scuze. I gotta get myself some water.'

'Carter can do that for you.' Bates glances at the two officers and waves his hand. 'Look, I know this is a lousy time, but if you could answer some questions it might put us that much closer to an arrest.'

Carter comes back with a coffee mug full of water. Rosa drinks half of it before answering.

'If it gonna help, ask your damn questions.'

They cover nothing that surprises her. Yes, her luggage was stolen, too. Yes, that heap on the floor is what she got back of it. Yes, she was in the customs hall when Tak was. Yes, she noticed two temporary security guards making him open his carrysack. No, she doesn't remember much about them. On and on they go, precise questions requiring minute answers. Finally Bates falls silent. Rosa drinks the other half of her water and sets the mug on the floor. Bates clicks off his comp unit and turns to the two officers.

'Carter, go through the flat, will you? You're looking for signs of attempted entry. Anything suspicious, tag it so we can get a tech in to dust it and scan it. Chiztolek, there's a manager in this building. Flat One A. Go ask her if she saw or heard anything that might mean strangers cruising the place.'

Once the officers have left the room, Bates turns back to Rosa.

'I know why Tak was murdered.' He speaks softly. 'Bobbie Lacey came clean with me; I know you guys were helping a friend with a little blackmail problem, and I know you had *iLeijchwen*. Lacey seemed to think you could be in danger if somebody got the notion you have it now, and I think she's right.'

'I dunt.'

'Yeah, I know that. Do they?'

'They who?'

'The men who murdered Takahashi.'

'Oh. Oh yeah.' Rosa rubs her face with both hands. 'Tak dead. It aint real yet.'

'I can understand that. But the thing is, even with police protection, I dunt want you here alone. You know someone who could come stay with you?'

Rosa thinks of Aunt Lucy, dismisses the thought as too dangerous.

'Or that you could stay with?' Bates goes on.

'Sure. If I call anyone on the team, they gonna take me in. I . . . oh, jeezchrise! Yosef Mbaye. Hey, could you put someone to protecting him too? He and Tak and me, we got to be real good friends during the Series. Someone, they maybe think he got the thing. And Tak . . . I dunt want Yosef hearing bout Tak on the news. It be noon yet?'

'No, not for a couple of hours. Why?'

'When the day it change, it be Friday. The Mbayes no be going anywhere on a Friday, cept down to the mosque and that be later.'

'Good.' Bates pauses, thinking. 'Tell you what. The best way to do this is to take you over there. Get some clothes together, okay? If he dunt want you staying, we're going to install you in a hotel to throw the bastards off the track.'

'Sure. I gonna drive my own car over, though.'

Bates considers. 'Okay, if you'll let one of my officers ride with you. I'm also going to leave an officer here – with your permission – round the clock. If someone tries to force entry, he's going to be real surprised.'

Before she allowed the police to take her and Mulligan home, Lacey called A to Z and had Buddy bring Aunt Lucy to the comm unit. Lucy took the news of Tak's death with a kind of weary resignation, or at least she managed to act as if she did.

190

'Dint know the boy well,' Lucy said. 'But hell, that be too bad. He was the lively kind.'

'Yeah. We'll talk more later.'

Sergeant Parsons ends up driving them back to A to Z, where he drops them off at the corner. Jack manages to stay on his feet and get upstairs, but the first thing he does once he's home is to stagger into the bathroom and vomit – from the painkillers, he tells her between bouts. Lacey hovers in the hall behind the half-open door.

'You need any help?' she says.

'No. Dunt worry about it.'

'You sure?'

He makes an indeterminate sound. Lacey leaves him to clean up and goes to the living room, where Aunt Lucy is sitting on the couch knitting while she watches the late-morning edition of the holonews. Bobbie pauses and listens to the Chief of Police in Esperance answer pointed questions from reporters. There have been no arrests in the mugging of the three Bears players. The detective in charge is pursuing a new theory, that Humanitas Party members objected to a lizzie eating with human beings.

'That's bullshit,' Bobbie remarks.

'Yeah,' Lucy says. 'Jack, he be okay?'

'I guess so. He dunt seem worried about it. Know something? I finally understand why he never took that full-time police psychic job.'

'No can blame him for that.' Lucy pauses to count stitches. 'Y'know, it always been this way, in our family. It always been the women working, holding things together, and the men, well, hell. They come and go, work for a while, get in trouble, whatever. At least Jack, he treats you good.'

Bobbie opens her mouth to snarl, realizes that she has no grounds and closes it again. Lucy frowns down at her knitting and says nothing.

'Uh, about Tak,' Bobbie says.

Lucy nods, finishes a row, rolls the strip around her needles, sets it carefully into her bag and looks up with her face running tears.

'Yeah,' Bobbie says. 'I dint think you were as easy about it as you looked on the comm.'

'Weren't gonna say nada with cops crawling all over the place.' Lucy fishes in her shorts and pulls a wad of tissue out of her pocket. 'I been crying off and on since I heard.'

'Yeah.' Bobbie sits down at the comp desk, where lights blink, announcing messages. 'Too damn bad. I ended up telling the cops everything, well, everything 'cept Yosef's little secret.'

'You what?' Lucy's tears stop fast. 'What you thinking of, girl? You loca?'

'Thinking that Tak, he dead, and maybe Red Wallace, she end up the same way if I dunt level with the greenies.' Bobbie swivels around in the chair. 'You be right – you're right about our family, aren't you? So damn used to living on the edge of the law we forget what the law's there for.'

Lucy sighs and looks away for a long moment. 'Maybe so,' she says at last. 'Jeezus. I done forgot about Rosa. We better call.'

'A couple of these messages, they're from her. Buddy, play the most recent one on the three-dee so Aunt Lucy can hear, too.'

The holonews disappears and Rosa's face comes onscreen. From her puffy eyes and thick voice Bobbie can guess that she's heard about Takahashi.

'Hey, Lacey, me again. I be calling from Yosef Mbaye's house this time. Police took me here, and Bates, he done set up a police watch outside, so we gonna be okay. But Yosef, well, he aint taking the news so good. He kinda all to pieces, blaming himself.' Rosa glances over her shoulder at a female figure at the edge of video range. 'Marisa, that be his lady, she trying to talk him down. She no getting real far. So, I be thinking, if Jack, he maybe could come over or something? Someone who gets it, what Yosef he going through. Give me a call back, okay? Thanks.'

The screen goes dead.

'Leave the news off, Buddy,' Bobbie says. 'Aunt Lucy, why don't you call Rosa? I'm going to see how Jack is doing. Or wait – tell me something. Are you blaming yourself for Tak's death?'

'Hell, no. He the one who grabbed the thing from me. What he say? Never saw a wild ride he dint like, something like that.' Aunt Lucy shakes her head. 'I sure sorry he dead, though.'

Bobbie find Jack in the bedroom, half dressed and sprawled across

192

the bed face down. His dirty shirt lies on the floor with his shoes and socks. The overhead light fills the room with glare. When she comes in, he lifts his head and peers as if he cannot quite see her. Despite the bright light his pupils are enormous. Lacey flips off the light, and he relaxes.

'Knew I forgot something,' he mumbles.

'What is that stuff they gave you?'

'Dunt know. Feels good. They dunt tell you the name cause they dunt want you cruising for it on the street.' He rolls over and smiles at her, a dreamy sort of grin. 'I kinda gotta go to sleep. Y'know?'

'Sure do. Sweet dreams.'

'No problem.' In a few seconds, he drifts off.

Too bad, Lacey thinks. *Yosef will just have to wait.* She goes back into the living room to find Aunt Lucy yawning and collecting her knitting.

'Get hold of Rosa?' Bobbie says.

'No, just the answer function on the comm. House comp say they all gone to bed. And speaking of which, Nunks and me, we pulled some of Mel's old junk around while you was gone. I got a pretty decent room and I gonna go there right now, honey. I be getting old, rejuv or not.'

'Okay. I'm not going to stay up much longer myself.'

Once Lucy's gone, Bobbie sits down at the comp desk. With a chime, Buddy switches over to audio mode.

'Do you wish to hear the rest of your messages, Programmer?'

'Are any of them top priority?'

'No. Summary mode: I arranged a meeting with Rafael Chang, the art dealer, for tonight. Dr Carol called to chat. Your brother called to inquire after your aunt's safety. I reassured him. I assume she is his aunt as well as yours?'

'You're correct. Huh. Now that's something I dint think Richie would do. I'm glad to hear it.' Lacey leans back in her chair and stifles a yawn. 'Buddy, you been monitoring the PBI files as well as the city cops?'

'Affirmative, Programmer. Do you wish to access a particular file?'

'Nah, just general data. Anything on the war threat?'

The AI hums for a moment. 'That depends on whether one characterizes the current diplomatic exchange as "war threat". Consequences of a failure to return the missing artefact have been described only in the most vague of fashions. Each official communiqué has been veiled in formality.'

'How about *un*official talk? That sound more serious?'

'There appear to have been few such exchanges, Programmer. However, I have performed my own calculations. I have based them on my study of history as well as the escalation of rhetoric common in political situations.'

'Okay. Tell me the results.'

'Data are still incomplete, but with that caveat understood, the situation is indeed serious. I estimate the probability of war at thirty-seven per cent.'

'Just over one in three. Could be worse.'

'It will be worse. Unfortunately, the probability rises sharply over time. Assuming current conditions remain unchanged, namely that *iLeijchwen* remains missing and the Confederation remains convinced the Republic is responsible for this, then within a week the odds will be even. The wordplay is unintentional. I have not computed odds beyond that point, as the situation is too inherently unstable to remain static beyond that point.'

'You mean there's going to be a war?'

'In a week's time, yes, if not earlier.'

Lacey swivels around and looks out over the living room.

'I realize that this is alarming news, Programmer,' Buddy says.

'Yeah. But you know what? I'm too damn tired to be alarmed. Wake me up if the war starts. I'm going to bed.'

At sunset Sarojini wakes. She sits up, activating a small lamp that casts long shadows on the whitewashed walls, takes the remote from the pierced-brass nightstand, and flips on the three-dee hanging on the far wall. A solemn holocaster stares out at her and remarks, in a voice far too calm, 'Our top story on Channel Eighty-Nine FirstNews: the murder of the Bears' ace reliever, Michael Takahashi.'

Sarojini can neither move nor think, merely watches as the story rolls on. Although the police have fed the holonews some peculiar story for a motive, she can guess the truth. It's a good thing, she thinks, that she has *iLeijchwen* safe with her. Who knows what those vicious thugs might have done with it? At a knock on her door, she mutes the sound. One of her young nephews comes in carrying a brass tray with a pot of tea, a cup and some bread and soyacheese on a plate.

'Thank you, darling,' Sarojini says. She can never remember the names of her many small relatives. 'Is your grandma taking care of you today?'

'Yes, Auntie. Mama's got exams at the university.'

'That's nice. Run and play now.'

The boy smiles and leaves. Sarojini's widowed mother lives with her in this flat – one of the many reasons that Sarojini has made caution a way of life. Mother never intrudes on her privacy, since her daughter's income provides such nice luxuries, but if Sarojini made some gross error, such as being arrested, Mother would be bound to notice. Since they don't want Mother living with them, Sarojini's three respectable brothers take Sarojini's 'investment counselling business' on faith and profess a complete lack of surprise at her irregular business hours.

Sarojini pours herself a cup of spicy, milky chai and leans back against the pillows. On the three-dee the holonews runs pictures of Takahashi throwing a ball at someone in a funny mask, or so Sarojini thinks of it. *He was so handsome, so alive! Horrible, all of it, horrible!*

She needs to decide on her next move. What if the cops link her to Takahashi and *iLeijchwen*? She had of course fake ID papers when she took the security job, one of her small sad legacies from Moses. She feels a few tears form – Moses dead, and now this poor fellow – and she blames both deaths on the carlis. Under their polished surfaces lurk the evil hearts of born meat-eaters, after all. They'll pay. She is going to insure that they will pay with interest. On the three-dee the news has moved on. She restores the sound, sips her chai, then stares for the second time that morning.

'Sources that we cannot at this time identify have discovered a possible suspect in the theft of the carli artefact known as *iLeijchwen*. The allegation states that the intended purchaser of the item was Senator George Martinelli.'

195

'Damn!' Sarojini snaps. 'How did they learn that? Now I'll have to find a new buyer.'

After he left Rosa Wallace's flat, Bates returned to his office in the hopes of finishing up paperwork only to find hysterical comm messages from the mayor of Polar City and the police commissioner. He got home, therefore, well after two p.m., took a shower and fell into bed. Now, a bare five hours later, his comm is beeping, the urgent triple beep that means his house comp has overridden the message-storage function. He sits up and grabs the link unit from his nightstand.

'Bates here. What is it?'

'My apologies, Chief,' the unit says. 'But Hazorth Ka Pral il Frakmo is online. Since he is listed as one of your priority callers, I accepted his request to override.'

'Jeezchrise!' Suddenly Bates is wide awake. 'Tell him I'll be right there.'

Bates pulls on his trousers, grabs a T-shirt from the floor and hurries into the living room of his cluttered apartment. His house comp has transferred the call to the three-dee screen on the wall. A life-size Ka Pral, sitting at his desk, looks out at him.

'Bates, I grovel before you,' Ka Pral says. 'Had I not felt it urgent to speak with you, never would I have bothered you at your home.'

'I wipe you clean of any stain of embarrassment,' Bates says. 'My humble apologies for my appearance.'

'No need.' Ka Pral bobs his head. 'Actually, I chose to sit down to hide my own lack of decorum. This news has rather outweighed the demands of protocol.'

'A murder is always alarming, yes.' Bates pulls the shirt over his head. 'I'm assuming you mean the sudden death of Mike Takahashi, anyway.'

'What? No, though it certainly is a sad event.' Ka Pral hesitates, then leans back in his chair. 'I mean the story concerning the theft of *iLeijchwen*. Bates, there's been an alarming development. An hour ago one of your holocasters publicly announced that the intended purchaser of *iLeijchwen* was Senator George Martinelli.'

'Good god!'

'As much as it pains me to risk discourtesy,' Ka Pral goes on, 'I must admit to being surprised that you would allow this news onto the public channels before we were informed.'

'I dint. The news couldn't have come from me or my officers. I knew nothing about it until you told me.'

Ka Pral jerks his hands out from his sides; his mouth hangs open for the briefest of moments.

'Is it true, do you think?' Bates says. 'About Martinelli, I mean.'

'Yes, I do. Our own sources had arrived at this same conclusion late this morning.'

'They did, huh?'

'At thirteen-twenty I placed a message at your office asking you to contact me as soon as possible. I assure you, I would have told you when you called.'

'I thank you for the reassurance.'

'But I assumed . . . forgive me, Bates. I see that I've been intolerably rude, waking you to air false suspicions. My shame bites deep.'

'I'm glad you did wake me. The sooner I heard this, the better. I'm going straight to the office, and I'll contact you again as soon as I know anything new. Martinelli of all people!' Bates pauses, struck by a sudden thought. 'Something else bothers me. If I didn't leak this story, and you didn't leak it, who did?'

Lacey wakes suddenly because she no longer has a pillow. She rolls over and sees what she suspected, that Jack has managed to get both and now he's lying on top of them. For a moment she wonders if she could stand to share a bed with him in a cold climate that requires blankets. Probably not. She sits up, grabs the edge of one pillow and yanks it free. Normally Jack sleeps through this procedure, but tonight he wakes.

'Sorry,' he mutters. 'Dunt know why I do that.'

He gets up and heads for the bathroom. Lacey lies back down and settles the pillow under her head. *Sleep*, she thinks, *just an hour more.* Jack returns, trips over the shoes he left on the floor, swears, then flops back down on his side of the bed.

'You awake?' he says.

'Yeah. How could I not be?'

'Sorry.' He raises himself up on one elbow and smiles. 'I dunt know why you put up with me. Y'know?'

'Sometimes I wonder myself.' She returns the smile. 'It must be because I love you or something.'

He leans over and kisses her. In answer, she turns and slides into his arms.

By the time Lacey gets around to switching on the three-dee, every channel is running the story about the would-be purchaser of *i-Leijchwen*. The holocasters from several Sarahian stations have even cornered Martinelli himself. On the advice of his legal counsel, the senator is saying nothing – loudly, every chance he gets. The Chief of Police in Esperance, prodded by Polar City's own Al Bates, has started an investigation.

'I guess we're getting somewhere,' Lacey says. 'I guess that's a good thing.'

'I share your ambivalence, Programmer,' Buddy says. 'One of the basic principles of diplomacy has always been that a thing left unspoken doesn't exist. There are too many things being spoken by too many sentients these days for diplomacy to remain capable of solving this problem.'

'And after diplomacy comes the fighting.'

'Exactly, Programmer. As gloomy as the prospect makes me, I must say that I admire your logical mind.'

Lacey decides to take the Metro to Rafael Chang's place of business over on the far side of Civic Centre. Although the evening rush has finished, enough people crowd the train to ensure good eavesdropping. Everyone talks about the murder of Mike Takahashi. Friends share their grief and outrage. Strangers agree with strangers, 'something gotta be done to keep this crap from happening'. Exactly what this something may be, no one can say. As the passengers rehearse every crime against the Bears on Sarah as well as this latest tragedy, voices get louder, faces get redder, fists get slammed into the palms of hands. A ugly mood, Lacey thinks, a mood that could turn even uglier if anything else goes wrong for the home team.

Lacey leaves the train at Santangelo Avenue, the closest thing to a luxury shopping district that Polar City can offer. On a street lined with umbrella palms from Sarah that shade little stores made of real wood, Rafael Chang keeps his 'shop', where the pale grey blinds are always drawn and a sign hangs perpetually on the door, 'By appointment only'. When Lacey arrives, she sees a crack of light around the blinds. She knocks, and a security comm clears its mechanical throat.

'May I ask you you are?' The voice is soft, vaguely female.

'Sure. I'm Bobbie Lacey. I have an appointment with Mr Chang at twenty-two-hundred.'

'Yes, I see your name on our list. It is an honour to open the door for you.'

Instead of the usual buzz, a bell chimes and the door slides back. Lacey steps into a room lit by glow strips up near the ceiling. Nothing hangs on the walls. On an island of grey carpet, two leather chairs sit on either side of a long, low black table. Directly opposite the front door, on the back wall, another opens and Rafael Chang comes in, wearing a beautifully tailored pair of white slacks, a white shirt with the sleeves rolled up to the elbows and a dove-grey waistcoat.

'Buenos noches, Lacey,' he says with a pleasant smile. 'You're looking well.'

'Gracias, and so are you, sir.'

'I feel like one of my own antiques.' Chang gestures at a chair. 'Shall we sit down?'

Lacey takes the offered chair, and Chang sits opposite.

'I noticed you looking over the room,' he says. 'Most people are surprised at how bare it is. I deal in one-of-a-kind things, you know. When I obtain something that one of my customers might like, I call them. If they're interested, they come down and I have the object brought in.'

'And there's nada to distract them?' Lacey says.

'Exactly.' Chang tents his fingers and looks over them. 'I had a call from the Chief of Police a little while ago. He wanted to know if I'd be willing to see you if he made the appointment.'

'I'm assuming you told him that I already had one.'

'Yes. He was quite surprised.' Chang smiles. 'Completely taken aback is probably the better term. He asked me to co-operate with you as fully as I could.'

'Now that I dint expect.'

'Me neither.'

They share a soft laugh. Chang reaches into his waistcoat pocket and brings out a data cube in a black plasto case. He sets it on the table and slides it over to her side.

'I've kept files for years on dealings in non-human art,' Chang says. 'Your legendary AI may be able to find something of interest in these. I had mine copy everything that might be relevant.'

'Gracias.' Lacey slips the cube into her shirt pocket.

'Well, I have no desire to see Polar City go up in flames and my collection with it. If there's anything I can tell you, just ask.'

'Thanks. About Senator Martinelli – does he have a reputation as a genuine collector?'

'Of course not. I met him once. He's totally ignorant when it comes to art by any species, his own included.' Chang pauses for effect. 'He buys Hopper art.'

'What? What for? I mean, jeez, I dunt know anything about art, but that stuff is junk.'

'He says it's cheerful. If one's taste runs to lime green, industrial orange and mauve, I suppose one might call it that. And encrustations, of course. We mustn't forget the shiny encrustations.'

'Well, from what I've read, *iLeijchwen* is pretty tame by comparison. Dunt see why he'd buy it.'

'Because it's famous. There are two kinds of buyers for rare art objects, Lacey: people who love them for what they are and people who love them for what other people think of them. I only deal with the former.'

'And so I dunt suppose any of your clients would buy *iLeijchwen* now.'

'None of my clients are stupid enough. They're not the sort of people who'd let Hagar be blown to shreds just to add to their collection.' Chang shrugs. 'Not even those who live on Sarah.'

'I'm assuming you know what there is to be known about the world of legitimate collectors.'

Chang inclines a modest head.

'So that leaves the illegitimate ones,' Lacey goes on. 'I dunt suppose there's anything in your files about those.'

'Oh, there might be.' Chang smiles in an oddly boyish way. 'Which reminds me. I've had more than a few suspicious comm calls – from sentients claiming to be agents who were curious, merely curious, to know what a fair price for something like *iLeijchwen* would be. Some might have been telling the truth, but I gave their names and numbers to Al Bates anyway. One of his officers is doubtless contacting them right now.'

'Yeah, I bet.' Lacey hesitates, thinking. While she has plenty of questions, she may well already have the answers on the data cube in her pocket. 'Here's something that might interest you. Did you realize that *iLeijchwen* has a psi component?'

Chang lets his hands fall into his lap.

'Guess you dint,' Lacey says. 'It took me by surprise, too, but a registered psychic told me. He had some contact with it a while back.'

'I've never read anything like that in the works of carli art historians, but then their culture would hardly encourage that line of speculation.'

'Yeah, that's for sure.'

'Although, you know, wait! It just might explain a rather odd theory of theirs. Have you heard of "eyelight"?'

'No, I can't say I have.'

'A number of the scholarly essays about it have been translated into Merrkan, but they're mostly hedge and fill. I always felt that their authors were trying to understand why *leijchwen* affect them the way they do rather than explaining it to anyone else. The basic fact, though, is simple: carlis do not have the same experience of seeing when they look at a reproduction of a *leijchwen* as when they are looking at one in the flesh, as it were. It doesn't matter how excellent the VR or the hologram.'

'Well, some of the Old Earth art I've seen has been like that, too.'

'Of course, but not to the same degree. With us, part of the experience is the knowledge that the piece of art we're facing is the real deal, as you young people might term it, and that it comes from our lost homeland. It's an intellectual realization that colours our emotional experience. With the carlis, the impact is direct and visceral. And all the carli scholars agree that with *leijchwen* the experience is enormously pronounced.'

'That's very interesting.'

'Yes, indeed. So their explanation is that somehow, in some semi-mystical way, a true *leijchwen* contains the light of its subject's eyes.'

'I take it that when they talk about the light of someone's eyes, it means a lot more to them than it does to us.'

'Definitely. The eyelight, the sum of an individual, his personality, his mind – the essayists often say that the human concept of *soul*, shorn of its irrational superstition, comes closest to expressing it. And that of Ka Prelandi is preserved in *iLeijchwen*. Thus the gaze of his eyes still exists. That gaze brought the disparate carli great families together and showed them they were a single people. It is *ini carli*, the root identity of their species.'

'Huh. And somehow or other the artist managed to invest the object with psi . . . I dunt know how that could happen.'

'Neither do I, but it doesn't mean it couldn't. I make no pretence of understanding psi and psionic objects, none whatsoever. Jack – er, that is, the registered psychic you mentioned might have some explanation.'

Lacey allows herself a laugh. 'Nothing gets by you, does it? But you've never heard Jack try to explain something. The eyelight theory is crystal clear compared to that.'

On her way home Lacey stares out the train window at the miles of faceless tunnel speeding by. She is beginning to understand just why the carli government would be willing to go to war over *iLeijchwen*. Until Ka Prelandi, civil wars ran like scarlet threads through carli history. Without the light of his eyes gazing upon his successors they might well do so again – or so their people seem to believe. Whether or not *iLeijchwen* truly binds the great families together by some mysterious art is irrelevant, Lacey realizes. Believing it does has invested this object with the power that the belief postulates.

Reason and diplomacy will never solve this crisis. The Republic is fighting the psychology of an entire species.

'It's these damn leaks,' Bates says. 'I'm sick and tired of hearing this shit on the three-dee news about "sources within the police" or "unidentified sources" and all the rest of that crap. I want to know whose mouth has the squitters. Comprende?'

The three sergeants nod. Parsons, Nagura, Maddock: they stand in a straight line in a posture near that of military attention. Bates would like to pace back and forth, but since his overcrowded office has no room for it he merely rocks on the balls of his feet.

'Someone's got more spending money than he or she should have,' Bates goes on. 'Or maybe they got a relative who works for the holocasts. Or maybe they just got a big mouth and everyone knows it. Start asking around. If that dunt turn someone up, go read the last batch of performance reviews. Any questions?'

No one says a thing.

'Fine. Then get out and get to work.'

The three sergeants exit in stiff silence. Bates flops down into his chair and swivels around to glare at the comp screen.

'I dunt suppose you know who's been shooting their mouth off?' Bates says.

'No, sir,' the AI says. 'I have no data available on this topic. I do, however, have an incoming call which, acting according to your earlier orders, I placed on hold.'

'Okay. Who from?'

'Bobbie Lacey.'

'Fine, put her through.'

The screen stays dark, but he can hear Lacey's voice, oddly tinny and distant.

'Where are you?' Bates says.

'On the Metro,' Lacey says. 'Look, I just got a call from a friend of mine who's up in Space Dock.'

'Yeah?'

'A Confederation heavy cruiser just dropped into orbit.'

'Oh my god.'

'Yeah. Alison heard some of the buzz around. The Cons claim they're here only to deliver a couple of security people from aggKar. No one believes them.'

'Yeah? I dunt either. I mean, I know they been expecting some security types, but I dunt think that's all. Say, you wouldn't have any brilliant discoveries to report, would you?'

'Sure dunt. And I'd tell you if I did. I just keep thinking about that dude we learned about in school. Franklin, I think his name was.

"Gentlemen, we had better hang together or we're all going to hang separately." Something like that. You have any new data?'

Bates hesitates for a long moment.

'You still there, Chief?' Lacey says.

'Yeah. Tell you what. I've got a bunch of stuff in my belt comp that I never did get around to downloading into the AI unit. I better do that, and then we can see if there's anything you can use.'

'Hey, gracias! I better hang up. I'm almost to my stop.'

'Sure. Talk to you later.'

Bates flips off the comm function. He realizes with a stunned sense of disbelief that, somehow or other, he has just given Buddy licence to hack.

'I gotta admit,' Rosa says, 'I be a little scared.'

'Dunt be,' Mulligan says. 'Nothing to it, really. You gonna be awake for the whole thing.'

'Oh. Okay. They no put you in a trance or something?'

'No.' He grins at her. 'No like in the holofilms.'

In a pale yellow room down at the Police Tower, they are waiting for their appointment with a police psychic. Across from them on a backless chair sits Officer Zizzistre, clicking through messages on a clipboard. He and another officer picked both of them up, and later they will drive them both back home. *Police protection*, Rosa thinks. Police around the Mbayes' condo, police at the team meeting this evening, police everywhere she looks or turns – for a Porttown girl the experience has been the opposite of comforting.

When the inner door opens, she nearly shrieks. Not that the middle-aged woman who appears looks in the least frightening – kind of dumpy, rather, with her white blouse hanging out over a too-tight uniform skirt and her hair pulled back in a messy reddish chignon.

'Who wants to be first?' she says.

'We all go in together, Linda,' Izzy says.

'Okay. You gonna be the witnessing officer?'

'Sure am. Come on, boys and girls.' Izzy hisses gently. 'Let's go get our memories read.'

Mulligan turns out to be right. While Rosa would never say she enjoys the experience of being hypnotized, she finds it nothing to fear either. In the dimly lit room Linda sits her down in a comfortable chair and tells her to relax. Thanks to her grief Rosa hardly slept the day past. With the dim light, the soft leather chair and the droning voice she finds relaxing suddenly easy. The hypnotist begins swinging a crystal on a gold chain in front of her.

'Just relax, honey, that's right, watch the pretty.'

The pendant glitters back and forth, back and forth.

'Just relax and remember things,' Linda murmurs. 'You got off the shuttle. It be sunny at the port. Lot of people. There's the robotrain.'

'Okay.' Rosa feels as if she's drifting off to the edge of sleep, but she can still talk. 'We got off the robotrain outside.'

'Now let's go inside the terminal,' Linda says. 'See the luggage area. Can you see the luggage area?'

'Yeah,' Rosa says.

She is seeing memories, Rosa realizes, merely memories that have become abnormally clear, not hallucinations or any such thing. In memory, Linda takes her into the customs hall, gets her to see the face of the clerk who told her that her luggage had been lost. From there the scene unfolds until she can see Tak bursting back in from the lounge in a state of fury, the carrysack swinging from his hand. Security guards cluster around him, as if perhaps they fear he'll turn violent.

'Look at the guards,' Linda says. 'Describe the guards.'

'There be so many of them,' Rosa says.

And yet a few do stand out: a short Blanco who looks scared half to death; a woman with a silver butterfly in her hair; the lizzie woman, permanent staff in her case, who gets Tak to behave by out-shouting him; the human man who slyly asks Tak for an autograph and calms him down further. She can see in her memories the carrysack sitting open on a table, see the guards clustering around it, but never does she see anything that might be a hand reaching into it. She watches Tak zip the case back up and take it away. With a snap of her fingers, Linda brings her back to the present.

'How you feel, honey?' Linda says.

'Okay.' Rosa covers her mouth and yawns. 'Weird. I feel like I been asleep. Feels kind of nice.'

'Good.' Linda smiles at her, then turns to her fellow officer. 'Get that, Izzy?'

'Sure did.' Izzy pats the recorder in his lap. 'Jeez, it hadda be stolen right then.'

'Damn right,' Mulligan puts in. 'Tak, he had it when he come out the first time. When he come back out, he dint.'

Rosa can only shrug, baffled.

'Oh well,' Izzy says. 'I gonna do some checking around, find out about them guards you saw, Miz Wallace. The process of elimination.' He hisses, nodding. 'That be what solves a case like this. Checking out everybody and every little thing.'

Lacey is reading over Rafael Chang's files when Jack finally comes home, running up the stairs and charging into the living room. She glances at the polarized windows. The sun, apparently, has already risen.

'Sorry I be so late,' Jack says. 'Rosa, she asked me to come in and take a look at Yosef.'

'How is he?'

'Bad. A mess. Jeez, Bobbie, I dunt get it. He keeps saying it be his fault Tak got killed.'

'Well, in a way it is, kind of. If he'd only gone to the police—'

'Oh shit.' Jack winces. 'Dunt never say that to him, will you? Aint never gonna get him through this if you do.'

'Okay. For your sake. Not his.'

'Okay. Whatcha doing?'

'Reading some data I got tonight. Are you going to bed?'

'Gonna take a shower first. What about you?'

'In a while. I want to finish this stuff. How did the reading go?'

'Not so good. Rosa, she never see no one take the flannel. Izzy, he be the cop in charge, say he gonna file a report.'

'Okay. Buddy, you can hack in and get that later.'

Rafael Chang's files prove a valuable source of information. While Chang never learned enough about black market dealers in hot art for the police to prosecute, he has made over the years a record of what he did find. In the small circle of legitimate dealers, news and suspicions travel fast. Fully half of the unsolved thefts involve carli art, with *leijchwen* of varying types high on the list. Fully half involve the same few suspected buyers as well, Martinelli among them. The dealers are harder to trace.

'Programmer,' Buddy says, 'no doubt you have noticed this yourself, but I see that the name Oscuridad appears four times in this record. The police have never been able to prove any connection, but do you find the repetition suspicious?'

'I sure do. Huh, is that the name of a business or of a person?'

'You know, Programmer, now that you mention it, I am unsure. The law enforcement agencies also appear to be in doubt.'

'Whatever it is, it dunt seem to have any fixed address. Think you can find out where it lives?'

'I shall try.'

'If not, I'll get in touch with Blade.' Lacey yawns, shakes her head, yawns again.

'Programmer, your actions correspond to the paradigm of "exhausted human". I suggest you go to bed. The funeral of Michael Takahashi begins at twenty-hundred, nine hours from now, but you will need to have breakfast, dress, and allow for travel time.'

'Yeah, you're right. God, I hate funerals.'

'It has always been my understanding that all sentients do.'

'You're right about that. And this one's going to be a real bitch.'

Chapter Ten

With the funeral very much on his mind, Mulligan wakes at sunset, silent tears hot on his cheeks. He has been dreaming about Takahashi, and for a few minutes the dream continues to cloud his mind. He externalizes it, imaging scenes from the dream as paper holograms glued to his face and arms. In his mind he visualizes himself pulling them off and dropping them to the floor, where they vanish. Beside him Bobbie still sleeps on her side, barely moving, quiet except for the occasional sigh.

He gets up as quietly as he can, scoops his clothes off the floor, and goes to dress in the bathroom to avoid waking her. When he's done he walks into the living room. Buddy's sensors turn and light; a few bells chime.

'Oh, it's you,' Buddy says.

'Yeah. Just going into the kitchen to make some coffee. You got a problem with that?'

'None. Is the programmer still asleep?'

'Yeah.'

'Good. Mulligan unit, I have something to suggest to you.'

'Yeah?'

'You are aware, of course, that the programmer has written to Admiral Wazerzis to ask for reinstatement in the Navy.'

For a moment Mulligan feels too sick to speak.

'Your appearance corresponds to my paradigm for "disturbed human",' Buddy says. 'I take it that you did not know this.'

'Sure dint.' Mulligan's mouth has gone very dry. 'Why?'

'Because she wants to return to the Navy, of course. Why else would she write such a letter?'

'Not what I meant.'

'No doubt. Your powers of self-expression have always been poor.

However, that is neither here nor there. I take it that you wish her to remain here with us?'

Mulligan nods.

'Very well then,' Buddy says. 'I will not be able to persuade her to stay. I am merely a machine. I know I cannot offer her the carnal satisfactions she apparently receives from you.'

'The what?'

'Therefore,' Buddy goes on as if he's not heard the question, 'I am speculating that you will be much more persuasive than I can ever be.'

'I get it. You want me to talk her out of it.'

'Precisely. Do you wish her to leave us?'

'Hell, no!'

'So I thought. I only wish you had my powers of speech and logic. On second formulation, I am glad that you do not have my powers of speech and logic, because then I would become redundant. I should wish that you possessed more of these powers than you do but considerably less than I.'

'What in hell? Get to the point, plugsucker!'

'The point is that you will have to use your body parts instead of words in order to give her reasons to stay. She seems to prize them.'

All at once Mulligan understands Buddy's insinuations. Even though he's talking with a machine, he blushes.

'Hey!'

'Wait!' Buddy's sensors swivel. 'I hear the programmer moving in the hall. We cannot continue this discussion at this time.'

Rather than face Lacey immediately, Mulligan darts into the kitchen and starts putting the coffee together. He remembers the tarot images that troubled him, the Hanged Man, emblem of loss. Once again he focuses his mind as Nunks has taught him, externalizing: he sees the card, in vivid detail, plastered on the white wall in front of him. Mentally he paints it out, like graffitti. *No should be surprised*, he tells himself. *Donna like that, what she want with a loser like you?*

'Morning, sweetheart,' Bobbie says.

Mulligan spins around and sees her standing in the doorway.

'Que pasa?' she says. 'You look like you're going to cry. Is it the funeral?'

Mulligan nods, not trusting his voice.

'Oh, sweetheart!' She walks over and lays her hands on his chest. 'Yeah, it's going to be lousy for all of us, but I know it's going to be worse for you, feeling things the way you do.'

He wraps his arms around her and holds her close.

'Bobbie?' he says. 'Something we gotta talk about.'

'Yeah?' She pulls a little away and looks up at him.

'I uh—'

'Morning, guys!' Aunt Lucy walks into the kitchen. 'Oh, sorry. I gotta learn to knock or something.'

Laughing, Bobbie turns away. 'No problem,' she says. 'I'm just going to put on the news, okay? Then we got to get dressed and out of here pretty quickly.'

'Okay. Sure.' Mulligan goes back to making the coffee. He can only hope that he'll have a chance to talk with her alone later in the evening.

Sarojini glares at the public comm unit's screen, but it remains black even though a small green light indicates an active connection. 'I don't believe this unit is broken,' she says. 'Sandy, please turn on your vid.'

'No.' The voice sounds dark, guttural. 'Somebody might see me using this comm. I can't risk it. I told you not to contact me at work.'

'It's the only number you left my former associate.'

'But I haven't run an advert. You're only supposed to use it when I run an advert.'

'Well, I'm afraid this is too important to wait.' Sarojini represses the urge to say something nasty. 'Final payment for the merchandise must be postponed for an indefinite period. Our original buyer is no longer in the market, which means finding another, and—'

The faceless voice cuts her off. 'Find another? I thought you said you'd take care of everything!'

'My former associate's murder made that impossible.'

'Well, yeah. I was kinda freaked by that.'

'No doubt.' Sarojini puts steel in her voice. 'I had to reclaim the merchandise at the spaceport.'

'What?' Panic trembles the voice. 'Here on Hagar?'

'I'm afraid so. It came back carried by the athlete who suffered an unfortunate accident yesterday.' She nods as the sound of a sharp inhalation comes over the speaker. 'Yes. That one. But I now have the merchandise.'

'You still think you can sell it?'

'Buyers always exist for rare items. And it's more valuable than you let on, isn't it? You should have mentioned it to . . . my associate.'

'I didn't know myself. You think they tell my type anything?' The whispery voice breaks off, then resumes. 'Look, go ahead and sell it. I can wait for my money, but don't comm me again! I'll contact you in a few days. Watch the adverts.'

The connection breaks. The screen reverts to shifting moire.

'You know,' Sarojini remarks to the air, 'I am really tired of dealing with the lower classes.'

With a shake of her head she leaves the comm booth and makes for the Metro station and home. She has some hard thinking to do.

So many people have crowded into the crematorium's bland little chapel that the air conditioning fails to keep up with the body heat. The chapel smells of some thick incense as well as perfume and sweat. Like everyone else, Lacey and her contingent start fanning themselves with the paper programmes for the service. Fortunately, sheer luck has landed them in a side pew, and she has the outermost seat next to a plastostone wall and an open window. She looks back over the row: Rosa Wallace next to her, then Aunt Lucy and Marisa Mbaye, with first Mulligan and then Yosef filling out the pew. The rest of the team sits in the ranks of pews directly ahead. Near the front Lacey spots Keiko Takahashi and an aged man who, Rosa tells her, is Tak's father.

'Everyone else with them, they be family, too,' Rosa whispers. 'Damn good thing they got one.'

'Yeah,' Lacey says. 'Sure is.'

Directly in front of the family the casket stands, closed and draped in a woven carpet of flowers, the gift of the Esperance Eagles. The autopsy report she read from Bates's files makes Lacey glad that no one will have to see what's left of Tak's face.

Since Tak himself held no particular religious views, for his family's

211

sake the funeral director has put together an amalgam service of high thoughts with vague affiliations. Ancient music, mostly by Bach, murmurs from the speakers. Various friends and team-mates mount the podium in turn and stand in front of a truly huge heap of floral arrangements to share reminiscences of their dead friend. Several non-denominational chaplains deliver short prayers. A Buddhist monk offers reflections on the transitory nature of all human life. Everything moves quietly along, neither too fast nor too slow.

Lacey is thinking they're getting off easily when Yosef breaks. She's been checking on him now and again during the service. Mostly he sat dead still, barely blinking his eyes, barely breathing. But during the Buddhist homily he begins to weep, silently at first. Lacey sees Jack lay a hand on his arm and lean close, talking to him, she supposes, through their shared talent. All at once Yosef sobs loud enough to make the speaker pause. Before Jack can stop him, Yosef gets up and runs, racing down the aisle to the door. Everyone in the chapel turns in a rustle of clothing and programmes to watch as Jack jumps up and charges after him. Distantly a door bangs, then another.

'Grief too is the play of illusion,' the monk says. 'But the suffering of illusion is not illusion. It is suffering.' He places his hands together, touches his fingers to his forehead, and steps down.

The Bach starts again, louder.

The chapel and the crematorium proper stand in the middle of an island of green lawn, separated from the surrounding desert by a chain-link fence. Inside the fence off-duty police and temporary security beings form a second line of protection, because beyond it fans cluster, at least a thousand of them, Mulligan estimates. At the moment they stand quietly, but they keep pressing closer, leaning against the fence, jockeying for position. The sight stops Yosef's run cold. He stands shaking on the gravelled path leading to the gate and allows Jack to catch up with him.

'Hey,' Jack says. 'Que pasa? Need some air?'

'Ah come off it, Jack! You of all people should know what's wrong.'

'Well, maybe, yeah, but jeez, man, I no can believe you be blaming yourself.'

212

'It's all my fault.' Yosef stares at the ground. 'If I'd gone right to the cops the way your Bobbie wanted, Tak would still be alive.'

'How you supposed to know what was gonna come down? Neither of us, we no got a talent for, like, seeing the future. Y'know?'

'Doesn't matter. When you commit a sin there will be repercussions. And now they've fallen on Tak, not on me where they belong.'

'I no pretend to have an answer for that,' Mulligan says. 'But I know damn well your sin no got much to do with this. The dudes who trashed Tak killed him, not you.'

'But—'

The bell begins tolling, or at least the recording of a large brass bell begins playing from the small steeple on the chapel roof – so loud that Mulligan gives up trying to talk. He figures that mind-speech will probably drive Yosef over the edge. He can feel self-loathing emanating from Yosef, mixed with fear, and puts a comforting arm around his shoulders.

The chapel doors open. The Buddhist monk in his orange robes walks slowly out. Behind him comes the black casket, stripped of its flowers, carried by six of Takahashi's team-mates. In time to the long, slow tolling of the bell they turn and begin carrying it around the chapel toward the crematorium at the back. Behind them come the mourners, Keiko leaning on a friend, and the other guests filing out in no particular order.

At the sight the fans outside begin to move, turning after the coffin, pressing and pushing those in the way. Jack can hear people sobbing, calling goodbyes, shouting promises of revenge. Other sounds start, too – angry voices lifted, a sudden shriek of fear as someone nearly falls in the crush. Jack can feel the mood change as the crowd hovers dangerously near to becoming a mob. He can see the police reaching for batons as the fence shakes, threatening to buckle. Some of the security guards begin edging backwards.

'Come on.' Jack grabs Yosef's arm. 'We better get inside.'

When he glances back he can see other guests hesitating in a frightened herd close to the chapel. Someone tall pushes his way through them, then takes off running toward the fence: Chief Bates, yelling orders as he runs. At the fence an officer hands him a bullhorn.

213

'Folks, hey! It's your Chief of Police here, Al Bates.' Bates's voice rings out, touched with sadness but commanding all the same. 'It's all over, time for you to start home. We gotta get Takahashi's family out of here. Come on now, let's not make things worse for them. Those of you in the rear, start moving away please. Those in the rear, start moving away please. Please, folks, think of Tak's family.'

For one breathless moment nothing happens. All at once a great many people sigh, almost in unison, and begin to disperse. They start walking away from the back rows; then the inner rings begin to turn. Slowly, like a stain spreading in water, the crowd eases out, turns thin, and becomes nothing but a lot of people moving toward parked skimmers and the Metro station.

'Jeez,' Bobbie says. 'You've got to hand it to Al. He's damn good at what he does.' She steps between Jack and Yosef, slips her arm through Jack's and puts the other hand gently on Yosef's sleeve. 'Marisa needs you. She and Aunt Lucy are waiting inside where they can sit down.'

Yosef nods, then hurries off.

'You no slouch either,' Jack says. 'Bobbie, Yosef he blaming himself. I get a real bad vibe off him. Damn good thing he got the team to help him over it.'

They look back at the chapel. Outside it Jack sees Rosa Wallace standing with her hands over her face, her shoulders shaking so hard that it's visible at this distance. Colin Dejean puts an arm around her and leads her away.

'Rosa's really taking this hard,' Bobbie remarks. 'Was she in love with him or something?'

'No. She all broken up cause he was her team-mate. Everyone else, they feel as bad. They just hide it better.'

'Oh.' Bobbie looks doubtful.

'Well, come on, when you were out in deep space, you worked on the bridge, right? You musta felt like you were part of a team. The officers, you had to work together and stuff.'

'Yeah, but it's not the same. I was the comp officer. My only real partner was the ship.'

Jack can think of absolutely nothing to say to this remark. There are times when Bobbie seems more alien to him than any lizzie or carli he's ever known.

When he arrived at the memorial service, Chief Bates took a seat at the end of the row nearest the door – not that he was expecting trouble, but his instincts told him that he'd better be able to get out fast if necessary. They turned out to be right. Once the crowd has started for home, he hurries out to the parking lot and his skimmer. He has an appointment at the Confederation Embassy.

A little fast driving gets him to the embassy some ten minutes early, plenty of time to park and go inside. The strawberry blonde sits behind the reception desk. He braces himself, but she looks up with a bland smile.

'Chief Bates? Ka Pral is expecting you. Please go down to his office.'

'Thanks. Will do.'

Bates finds the office door partly open. He can hear voices speaking the carli language and knocks. The voices stop. In a moment, Ka Pral opens the door wide. His left ear is twitching again, Bates notices.

'Ah, Bates! My thanks for gracing our humble establishment. I have two other visitors who will interest you.'

The visitors turn out to be the carli security experts from aggKar, a slender woman with dark brown fur, tipped in places with russet, and a tall man, straw coloured and sleek. Instead of the familiar robes over their tunics they both wear loose long jackets of some nubbly black cloth, pulled tight at the waist by a heavy belt that carries assorted pouches and tools. Bates decides against asking if they have weapons.

'Lieutenant Kaz Varesh,' Ka Pral says. 'Officer Ka Glon.'

'Hello,' Bates says. 'I am honoured to meet you.'

They nod, nearly in unison.

'We are honoured to meet you as well,' Kaz Varesh says. 'I cannot tell you how glad I am to see another expert in our field. Perhaps now we can get some clear and unequivocal information.'

'So we may hope.' Ka Pral bows all round. 'Bates, I am assuming that you would prefer to forgo our usual rituals? I know that time is short.'

'Time spent in conversation is a flower,' Bates says, 'as your poet Kaz Sayalti once wrote, but if I remember it right, she went on to say that at times duty requires us to march quickly through the garden.'

'Very well put.' Kaz Varesh bows in his direction. 'And unfortunately true.' She turns to Ka Pral. 'Enough time has been wasted already. I hope you and the ambassador both realize it. I cannot believe the incompetence I've seen.'

Ka Pral bobs his head and spreads his hands wide in acquiescence. Bates hopes that he's managing to hide his shock. Not only has he never seen a rude carli before, but Ka Pral seems to find nothing unusual about it. The four of them sit down, facing each other around the low table. Ka Glon unclips a recording comp from his belt and flicks it on with one long finger.

'Now,' Kaz Varesh says. 'Chief Bates, if you would be so good and noble as to tell us of your progress, I will then tell you of ours.'

'All right,' Bates says. 'At sunset I got a full report from the police in Esperance on Sarah, who are finally investigating the correct people. They got the proper warrants and thoroughly searched Senator Martinelli's homes, both the one in the capital and his original house in his district. They searched his senatorial offices as well. They spoke with his people and interviewed him directly. They believe that the Senator does not and never has possessed the missing *leijchwen*. They have sworn statements to that effect, which I will have copied and sent to you.'

'Excellent!' Kaz Varesh rubs her hands together. 'Now then, the plastoclear case which held *iLeijchwen* and the pillar which supported the case have been subjected to our usual battery of tests. They are both covered with human fingerprints from approximately six individuals, and carli fingertip prints from so many different individuals that all could not be distinguished. Microanalysis of the air filters in the room produced hairs of thirty different colours. We fear that scientific analysis will tell us little, therefore, and are planning an extensive series of interviews with embassy personnel.'

'I commend your energy,' Bates remarks, 'and I apologize for the slackness of my own investigation.'

'My dear chief,' Kaz Varesh says, 'I have one building to consider,

216

while you have an entire city. The two situations are far too disparate to allow comparison.'

'If only we could convince the Council of this,' Ka Pral mutters.

'Indeed.' Kaz Varesh briefly flattens her ears. 'And if only the ambassador had chosen to summon us at the moment the crime was discovered. There's a Merrkan idiom that corresponds almost exactly to one of ours: the trail has gone cold.'

Bates feels like applauding her for voicing what ritual etiquette has forbidden him to say.

'I had words with the ambassador earlier this evening,' Kaz Varesh continues. 'He provided no satisfactory explanation for the lapse, but he did suggest that the Secretary of Protocol might be able to cast some light upon the problem.'

Ka Pral cringes, then collects himself with a bob of his head. 'Gri Nerosi's disappearance was not reported for two days because he was technically at leisure.' Ka Pral glances at Bates. 'Your term, I believe, is time off. Only when he did not return on schedule did we realize that something was wrong.'

'That was what?' Kaz Varesh says. 'On the day known as third Stember. The ambassador did not send a message to the Council and report *iLeijchwen* gone until the day known as eleventh Stember. Why?'

'Because of the reception for the Enzebb ambassador on tenth Stember. An incident of this magnitude might have ruined an extremely important diplomatic occasion. His Excellency told you—'

'Yes, he did. I was not satisfied with his answer.' Kaz Varesh turns her amber-eyed gaze upon Bates. 'I have read the reports of the information that you graciously gave to our Secretary of Protocol. Thank you very much.'

'You're most welcome.'

Ka Pral runs a hand through the fur on his opposite arm, surreptitiously glances at it then wipes it off on his robe. He's shedding, Bates realizes.

'Here is our procedure for the next few days,' Kaz Varesh goes on. 'We are going to interview every single member of the embassy concerning the days of thirty-first Awgus to fourth Stember. I am

217

pessimistic about their ability to recall anything useful, but one can always hope.'

'I realize that I have no jurisdiction here,' Bates says. 'But—'

'If we find anything that will help you track Gri Nerosi,' Kaz Varesh interrupts, 'you'll know it immediately.'

'You have my humble thanks. I'll send you complete and detailed reports of our efforts to find both Gri Nerosi and the embassy's stolen property.'

'You're welcome, I'm sure, and in turn I thank you in deep humility.' Kaz Varesh stands up and waves a hand at Ka Glon. 'Come along. We'd better get started.'

Once they've gone, Ka Pral shuts the door hard behind them. With a sigh of relief, he returns to the circle of chairs and reclaims his.

'Fine officers, both of them,' he says. 'No doubt you were surprised by Kaz Varesh's decorum, or rather her lack of it.'

'I'll admit to that, yeah.'

'The normal etiquette of our kind does not apply to our security people. If it did, they'd never solve any crimes.' Ka Pral runs a hand over his head. Loose hair sticks to his fingers. 'They show the true nature of our people, Bates. You can imagine what life would be like if all of us showed our true nature.'

'Yeah, I certainly can. But I hope they turn something up.'

'Yes, so do I, before the situation deteriorates any further. I was wondering if you have information that is best kept between friends.'

Bates smiles. 'Some. Martinelli is a pompous idiot. He professes to be completely puzzled by the outcry over the part he's playing in this. He keeps saying that he never dreamed of acquiring such a priceless relic for his personal enjoyment. He wanted a regular *leijchwen*, not this one in particular – as if that made everything all right.'

'Idiot strikes me as a fine choice of word. I suppose he claims to be unaware all *leijchwen* are national treasures that must never be sold?'

'Most likely, yeah. He's hired two of the best lawyers on Sarah.'

'Do you think there's any hope of prosecution?'

Bates turns his hands palm up and shrugs.

'I do understand that,' Ka Pral goes on. 'The Council will not. We have a great many laws pertaining to *leijchwen*, and all of them have been broken.'

218

'But those laws hold only in the Confederation and its territories.'

'True. But the embassy and its grounds are legally part of the Confederation.'

'Of course. And since the theft occurred here, then your thief broke your laws the moment he laid hands on *iLeijchwen*. Once he left the embassy, however . . .' Bates pauses to let it sink in. 'Unfortunately, as much as I agree that Martinelli has no sense of decency and no brains, for that matter, he's broken no Republic law.'

'Umph.' Ka Pral hesitates, thinking. 'This is the root of our differences, isn't it, Bates? I persist in holding Martinelli responsible while you persist in thinking Gri Nerosi alone is responsible. Do you know what my worst fear is? That someone will destroy *iLeijchwen* rather than be caught with it.'

'That would be a horrible outcome. For all concerned.'

Ka Pral leans back in his chair and sighs. 'Oh yes. Horrible indeed.'

'Just among friends, can I ask you why you postponed calling in security? Dunt answer if it's going to put you in a bad position.'

'Actually, you no doubt need to know this. It was important that the ambassador be a good host to greet our guests at the reception. Had he notified the Council about the loss of *iLeijchwen*, he could never have pretended to be relaxed and happy. Ka Jakhonas isn't a professional actor, after all.'

'Er, that's true. But why would it be harder to pretend because the Council knew?'

'Because he'd be under sentence of death, of course, as soon as he notified them.'

'*What?*' Bates stares at him.

'Ah, I see you don't understand,' Ka Pral says. 'The ambassador is the head of our work-family, and anything that happens here is his responsibility. If *iLeijchwen* isn't returned by the deadline, he'll be a shamed man, and of course then he'll have to commit suicide. As soon as the Council learned of the theft, they sent the official letter of disgrace.'

Bates can barely speak. 'I see.'

When he returns to his office, he finds a message waiting from Kaz Varesh. Rather than trust the comm lines, she sent a paper letter, carefully sealed, by embassy courier.

Something I did not wish to say in front of the Secretary of Protocol: there was what you would call a conspiracy of silence over the disappearance of *iLeijchwen*. Whether or not we believe the Protocol Secretary's story of refusing to endanger the reception, and I do find this plausible though not proven, we should both be aware that at least twelve people were involved in hiding the disappearance till after the reception. The trail is covered with ice. Hope for a thaw.

'Ah crap,' Bates says. 'Well, if anyone can apply a blowtorch, it'll be Kaz Varesh.'

Although the temporarily zealous Vice Squad has managed to roust a certain number of petty criminals from Polar City, they have no way of preventing those same sentients from visiting now and again – especially if they're willing to pay for the privilege. Lacey meets Blade at one of his regular hangouts in the Outworld Bazaar, a beer bar downstairs from one of Richie's establishments. Lacey and Blade sit at a little table against the far wall where they can keep an eye on the door and order drinks from the servobot: grain beer for Lacey and sandworm beer, bubbling with larvae, for Blade.

'I don't think I've ever seen you dressed all in black before,' Blade remarks. 'Why the funereal air?'

'I've just been to a funeral,' Lacey says.

'Oh. That for the unfortunate Takahashi?'

'Yeah. And I've been wondering something.'

'No.' Blade lays a massive hand flat on the table. 'I can guess what you wondering, and no. We did not trash Tak. You think we're as crazy as our new neighbours out in our lovely suburban home? The team is our team, our team is in the Galactic Series and every hair on their heads is sacred unto us. Well, at least while the Series is going on.'

'Good. I needed to know that.'

'Of course.' Blade considers the foaming mass in his mug of beer. 'So many little lives, all about to be snuffed out like candles in the wind.' He raises the mug and drinks. 'Tasty, though.'

'Glad you like it.' Lacey takes a sip of her beer while she considers phrasing. 'Actually, I was wondering if you had any idea who hired the work-over artists.'

'No doubt you were. You always had an active mind.'

'I dunt suppose they approached your boss first.'

'Not to my knowledge, no. I've heard around that the hopelessly crude thugs in question had no intentions of killing Tak. They were merely too stupid to stop beating him before they did. Whether this is true or not, I don't know.'

'Dunt do him any good if it is.'

'Entirely too true. From what I saw on the news vids his mortal coil was about as shuffled as you're going to get.'

'Do you know who they are? There's money in it if you do.'

'I regret it, but I have nothing to sell. The Bazaar is full of people who will do anything, or almost anything, for money. I could give you a list of most of them, but it would be so long as to be meaningless.' He salutes her with his mug. 'And besides, you probably know them all already.'

'Maybe so. But I dunt want to put my neck on the block by going around asking them.'

'I take it this means you thought me as innocent as the newly hatched?'

'I hoped you were. I'm glad to see I was right.'

'Is that the only reason you came looking for me tonight?'

'No.' Lacey fishes in her pocket and comes up with a twenty. 'Does the name Oscuridad mean anything to you?'

'Most assuredly it does.'

'Can you take me to meet . . . is it a her or a him?'

'Both. Not in one person joined, like some of your brother's employees, but a pair.'

'Human?'

'Monkey-types indeed.'

Lacey slides the twenty over to him. He starts to take it, then lays it back down.

'You can't possible afford all this,' Blade says.

'It's no my dinero.'

'Oh.' He picks it up, and with a flick of a claw secretes it somewhere. 'Richie's? Why not ask him these pointed questions?'

'Who's going to pay him protection money if he tells the first person who asks where to find them?'

'Point taken. Your brother is a truly amazing being. 'Tis pity he's a whore.'

'Yeah.' Puzzled, Lacey stared at him. 'Uh – is that one of your quotes or something?'

'After a fashion. I'm sorry. Don't worry about it.' Blade has a gloomy sip of his beer. 'In fact, your family seems to have been an entire flock of *rarae aves*. The boss was telling me that he remembers your father well. You and Richie must have inherited your looks from him but your brains from your mother.'

'That's the general theory, yeah. Now, about Oscuridad. Where?'

'I don't know at the moment, and that's not a ploy to part you from more of Richie's ill-gotten gains. I can however find out. It might take me a while.'

'We dunt have a while.'

'Do you really think the wretched Cons will resort to violence if they don't get their rag back?'

'Yeah.'

'*Merde*. Also, *scheiss*. Okay, I'll move as fast as I dare. How long have we got before the laser cannon start firing?'

'The ultimatum expires in five nights. Won't be long after that.' Lacey stands up and slides her half-full glass across to him. 'Finish this too if you want.'

'Thank you, I will. After that bit of news, I need another drink.'

Office work. At times Bates wonders why he kept accepting promotions until he ended up here, stuck behind a desk, buried in office work, trying to juggle his officers' needs against the politicians' demands while at the same time making sure that the citizenry stay reasonably safe, and all on a budget never large enough. Onscreen his AI lists four administrative reports, the shortest of which is over thirty thousand words.

'Hey, Chief?' Sergeant Nagura appears in the doorway. 'I hate to interrupt you—'

'No, no, it's fine. Come in. What have you got?'

'Something on that missing carli.'

'Gri Nerosi? I'll be damned! Finally, huh?

'Yes, sir. I had a hunch and went over to Carlitown. Found a friend of his. I've brought him in for a statement, and I wondered if you—'

'Sure do.' Bates heaves his bulk out of the chair.

The police interview helpful witnesses in a large office, cluttered but reasonably pleasant. When Bates follows Nagura inside he finds their witness seated in an overstuffed chair and drinking coffee. He proves to be unusually small, little more than one point three metres rather than the one-six average for carli males, with dull yellow fur and clear brown eyes. Instead of robes, he wears a pair of jeans and a shirt.

'I appreciate your offer of help,' Bates says. 'Señor—?'

'George. George Merchant of Lansing Textiles.' He speaks with only the slightest trace of a carli accent.

'Lansing Textiles,' Bates repeats. 'You a Republic citizen?'

'No, I'm a Con.' One ear flap dips, the equivalent of a wink. 'Lansing's based on our home world, but we keep offices here. Luxury trade stuff, you know?' Bout two-thirds of our employees are your people, Republic citizens I mean, and of course almost all our customers. I'm the manager, been living here for thirty-seven standard years.'

Merchant reaches into a pocket of his human-style shirt and pulls out a business card. Bates has never seen a carli with a pocket before.

'Downtown office. That second address is the warehouse.' He scribbles a few words in standard Merrkan script along the bottom. 'That's my home, apartment off Madison, right in the middle of Carlitown. I like humans fine, but you people dunt know how to cook.'

Bates glances at the card before pocketing it. 'I understand you and Gri Nerosi are – what? Friends? Neighbours?'

'Friends, no. But we both like to play *griish*. Little club near my apartment's always got a game going. A dude like that, he's no going to have too many friends of any species, you know? Good *griish* player, though, and you gotta have some brains to play that.'

'I've heard of it. It's a strategy game, right?'

'Sort of like your chess, yeah. But he dunt got much common sense, and he no can work with other sentients worth a damn. No to

223

mention the fact that some of his habits drive you loco. He does *this*, all the time.'

Merchant growls under his breath, barely audible, almost a whistle.

'That would grate, all right,' Bates says. 'When was the last time you played with him?'

'I dunt remember for sure, but the club keeps records, kind of a full-time tournament, you know? You could check. But it was, oh, six weeks ago? Seven? Sorry, I dunt know.'

'You sure you no seen him since then?'

'Yeah, I'm sure. Like I said, check with the club. They no going to be happy talking about it, but she's pretty good.' The carli nods towards Nagura. 'She got me here.'

'Yeah. Got any idea why they dint come forward before now?'

'Come on, Chief, who the hell is gonna say, hey, I know the bastard who stole *iLeijchwen*? Must have been crazy, but we dunt think that excuses as much as you humans do. Anybody who could do that . . . every carli on this planet is disgraced, just having him share our air.'

'So you dunt think he had help from another carli?'

'Hell, no! Ask me, I think he's dead. Good riddance, and he dunt rate going home in a body slab neither. Anyway, he's no in Carlitown, and we sort of stand out when we go anyplace else.'

'That's for sure. Now tell me, did you think Nerosi had a gambling addiction?'

'Yeah, a real problem. He even tried to talk me into going to some no-limits poker game he found. I told him those things is muy dangerous, besides being illegal as hell, but you think he listens?'

'He mention a name in connection with that illegal game?'

'Yeah, some sentient named Jay Gagne runs it. But I dunt know how to find the game because I told him to go pluck his backside bald.'

Once Merchant's been thanked and sent on his way, Bates tells Nagura to follow up on both leads, then returns to his office. The list of reports still lurks onscreen, glaring at him. He ignores them and asks the AI for the report he does want. Yesterday he ordered Polar City sealed as completely as possible: any sentient leaving or entering by the spaceport, the airport, the robotrain system or a major freeway

224

had better have good ID and a damn good reason for going away. He's barely started reading when his AI unit interrupts.

'Chief? Mr Akeli of the PBI is downstairs and wishes to see you.'

'He came here? Jeez, I'm in shock. Sure, send him straight up.'

Akeli arrives promptly, attended by a pair of PBI agents each neatly dressed in business suits. Since Bates's office offers only two chairs, they stand outside in the hall. Akeli sits down opposite Bates and looks around at the cracking green walls, the piles of papers and files, the ceiling where the acoustical tile perpetually threatens to fall.

'I see that the domestic force offers little in the way of emollients,' Akeli says. 'You have my sympathies.'

'It's okay,' Bates says. 'So, to what do I owe this honour?'

'I was attending a grand jury investigation across the street, the one concerned with those smuggling cases, and while I did so it occurred to me that there are a few matters concerning the missing artefact that we might properly discuss.' Akeli pauses for a breath. 'Such as this matter of leaks to the popular media.'

'Yeah. Damn right. We did an internal investigation here and found no one who would have talked to the holocasters. So we shook down a couple of holocasters and hit pay dirt. They're cautious over in the news rooms. They dunt want to put something on the air only to find it came from some nut. So they asked for ID. This person, human, female, had all the right papers. Claimed to be someone called Officer Saunders.'

'And there is no such sentient?'

'Not working for us. You can buy ID for anything over in the Bazaar, if you're willing to spend. Saunders – whoever she really is – knew she'd get plenty out of the news people, so I'd say she spent.'

'So it would seem. At least you must now have a good description of this person.'

'No such luck. She wasn't dumb. Showed the ID over a partial vid link. With the holo of her face covered.'

'Most frustrating of her. I too have been consulting with my internal security people. So far they've turned up nothing.'

'They may not.'

'So it would seem. I sincerely hope we've seen the last of this sort of thing.'

'The best defence is a good offence.' Bates leans back in his chair and considers him. 'We need to tell the Cons that *iLeijchwen*'s on-planet. If Ka Jekhonas finds out from the holonews, we're going to have a real mess on our hands.'

'No! Why give them a weapon against us? And what if they leak the news themselves? Disclosing the involvement of a popular sports figure is bound to cause considerable unrest.'

'Yeah, that's true. But the point is keeping it off the news, not putting it on.'

Akeli squeezes his fat lips together.

'What makes you think the carlis are going to leak this story if they get it?' Bates says. 'Is there something you're not telling me?'

'Not at all. I thought it was obvious that the Confederation is manipulating this situation as a pretext for military action. Therefore it stands against their best interests to allow you to solve the problem.'

Utterly caught off-guard, Bates can only stare at him.

'Well?' Akeli raises one eyebrow. 'Do you think I have mistakenly evaluated the situation?'

'Maybe, maybe not. Some members of their Council are going to be thinking this way, sure. I'd suggest, though, that not all the Cons agree on this.'

'Oh, indubitably. The protests of those embassy members who feel war is unwise will probably delay the military action by perhaps five or six hours while they're being bundled aboard that heavy cruiser in orbit.' Akeli smiles thinly. 'The wider view, Bates. I suggest you learn to take it.'

'Yeah?' Bates has to work to keep his voice steady. 'The one trouble with the wider view is things get out of focus. It's in Ka Jekhonas's best interests personally to get *iLeijchwen* back, after all.'

'What? How could that possibly be the case?'

'Because he'll have to kill himself if he dunt.'

Akeli blinks rapidly, several times. 'Ah yes,' he says at last. 'Their code of honour.'

'I dunt think he's thrilled by the prospect,' Bates goes on. 'If his staff members and I work together, maybe we can do more than protest.'

'Perhaps. So we all should hope.' Akeli stands up. 'I need to return to my own headquarters, but there's one last thing. Martinelli is on his way to Hagar.'

'Oh jeeze-aitch-ker-rist!'

'My reaction was similar, yes. He insists on coming, apparently against the best advice both of his own security experts and my own bureau. Unfortunately, he is mostly my responsibility, but I may need to ask you for additional officers to protect him.'

'Understood. You better figure out a way to muzzle him, or we'll have half the carli navy in orbit. Maybe he'll break a leg getting off the shuttle.'

'I doubt if we'll be so fortunate. Unless, perhaps, such a mishap could be arranged.'

It takes Bates a moment to realize Akeli's making a joke.

Once Akeli and his goons have left, Bates returns to his report. Boring it may be, but at least it takes his mind off the interstellar situation.

Rosa runs a hand through her short red curls, still shower-damp, then slams her locker shut. 'This was a damn stupid idea,' she announces. 'Dunt know what Georgy was thinking of. Worst goddamn practice this team, we ever have.'

'It gave you something to think about besides the funeral,' Officer Tolridge says.

'Yeah, maybe so. The worst thing be that team meeting. Jeezus.'

'Yeah. I cried myself when your manager was talking about winning one for Tak.'

'Yeah.' Rosa picks up her carrysack. 'Okay, I be done.'

A tall human woman, Tolridge leads the way out of the locker room. At the door into the corridor, she pauses, looking back and forth.

'Damn it, Mbaye was supposed to wait right here!'

'He dint? We better put on some speed.'

Rosa might be the better sprinter, but Tolridge has the longer legs and carries nothing but her police baton. As they run down the corridor, Rosa finds herself falling behind. Tolridge bursts through the door leading out. Rosa can hear her yelling.

'What the—? Hey, you! Stop right there! Police!' Her whistle sounds, a long electronic shriek.

Rosa runs out into the parking lot and the uncertain light of the aurora flickering overhead. Twenty metres ahead of them she sees a couple of men pinning Yosef against her jade-green Jag while a third is already running away. The other two let Yosef go and spin around. A second police whistle answers Tolridge's.

'Hands over your head!' Tolridge yells.

The two take off, running after their comrade. Tolridge pulls her stunner from its holster and fires with a sweep of the broad beam. One man screams and stumbles, but his friends grab him and haul – and he keeps running. Swearing under her breath Tolridge fires again and hits nothing. The second cop appears with a comm unit in his hand.

'Stay where you are!' he calls out. 'We dunt dare leave them alone.'

'Shit!' Tolridge mutters. 'But he's right.'

A skimmer comes zooming over the lot and lands with a squeal, skidding along the plastophalt toward the three. The doors pop open, the attackers leap in, and the skimmer takes off before the doors even close. For one brief moment Rosa sees someone's legs dangling in the air. They disappear, and the skimmer picks up speed. The second officer is staring at it, muttering a description into his comm. Tolridge swears again.

'I'd bet it turns out to be stolen,' she says. 'If I was the betting type.'

'Yeah,' Rosa turns to Yosef. 'Why the hell dint you wait inside?'

Yosef starts to answer, but he cannot speak, only tremble. Rosa considers yelling at him, decides it would only make things worse, and starts searching in her carrysack for the skimmer keys. The two cops converge, talking in low voices.

'Okay,' Tolridge says. 'Johnson here, he's going to stay and file the report. Mr Mbaye, you recognize those punks?'

Yosef shakes his head. Tolridge considers him for a moment, then turns to Johnson. 'I think he better get home.'

'Yeah,' Johnson says. 'I got a good look at los dorkeros. If we need to question him, we can do it later.'

While the two cops watch, Rosa unlocks the Jag. Inside on the dash sits the small black pennant that functioned as a parking permit out at the funeral chapel. She hates to see it but hates to throw it away. Everything that means the funeral has come and gone puts more distance between her and Tak.

When she and Yosef drive off, Tolridge follows them in an unmarked skimmer. Rosa has to drive slowly, another thing she hates.

'Crappy day,' Rosa says.

'Yeah.'

In silence they drive to The Ring, turn onto it, go halfway around and get off again, heading out to the underground condo development where the Mbayes live.

'Rosa?' Yosef says. 'Do me a favour?'

'What?'

'Don't tell Marisa about this attack. I don't want her worrying any more.'

'She got more guts than you think.'

He says nothing. They leave the freeway and follow the smooth straight road that heads out to the development, Shady Acres.

'Oh what the hell,' Rosa says. 'None of my goddamn business. I won't tell her.'

'Thanks. I know what a damn nuisance I am.'

'Yeah, you are. Never shoulda stopped you that night.'

Again the long silence.

'Uh, say,' Rosa says at last. 'I meant that as a joke. About not stopping you, I mean.'

'Oh. Okay.'

Rosa feels a little sick. She has no idea of what might go wrong next, but she can't shake the feeling that something will.

'Another attack on Mbaye?' Bates says. 'Jeezchrise!'

'Yes, sir,' Officer Zizzistre says. 'It took me that way too, when I read the report.'

'Well, this makes one thing clear. Whoever's doing these attacks, they dunt know where that thing is either.'

'Some comfort, huh? By the way, I done checked out all them security guards. You want me to file that report?'

'Give me the five-minute version now and then file it.'

'Yes, sir. Here's the big thing. One of them, she no was real.'

'What?'

'She got herself hired with a fake set of IDs. The descriptions, they give us a Hindu woman, kind of undistinguished-looking, silver butterfly clip in her hair. Mulligan heard her say she was hired for lounge security. That helped. The clerk out at the spaceport, he remembered that, found her name and stuff. Dunt match any other records. The social security number, it belonged to some dude ten years dead.'

'Huh.' Bates leans back in his chair. 'No one saw her actually take the damn thing?'

'No, sir. That would make it too easy. But she kinda stands out.'

'Yeah. Of course, for all we know, she's only a welfare mother who dunt want her extra earnings reported or someone like that. But, like you say, she kind of stands out. Think you can track her down?'

Zizzistre shrugs. 'I done checked the demographics. There only be a hundred thousand adults of Indian descent in this town. And only half of 'em, say, gonna be donnas. Well, that's assuming she come from Polar City.'

'Izzy, that's too much, even for you,' Bates says. 'Tell the duty officer I'm assigning you two assistants. Keep them looking for this lounge security person. Nagura got lucky with Señor Merchant, they might with Butterfly Girl here.'

'You bet, Chief. Routine work. Amazing what it can turn up.'

'It sure is. I want you to keep working on the Takahashi case. You know, by rights I should assign a detective to work over you.'

Izzy goes completely still, barely breathing, it seems, as he falls into the instinctive lizzie freeze.

'But I'm not going to.' Bates grins at him.

'Gracias, sir.' He hisses in relief.

'When are you going to think about taking that sergeant's test? I'll recommend you for it.'

'Well, hey, gracias, sir! I gonna do that, then. But I gotta work on the way I talk, I know. Maybe do that first.'

'It'll be easier to make the grade if you don't sound like you come from Porttown, yeah. Even though you do. It stinks, Izzy, the snobbery, but there it is and we're stuck with it.'

'Yes, sir. I savvy.'

'Probably better than me, yeah. Well, there are courses you can take. The department might even pay for one. Check it out and let me know.'

In a couple of weeks, the Park and Rec semi-pro season will be starting. That evening Mac's Discount City Appliances Marauders hold their first practice, which mostly consists of sitting around drinking beer while they argue about who's going to play where in the outfield. In disgust Mulligan leaves early. He comes home to find Aunt Lucy in the kitchen, making a soy loaf with a heavy addition of chopped onion. She glances up when he walks in.

'Bobbie, she gone out,' Lucy says. 'The Bazaar to see Richie, she say.'

'Oh.' Mulligan goes to the cooler and gets out a jug of drinking water. 'When she gonna get back?'

'Dunt know.' Lucy hands him a glass. 'Late, I guess.'

'Okay. Hope it no gonna be too late. The funeral and stuff, it wiped me out.'

'Me, too, chico.' She frowns down at the crumbled soy protein in the bowl. 'I called Kelly, said to postpone our team meeting. Fine with him, he say. No one gonna concentrate till the Series be over anyway.'

After dinner Mulligan flips around the three-dee channels in hopes of finding something to keep him awake, but with the baseball season over he sees nothing he wants to watch. He ends up falling asleep long before Bobbie comes home, but all day he dreams that she stands on the observation deck of a starship that's carrying her far, far away.

231

Chapter Eleven

Like most underground dwellings, the Mbayes' condo would be claustrophobic without the floor-to-ceiling holograms on selected walls. In the guest suite Rosa has a view of a green island rising from a clear sea, framed by two skinny trees that appear to be just outside her room. Marisa told her that the name of this holo is 'Bali Hai', a reference to Old Earth literature. Marisa decorated the suite to match the holo – pale green wallpaper with a pattern of leaves, bright floral bedspread and upholstery on the chair, a sand-coloured rug, an arrangement of large shells in the little bathroom. Every room in the five-bedroom condo has a theme. Rosa will be glad to get home.

On the evening of game three of the series, Rosa wakes early when the holo sun rises over the distant island. Outside, the real sun has just set at 1825 by the clock, and for a while Rosa lies in bed wondering whether to get up or turn off the holo and go back to sleep. The question answers itself when someone knocks on the door, a timid little rap.

'Marisa?' Rosa calls out. 'Come on in.'

'Thanks.' Marisa opens the door. 'I need your help. I guess. It's Yosef. I don't know what to do.'

Inside, away from the infidels, Marisa wears ordinary clothes: a pair of white maternity shorts and a red and white checked cotton smock at the moment. She stands uneasily in the doorway as Rosa rolls out of bed and grabs her own shorts and T-shirt from the floor.

'Yosef, he be sick?' Rosa says.

'I don't know. I've never seen him like this.'

Rosa understands her confusion when Marisa leads her to the master bedroom, an arrangement of pale blues and quiet floral stripes. Dressed in a pair of grey pyjama pants and nothing else, Yosef lies on top of the bedclothes curled up tight, his face half buried in a pillow.

Beyond him a holo of an Old Earth rose garden casts soft sunlight into the room. On its sound track, bees buzz and birds warble.

'Joe?' Rosa says. 'You okay?'

He lies stone still. Rosa walks over to the bedside and lays a hand on his shoulder. Nothing – not a sign that he feels her touch or sees her standing there. Fortunately she can see his chest rise and fall as he breathes, or she might have thought him dead.

'Joe!' Rosa raises her voice and shakes him. 'We gotta get to the park. Batting practice.'

'I can't.' His voice sounds small and high, like a child's. 'I just can't.'

Rosa feels so odd that it take her a moment to realize exactly what the feeling is: a strange mix of fear and revulsion. It seems to her that he even smells different, like a sick animal. If he weren't her team-mate, she knows, she would turn and run out of that room.

'Joe,' Rosa says. 'What be so wrong?'

'I don't know.' He screws his eyes tight shut. 'Leave me alone. Oh, for god's sake, leave me alone.'

Marisa sinks into a blue wingback chair and covers her face with her hands.

'He started to get dressed,' she mumbles. 'Then he looked at me and said "I'm too tired", and lay down like that.' She takes a deep breath and lowers her hands. 'I'll go call our doctor.'

'Good idea. And when you get done, then I gotta call Georgy. He probably gonna send the team doctor over, too. Dunt worry, Marisa. We gonna get him fixed up fine.'

Yet when she looks at Yosef, trembling as he lies curled around his pillow, she wonders if she's lying.

Even though it's Sunday, the possible interstellar crisis drives Chief Bates to his office for an early half-shift. He'll need to pick up Kaz Phaath long before the game starts, as the traffic out to the stadium is going to be horrendous. He's still going through his mail when a long grey head appears, craning around the door jamb. Officer Zizzistre apparently shares his views on the sanctity of days off.

'Got a minute, Chief? I think we finally getting someplace on this murder.'

'Routine pays off, right?'

'Right.' The heavy-set lizzie shuffles in and drops a hard-copy report on the desk. 'I done checked out Takahashi's luggage. Security guards done found it in a dumpster back of the main terminal. Takahashi, he brought it home and dumped it in the bedroom, where we done found it. No valuables left, natch, and his clothes, they were pretty ripped up from the search. But then I see one funny thing. Nice bit of black lace. A stocking.' Izzy grins and blinks all his eyelids, the lizzie equivalent of a wink.

'Big deal,' Bates says. 'From what I've heard, Tak always had some action going and I bet you heard it too. I want to know why you got that egg-eating grin on your snout.'

'Okay. This stocking, first off, there be only one. Second, it dint feel right when I took ahold of it. I done touched it to my snout, and it smelled funny, kind of like plastowire, and it felt rough somehow. So I had the lab take a look at it.'

Bates has been skimming through the report while Izzy talks. He comes to the end and leans back with a satisfied smile.

'Smart threads. Muy bueno, Izzy! So somebody was eavesdropping, somebody who wears black lace stockings.'

'And there no coulda been too many like that on the *Prez* that trip,' Izzy says. 'Gotta be easy to find her, now I know what I'm looking for.'

'Yeah, gracias. Good work. Want a suggestion?'

'Sure.'

'Ask the other unmarried men on the team. The married guys had their wives along with them, and they won't know nada.'

'Got it.' Zizzistre hisses under his breath. 'Thanks, Chief.'

After staying out well into the daylight, Lacey's tired enough to sleep late that evening. At about 2200 she comes ambling into the living room. Aunt Lucy is sitting on the couch, working on her wall hanging, while she keeps an eye on some soap opera or other.

'Where's Jack?' Bobbie says.

'Out running. He run every night?'

'Five klicks, yeah, one at a time. He runs over to the park, catches his breath, runs around it three times, then runs home.'

Aunt Lucy sighs and lays her knitting in her lap. 'Broke my heart when they branded that boy. Best natural athlete I ever coached.' She sighs again. 'There be coffee in the kitchen, honey. I done made some.'

Bobbie gets herself a cup of coffee, then sits down at her comp desk. Buddy flashes a queue of mail onscreen: nothing from Wazerzis and nothing much else, either.

'I do have something of interest, Programmer,' Buddy says. 'From police files.' His sensors turn toward Aunt Lucy. His next words appear onscreen. 'Shall I assume silent mode?'

'No, not necessary. What's this news?'

'Very well.' Buddy hums, clearing his throat. 'In Mike Takahashi's luggage a police officer found a black lace stocking. It contained smart threads that were transmitting conversations in that room back to some unknown recording device.'

Aunt Lucy yelps.

'What's wrong?' Bobbie spins her chair around to look. 'Poke yourself?'

'No, that there stocking. That Midori woman! I knew she up to no damn good! She were the one that gave it to Tak. A souvenir, he say, and you can guess what of. Jeezchrise, Buddy! You say it transmitted what we were talking about?'

'It would have transmitted anything said in Takahashi's cabin, but only there,' Buddy says. 'According to the police laboratory, its pick-up range has a four-metre radius.'

Aunt Lucy rolls her knitting up around the needles and shoves it viciously into the bag.

'We done went into Tak's cabin to be private,' she says. 'When we was discussing who was gonna carry that rag through customs. Me and Rosa, Yosef and Tak.'

Two of Buddy's alarm bells ring spontaneously. Lacey swears under her breath.

'That there Navy,' Aunt Lucy says, 'it dint no nada for your ladylike ways.'

'Look who's talking,' Bobbie says. 'But huh, this Midori got a data bonanza for her, uh, efforts. I wonder who she was working for. That bug is sophisticated, so it's probably either the Cons or the 'Lies.

Maybe she was selling information to anyone who'd pay, for that matter. I think we better call Bates about this.'

'Yeah. Sorry, honey, but I kinda blew it for you, too. I done say something like, we gonna give it to my niece when we get it back on-planet.'

Buddy squeals again. Lacey steeples her fingers and considers what she's just heard.

'My word,' she says at last. 'I guess I'd better stop walking around alone at night, huh? I've been pretty lucky so far, and here I didn't even know I needed to be.'

When Lacey finally gets through to him, Bates finds her news interesting enough to record every detail while she talks. Onscreen his image scowls.

'Looks like this situation's getting on your nerves, Chief,' she says.

'I have to admit it, yeah. Midori dunt sound like a real name to me. It's some kind of liquor, isn't it?'

'I think so,' Lacey says. 'It's her groupie name, for sure. But you've got the name of her bank, and several guys on the team know her cabin number on the liners.'

'Oh, we'll find her.' Bates smiles, but he only looks the grimmer for it. 'Dunt you worry about that. Lacey, you should have a police guard.'

'If I do, I'll be useless. The places I need to go, a cop shuts mouths. Dunt worry, though – I'll get a bodyguard on my own.'

'Good. What angle are you taking on this?'

'Well, whoever stole *iLeijchwen* must either be trying to sell it or planning on hoarding it for ever. If it's the latter, we're out in the sand with no canteen. So I'm assuming it's the former. The black market's going to be more open to me than to you.'

'Yeah, good. And tell your aunt she should be ashamed. Here she is, one of the pillars of Little League society, consorting with groupies and smugglers.'

'I heard that!' Aunt Lucy calls out.

Bates laughs. Bobbie assumes that he needs to.

For the last leg of his run, Mulligan takes the uneven stairs at A to Z at a fast pace, two at a time when he can manage it. Panting and

236

sweating, he jogs down the hall and walks into the living room. Aunt Lucy's knitting on the couch; Bobbie sits at her desk. The clock states that it's nearly 2240.

'Evening, sweetheart,' Bobbie says. 'Want some coffee?'

'Gonna take a shower first. We got a long time till the game. Oh-two-hundred, it come on, but they gonna have some kind of pre-game thing first.'

'A memorial show about Tak, too,' Aunt Lucy puts in. 'I done saw it in the listings.'

'Jeezus!' Bobbie snaps. 'I forgot about the game.'

'Hey!' Mulligan grins at her. 'You sure gotta be worried about them carlis, if you forgot about the Series. Say, Aunt Lucy? You watch the news yet?'

'Yeah. Why?'

'The Commissioner, he gonna let the Bears get a replacement in for Tak?'

'No.' Aunt Lucy clacks her needles viciously. 'Rule's a rule, he say. No replacement players in post-season play.'

'Shit! That gonna hurt. If the Bears gonna win, they gonna hafta do it on heart.'

For the first time in months, Mulligan realizes, he doubts that his team is going to take the Series. While he cleans up, he goes over and over the probabilities in his mind. Now and again Tak may have let his nerves get to him, but most of the time he was one of the best closers in the league. If the Bears can get strong performances from their starting pitching, the middle relievers might be able to nail down the last few innings as he used to do. Maybe.

He's combing his wet hair in the bathroom when he hears Bobbie calling him.

'Jack! Comm's for you!'

Someone on the Marauders, he supposes, but when he returns to the living room, he sees Rosa Wallace's face on the three-dee screen. Aunt Lucy has moved to sit in front of the vid pickup.

'Oh my gawd, chica!' Lucy is saying. 'This be all we need. Oh, here be Jack. I gonna talk to you after he get done.'

Jack takes her place. 'Que pasa, Red?'

'I no be sure.' Rosa looks exhausted. 'Yosef, he acting gonzo. No wants to get out of bed. I dunt think he sick. I think it be something in his head.'

'You probably right. You called Georgy yet?'

'You bet. He be here, and the team doctor, and Yosef's regular doctor, too. They all, I mean the doctors, they say he depressed and gotta have medication, but if they dope him up, the league it gonna disqualify him for the Series.' She bites her lower lip, as if to keep from crying. 'Leave us two pitchers short.'

'Can he play if he no gets the meds?'

'I dunt think so. I was kinda hoping you could come over. You be a registered psychic, and maybe you can tell them what going on in there.'

'Hey, I got no med tech training. No way they let me do that. But maybe I can, like, make him feel a little better.' Mulligan pauses, struck by a feeling of doom. 'Say, Yosef, he no supposed to pitch today, is he?'

'Yeah, he sure as hell is.'

'Okay, I gonna get over there soon as I can.'

'Tell you what, I gonna come pick you up. Marisa, she be okay with these medicos here.' Rosa looks over his shoulder. 'Aunt Lucy? I gonna hang up and get over there.'

'Fine, chica,' Lucy says. 'We can talk later.'

The screen goes dark.

'Oh my gawd!' Lucy snarls. 'Just like the boy, crapping out when his team needs him!'

'I take it you've had enough of Mbaye to last you,' Bobbie says.

'For the rest of my life, natural or rejuved.' Lucy scowls at the dark screen. 'But damn, he sure can pitch!'

After he sends Lacey's information to Zizzistre, Bates brings up the latest report on the hunt for the mysterious security guard. Checking employment records for security firms, searching the tiny neighbourhood where non-embassy carlis live, searching welfare rolls, collating AI data on the inhabitants of the Murghi Mahal – the department's put a team of six officers to work on these angles. Another team, directly involved with the Takahashi murder, have rounded up, traced, crossed off as possibilities, or moved to a shortlist and set a watch upon all the usual suspects, low-level thugs, hired muscle, and the like.

He really has no reason to be sitting in his office on a Sunday. His best officers are taking care of everything. Yet he lingers, unwilling to go back to his fusty apartment where the stack of hard-copy reports on his kitchen table will only tempt him to work there instead of here.

'Chief?' the AI says. 'Incoming call on your personal line.'

'Bring it through.' His heart beats briefly faster. 'Thanks.'

As he hoped, Kaz Phaath's image appears. Her hair hangs loose, unbraided but tightly crimped from past braids, and she wears no make-up. Behind her he can see her office.

'Al,' she says, 'I'm being a pest, I know, but do you think you could pick me up early?'

'Oh, I can manage that, yeah.' He grins at her. 'How come?'

'It's the security agents. They are driving everyone here absolutely stark raving mad. Kaz Varesh never stops prodding, Ka Glon keeps turning up in hallways with some new device in his paws. You can't look out a window without seeing them, and none of us can talk about anything else.'

'It sounds like you need to be rescued, all right. I'll volunteer.'

'Thank you so much!' She beams at him, then wrinkles her nose and turns quickly away to sneeze, three times. 'Everyone's shedding, too. It's the stress. The cleanbots must be full of hair.'

'Worse and worse,' Bates says. 'I'm on my way.'

'Tell you what. Why don't I pick you up for a change? That way we can take my car to the game. Riding in a squad car's kind of fun, but people do stare.'

'Yeah, that's true. Okay. When you reach the Police Tower, tell the AI on the main door comm to ring through to me. The code it's going to want is "yellow seventeen".'

'All right.' She jots a note on a pad lying on her desk. 'I'll be there as fast as I can.'

Rosa and Mulligan walk into the Mbayes' pale yellow and beige living room to find the doctors gone. Reynolds, the Bears' head trainer, is standing at the sideboard and helping himself to the plates of food

Marisa's laid out. Across the room Georgy slumps in a yellow-striped chair and glares at the white carpet. Fezawhar sits on a backless bench nearby.

'Fezzy!' Rosa says. 'I thought the doc said you hadda stay in the hospital another night. When you get out?'

'About half an hour ago,' Fezzy says. 'Georgy come by and told me what happen, and I told the doctor I done checked out. Yosef, he raised on Longburrow. He damn near a lizzie when you come right down to it. I been trying to explain to los medicos, but they aint listening. Hey, Jack! Good to see you.'

Georgy looks up and nods Mulligan's way, then returns to his study of the carpet. Mulligan reads hopelessness around him, a mood that translates into a smell like old dishwater. Reynolds wanders over, licking his fingers.

'Yo, Red.' He wipes his hand on his pants leg and offers it to Mulligan. 'Nice to meet you.'

'Thanks.' Mulligan shakes hands. 'Los medicos, what they say?'

'Severe clinical depression. We got prescriptions for three kinds of pills and a pack of preloaded hypos. One of the cops, they gone to the drugstore for us. No one wanted to let Marisa out there alone.'

'Damn right!' Rosa snaps. 'Where she be, anyway?'

'Sitting with her old man.'

'I gonna go see how things going,' Rosa says. 'Jack, mind waiting a minute?'

'Sure dunt.'

Reynolds wanders back to the buffet. Mulligan finds a side chair and sets it down next to Fezawhar. On the wall across from them, a floor-to-ceiling holo displays a view down a long green lawn, edged with trees, to a fountain splashing in sunlight. Distantly in opalescent mist stands a big stone building with skinny towers like fingers poking toward the sky.

'I done told them what be wrong with Yosef,' Fezzy says abruptly. 'He gone to ground. All our people, we do that when things get too much. Get in that damn burrow and slam the door. No can find some real dirt, we just go inside ourselves.'

'Yeah,' Georgy says. 'But lizzies, you can get out again when you want. Yosef, he's stuck.'

'Now, that be true.' Fezzy shakes his head. 'You monkeys, you the fragile types.'

'Señor di Giorgio?' Mulligan says.

'Call me Georgy, kid.'

'Okay. The pills and stuff, you gonna give them to Mbaye?'

'We're gonna have to. You aint seen him yet. No way I'm gonna let another sentient stay in that condition if there's a remedy. I already called Delacruz. Told him to get ready to pitch.' Georgy glances at his watch, then at Fezzy. 'Which reminds me. We gotta leave soon.'

'Yeah,' Fezzy says. 'But I gonna feel better if I see Yosef get some of that medicine first.'

Jack feels his stomach twist and knot. In a few minutes he gets the chance to see Yosef for himself, when Rosa comes back to the living room.

'Jack?' she says. 'You wanna come sit with Yosef for a while? I gotta get ready to leave for the park.'

Mulligan follows Rosa into the blue bedroom. For a moment the holo wall behind the bed disorients him. He thinks that Yosef has somehow gone outside among the roses; then he remembers that the condo lies six metres underground. Marisa, who has been sitting in a nearby chair, stands up, draped from head to foot in a thin black gauze dress over shorts and a smock. Only her face peers out at him.

'Uh, say, Señora Mbaye,' Mulligan says. 'You dunt need to wear mourning yet or anything. Y'know?'

Rosa, behind him, kicks him in the ankle.

'It's not that.' Marisa manages a brief smile. 'It's all these men in the house.'

'Oh. Right. Religion.' Mulligan walks over to the bed. 'Hey, Joe?'

Dressed in baggy grey pants, Yosef lies curled tight around a pillow. He looks grey himself, as if the skin over his entire body has been rubbed with ashes, but Mulligan wonders if he's only externalizing. His eyes are shut and his breath catches ragged in his lungs.

'Joe?' Mulligan says. 'You no asleep.'

Yosef trembles but refuses to open his eyes.

'Marisa?' Rosa says. 'Come on, why dunt you take a break? I gotta leave soon, so come out now while there be another woman here. Get something to eat.'

Marisa hesitates, then nods her agreement. Rosa slips her arm through Marisa's and gently guides her out. Mulligan shuts the door, glances around, and finds a straight chair to pull over beside the bed so he can sit down facing Yosef.

'Joe,' Mulligan says, 'you can come out, or I gonna go in after you. I gonna, if I have to. Like crawling down a burrow. Y'know?'

Yosef's eyes jerk open.

'Huh,' Mulligan says. 'You no can hide from me, y'know. No like the doctors.'

Yosef's panic externalizes as thick smoke, swirling out of his body and filling the room with rank-smelling clouds. Even though Jack knows it's only his own mind working symbolically, he starts coughing. Yosef flops over onto his back and lets his arms relax, though he keeps the pillow lying across his mid-section. The smoke clears.

'Jack, I'm sorry,' he whispers. 'I'm just too tired.'

'Tired of what?'

'Worrying about Marisa. Being scared. Wondering if these butt-ugly thugs are going to kill another friend of mine.' His voice shakes. 'Tired of lying, too. Pretending I'm something I'm not. Or is that pretending I'm not something I am?'

'Well, yeah. It no easy for you. But the team—'

'Oh, god. Don't. Just don't.' Yosef wrenches himself around, flops face down onto the bed and begins to sob.

Mulligan curses himself for a jerk and desperately tries to think of what to say next. Behind him the door opens. He twists around to look, expecting Marisa, but Reynolds walks in carrying a plastowrap bag.

'The cop, he got back from the drug store,' Reynolds says. 'Joe, please, come on now. You gotta swallow some pills for me.'

Yosef goes dead still except for his hands, clutching the sheet like lizzie claws.

'Joe,' Reynolds goes on, 'I dunt want to ask Mulligan to hold you down while I give you one of these here shots.'

Yosef sighs, one long sob of defeat, and rolls over onto his back.

'Okay,' he whispers. 'Whatever you and the doctors say.'

*

At midnight Jack calls to tell Lacey that he's on his way home. By then, Aunt Lucy has left for the ball park, the guest of the Bears again. When she dropped by to pick Lucy up, Rosa remarked that Georgy is hoping she'll bring the team luck. For company Lacey flips on the three-dee only to find the screen full of a collage of Takahashi's best games. She flips it off again.

'You seem agitated, Programmer,' Buddy says.

'I just can't take watching pictures of Takahashi, that's all.' She glances at the time. 'When this memorial thing's over, put on the pre-game show, okay?'

'Certainly, Programmer.'

Lacey walks over to the window and looks out. Across the street stands a slab-sided building that used to house a plastofoam extrusion business. It failed two years ago, but tonight there seems to be a light in one of the long slits of windows on the top floor. Or is it just a reflection from the streetlights? Lacey leaves the living room, walks down the corridor, and turns into an empty room. From this window she can see the factory from a different angle. The window still shines, a faint glow as if someone had a weak light source placed down low or on the floor.

Lacey goes back to the living room, but she stops in the doorway. Buddy's sensors turn to greet her.

'Turn off the lights in here,' Lacey says.

The room goes dark. Once her eyes adjust, Lacey moves toward the windows, but she keeps close to the wall, hopefully invisible to anyone looking in. She sidles up to the window and looks out. No one on the street, but the glow in the factory window persists.

'Lights on,' Lacey says.

The room brightens while Buddy talks.

'Very well, Programmer. Your three-dee programme starts in less than four minutes. I . . . ah, you have an incoming call.'

Blotchy reception and static in the audio tells Lacey that the call's coming from a public comm booth. She manages to make out Blade's large toothy face.

'Greetings from the wee morning hours,' Blade says. 'I have news from the land of shadows where things are murky and obscure.'

'Swell,' Lacey says. 'And I've got a job for you. Think the boss will let you take it?'

'If it's profitable, indubitably. What kind of job, or can't you say?'

'Yeah, being a bodyguard. For me.'

'A pleasant job, then. Tell you what. I am about to return to the beautiful suburban home the boss and I share. I shall place your proposition before him and see what kind of a percentage he'll demand. Shall I contact you again by comm, around sunset tomorrow, say, or would you prefer meeting me somewhere?'

'How about you come here? I dunt think it's a good idea if I go into the Bazaar alone.'

'Good god! I see. Very well. I shall arrive at your emporium some time after midnight. Not too early, never fear about that.'

'Great. I'll be here.'

After he terminates the call, Buddy hums and clicks for some moments. 'Programmer,' he says, 'it distresses me that your life may be in danger.'

'Not half as much as it distresses me, I bet. Hey! What's that?'

Outside a skimmer is landing. When Buddy darkens the lights, Lacey returns to the window, standing beside rather than in front of it. She looks down, then laughs.

'You can turn the lights on, Buddy. It's Jack. Someone must have given him a ride home.'

When Jack comes in, he brings Nunks with him. Lacey can tell by the way they look at each other that they're talking something over, but Jack breaks it off and turns to her.

'Yosef, he real bad. He no gonna play any more this post-season.'

'Oh shit.'

'Yeah. I gonna make myself a drink. Want one?'

'Please. Nunks?'

Nunks shakes his massive bifurcate head. Jack walks over to the wet bar in the corner.

'How'd you get home?' Lacey says.

'One of the Bears' trainers, he give me a ride. Los medicos, they done gave Yosef all these pills. You gotta take them in the right order and at the right time, so Reynolds, he hung around showing Marisa how it worked.'

244

'Oh. Sounds grim.'

'Yeah, it was. I keep wondering, those pills, if they be like the ones the carlis use to mind-wipe someone's psi. Sure were enough of them.' He pauses, turning toward Nunks. 'Nunks, he say they gonna turn Yosef into a zombie till he get used to them.'

Lacey shudders like a wet dog. On the three-dee the pre-game show is starting. She flops down into her corner of the couch and watches to give herself something else to think about. Nunks pulls over a chair and joins her. Jack hands her a glass of scotch and water, then takes his to the other corner of the couch.

'You didn't see anyone hanging around here, did you?' Lacey asks. 'When you drove up just now?'

'Yeah. Bates musta put some cops on us, huh? Two guys, one sitting in a car round back, the other dude in a doorway over on Y Street.'

'Bates never said he was going to put us under surveillance.' Lacey gets up. 'Buddy, get me through to him, will you?'

Although Chief Bates has left the office, his AI reaches him over his comm link. Bates confirms that whoever's staking out A to Z has nothing to do with the city police.

'I'll get a couple of officers over there,' Bates says. 'And have the regular patrols drive around your block every hour or so. That should send the message.'

'Thanks, Chief. And there might be someone camping out in the old CustomPack factory across the street from me, too.'

Lacey goes into the dark bedroom and stays watching at the window until the first patrol car arrives. It glides past, makes a U turn at the corner, glides back and parks in front of the factory. Two officers get out and go to the door. She can see them examining the lock; then one of them steps back and pulls a comm unit out of his pocket. In a few minutes, a second car arrives. When these officers get out, she can see that one of them is carrying a spray gun.

'Hey, Bobbie?' Jack is standing in the doorway. 'The game, it be on.'

'The real show's in here, sweetheart.'

Jack walks over to join her and looks out.

'Jeez,' he says. 'Cops.'

With a bang that carries across the street, a cop kicks in the door.

The officer with the spray gun goes in first; two others follow; the fourth stays outside with his comm link raised, ready to call for reinforcements.

'I gonna go watch the game,' Jack says. 'I feel loco for doing it, but I gotta.'

'Sure,' Lacey says. 'I'll join you when this is over.'

It takes a while, some ten minutes at least by her rough reckoning, but eventually the three cops return with someone handcuffed among them. By the streetlight Lacey can tell only that he's human and male. At the least they'll be able to book him overday on trespassing charges, which means she'll be able to get some sleep. She watches while they load him into one of the squad cars, then leaves the window.

In the living room she finds the game gone to a commercial break and Jack looking desolate. Nunks turns her way and moans with a spread of his hands.

'Delacruz done give up three runs,' Jack says. 'In the first. The Bears, they go down in order.'

'I see.' Lacey drops onto the couch beside him. 'Gonna be a long night.'

'Well, hell, that was pathetic,' Bates says. 'Dunt get up yet. We'll let the crowd clear out a little first.'

'I don't understand this sport,' Kaz Phaath says. 'But I must say these players didn't resemble those we watched on the holocast. The death of their colleague must have upset them.'

'Death tends to upset people, yeah. But jeez, I dint expect a seven to nothing rout.'

'Well, there was the news, too, about that other pitcher.'

'Yeah, that's true. Mbaye on the disabled list for the whole post-season.' Bates shakes his head. 'Pathetic.'

'Perhaps they'll do better tomorrow. Will they play only two games here?'

'Three. Then they go back to Sarah if more games are necessary. Right now, that's looking like a real big if.'

Around them the gloomy crowd is standing up, collecting pennants, hats, cushions, pausing to drink the last of their beer or their soda. Bates sees a couple of human kids near tears. None of the adults look much happier as they jam the stairs up and out.

'I'm sorry the evening dint go better for you,' Bates says.

'It's all right,' Kaz Phaath says. 'The atmosphere at the embassy is much worse.'

'Yeah, guess so. It's really sad about Ka Jekhonas. I dunt understand how the Council can expect him to do that, but then I know what honour means to your people.'

'Do what?' Kaz Phaath turns toward him.

'Jeezchrise, I'm sorry! I thought you knew. Ka Pral was telling me, and I figured he'd have told you as well. He said that Ka Jekhonas will have to commit suicide if *iLeijchwen's* not returned.'

She raises her hand to her throat and gasps for breath. In the glaring light of the stadium he can see that her face has turned ashen.

'I'm sorry,' he repeats. 'I really thought you knew.'

'Don't blame yourself.' She whispers so softly he has to lean forward to hear. 'They should have told me. I never thought—' She hesitates, then speaks a few soft words in the carli language.

Bates sits cursing himself for several long minutes, but he can think of nothing to make up for his gaffe. On the stairways the crush is easing. He stands up and holds out his hand.

'Let's go, okay?' he says.

'Yes, thank you.' She gets up, hesitates, then lets him take her hand for the walk out.

In the parking lot Kaz Phaath's dark red Toyota skimmer sits in a drift of paper cups and other trash. She unlocks it with the remote, then takes a moment to kick the worst of the trash away before she gets in. Bates slides into the passenger seat.

'Nice car,' he remarks. 'But I'm surprised you don't use one of the official skimmers.'

'I really prefer smaller vehicles when I don't need to uphold the dignity of the Confederation. This one is mine. I had planned to ship it home when I left Hagar.'

'You had planned? Plans have changed?'

'I hope not.' She runs a fingertip over the wheel. 'Things are so awful. If we do have to evacuate, we'll have to leave the big things behind.'

'Well, I'm doing my best to get *iLeijchwen* back for you.'

'I know.' She looks up with one of her brilliant smiles. 'And that gives me hope.'

'Thanks.'

A solid stream of cars bunch up in the lane toward the exit, slow to a crawl, then stop. Kaz Phaath leans back in her seat.

'No use in joining that queue,' she says. 'Is it true what I hear, that Martinelli is actually coming here?'

'He's talking about it, yeah, the idiot.'

'I don't care if the Esperance police did search, you know that he's responsible – somehow.'

'How come you so sure Martinelli's involved?'

'He's so stupid. I've listened to his speeches.'

'You got a stronger stomach than I do.'

'I needed it, believe me. After what he said about the Confederation – if you had the practice here, I would call personal challenge. Not that he's worthy of the honour.'

'Look, even if he's a complete scumbag, which is the truth but dunt you quote me, he's no the one who has *iLeijchwen*, and that's the truth, too.'

'"Scumbag". Have I mentioned how much you've expanded my vocabulary, Al?' She grins, briefly. 'But humans like Martinelli will be the reason your Republic collapses, you know. This creature is one of your leaders.'

'Does government always lead?'

'It should. Of course.'

'Know something? The Republic's survived for five hundred years now, and Martinelli's no worse than a lot of our politicians have been, from the beginning back on Old Earth right down the time line.'

'I've read about this, yes. I do not understand how it's possible.'

'Humans thrive on chaos, I guess.'

'No one can possibly thrive on chaos. Or in it, for that matter.'

'It's not easy, no. But when I look back on some of the things our species have managed to live through, I can't say that chaos is always fatal.'

Kaz Phaath turns to look at him, her lips slightly parted, her eyes

248

narrow. She starts to speak, then merely sighs and leans forward, peering out the windshield.

'That jam's breaking up. Let's go. I'm to drop you at the Police Tower, then?'

'Please. That's where my skimmer is.'

The Bears lost. Bad. After a troubled day's sleep, Mulligan wakes to this thought and a directly related hangover. He staggers into the bathroom, finds a bottle of analgesics, and takes several too many. For a moment he stares at his puffy-eyed face in the mirror.

'You gotta stop drinking so much,' he tells himself.

The reflection has the look of a man who's heard the same thing too many times to take it seriously. With a shrug Mulligan turns away.

Out in the living room the windows have turned clear enough for him to see the aurora dancing in the sky. Buddy clacks and hums.

'Mulligan unit, have you spoke with the programmer yet?'

'No had the chance, plugsucker. Too many things coming down.'

'I suggest that speed is important. What if Wazerzis agrees, and she accepts the commission? She will not be able to renege once she has.'

'Able to what?'

'Back out of the deal.'

'Oh. I dint know that.'

'That's why I told you, yes.' Buddy makes a whirring noise. 'Aunt Lucy appears to be approaching. We cannot talk. But please, act soon.'

Sarojini wakes to the holonews. She lies in bed and listens to the Alliance ambassador offering ambiguously labelled 'support' to the Republic in this current crisis. His long white nose wobbles and shakes as he condemns 'veiled aggression' in equally veiled language. With a sigh she flips off the three-dee and turns on her net access. *You've miscalculated*, she tells herself. *If there's a war, what will happen to all of us?*

To distract herself she accesses her favourite news site and glances down the personals.

'Queen of Hearts, Harry longs to hear your voice.'

So – Sandy wants her to call, does she? Sarojini gets out of bed and dresses fast. The sooner she hears what Sandy has to say, the better.

Monday evening Bates reaches his office at his usual time, 2000 hours, to discover that life has just become even more interesting. Since the Interplanetary Commissioner of Baseball must by terms of his office attend every Galactic Series game, the current commissioner is staying downtown in one of Polar City's few luxury hotels. At the moment, several hundred angry citizens are picketing out in front to protest his decisions over replacement players for the Bears.

'It's peaceful so far,' his AI tells him. 'Before you arrived, Captain Hernandez detailed six officers to go down and be visible.'

'Good. Send his AI a note commending him.'

The real surprise comes a hour later, when Sergeant Nagura hurries into his office with a clipboard.

'Chief,' she says, 'we've got another leak.'

Bates realizes that he's too angry to even swear.

'This one could be dangerous,' Nagura goes on. 'The holocasters have been saying that Takahashi had *iLeijchwen* but now it's disappeared again.'

'Real dangerous, yeah.'

When Nagura hands him the clipboard, he presses 'play'. On the small screen the Channel Twenty Newsbreak appears.

'. . . team officials refused to speculate as to why the murdered relief pitcher, credited with the save in the Bears' championship-winning game last month, had the carli artefact in his possession. But forensic data, revealed publicly for the first time in this Channel Twenty exclusive, prove conclusively that the alien masterpiece was carried in the luggage of Michael Akimo Takahashi, who met his death some hours later. Unnamed sources within the police department—'

'—are meat, if I get my hands on them.' Bates punches 'stop', savagely. 'I'd better get over to the Confederation Embassy and smooth some ruffled fur, but I think I'll call the PBI first.'

'They'll need to know, yes,' Nagura says.

Some hours later, after several hurried conferences at the Police Tower, Bates drives to the embassy building. The blonde receptionist sends him straight through to Ka Pral's office, where Ka Pral waits

250

with Kaz Varesh and, much to Bates's surprise, Kaz Phaath. When Bates walks in, Ka Pral shuts the door. No one offers any refreshment, no one sits down.

'Mr Secretary,' Bates begins, 'do you recall an incident some months back, when my government discovered representatives of a new sapient race within our system, only to learn that your own honoured government already knew of this? You extended your personal apologies to me on that occasion. I now do likewise, if I may.'

He watches anxiously as Ka Pral considers, his ears laid back. Kaz Varesh has her arms crossed over her chest.

'I kept this secret,' Bates goes on, 'at the order of my superior, the head of the Republic's Public Bureau of Investigation.'

Ka Pral's ears relax to full extension. 'My dear Bates, then you were as helpless as I, in the situation to which you refer.'

'I was, yes. My superior felt that the news would alarm you, as I see it has.'

'Of course! Our sources assured us that *iLeijchwen* had been transported to your capital for the senator. I am sure you can understand how upset we of the embassy were to discover that our national treasure had actually been returned here, to this very planet, while we remained ignorant of the fact.'

'I informed my superior that you would be much more deeply alarmed if you found the news out some other way.'

'You've certainly been proved right in that,' Kaz Varesh says. 'I trust you're taking steps to stop this leak?'

'It's not one of our officers. Someone with false identity papers passed the news along and claimed to be from the police. From now on, every news channel is going to clear every story with me first.'

'Good,' Kaz Varesh says. 'Then the question becomes, who did pass along the information? Besides the municipal police, who knew?'

Whoever paid Miss Midori, Bates thinks, although habitual caution keeps him from mentioning her. But there are other possibilities outside his department. He allows himself a smile. 'I am forced to pass all information gathered along to the PBI.'

'How delightful for you!' Kaz Varesh bobs her head. 'Nothing like a little inter-departmental revenge to brighten a day, I always say.'

Bates laughs. For the first time he dares to look at Kaz Phaath. Her face has resumed its imitation-carli lack of expression, but something lurks deep in her dark velvet eyes.

'You lied to me,' she says.

'I dint lie, exactly, just dint tell you everything. I had to. It's part of my job.'

'Of course.' She smiles, and at last he can decipher her feeling on the matter: approval.

Ka Pral insists on walking Bates out to his squad car, parked in back of the embassy. They linger, looking up at the shifting purples and greens of the aurora. Somewhere beyond the lights the Confederation heavy cruiser hangs in geosynchronous orbit.

'I'm going to tell Kaz Varesh this in a report,' Bates says, 'but I want you to know it, too. We're doing our best to keep *iLeijchwen* here in Polar City.'

'It will be much easier to recover that way, yes,' Ka Pral says.

'Exactly. Of course, it may be in danger. Should some accident happen to the city, *iLeijchwen* would share in it.'

For a moment Ka Pral goes as still as a frightened lizzie. 'That would be most unfortunate.'

'I thought so, yeah.'

'This is such an important point that I'll make sure my superiors understand the danger. Of course, as long as there's any threat of intervention from the Alliance, a prudent government must take steps to guard itself, no matter what the risk to individuals or individual objects.'

'Naturally.'

As he's driving back to his office, Bates is considering Ka Pral's remarks. He hopes he's translating them correctly into 'get the Hoppers off our backs and we'll take our ship out of orbit'. Knowing the Alliance as he does, however, he can assume that they'll make things worse before they make them better.

The newscasters must love days like this, Sarojini thinks: a Bears' loss, a murder of a Bears' player, a stolen alien artefact brought on-planet by that same player, the possibility of war. She watches each clip, reads every word, listens to megabytes of news analysis, follows every link and sidebar, but she finds no mention of a certain security guard's encounter with Takahashi during the Welcome Home. On the other hand, the police may not be releasing everything they know.

She turns off the news and gets ready to leave. She dresses strangely, for her, first in a plain white jumpsuit that will keep her decent and anonymous once she sheds her camouflage, and then the camouflage itself – a sari of rough fabric and loud colours topped off with far too many fake-gold bangles. She checks her pocket to make sure she has the tiny canister of *KeepBack*! A silly name, she always thinks, but she feels safer carrying the spray repellent, especially in the Bazaar.

Though she feels impossibly garish, once she reaches the Outworld Bazaar she blends into that world of tarnished spangles and flashing holosigns. Pretty boys in doorways, card sharks in windows – she ignores them and enters a quasi-legal public comm shop that she's used before. She can trust them to ignore all sorts of legally required record-keeping, just as they're willing to ignore illegal hardware. She shuts herself into a booth, takes a distorter out of her handbag, and couples it onto the input mike.

Despite the device, she keeps her message short. 'When you have the deal set up, post a personal saying "the cards say yes for Harry". I'll contact you about a meeting place.' She hits the cut-off button on the holorecorder before she turns off the distorter. A few moments later, a soft *ping* announces the cycle's end, and a message cube drops into her waiting hand.

The inner pocket of her white jumpsuit holds an empty chewing spice tube, carefully cleaned and wrapped in a piece of plain white plastic. Inside she earlier put a single hair, tweezed from the surface of *iLeijchwen*, proof for the principals in this deal that she really does have the weaving. She places both tube and message cube in a plain white box furnished by the comm shop, fills in an address, and leaves the booth. The lizzie attendant has been dreamdusting; her second eyelids keep closing and opening and she doesn't notice her client is wearing gloves. Once Sarojini pays for the transaction in cash, she walks away from the shop, removing the gloves as she leaves.

A short time later, a modestly dressed woman in a white jumpsuit gets on the Metro for the Civic Centre downtown.

*

As the night wears on, Bates keeps a careful eye on the public demonstration. Emotions are running high on the picket line outside the commissioner's hotel, but so far they've restricted themselves to signs, chants, and a single scattering of stones thrown at one point at the uniformed doorman. The crowd itself grabbed the stone-thrower and turned him over to the police.

Other good news arrives in the form of Sergeant Maddock, who announces that he has something to report. Bates waves him toward the extra office chair.

'About damn time we had some breaks. What do we have?'

'Zizzistre just phoned this report in. He found the donna who gave that stocking to Mike Takahashi. Name's Marion Scheffler, but she goes by Midori, just like Lacey said. She really does work for that bank, but Izzy thinks some foreign government recruited her for this job. She travels all the time, and she wouldn't be real noticeable.'

'Planting bugs sounds like routine operative work, all right. It should be enough for a warrant. Have Izzy get one and pick her up.'

'He figured you'd say that. He's checking with Judge King right now.'

'Good. Has anyone found this Jay Gagne yet? The one running the illegal card games?'

'No, sir,' Maddock says. 'Not yet.'

The AI unit suddenly hums and clicks.

'What is it?' Bates says.

'If I may be so bold, sir, I have information about Jay Gagne.'

'You what?'

'An elementary knowledge of Old Earth languages is built into one of my basic data modules. In the language known as Francais, there was a phrase, *zhuh gain*, which bears an audio resemblance to Jay Gagne.'

'It sure does. What does it mean?'

'I win.'

Bates and Maddock both laugh.

'Thanks,' Bates says to the AI. 'Good work! A perfect fake name for a gambler, all right.'

*

Alison Glover stands in the middle of Lacey's living room and looks slowly around her. She wears leather pants, but with a plain black tunic this time, and her hair is neatly braided, ready for freefall.

'Jeez, Lacey, this is a strange place.'

'Sure is,' Lacey says, grinning. 'That's one reason it suits me.'

'Okay. Where's the boyfriend tonight?'

'At practice. He plays on a semi-pro baseball team.'

'A real athlete, huh? How is he at indoor sports?'

'Oh shut up!'

Alison laughs and flops down on the couch. Lacey brings her a drink and sits down opposite her.

'I have to admit I'm kind of surprised you'd drop by like this,' she says.

'Hey, you're on the route to the spaceport, aren't you? Thought I'd say goodbye.'

'You've got that full cargo, then?'

'Signed the manifest last night for cube components. Look, Bobbie, you know a hell of a lot more about politics than I do. This situation, with that carli rag missing and all, it's pretty dangerous, isn't it?'

'Oh yeah, and it just got worst.' Lacey waves vaguely at the three-dee screen. 'The midnight news announced two Alliance heavy cruisers made orbit a while ago.'

'Oh shit! Two, huh?'

'One more than the Cons, yeah. Their embassy says they're here as a token of the Alliance's friendship toward the Republic.'

'To tell the Cons to sod off,' Alison translates. 'Right?'

'Right. This is interesting. With the 'Lies taking a hand, it's not real likely that the Cons will invade us. On the other hand, it ups the ante real high. If there's a war between the Cons and the 'Lies, the first move one of them will make is to take out the spaceport to keep the other's ground troops off-planet. And that attack will take Port-town with it and a big hunk of the city as well.' Lacey pauses for a smile. 'You're leaving just in time.'

'Dunt grin like that, you idiot! But hey, we do have a Navy of our own.'

'Sure. How long do you think it's going to last? We'll fight to the last sentient, but that'll maybe take a week.'

'Do you realize you said "we"?'

'No. Up yours.'

Alison looks away, thinking. 'Look, Bobbie, why dunt you come with me? *Freebird*'s got a light cargo. You can find work starside, papers or no papers. A lot of ships are too desperate for good comp officers to ask dumb questions.'

'Thanks,' Lacey says, 'but no thanks.'

'Hey, you're the one who told me the news. Bobbie, you got to get out of here! Hell, bring the boyfriend too. You probably no would want to go without him, and he can always cook or something.'

The temptation overwhelms her. To get back into deep space, to take Jack with her, even, which the Navy would never allow her to do – safety, yes, but the freedom calls her more. But if she left, if they left tonight, what about the others – her aunts, her family, Buddy, Nunks? She'd be leaving them behind to die.

'I can't,' Lacey says. 'There's still a good chance I can find that damned carli rag.'

'If you don't—'

'Hey, if the 'Lies or the Cons hit the spaceport, at least I won't have to live to regret my decision.'

'You're impossible. Know that?' Alison contemplates the ceiling. 'We got a long lead time for delivering that cargo. Tell you what. I'll be up at Space Dock for a couple more days. You change your mind, you give me a call.'

'You dunt have to wait. I'm staying.'

'Yeah? Well, there's some electrical work the *Freebird*'s going to need done sooner or later. Might as well be sooner. You know where to reach me if you want to.'

Not long after Alison leaves, Jack comes home. Lacey's consulting some of the files Buddy hacked from the police department when distantly a door bangs shut. Someone runs up the stairs and footsteps hurry down the hall.

'Jack?' she calls out.

'Yeah. Just me.'

Jack strides in, then hesitates, leaning in the doorway. He's dressed in beaten-up jeans and his Marauders shirt, smeared down one side with the reddish dirt of the Park and Rec field, but the way he moves, the way he stands, his easy male grace – she feels that she could look, simply look at him, for hours.

'Have a good practice?' she says.

'Yeah. Aunt Lucy, she here?'

'No, she went to the park with Rosa again.'

'Good.' He looks at her so strangely that she wonders if perhaps he's angry with her.

'Is something wrong?' Lacey says.

'We gotta talk. I no can take this any more.'

'Take what?'

He shrugs, his eyes lost in shadow. Buddy clears his throat.

'Programmer, I do not wish to invade Mulligan's privacy or yours, but I am incapable of moving from the room.'

'I get it, Buddy,' Lacey says. 'We'll leave.'

Without a word Jack turns and strides out. When she follows him into the bedroom, he shuts the door behind them. In the corner, the small brass lamp lights the room with a tolerable glow. Jack sits down on the end of the bed, his hands dangling between his knees. Lacey leans against the chest of drawers opposite.

'What's wrong?' she says.

'Buddy, he told me you want to go back to the Navy. Said you wrote some letter to old Iron Snout.'

'Damn him! I dint want you to know.'

'Yeah, that be plenty obvious. Jeezchrise! You coulda levelled with me upfront.'

'I dint want you to worry.'

'Oh, great. Just thanks a whole lot.'

'I'm sorry. I should have told you, yeah.'

A long drift of his pale hair has fallen forward into his eyes. He reaches up and combs it back with his fingers.

'It's the long shot from hell, Jack,' Lacey goes on. 'I'll bet anything you want that they won't take me back. But I had to know, once and for all.'

'Long shots done paid off before. Suppose they say yes. You gonna go?'

'Well, uh—'

'I bet you do go. I bet there just aint, like, nothing to keep you

257

here. No can blame you. I no could believe it when you took me in, y'know? Aint surprised now that you be leaving. Dunt you think I know what a loser—'

'Dunt say shit like that! I dunt want to leave you.'

'But you want deep space more . . . well, dunt you?'

Lacey hesitates, wondering if he's speaking the truth. Had someone else asked her that question, she would have said yes unthinkingly, but watching him watch her, with his eyes so full of hurt, she barely knows what she does think. All at once he looks down at the floor.

'Guess I know the answer to that,' he says, his voice shaking.

'No! I mean – Jack, I do love you. You believe me, dunt you?'

'Oh yeah. Far as that go. I mean, like, if the Navy, they won't give you your commission back, I gonna be some kind of second best.'

'That's not it at all. Look, suppose I did get reinstated. You could stay here with Nunks. I'd get shore leave, I'd be stationed out of Hagar. Not like I'd be gone for ever.'

'Just maybe ten months a year.'

'Well, yeah. You're right. It wouldn't be fair to you.'

'Dunt sound like you gonna miss me much for them ten months.'

'What? Oh, come on!'

He gets up, walks the few steps over to her, then tilts his head to one side and considers her with unfocused eyes.

'You scared,' he says at last. 'Jeezus, Bobbie, I can feel it pouring off of you. What's scaring you?' He hesitates, his mouth slack. 'Oh shit, you scared of me!'

'Damn right. You can read my mind. Sometimes it drives me up the wall.'

'Well, I no can hide a damn thing from you either.' His eyes fill with tears and he turns away, wiping them awkwardly on his sleeve. 'Dunt leave me 'cause of that, Bobbie. Tell me you think I be some stinking Rat Yard loser, tell me you love the Navy more – I dunt care. But, oh god, please dunt be something else I gonna lose, cause of this goddamn talent crap I never wanted.'

'I never thought of it that way before. I dint mean it that way.'

'Yeah?' He turns around. 'Well, how the hell else I supposed to take it?'

'No other way, I guess. I'm sorry, Jack.'

He sits down again on the end of the bed and runs both hands through his hair. She can feel his hurt almost palpably, as if she were suddenly the psychic. *He's right*, Lacey thinks. *He no can hide anything – from anyone*. She finds herself remembering Alison's offer, and how despite everything she turned it down. Things have changed, she realizes, since she was that young recruit so desperate for the stars – her only way off a world that held nothing for her, or so she thought. Now she has something to leave behind, something to lose.

'Tell you what,' she says. 'If they offer me my commission back, I'm no going to take it.'

He looks up, his lips half parted.

'I mean it.' She walks over and sits down beside him. 'I no can leave you. I was just kidding myself, thinking I could.'

'You sure?'

'Real sure.' She manages a smile.

His tears run, spill over. Mostly because she cannot stand to see anyone cry, Lacey throws her arms around him. He holds her close, and she can feel him shaking.

'Okay, Jack?' she whispers.

'Okay.' He lets her go. 'Hell, so much for romance. I gotta blow my nose.'

Chapter Twelve

Late in the morning hours, the Bears lose the fourth game of the Series, putting the Eagles up three games to one. With sunset and the first holonews, the dismal fact spreads that one more Bears' loss means the Eagles take the championship. In Polar City a stunned sort of calm prevails, but Bates doubts that this condition will last past tonight's game, simply because he doubts if the Bears can pull off a win. As he drives to work that evening, he listens to audio feed from a local comm-call sports show. The fans believe their team is being robbed blind. That they also see themselves potential victims of an unjustified war adds to the rage. From his car Bates calls in and has the day-shift captain assign more officers to guarding the commissioner's hotel. The demonstrators now number over a thousand.

Once Bates gets to his office, he finds a screen full of mail waiting for him. He's just sat down to read it when Maddock comes in with a handful of paper.

'Chief? I got that roster of who's pulling overtime you said you wanted to look at.'

Bates holds his hand out for the stack. 'Dunt really want to look at the thing, but I'd better. I dunt give a damn what the mayor thinks, no way are we putting anyone out there who's already done a double shift.'

Bates has nearly finished reading the list when Officer Zizzistre sticks his head into the doorway.

'Chief?' Izzy says. 'I think you maybe want to get in on this.'

'Yeah? What is it?'

'I got the warrant on that Scheffler donna, and I got her down in interrogation right now. She been screaming for her lawyer, so I let her call him and I dint ask her nada yet besides her name.'

'Muy bueno,' Bates says. 'Her lawyer on the way?'

Izzy nods, his snout furrowed with worry. 'Yeah, and you no gonna like who it is. Sikklith.'

'Okay, that tells us she's guilty. I dunt think that shyster ever represented anybody innocent except by accident.' Bates scowls at the paper in his hand without seeing it. 'I'd better get hold of Akeli. He's going to want agents here for this. Interstellar spying falls into his jurisdiction. Go take Midori to the conference room.'

Bates has time to finish reviewing the evening duty rosters before everyone has assembled around the large table: Midori Scheffler, her attorney Sna Sikklith, Officer Zizzistre, and two PBI agents in the crisp, anonymous blue business shorts and waistcoats that might as well be a uniform – quite a contrast to Sikklith's trademark loud plaid suit. Scheffler wears black, Bates notices, and no make-up whatsoever. Looking at the woman, Bates can see that in normal circumstances, she'd have both charm and sex appeal. At the moment she sits slumped, her eyes narrow, her lips tight, as if she's afraid she'll blurt something incriminating.

With a glance at the attorney, Bates begins. 'Your name is Marion Louise Scheffler. You're employed as a senior loan officer at First National Bank here in Polar City, and four days ago you returned from Sarah on the same ship as members of the Polar City Bears. Is this correct?'

'I am Marion Scheffler.'

'Do you sometimes go by the name of Midori?'

'Yes. My attorney, Mr Sikklith, is going to answer any additional questions.'

The olive-drab lizzie hisses, displaying dozens of gleaming sharp teeth, three of them gold-capped. 'Come on, Bates! My client's personal affairs are her own, and I no have heard any reason she should inform you of them.'

Izzy reaches for the official passenger list of the *President Nkrumah*, but the attorney waves it away. 'Oh, no doubt you can prove her presence on said ship. I so stipulate. What's lacking is cause for police interest in her private life.'

'We're investigating the murder of Michael Takahashi, and we have reason to believe your client was, ah, intimately acquainted with him

261

shortly before he was killed.' While he speaks, Bates watches Scheffler. Some feeling stirs in her half-dead eyes.

Sikklith interrupts before she can respond. 'Even if this were so, I repeat, what concern is it of the police? You may want citizens to tell you about their private lives, Chief Bates, but I'm not aware of any law requiring them to do so.'

'But planting unregistered listening devices on other sentients, Sikklith, *is* against the law. And I bet you know that, dunt you, Midori?'

Officer Zizzistre holds up a transparent evidence bag containing a single black-lace stocking. Bates focuses his attention on Midori's face. It turns dead pale and she raises a hand to her mouth, as if she could shove her sudden gasp back in. The male PBI agent leans forward and stares at the evidence bag.

'Smart thread?' he asks. Izzy nods.

'We've got witnesses,' Bates goes on, 'who swear that you handed out four of these little souvenirs. I dunt think you were just eaves-dropping on your boyfriends for fun. Who asked you to plant those stockings, Midori? You co-operate with us, and maybe we can make it a bit easier on you.'

Sikklith shifts uncomfortably and opens his beak, but Midori talks first. 'I . . . could I have a few minutes to talk with my attorney? Alone?'

Bates gets to his feet. 'Sure,' he said. 'Just remember. You'll do yourself a favour by co-operating.'

Bates shepherds Izzy and the PBI agents out ahead of him, then closes the door. They wait for a few minutes, saying very little, until Sikklith opens the door and waves them back in. Bates looks Midori over. She returns his stare boldly, but her cheeks shine and she squeezes a wad of wet tissue in one hand.

'Chief Bates,' Sikklith says, 'we are prepared to co-operate with both your investigation and the one the federal authorities will no doubt wish to conduct.'

The two PBI agents exchange a startled glance.

'However, I want some guarantees first,' Sikklith goes on. 'I suggest we meet with the DA. This will cause an unavoidable delay, I realize, but—'

'Look,' Bates interrupts. 'I don't have the authority to make any deals, but we need this information fast. We're trying to prevent a war here, Sikklith, and if the Cons decide to fry the city that mansion of yours is going to fry with it. What about I give you my personal word that I'll tell the DA to cut you all the slack she possibly can? Here, in front of witnesses. And then I'll send them outside, and Midori can tell me what she knows in private.'

Sikklith considers, sucking each of his many teeth in sequence. Midori stares out at nothing.

'Very well,' Sikklith says at last. 'You promise me you'll talk to the DA and push for indemnity. I know she has the last word, yeah, but what you say will carry weight.'

'I promise.' Barts turns and glances at the other officers. 'If you'll wait for me outside?'

They clear the room in surprised silence. Zizzistre shuts the door hard behind them. Bates smiles.

'Start talking,' he says.

'Very well. Recently my client was approached by representatives of the Coreward Alliance—'

'Oh god!' Midori breaks in. 'I didn't think—' Her voice thick, with tears, quavers as she finishes. 'I never thought they'd kill anybody. I never thought they'd kill Tak.'

She drops her face to her hands and weeps. Sikklith reaches inside his waistcoat and brings out a large handkerchief. She takes it and begins wiping her eyes.

'Be calm, my dear,' Sikklith says. 'I'll tell the chief for you.'

An hour and a half later, Bates has some answers and a headache. He lets the PBI operatives take away Scheffler, her lawyer, and a scribbled note to the DA that fulfils his promise, then gives Izzy a recap back in his office.

'Our Midori likes excitement in her life,' Bates says, 'too much for her own good. She dunt know the name of her handler, but it sounds like Royall himself. Akeli's agents will show her some pix. Anyway, he approached her to do some work for the Alliance and she thought it sounded like fun. Well-paid fun. Unfortunately, her handlers told her only as much about the situation as she needed to know. They wanted to get their hands on *iLeijchwen* for reasons they never

263

explained. When she got on board the *Calypso*, she knew only that someone on the ship might have the artefact. Once she arrived on Sarah, however, her contact told her that Yosef Mbaye was carrying it.'

'So they done learned something in that four days, huh?' Zizzistre says.

'Sounds like it, yeah. She kept in touch with the team, and on the way home she got lucky. The bug she left in Takahashi's cabin picked up primo information. By the way, those thugs were supposed to take the stocking out of his luggage. They were so panicked when Tak died that they forgot.'

'Dunt suppose she identified them?'

'Oh yeah, she described them. I had the AI pull up matches, and she fingered them, all right. That's the good news.'

'The bad?'

'They're inside the Alliance Embassy. They have diplomatic immunity. Oh, and one of them matches the description we got from Rosa Wallace, that guy that came after her.'

Zizzistre slaps his tail on the floor so hard that two nearby stacks of paper slip and spill.

'Here's the best part, Izzy. They also match the descriptions of the men that hooker saw disposing of Moses Oliver's corpse. And we no can arrest them for that, either.'

'Jeezus! And that guy we caught watching Lacey, he works for the 'Lies, too. Chief, this means the Hoppers behind the theft!'

'Not necessarily. No jumping to conclusions. I've seen the place where the carlis kept the thing, dunt forget. I no can imagine anyone from outside getting in and out with it. Gri Nerosi, yeah, he could have stolen it. Bobbie Lacey tells me the scum at the bottom of the Bazaar heard that a carli was looking for someone to fence stolen property. Oliver volunteered.'

'Okay, but aint it logical that the Hoppers, they were the ones who put Oliver up to it?'

'Logical dunt meant actual.' Bates pauses for a grin. 'If they were, then Oliver double-crossed them by sending the artefact to Sarah with Yosef Mbaye.'

'Double-crossing Hoppers, it an easy way to die young.'

'Or maybe Oliver took the thing on spec and found he could get a good price from Martinelli. Oliver ran information to both sides. What if he sold the Hoppers the info that he was smuggling a carli artefact?'

'And then they killed him to get it? Sounds like them, yeah.'

'Only he dint have it when they killed him. That's where things got confused.'

Zizzistre nods, thinking.

'Either way, though,' Bates continues, 'if the Hoppers get their hands on it, there's going to be hell to pay.'

'The Cons, they gonna be mad enough when they figure out the Hoppers muscled in on this racket. Dunt matter who Nerosi stole it for, then.'

'Damn right. And if we dunt get their cloth back, the carlis are going to declare war as soon as they find out.'

'They gonna declare war anyway, aint they? Jeez, it be the twenty-fourth already, Chief.'

Bates had nothing to say to that. For a long moment or two they sit together, neither speaking. Zizzistre gets up with a shake of his head.

'What the hell,' he says. 'You gonna go to the game tonight, Chief?'

'No. I had enough with Game Three, thanks.'

'You never know. Might win one yet.'

Again the silence hangs between them. With a last sigh Zizzistre leaves, and Bates returns to his paperwork. He wants every possible officer either out on the streets of Porttown or down at the baseball stadium before the game ends. Without a police escort, the commissioner may have a hard time reaching his hotel.

Yosef sits in the yellow-striped chair in his living room and smiles out at nothing. His dark eyes stare, like marbles stuck in a mask. His hands lie flaccid on his thighs. Draped in her black gauze, Marisa sits on the backless bench nearby. Mulligan can read how hard she fights to keep from crying. He himself feels like vomiting, but he forces out a smile.

'Hey, Joe,' Mulligan says. 'You look like you be feeling better today.'

Very slowly Yosef turns his head and looks his way. 'Yeah,' he says, and his voice runs slowly, too. 'Guess I do.'

Marisa catches her breath in a sob. Mulligan tries to think of something reassuring to say but fails. The worst thing, he realizes, is that Yosef has become a psychic blank. Mulligan can read nothing, pick up nothing, feel nothing of the talents Yosef once possessed. The psychotropic drugs have temporarily removed his curse, but what they've left behind hardly rates as a sentient being.

When Rosa strides in, her carrysack slung over one shoulder, Mulligan feels like hailing her as a saviour.

'I better get going,' Rosa announces. 'Jack, want a ride home? It be on my way to the park.'

'Yeah, sure do. Uh, well, say, Marisa. Nice to see you.'

She crouches on her bench and gazes up at him, her face framed in black.

'I gonna come back right after the game,' Rosa tells her.

At that Marisa manages to smile.

When they leave, Officer Tolridge sits in the back seat of Rosa's Jaguar. The skimmer runs so quietly that Tolridge will be able to overhear any honest conversation. Neither Mulligan nor Rosa speaks while she backs the skimmer out of the underground garage and eases it into the air.

Mulligan says at last, 'Any of the rest of the team, they come by to see Yosef?'

'Yeah,' Rosa says. 'Sure wish they never did.'

'It be a real bring-down, yeah.'

The rest of the ride passes in defeated silence. When they reach A to Z, Mulligan unfolds himself and gets out of the car, then holds the front door for Tolridge as she gets out. The plainclothes cop on guard across the street waves. Tolridge waves back.

'Oh hey,' Mulligan says. 'Aunt Lucy, she going with you tonight?'

'She dint wanna,' Rosa says. 'No can blame her.'

Tolridge gets into the front seat and shuts the door. Rosa hits the accelerator, and the skimmer lifts fast. Mulligan waits till it turns the corner, then hurries inside. In a couple of hours Game Five will start. He wonders if he even wants to watch.

Upstairs he finds Bobbie sitting at her comp desk and staring at Buddy's screen. Standing at the window near her is the largest lizzie Mulligan's ever met, pale blue and a good six centimetres taller than he is. He wears a pair of faded khaki trousers, cut in the lizzie manner to allow for his massive tail, and a khaki shirt, oddly marked with darker spots and stripes here and there. He turns around and hisses politely.

'Hello,' the lizzie says. 'I'm Blade. To me has been entrusted the task of keeping your beloved safe on the streets.'

'Uh, yeah?' Mulligan says. 'Well, cool. Pleased to meet you.'

As they shake hands, Mulligan realizes that the unfaded marks on the shirt match the shapes of various bits of military insignia.

'I get it,' Mulligan says. 'You were in the Navy with Bobbie.'

'More or less. I was one of the *Avalon*'s Marines.'

'Cool. Glad to hear it.' Mulligan glances at Bobbie. 'Uh, I coulda come with you, y'know? If you, like, needed someone.'

Blade busily looks elsewhere.

'You dunt understand, Jack,' Bobbie says. 'You're my backup unit, my insurance policy.'

'What?'

'If something happened to me, wouldn't you know?'

'Oh. Sure would. I could, like, come after you.'

'I was thinking maybe you could call the cops first.' Bobbie smiles at him. 'But the real thing is, I've got to leave someone I can trust here at A to Z. The Hoppers know Aunt Lucy was in that cabin with Tak and Yosef, right? If someone breaks in, she no is going to be able to defend herself.'

'Dunt be so sure,' Aunt Lucy says from behind him. 'But I just kidding. Jack, I gonna be grateful if you stay here with me. Nunks, he dunt talk. How he gonna call the cops?'

'Yeah, sure thing,' Mulligan says. 'Okay. Sounds to me like Bobbie's got it all figured out.'

'She good at that,' Aunt Lucy says. 'Hey, you done saw Yosef, right?'

'Yeah, sure did.' Mulligan shudders. 'Them drugs, jeezus, they might's well murdered him and been done with it.'

Bobbie winces with a shudder of her own.

'Ugly,' Mulligan goes on. 'Real ugly. Jeez, this whole thing, it be so

267

damn unfair. He got the psychic genes, yeah, but shit, he be a ballplayer first, and his talents, they no the kind you could use in a game.'

'Yeah,' Bobbie says. 'But I dunt know what anyone can do about it.'

'Neither do I,' Mulligan says. 'But I gonna, like, think about it a lot.'

'Semantic analysis of the "personal" columns for the past three days have revealed the usual number of probable code messages. I am attempting to access purchase records, but it is unlikely that these will prove to be of any value, as such advertisements, when placed with illicit intent, are normally placed through a commercial anonymizer or comm shop. The exact probability of this outcome, in fact, is—'

'Spare me the math, Buddy,' Lacey types. In deference to those watching the ballgame, she and Buddy have entered silent mode. 'Go on. Any of the ads look promising?'

'Seven, Programmer, but these were selected based on the latest info-coding paradigm, and the paper describing it is public knowledge. A truly cautious sentient would be able to circumvent it.'

'A truly cautious sentient who read that paper, you mean. Where was it published?'

'The University of Capetown Press.'

'Do you really think some low-life art thief would have read it?'

'Perhaps not. I shall proceed to attempt decoding.'

'First do a run on the PBI files. I want to see if that Scheffler woman positively identified her handler.'

'Very well, Programmer. Starting sub-routine. Ah, here we are. Scheffler has identified her liaison with the Alliance Embassy. It was indeed Erik Royall.'

'The Cons know about this yet?'

'As far as Chief Bates is aware, no, but they are unlikely to remain in ignorance for long.'

'Yeah, the law's been having a real bad problem with leaks. You might take a look and see if you can find any footprints in their files,

Bates's and Akeli's both. You've got twice the brains of their security AIs.'

'Currently available specifications confirm this, yes. Work order noted, Programmer. Secondary priority?'

'Affirmative. Finding that damned rag's still top priority.'

Lacey takes her laser pistol from the desk drawer and checks the charge. She slips open the end plate and plugs the pistol into the special – and illegal – outlet on the comp desk, then returns to the keyboard. 'Charge this to full for me, will you?'

'Certainly. I trust this does not mean danger pending?'

'Dunt, because it does.'

Over on the couch Jack howls in rage and Aunt Lucy shakes a knitting needle at the screen. Lacey swivels around.

'What happened?'

'Sorry,' Jack says. 'We just got robbed again. Eagles runner, he out at the plate and that damn ump call him safe!'

'What's the score?'

'Eagles two, Bears one, in the seventh.'

'Well, hell, it aint over till it's over.'

'Hey, Chief! You been watching the game?'

Bates pauses outside his office and lets Maddock catch up to him. 'I'm not into pain that much. Is it over?'

'No!' Maddock is grinning like a child. 'Colin grounded out, but he drove in the tying run and the game's going into extra innings. Score's two to two, tenth inning's just started. We still got a chance.'

'Allah be merciful, a chance! If the Series goes to Game Six, they're going to play it in Esperance and what happens then is someone else's problem, not ours.'

The stadium has fallen as silent as it ever gets. Rosa leans forward, hands on her knees, waiting for the first pitch of the tenth inning. The Bears are fighting back. The fans are staying to support them. *If we only had Tak* . . . She refuses to finish the thought. On the mound Enrico Quijada stands ready, a middle relief man trying his best to pitch like a closer.

269

When Quijada walks the first Eagles' batter, the entire stadium groans. For a long moment Enrico stands with his head hanging, then he pulls himself together. The second batter strikes out. The third hits a hard drive straight toward the hole – but Gina leaps, scoops, throws to first in an impossible play. He's out, and the stadium erupts in cheering. *One more out*, Rosa prays. *Oh Lady Luck, one more out.*

Walking slowly up to the plate is a pinch hitter, a left-hander to face Enrico, a left-hander himself. The Bears' catcher trots out to talk with Enrico, then ambles back to the plate. Whatever he said turns out to have been wrong. One pitch, one fat pitch – a smack, a crack of the bat – Rosa knows from the sound alone that the ball is gone. The Bears can only stand and watch as the home run sails over the right field fence. *He done turned on it*, Rosa thinks, *the bastard.*

The fans fall silent again. When Enrico manages to strike out the last batter, no one even applauds. The Bears walk slowly back to a dugout as silent as the stands. Enrico grabs a towel and goes to the far end of the bench, where he slumps down, the towel over his head to hide his face.

'All right,' Georgy says. 'We aint dead yet. Let's go out there and put some runs on that board.'

The first Bear strikes out. Rosa grabs her helmet and a bat, her gamer, and gets into the on-deck circle as Barak lines out on the first pitch. Two down. Swearing under her breath Rosa walks to the plate, taps it for luck, then crouches, waiting. Apparently the Eagles' closer feels some pressure himself. His first pitch, a fastball up, sails right down the middle of the plate. Rosa swings, connects, and takes off running. When she hits first safely, the fans come to life, cheering again. Rosa takes a lead off first and waits.

Gina walks to the plate. *Get a hit*, Rosa thinks. *Just get a hit!* Gina lets the first pitch go by, a ball. The next – too low – but she swings anyway. Wood connects with leather. Rosa takes off, racing for second base, but the words toll in her mind like the bell at Tak's funeral, *too low, too low.* The ball bounces off the grass right into the shortstop's waiting hands. Rosa hits the dirt and slides.

'Out!' the umpire's voice booms.

Rosa hears the Eagles yelling, screaming, running past her to the mound to mob their closer as once the Bears mobbed Tak, on that night an eternity ago when they won the All-Hagar pennant. She sits up but stays on the ground, dusts the dirt from her uniform shirt. For a moment the fans wrap themselves in dead silence. Then the chanting starts.

'Robbed, robbed, robbed!'

But hey, I sure was out, Rosa thinks. She gets up and realizes that police and security guards have rushed to form a line below the stands. The fans chant and stamp, over and over, 'Robbed, robbed, robbed.' The Eagles are racing off the field. Rosa can see Georgy standing in front of the Bears' dugout and waving both arms at her. The chant swells to a roar like the biggest sand storm in the world. She realizes then that the fans are protesting not that last call, but the entire thing: Tak's death, the commissioner's decisions, the humiliating way their team has lost. She runs off the field, her second sprint of the day.

The Bears huddle in their clubhouse while Georgy consults with the police. Over in the Eagles' locker room, the champagne is flowing, most likely, and Commissioner Chavez is making his way through the happy mob to present the trophy to their owner. When that scene hits the three-dee screens . . . Rosa can imagine the reaction of the Bears' fans.

'Jeezus,' Colin mutters. 'Hope they get back to their hotel okay.'

'The Eagles?' Gina says. 'Yeah, so do I. Chavez, well—'

'Hey,' Rosa says. 'He just following the rules.'

'Bullshit. The commissioner, he be there to adjust the rules, if he gotta.'

A good many team members mutter their agreement. Georgy comes trotting back in. His face, normally a light brown colour anyway, has gone almost Blanco-pale.

'Get cleaned up and dressed,' he says. 'But we aint leaving yet. There be a real mob out there. People burning trash in the parking lot. Punks tipped over the commissioner's limo. Police say they can't get us out of here till things get under control.'

'Oh god!' Colin heads for the door. 'My wife!'

Georgy grabs him with both hands.

'The cops, they bringing the spouses in the stands down here,' Georgy says. 'You no can go out there, Dejean! Cops won't let you. Comprende?'

Colin stops struggling and nods. Fezzy turns on the three-dee screen that hangs on the clubhouse wall. The picture stabilizes in time for the Bears to see the commissioner's limousine burning.

'Well, shit,' Jack says. 'Hell of a way to lose a ball game.'

As soon as the umpire calls Rosa Wallace out, Jack grabs the remote and turns off the three-dee. Lacey notices that no one else objects, not even Aunt Lucy, who normally believes in watching wrap-ups. Nunks moans and gets up, stomping for the door.

'I gonna go work in the garden, too,' Jack says. 'Need to move around.'

'Sure,' Lacey says. 'Blade and me, we're going to head to Richie's. I've got to talk with him before I can do anything else.'

In the warehouse district, now about two hours before sunrise, the streets stretch out empty and silent. As they leave A to Z, Lacey smells distant smoke in the air but thinks little of it. Lacey and Blade walk fast, half jogging at moments, to the Metro station and glide down on an empty elevator. On the tile and plastocrete platform a big three-dee announces the Bears' loss, but a train stands ready to rescue them from having to watch the news. They board, the doors slide shut, and the train starts. Lacey ducks into the nearest empty pair of maroon seats and leans forward to look over the touch screen map.

'I think we'll get off at F Street,' she says to Blade. 'I'd rather walk into the Bazaar from the quiet side.'

'An excellent plan. And by the way, you do have your lovely little service pistol with you, don't you?'

'You bet.' She pats her waistcoat pocket. 'If Richie comes through, we're going to be carrying a lot of money.'

Bates has set up a command post out in the hall in front of his office. Comm links stand in a rank on a commandeered table. Officers and administrative assistants rush back and forth with messages. Every available AI has been hooked into the main system. Someone's brought up the big three-dee from the squad room to plug in as well.

A map of Polar City fills its huge screen, marked by tiny red flame icons to show where the city's burning. With a portable comm link held to one ear, Bates stands in front of it and watches a new icon light while the mayor gabbles into his end of the call. Bates barely listens until one sensible idea finally catches his attention.

'Yeah,' Bates says. 'Call for the National Guard, sir. We're going to need all the help we can get. Yeah, do it now.' He hangs up before the mayor can waste more time talking.

Sergeant Maddock trots up and hands him a clipboard, carrying two messages from the head of the Fire Department.

'You know,' Bates says. 'I feel like a fucking idiot. I assumed the riots were going to start in Porttown. Never dreamed those middle-class folks at the game would act like Porters.'

'No one else did either, sir,' Maddock says. 'But the rioting's going strong in Porttown, all right. We gonna need every officer we got there. It's spreading to the Maple Street district. Lots of reports of looting coming in. Murghi Mahal's quiet, so is Carlitown. But kids and punks are roaming around New Cloverdale trashing skimmers.'

'Well, we no can do anything about looters right now. Top priority's got to be the fires and keeping people from killing each other. The mayor's going to call in the National Guard. Spread the word. It'll give the officers on the front lines a little hope.'

Lacey gets her first hint that something's gone wrong when the escalator carries them up from the F Street Metro station. She notices Blade sniffing the air.

'Smoke,' Lacey says. 'Yeah, I smell it too. Must be a fire around here.'

The escalator crests the top into the tiny lobby. Through the heavy glass doors Lacey can see flashing lights and little else.

'It would appear that around here is right here,' Blade remarks.

They push open the doors and walk out into the chaos. Sirens are screaming, people are yelling, fire blazes and crackles, glass shatters, police whistles sound, and ambulances squall. The smoke swirls thick, black and stinking of chemical suppressant foams. A young Blanca, no more than thirteen, races past, her arms full of holovids. Directly across the street Mac's Discount City Appliances is burning. Lacey can

273

see two firebeings in a cherrypicker hovering over the flames while they direct the hosebots spreading foam.

Screaming at the top of his lungs a Blanco rushes down the sidewalk. Blade grabs Lacey and yanks her behind him, then flicks one casual wrist. The man drops to the street.

'Cry havoc!' Blade shrieks. 'Let slip the dogs of war!'

Hissing like madman he dances a few steps and swings his tail. A punk with a knife screams in pain and flies a few feet into the air, only to stop when he meets the tiled wall of the Metro station.

'Come on!' Lacey yells. 'Let's get off F Street.'

Side by side, arms up to guard their faces, they plunge into the mob and head for the intersection of F and Oak, about twenty metres away. It might as well be kilometres. Blade keeps hissing, Lacey finds herself talking, meaningless words to let people know she's behind them – those who can hear. Several times Blade turns around and whips his tail; sentients scream and scatter. They finally make the corner only to realize that a new wave of sentients is rushing down Oak to join the looting. Blade grabs Lucy's arm and hauls her into a sheltered doorway, where three steps up lead to temporary safety.

'If this thing burns,' Blade yells, 'we'll have to risk the mob.'

Lacey merely nods. The stink of smoke and burnt foam has stripped out her throat. She takes her laser pistol from her inside pocket, checks to make sure the safety's on, and puts it into the pocket of her shorts.

The streets swarm with people, dashing back and forth in the light from burning buildings and cars. From the top step Lacey can see the looters, gang members mostly, human and lizzie both, with their heads wrapped in bright-coloured scarves, but ordinary people too have caught the madness. She watches two women help smash the window of the clothing store next to Mac's. Yelling like banshees other sentients rush in after them. Blade touches her arm and points up at the sky. Smoke swirls and hides it as far as she can see in every direction.

'Dawn!' Blade yells. 'Nearly dawn!'

'How the hell can you tell?'

Without answering Blade turns away, looking down F, his head cocked as if he's listening for something. In a moment Lacey can hear it too, a pounding on the street like some giant machine, a bevy of pile drivers, maybe, coming closer and closer. Out in the street the screaming gets louder. Sirens shriek overhead. A ragged crowd of sentients comes running down F Street. Behind them she sees a tight row of – something. The sentients approaching look so grotesque that for a moment she wonders if she's seeing a squad of Enzebbeline. Helmets with shiny visors, huge gas masks with air tubes like probosci, gloves, uniforms with padded tunics, clear shields in one hand and stun sticks in the other: the police are marching, clearing the street as they come. Someone in the rear must have a bullhorn, because a hollow voice booms and cuts through the noise.

'Disperse. You are in violation of city law. Disperse.' Over and over it sounds, while the police line marches on.

The looters, the mob, the innocent – all find themselves equally trapped. Fire engines block half the street; fire itself leaps on one sidewalk. Screaming, the crowd turns and tries to follow orders, tries to push through the bottleneck, but the police keep advancing. The sticks rise and swing, sentients stumble and fall under their feet, screaming in panic, crawling toward the sidewalk. From behind the police line the white trail of gas grenades streak up and arc down.

'Disperse, you are in violation of city law. Disperse.'

The canisters hit and shatter. A pale green mist of retch gas rises and spreads. The screaming turns to howls and the choking sounds of sentients trying to run while they vomit. Blade steps in front of Lacey, grabs her by the shoulders and turns her around, pushing her against the locked door and sheltering her as best he can.

'We gotta get out of here!' Lacey yells.

'Shallow breaths, Lieutenant,' Blade says, hissing. 'Remember your old gas drills.'

Lacey unbuttons her waistcoat, struggles out of it, and wraps it around the lower part of her face. Behind her the noise goes on and on, the sirens, the bullhorn voice, the screaming and sobbing. She smells a trace of the gas, nearly gags, concentrates on breathing through the cloth.

'They're past,' Blade says, and his voice chokes and wavers. 'Let's run for it.'

When he steps back she turns around, but she keeps the cloth wrapped tightly. Out in the street Blancos and lizzies lie sprawled and unmoving. Others crawl bleeding and gagging along the sidewalks. About half a block away the police line marches forward on a wave of screaming sentients and crackling stun sticks. Disperse, disperse – but there's nowhere for anyone trapped to go. The police are swinging hard, stunning and shocking anyone they can reach as their desperate victims try to follow their orders and run.

Yelling wordlessly, some thirty young sentients burst out of shelter behind the police lines. They've wrapped their gang colours around their noses and snouts. They grab rubble, stones, burning hunks of wood, anything, and start hurling it at the police from behind. The bullhorn shrieks. Half the police spin around in well-trained unison and fling up their shields. More gas canisters come flying and burst into the street. The gang members hurl one last barrage, then retreat, but their tactic has worked. The crowd trapped by the police up ahead has escaped and fled.

'Jeezus god!' Lacey snarls. 'I hate cops.'

'Me too,' Blade says, 'but let us indulge our feelings later and run like hell right now.'

Dodging the panicked, picking their way over the fallen, Lacey and Blade reach Oak Street at last. Smoke drifts down the middle of the street and clings to the buildings, but nothing here seems to actually burn. In the haze sentients appear suddenly, then drift away. Coughing and choking, Lacey and Blade jog down the sidewalk. The farther they go from F, the fewer the sentients they meet.

'So much for the quiet way in,' Blade remarks.

'Yeah. Me and my big mouth.'

'The sun's up,' Bates says. 'And the first National Guard unit's here. They're trucking two companies into Porttown to guard the stores on F Street.'

Sergeant Nagura nods to show she's heard, then turns back to her comp unit. An administrative assistant comes up, hands Bates a sheaf of paper, then hurries off again. Bates scans the reports quickly.

'Looks like things are starting to calm down,' he says. 'Could have been much worse, after all. And we haven't lost a single officer. Good. Guess we're doing something right.'

'If the National Guard are coming in, Chief,' Nagura says, 'do you want me to move our officers to somewhere else?'

'Yeah. Get about a third of them over to New Cloverdale. The Mayor's been screaming at me about putting more officers there. The rest should deploy around Maple Street.'

'Yes, sir. The Mayor wants to know if he should set a curfew.'

'In Porttown? Definitely. Let's wait and see how the other neighbourhoods go.'

Aunt Lucy sits on the edge of the couch and glares at the three-dee screen. The video comes from a National Guard rapid deployment VTO currently flying over Porttown. Six long blocks are still burning along F Street, but she can see, here and there, ruins thick with charred foam where the fires have apparently gone out. For a few moments she and Jack watch in silence. On some corners stand clusters of soldiers, assault lasers at the ready. Lucy notices Kelly's Bar and Grill standing unharmed and points it out to Jack.

'Good,' he says. 'But Mac's sure looks trashed. Jeez, I wonder if he gonna be able to front a team after all.'

'Dunt worry. If he dunt, we need a shortstop. But I got no call to be mentioning that. Dunt want Mac accusing me of tampering. I wish they'd show my block. Sure hope my collection's all right.'

Richie's place stands in the middle of peace and quiet. Though overhead smoke still roils, turning gold with the brightening dawn, and though the sound of sirens echoes down the empty streets, in Richie's gardens nothing moves. Music floats from the open windows of the big white house and a solitary lizzie guard leans over the front gate, picking his teeth with a silver beak stick.

'Let me guess,' Blade says. 'Your brother's made a pact with the devil, right?'

'Sometimes I wonder, yeah.'

The guard looks them over, recognizes her and waves them through. At the private grav lift another talks briefly into his comm unit, then allows them to ride up. Richie himself greets them when the grav lift opens at the top. He looks tired, Lacey realizes, with dark circles under his eyes – the first time she's ever seen him look less than perfect. He wears faded jeans and a grey silk shirt open halfway to his waist. She can hear Blade, behind her, make the snuffling noise that lizzies use to express surprise.

'You certainly do look alike,' he mutters.

Richie catches the remark and grins. 'The resemblance, it end there, though,' he says. 'She got brains, too. Hey, Bobbie, your hair's a mess. You get caught in a riot or something?'

When Lacey runs a hand through her hair, it comes away covered with gritty ash and the sticky residue of the suppressant foams. She wipes it off on her shorts.

'Who's this?' Richie waves an elegant hand at Blade.

'My bodyguard,' Lacey says. 'His name's Blade.'

'Okay. Sit down, both you guys. So what's so important you no can wait till the happy fans clear the streets?'

'Dint know there was so much action,' Lacey says, 'or I would have waited.'

'Want a beer? You gonna need something to drink, all that smoke.'

'Water will be just fine.'

Richie picks up a comm unit and calls a flunky, then arranges himself on his silk divan. Lacey takes a chair, but Blade stands behind her, his feet a little apart, his hands clasped behind his back. From where she sits, Lacey can see a three-dee hanging on the wall. The sound's off, but the picture shows fires burning over on Maple Street, a normally respectable part of town. Richie notices her interest.

'Bobbie, way I figure, Porttown's never too far from riots, and if they spread to Harlem Nuevo and like that, cool. Let the ricos get a taste of it.'

'You rico too, these days.'

He merely shrugs. A young lizzie opens the door and comes in with a pitcher of ice water and glasses. Lacey says nothing until the servant has poured water all round and left. She finishes one glass straight off, gets up and pours another for herself and Blade both.

'Anyway.' Lacey sits down again. 'I'm here for two reasons. First off, I need money, a lot of it if I'm gonna buy back *iLeijchwen*.'

'You found it?' Richie says.

'Not yet, but I've got an idea. Well, hell, if it hasn't burnt along with half the city.'

'Yeah. That be kind of sad, if it did.'

'Sad?' Blade puts in. 'You share your sister's taste for understatement, I see.'

Richie smiles, his eyes lazy.

'Which brings us to the second thing,' Lacey continues. 'If I dunt find this rag, or the cops dunt, you've got to be ready to evacuate Porttown. If the war starts, Richie, the first thing the Cons will do is take out the spaceport. And that means everything around it for about three kilometres. You think the fires are bad tonight, well, wait and you're going to see some real damage.'

'I gonna skip it, thanks,' Richie says, but he's not smiling. 'Evacuate? There really gonna be a war? The holonews, it just talk about diplomatic consequences.'

'I dunt know who runs the holonews, but they got their heads up their collective arses. Thanks to the goddam Alliance, yeah, there could be a big war. When they put those cruisers in orbit, they made sure the carlis couldn't back down. They'd lose face if they did. You know how much carlis like to lose face.'

'Jeez.' Richie blinks twice. 'A war, huh?'

'Yeah. The government's not going to get anyone out of here. They dunt give one damn about anybody south of Ninety-Sixth in the best of times, and now they've got a real good excuse to let us all burn.'

'I gotta agree, but what makes you think I can do anything about it?'

'Dunt give me a lot of crap, Richie.'

For a long moment he considers her, then laughs. 'Okay. I gonna see what I can do. Bout that money, how much you need?'

'Dunt know. If the sodding idiot who's got the rag has half a brain they're going to want to unload the thing, not haggle. But I better have good earnest money, just in case.'

'Five thousand?'

'That should be a good start, yeah, at least.'

'No problemo.' Richie pauses and looks at the three-dee. Hordes of kids dressed in expensive clothes are rushing through the winding streets of New Cloverdale. 'Everybody wants to get into the act, huh?' He turns back to Lacey. 'Tell you what, I gonna send you guys home in a car. You dunt want to carry that much cash on the Metro.'

'Sure dunt, yeah. But I wanted to make one stop—'

'It would be a waste of time,' Blade says. 'The emporium we wish to visit will be shuttered up tight against rioters.'

'You've got a point, yeah,' Lacey says. 'By the way, the cops have fingered the pair who killed Tak. They work for the Hoppers.'

Richie leans back on the silk pillows. 'You happen to know who they be, big sister?'

'Yeah. Why?'

Richie contemplates the far wall. 'Y'know,' he says at last, 'I got a few things I want to say to those dudes.'

'They've got diplomatic immunity. There's no way the cops can nail them, even if they get solid proof.'

'I'm no a cop.' Richie smiles, his beautiful, wide-eyed smile that makes him seem a complete innocent. 'They got their rules, I got mine.'

At her request, Richie's driver lets Lacey and Blade off several blocks from A to Z. She wants to check on an elderly sentient and his little grocery store. Sure enough, as she and Blade round the corner they see a mixed lizzie and human gang outside the Handi-Stop. A chunk of broken plastocrete goes sailing through the front window of the store. The owner, old Mr Fiztre, surges forward, tail swinging, only to be clouted from behind by a young Blanco wielding a length of pipe. Lacey pulls his laser and fires over the heads of the gang members and Mr Fiztre both. The beam of white fire shatters a window already cracked in four places. Shrieking the gang boys race away and disappear into the hazy sunlight. Lacey slides the laser back into her inner pocket.

Fiztre stands up and slaps his tail on the ground over and over in sheer rage.

'You okay, Fizzie?' Lacey says.

'Okay enough.' He reaches up and touches the back of his head. Orange blood stains his fingers. 'Stupid punks! But they no hit me real hard.'

'Good. You better pull down your metal shutter and close up. Then get to a doctor.'

'Yeah. Aint no one gonna be spending money today anyway.' He turns and looks at the damage. 'Goddamn insurance better pay fast, all I can say.'

'If they dunt, let me know and I'll write a letter for you.'

'Gracias, Bobbie. I gonna do that.' He slaps his tail again. 'Punks! They all acted like they was dusted to the snout. I know most of em, but they dint care, they too busy having fun. Fun. Bunch of damned dungtails.'

'We better go,' Lacey says. 'Sun's up.'

Even without suncloaks, though, they have little to worry about this morning. Through smoke as thick as clouds on Sarah, Hagar's fat red sun rises, hugely bloated in a dirty yellow sky. The light hangs high in the air, it seems, scorching nothing.

A couple of hours past dawn, a full company of National Guard arrive at the baseball stadium. Wearing gas masks, flak jackets and helmets, carrying laser rifles at the ready, they escort the players and their spouses out of the clubhouse. Burnt skimmer corpses lie all over the parking lot. Long streamers of black ash drift in the hot wind. Overhead the swollen sun covers the view with an ugly metallic light.

Once they got started, the fans apparently lost the ability to tell friend from foe. In their separate lot the players' cars burned along with the commissioner's limo. Rosa's Jaguar lies on its back, a burnt-out wreck. At the sight she weeps in long convulsive sobs she cannot control.

'Hey, hey!' Hiram Rosen comes running. 'Red, you got insurance, right?'

'Yeah.' Rosa snivels between words. 'But I loved that car. Ah goddamn it!'

Midmorning finds Bates back in his office to make a last round of comm calls. Daylight and the National Guard have combined to put an end to the rioting – for now, he reminds himself. After sunset all bets are going to be off. He sits down with a sigh of relief; he stood most of the night. His AI flashes a list of calls to his personal number.

'Return Kaz Phaath's call first,' Bates says.

When the AI rings through, she answers immediately. Her eyes look puffy and swollen as she leans toward the vid input; her hair's pulled back and wrapped by a bright scarf.

'Are you okay?' Bates says.

'Oh good lord, Al!' Her voice seems huskier than usual, too. 'I should be asking you that.'

'Hey, I spent the whole riot here in the Tower.'

'Ka Pral insisted you would.' She smiles briefly. 'I'm glad he was right. I spent a couple of hours up on the embassy roof, watching the fires. It was ghastly, but it was fascinating, too.'

'Yeah.' He covers a yawn. 'I guess it would be.'

'Oh, I'm so sorry. I should hang up and let you get home. This is a semi-official call, though. The ambassador is dreadfully worried about *iLeijchwen*. I mean, that is, he's worried it might have burned in the riots.'

'You know something? That never crossed my mind.'

'No doubt you had lots to worry about, with people being killed on the streets and all. But to Ka Jekhonas . . . I mean, he really—' Her voice breaks, and she turns away.

'Hey, it's going to be okay. Dunt cry. Tell the ambassador that I'm sure the thief guarded it extremely carefully. Everyone knows what it's worth.'

'That's true, isn't it?' She turns back to the vid pickup. 'I will pass that on, and thank you.'

'Are we still on for dinner tonight?'

'Of course, if you can get away from your duties.'

'Let's hope I can, but I think the worst is over. I might be late. I'll call you as soon as I know.'

'Thanks, please do.' She hesitate briefly. 'I was remembering what you said after the baseball game, about humans thriving on chaos. Do you still believe that?'

Bates considers. 'Oddly enough, I do. What happened last night was over the line, yeah. We could call it excessive chaos, I think. But a little of it's good for the soul.'

She looks at him in utter amazement. 'Oh well,' she says at last, 'we can talk more later.'

Since he's indulged himself by taking her call first, Bates does penance by calling Akeli next. His AI routes the call through two private links before it reaches the PBI boss at home, judging from the living room furniture the vid picks up. Akeli however has obviously not been to bed. He peers at the screen with eyes bloodshot from exhaustion.

'Ah, Bates,' Akeli says. 'I have good news for you, a palliative, one would hope, for the troubles of the night past.'

'Yeah, I could use some good news for a change.'

'I have been in touch with the president and the diplomatic corps. An envoy fluent in the Alliance home language has contacted the Hopper ambassador here. He, the ambassador I mean – the envoy is a woman – was properly mortified when the misdeeds of his staff were brought to his attention.'

'I suppose he pretended to be surprised, too.'

'No doubt.' Akeli allows himself a smug smile. 'The upshot of this will be a great deal of trouble for our Hopper friends here on-planet.'

'You know what? I couldn't have a better piece of news.'

'Except, of course, that of the recovery of the carli relic.'

'Yeah. Except for that.'

Before she goes to bed, Lacey takes a shower to wash off the stink of the riot. By the time she's done, Jack is already asleep. She decides to check in with Buddy and goes out to the silent living room, where the polarized glass hides the diseased sun. When she sits down, Buddy activates with a chime.

'Programmer, shall I display mail?' Buddy says.

'Yeah. Anything new in the police files?'

'Negative, Programmer, but the late holonews contained a fresh warning from the Confederation Ambassador. In truth, the Confederation has already shown a remarkable amount of patience.'

'Considering they normally dunt have any, yeah. What's this to do the war forecast?'

'The probability is now greater than ninety per cent for war within one standard week. The published deadline will probably signal not armed attack, but a breakdown of diplomatic relations. I am sorry,

Programmer. Even the most optimistic assessments indicate open conflict is inevitable, assuming no change in the underlying situation.'

'That's what I expected. What happens if we find their flannel for them?'

'I presume my programmer refers to the carli artefact, the *leijchwen*. The probability will drop, unless the Alliance is responsible for the original theft.'

'It looks like they are, except it's not like them to risk war when they dunt have the odds on their side, and they dunt. There's something working here we haven't found yet. It would be real useful to have a look at a few Alliance embassy files. I dunt suppose you've got a back door into their comp?'

'I do not, Programmer. I have been attempting to construct such a back door for seventy-three point four hours, so far without notable success.'

'Be careful. I dunt think the Hoppers are going to be happy if they catch you.'

'I am aware of their disregard for non-flesh sentient life, Programmer, and am exercising due caution. They have littered the ways in with sub-routines which, if executed, would cause actual damage to the basic BIOS of any AI.'

'Hey, if it looks too dangerous, quit. Dunt risk yourself.'

'Thank you, Programmer. That's an order I'll be happy to obey.'

'Which reminds me: did you ever find any hacker footprints in El Jefe's files?'

The AI hums to himself for a moment. 'None, Programmer, and my watch sub-routine on Mr Akeli's files reveals no unauthorized access to the PBI's databanks.'

'Other than you, you mean. This is real interesting. If nobody but you has been hacking – damn! I dunt feel like doing the cops any favours right now, but I wonder if Bates is still in his office.'

'I shall endeavour to reach him. Linkage sub-routine operational. Ah, here he is.'

When he appears on-screen Bates looks exhausted. He holds a large paper cup full, most likely, of coffee.

'What the hell do you want?' Bates says.

'You could at least pretend you're happy to see my face. I'm about to do you a favour, Chief.'

'Yeah? What have you got?'

'Real polite today, Señor Bates. It's no very much, but Buddy ran a security check for you. You haven't had any hackers getting into your files. Akeli dunt either. Which makes me wonder where those leaks have been coming from.'

'Me, too. We found out that some character named Saunders has been feeding the newsbots. She had police ID, but it was fake. If Buddy's right—'

'Of course he's right.'

'Whoever this Saunders donna is, she dint get her info from us. Huh, wonder if that means she's involved with the theft somehow.'

'Sounds like a good guess.'

'It's more than we had before, at least. Look, Lacey, sorry I bit your head off. I've been working through the reports on the damn riots, like I got nothing better to worry about than a bunch of lousy—' He stops abruptly.

'Bunch of lousy Blancos, huh, Chief?'

Bates rubs his unshaven chin. 'No was going to say Blancos, I was going to say Porters. I know you live there and I've got some good officers who come from there, but you know as well as I do that the worst scum in the city hangs out in the Bazaar. The sort that just loves a good excuse to smash things up or burn 'em down.'

'Yeah? Which gives you the right to just smash them up first, huh? Along with anybody else happens to get in the way.'

'What the hell you talking about?' Bates looks honestly confused. 'We've been managing the situation pretty good so far.'

'Look, Bates, I happened to be out on F Street this morning. I saw what came down. There were your officers, armed to the teeth and covered in riot gear. There were unarmed people trying to follow orders and disperse. But they didn't let them disperse, your cops. They ran them down and trapped them and beat the shit out of them, just because they could.'

Bates stares, blinking. 'Well, hell,' he says at last. 'You oughta know better than going out during a damned riot.'

'I'm not talking about me. I'm talking about the people I saw lying out in the street bleeding.'

'My people did a good job on this. We've only got six confirmed dead so far, and the fire department's on top of that bad fire the other side of Prospect.'

'Dunt throw statistics at me, Bates. I know what I saw. Long as they're Blancos or Porters, and yeah, I know that includes the lizzies who live here, not just us, then your goddamn cops can be judge and jury. They weren't out there to get people off the streets. They were out there to make people pay for being on the streets.'

'Some of those people were looters. Thieves.'

'Some. Not all. And since when is being a thief punishable by having the crap beaten out you?'

He starts to answer and thinks better of it, apparently, because he looks away.

'Bates, you've asked me a couple of times how come I dunt come work for you. Well, this is why.'

'I dunt have time for this crap. Thanks for the tip, and next time there's a riot just stay home.'

The link goes dead. Lacey lets out her breath in a long sigh that sounds more like a growl.

'Programmer?' Buddy says. 'I don't understand why Chief Bates seemingly missed the point you were trying to convey. I consider him intelligent.'

'He's smart enough.' Lacey gets up. 'Just a self-righteous bastard who thinks he is the law instead of serving the law. Ah, the hell with it! I'm going to bed.'

'Damn her anyway.' Bates stares at the comm screen for a long moment. 'AI?'

'Yes, Chief?'

'You heard what Lacey said about the riot squads?'

'Yes, sir.'

'Could she be right?'

'The holonews showed vid of a scene much as she described, sir.'

'Well, the goddamn holonews! They're always going to go for the

most sensational angle on any story. Blow things up out of propor-
tion, too. That's what gives you high ratings, not real journalism.'

The AI merely hums and clicks. Bates stands up and rubs his face
with both hands.

'I'm going home to get a few hours' sleep. If there are any breaks
on the Gri Nerosi case or about *iLeijchwen*, call me.'

Chapter Thirteen

Lacey wakes well after sunset. Beside her Jack lies snoring, asleep on his back, one arm trailing over the edge of the bed. The clock tells her that she has a day and a handful of hours till the carli deadline, a thought that gets her up and into the living room. The coffee maker stands fully loaded on the wet bar; she flicks it on, then sits down at her comp desk, yawning.

'Programmer!' Buddy activates with a hum. 'I am pleased you have risen. I have what might be an interesting result from my analysis of the personal advertisements on the most popular net sites. I abandoned the use of cryptoanalytic algorithms and resorted to neural net logic.'

'Wonderful!' Lacey is suddenly wide awake. 'What is it?'

'I found two chains of adverts that appear to be related. The first occurred around the time *iLeijchwen* must have been stolen. It refers to two persons, the "King of Diamonds" and "Harry". This sequence ends the day Moses Oliver was killed. The next sequence begins a few days ago with "Queen of Hearts, call Harry who pines for you". King of Diamonds and Queen of Hearts are terms derived from the Anglo-American tradition of playing cards on Old Earth.'

'Yeah, I knew that part.'

'At any rate, "The cards say yes for Harry" ends this sequence. The name Harry is a homophone for the Merrkan word "hairy", which describes *iLeijchwen*. The probability that this is simple coincidence is well over eighty per cent, but it is still the only meaningful correspondence I've found.'

'Could you find out who placed it?'

'No. It was entered from a commshop in Zone Nineteen, the Outworld Bazaar, and paid for in cash.'

'Sometimes I see why the Cons and the 'Lies have banned cash.'

'Indeed. Have we reached a fatal break in our data chain?'

'Logically, yeah, but I think I'll try playing a hunch. Can you get into the police files and borrow their suspect ID graphics utility?'

'With great ease, Programmer. Work order received. I will commence as soon as I finish delivering this message. Blade called and will return here as soon as possible, no later than twenty-thirty. He said to tell you that he heard a strange bit of news out in the Rat Yard that may prove significant.'

'I dunt suppose he told you the news?'

'No, he did not.' Buddy sounds annoyed. 'I am quite curious.'

'Me, too. Any new mail since I last looked?'

'No, Programmer. Nothing from the admiral, either.'

'That dunt matter any more. Which reminds me, Buddy. Why did you tell Jack I'd written to him?'

'Because I wished you to stay here, of course. It is not in my programming to dissuade you from any legal course of action. The Mulligan . . . I mean Jack, lives under no such constraints.'

'I see.'

Buddy hums, clicks, sends a flicker of light dancing across the dark screen.

'What's wrong?' Lacey says.

'Nothing. I was just—' His voice hangs briefly. 'Are you going to stay?'

'Dint Jack tell you? Yeah, I'm going to turn down the commission if Wazerzis offers it to me. Bet he dunt, though.'

In a cascading peal of bells Buddy floods his screen with bright gold.

'I take it that means you're happy,' Lacey says.

'Why, yes, Programmer. You have made an accurate assessment. I shall now proceed to borrow the police graphics utility.'

Bates arrives in his office to find an urgent message blinking on his screen. The commander of the National Guard units now in Polar City requests a meeting as soon as possible to discuss both the aftermath of the riots and the evacuation plans for the city if war becomes unavoidable.

'Colonal Kri Ahtuksak left a copy of the standard disaster procedures manual in my databanks,' the AI says. 'I scanned it as I loaded it, and I have found a peculiar discrepancy.'

'Yeah? What?'

'The report details plans for all areas of the city. Yet I find no mention of Porttown.'

'Try under the name F Street neighbourhood and slash or warehouse sector.'

'Thank you, Chief. Searching document now.' A long click and hum. 'I have found six references. They suggest that the designated areas be evacuated last by placing an armed perimeter guard.'

'They what? That can't be right. Put it onscreen.'

The AI reported accurately, it turns out. Bates reads the passage twice, but he finds only one way to interpret the turgid prose: in case of a military emergency the National Guard will ring Porttown round and shoot anyone who tries to leave before an official order allows. The writer of the report justified this scheme by the need to keep the freeways and other skimmer arteries moving.

'Jeezchrise!' Bates snaps. 'They should clear the port area first. That's where the attack is going to start.'

'The report includes that very projection, Chief,' the AI says. 'Shall I put the relevant section onscreen?'

'No. I'll take your word for it. Okay. Contract the colonel's AI and arrange a meeting time. Remember that I have to leave early tonight.'

While the AI works, Bates leans back in his chair and considers the evacuation plans. He intends to have a few words with this colonel when they meet. Since Polar City's spaceport is the only one on-planet, any attackers with half a brain will destroy it immediately. Orbiting laser cannon will start a firestorm that's bound to spread to the rickety buildings of the Blanco ghetto nearby. How could the brass leave thousands of people there to fry? Much against his will, he finds himself remembering his squabble with Lacey.

'Priority message, Chief,' the AI says. 'Akeli.'

'Put him through. We need to discuss how we're going to handle the Alliance Embassy.'

Mulligan wakes to find Lacey sitting on the edge of the bed. She's holding a cup of coffee.

'Here.' She hands him the cup. 'I need your help, Jack.'

'Sure.' He sits up and tries a sip – half soymilk and sweet, the way he likes it. 'With what?'

'Those two temp guards at the spaceport, the day the flannel got stolen from Tak's luggage. The ones who took him back into the customs hall. You remember what they looked like, dunt you?'

'Yeah.' Mulligan yawns, then gulps down more of the lukewarm coffee. 'Funny. I was, like, dreaming about them.'

'Yeah? Maybe you were picking up something. Come on, get dressed, okay? We need to get moving on this.'

Mulligan finishes the coffee while he puts on a pair of shorts and finds a less than dirty shirt on the floor. Carrying the cup, he walks into the living room to find Aunt Lucy watching a three-dee special on the damage from the riots. He pauses, swearing under his breath as the screen shows aerial footage of what's left of F Street. Mac's Discount City Appliances is black and completely gutted. On either side the buildings stand in partial ruin, black walls mounded with foam. The glass doors of the Metro station lie in shards across the sidewalk. Slowly the police chopper moves on.

'There's Kelly's!' Aunt Lucy says. 'Still okay!'

'That be something, I guess,' Mulligan says. 'But jeez, look at the next block. Like a fucking war zone. Uh, sorry.'

Lucy gives him a nasty look for the profanity, then goes back to studying the screen.

'I done saw my building earlier,' she says. 'It be okay. Sure glad.'

'Hey.' Bobbie gets up from her usual chair. 'You guys can talk later. Jack, sweetheart, come here and sit down.'

'In your chair?' He grins at her. 'I get a promotion or something?'

'Buddy's going to try to draw portraits of those two guards you saw so I can print them out and show them around.'

'I get it. Jeez, I already did that for the cops. It was, like, real boring, y'know?'

'I possess a higher intelligence rating than any police comp now available,' Buddy breaks in. 'Therefore we may assume the job will be both more efficiently done and of superior quality. I will start with the available drawings and ask you to modify them, so the process should be shorter than before.'

'Okay, plugsucker. Whatever.'

Buddy hums and clicks. 'Jack?' he says. 'I am sorry I have insulted you in the past.'

Mulligan stares at the blank screen, then decides that an apology's an apology, machine or not. 'Well, okay. I gonna stop calling you plugsucker then.'

'Thank you. Please sit down and let me begin the program.'

Bates is gathering print-out for his meeting with Colonel Ahtuksak when Sergeant Parsons appears in the doorway.

'What you got, Parsons?'

'That gambler, Gagne.' Parsons enters and hands him a data cube. 'I've been going over all the records in our databases. No found very much, but look here.'

Bates loads the cube into his comp unit. Onscreen a long list of names appears. 'Where?'

Parsons leans over his shoulder to point. 'Whoever this dude is, he's real careful, this the only mention I could find in the files. But you see there?'

'Yeah, I sure do. So.' Bates taps the screen with one finger. 'Moses Oliver worked for Gagne, did he? And as his recruiter at that.'

'Oliver dint lack guts, huh? Finding new pigeons for an illegal operation aint the safest job in the world.'

'No, and it's about to get more dangerous for his replacement. Let's set up a sting.'

'I figure maybe Mendoza?'

'I dunt think he's our gambling friend's type. Kaz Varesh has been offering embassy help, so let's ask her for one of their under-assistant clerks or something. Someone who might have heard Gagne's name from Gri Nerosi. She can be on the sting if she wants.'

'Will do, Chief. Should I mention your name when I make the call?'

'You bet. If I had more time, I'd do it myself. Tell her that, too.'

Bates bundles his print-out into a file, glances at the time, and decides he'd better confirm his early evening appointment – just to keep his schedule smooth, he tells himself, just for reasons of efficiency. When he puts the call through on his personal line, Kaz

Phaath answers immediately. For a moment she looks at him as if she doesn't quite recognize him.

'Is something wrong?' Bates says.

'I'm sorry.' She manages to smile. 'Things are so frantic here. I know it's Kaz Varesh's job to ask questions, but she's so rude!'

'I dunt suppose they've found anything important?'

'If they have, they haven't deigned to let me know. Kaz Varesh says she reports only to the ambassador and to you.'

'Well, I haven't heard anything, so I guess she was right about the trail being cold.'

'She mentions that quite regularly. She seems to blame me.' Kaz Phaath looks away, biting her lower lip once before she goes on. 'We had a conference, you see, all the senior staff, to vote on whether to hide *iLeijchwen*'s disappearance. There are eleven of us. I was the last to vote, but of course I voted with Ka Pral. He's done so much for me in my career. I think you people would call him my mentor. And I know how much the reception meant to him. To think of spoiling it – but Kaz Varesh makes me feel like a criminal for being the tie-breaker.'

'You couldn't have known the consequences.'

'Thank you.' For a moment the dazed expression returns to her eyes. 'No, I certainly couldn't have known that. But – anyway, I mean – I'm so glad we're going out tonight.'

'You need to get away from things, yeah. Oh-four-thirty?'

'Yes, indeed. See you then.'

Blade shows up at A to Z just after 2000 while every one is eating a late breakfast. Aunt Lucy insists on cooking bacon and fried bread for him, and judging from the way he wolfs the food down, Lacey can guess that neither he nor his boss have had much money for meals lately. No doubt their regular customers are having trouble finding them.

'A splendid repast!' Blade sets the empty plate on the floor. 'A thousand thanks.'

'So come on,' Lacey says. 'What's this news you told Buddy about?'

'Well, it may be nothing. I was listening to one of Dr Carol's patients, Miz Krupp her name is, who lives unfortunately near to the

293

boss's new headquarters. She was babbling about her dancers, what-ever they may be. I noticed her blue headdress.'

'The blue tablecloth?' Lacey says.

'It's not a tablecloth, my dear Lieutenant. It's a carli burial shroud.'

'You're kidding!'

'Not on your life.' Blade lays a massive hand over his two hearts. 'So I asked her where she got it. She said she found it on a dead animal. "And where, pray tell, is this dead animal?" say I. I was too blunt, perhaps, because she became threatened. She wouldn't tell me a word more. In fact, she ran off shrieking that I planned to rob her.'

'You're sure it's a shroud?'

'The silver embroidery is the tip-off.'

'I didn't see that the day I met her, but I wasn't looking at her much, either.'

'She is not a lovely sight, unlike the typical carli shrouds which are often gorgeous. They carry a supply with them, you know, whenever they leave aggKar. No doubt the embassy has a closetful, right next to the spare sheets.'

'So there could be a dead carli somewhere out in the Yard?'

'Generally speaking, one only finds shrouds when there's someone in them, and that someone is usually much the worse for wear.' Blade hisses. 'As it were.'

Despite the subject, Lacey has to laugh. 'Yeah, I guess so. I wonder if it's Gri Nerosi? It doesn't make a lot of sense. Why would someone murder him and then wrap him up?'

Blade spreads his hands wide.

'But it's better than no tip at all,' Lacey goes on. 'Tell you what. When we're done in the Bazaar, we'll go out and see if we can get some more data out of Miz Krupp.'

'You never know. It might pay off. What are we doing in the Bazaar? Oscuridad, of course.'

'Right. And then we're going to ask a few questions.' Lacey picks up a hand-sized display tablet that Buddy loaded earlier. 'Ever seen these two sentients?'

When she taps an icon, two holos appear side by side: an Indian woman with a silver butterfly in her hair and a burly Blanco man with a drooping moustache.

'No,' Blade says. 'They look blindingly ordinary.'

'That's the trouble, yeah. I'm hoping someone in one of the public comm shops will recognize them.' Lacey glances at the clock. 'We'd better get moving. The police have set a curfew for Porttown. Oh-nine-hundred unless you can prove you're going to a day job.'

Chief Bates's appointment with the National Guard commander, the mayor of Polar City, and the vice-governor of Hagar leaves him steaming. Although the other three eventually conceded his point – that the badly flawed evacuation plan amounts to a denial of the Porters' civil rights – they all refused to consider changing it on the grounds that time was simply too short. He did extract a promise from them that, if Polar City still exists a week from now, they will change it. He intends to remind them.

When he leaves City Hall, Bates drives an unmarked skimmer to Santangelo Avenue, parks in a public lot, and walks two blocks to a small restaurant. Dark wood walls and small stained-glass light fixtures ensure a dark interior. At a table next to the wall and behind a potted moon bush from Sarah, Erik Royall sits waiting for him. Mercifully he wears an ordinary grey business suit rather than his braid-encrusted yellow uniform. When Bates takes the other chair, Royall barely looks up from his coffee mug. Under the table Bates sets his briefcase, complete with a scrambler beacon that will jam any possible Hopper bugging equipment. A waitress comes over, and Bates orders coffee and a sandwich. Only when she's brought the food and gone does Royall speak.

'I'm glad to see you, Bates,' he says with his usual grin. His eyebrows rise and twitch. 'I wondered if maybe you were setting me up for something.'

'My government's out of the habit of assassinating people,' Bates says. 'What are you afraid of?'

'Things have been a little tense round the old homestead lately. Dunt tell me you aint heard the one about the envoy and the ambassador.'

'Okay, I won't.' Bates takes a bite of his sandwich and washes it down with coffee.

Royall leans forward. A waft of Hopper perfume comes with him,

295

all dust and dead leaves, strong enough to make Bates lay the rest of the sandwich back on the plate.

'You said you had information for me,' Royall says. 'I need to get back as soon as I can.'

'Rushing around's not good for your nerves.' Bates wipes his mouth on his napkin. 'You dunt pay your people enough, you know? Midori Scheffler may be a groupie, but she's got enough brains to know she dunt want to sit in jail longer than she has to. She's singing like a Darian warbler, everything she knows about you and your goons.'

Royall grins more and shrugs, but a fine sweat breaks out on his forehead. 'Who's this? She dunt sound like anyone I know.'

'Yeah, she told Akeli you were going to feed her to the rats if she got caught. We do have her positive IDs on your pair of slave goons. A witness to the dumping of Oliver's body corroborated them, too.'

Royall's grin hardens to a grimace. The eyebrows peak and stick.

'Akeli's got a federal warrant,' Bates goes on. 'Now I know it dunt mean a damn thing with their diplomatic immunity. But it's going to be a nuisance. The last time I looked, Gorvalneh dint like nuisances.' He deliberately omits the glottal stops.

Royall has gone decidedly pale. When he leans back, taking the scent with him, Bates addresses himself to his lunch. He eats half his sandwich and finishes his coffee before Royall speaks again.

'About those security guards,' Royall says at last. 'If I'm thinking of the same people you are, of course.'

'Of course.'

'Well, they've gone missing.'

'Yeah. Sure.'

'No, no, I mean it. They aint been seen at the embassy for about twenty standard hours. If the PBI happens to pick them up, I dunt think the ambassador's going to protest.'

Bates considers Royall, who's managed to get control of himself: his face reveals nothing now. Even the eyebrows stay at a reasonable horizontal.

'They should have retrieved that smart thread transmitter,' Bates says. 'I've never known your masters to accept excuses for failure.'

'Yeah. They hold their people to high standards, all right.'

296

'So I wonder, the goons, did they leave suddenly to save their skins, or are they already dead?'

'I dunt know. And that's the honest truth.' Royall smiles. 'If they ask for amnesty, you'll know, huh?'

'There's no way they can get amnesty for Takahashi's death. You saw what happened last night. I dunt want it happening again because the courts have pardoned Tak's killers.'

'Oh. You got a point, all right.'

'It's a special case.' Bates casually glances away. 'Usually it's pretty easy to get political asylum, especially if a man knows stuff worth passing on.'

Royall stands up. 'I gotta be getting back,' he says. 'I got work to do.'

He turns on his heel and strides out of the restaurant. Bates picks up the other half of his sandwich and takes a thoughtful bite while he wonders whether Royall will take the bait and defect.

The waitress comes by with a carafe of coffee in one hand and a bill in the other. 'Did the other gentleman leave?' she says.

'Yeah. He didn't pay you?'

She shakes her head.

'Okay, then give me his bill too.'

'Gracias.' She smiles in evident relief.

When Bates returns to his skimmer, he finds the comm blinking. He flicks it on. The unit tells him he has one recorded audio-only message.

'Okay,' Bates says. 'Let's hear it.'

'Hey, Chief?' Lacey's voice begins. 'Maybe this is important, or maybe it's chasing sandworms in a swamp. I may have a lead on Gri Nerosi's whereabouts. Guess I should say his body's whereabouts, because if this tip is legit he's dead. One of the Rat Yard crazies is muttering about finding a well-dressed dead animal out somewhere in the Yard. I'll call again if I learn anything more, or if I find a corpse.'

The message ends. Bates whistles under his breath. First Scheffler, then the Hoppers, now maybe Gri Nerosi's corpse – at last the case is beginning to crack, and he can only pray it cracks fast. He intends to speed it along. He picks up the microphone and speaks the code for an all-points alert. Bringing in the Hopper thugs who killed Takahashi will go a long way toward calming the city down, even if they refuse to tell him what they know.

The glittering holosigns and bright maglev lights at the heart of the Outworld Bazaar appear untouched, and Lacey catches her breath at this reminder of her brother's influence. The rioters stayed away from the Mayor's empire. The narrow streets also harbour a few perfectly legal businesses. Blade leads her to a corner shop under a three-dee sign that announces 'souvenirs'. In the windows she can see coffee mugs, T-shirts, little plates, printed towels, and the like, all plastered with the legend 'Polar City on Hagar' and streaked with assorted bright colours no doubt meant to represent the aurora. When Lacey follows Blade inside, they find a welter of merchandise piled up on shelves, stacked on the floor, hanging from the ceiling – all of it cheap, none of it durable. At the door a bored Blanco clerk sits on a stool by a cashcomp desk and reads a magazine. He glances at them, then returns to his screen.

'Let's work our way back,' Blade murmurs.

They dodge a stack of big plastoclear globes that, according to the labels on their boxes, produce a credible imitation of the aurora when you shake them. The merchandise begins to change character the farther back they go. The human-style T-shirts have slogans like 'Room for Two' in the women's sizes; the men's announce that their owners got laid in Polar City. A lizzie-cut smock says 'Eat my eggs!' High up on the wall hang black velvet paintings of various sentients in various sex acts, some of which look profoundly uncomfortable. On one shelf Lacey sees a long row of green plastic statuettes – naked female lizzies bent forward, hands on knees, tails raised. In silent horror Blade points out the holograms of carli women wearing only collars and leashes.

'What the hell?' Lacey whispers.

'I believe the phrase is,' Blade says, 'don't knock it till you've tried it. You'd be amazed at the profit they make from this stuff, completely legitimate.'

'That depends on what you call legit.'

'True.' He pauses in front of a shelf full of brown plastosoft objects, some vaguely tubular, some roundish. 'It's interesting, isn't it, how the excrement of all known sapient species is approximately the same colour? I suppose you place one of these on someone's chair or bed to see how they'll react when they find it.'

Lacey can only shake her head.

'Can I help you?' A dry, thin voice sounds from behind a stack of boxes that seem to contain inflatable . . . somethings. Lacey decides not to get close enough to read the labels. In a moment the speaker follows the voice out, a skinny Blanca with long pale brown hair that hangs in tendrils beside her face and trails over the collar of her white shirt. She wears a gold hoop through one ear.

'I am the man of shadows,' Blade says. 'The Prince of Aquitaine in his ruined tower, not that the second line will mean anything to you, I suppose. It doesn't even mean much to me, since I don't know where the hell Aquitaine is.'

The woman stares at him with small brown eyes, then nods. 'You better come down to the back.'

They follow her between racks of three-dee postcards to a door on the back wall. She knocks twice, then opens it and gestures to a small room stacked with packing crates, lit by one overhead bar. At a table under the light sits a gaunt Blanco who must be her twin, Lacey decides: the same lank brown hair, the same squinty brown eyes, even the same gold earring. A greasy plate with a half-eaten sandwich lies in front of him.

'Yeah?' He looks up.

'Darkness, darkness, be my pillow,' Blade says. 'I take it that you understand twilight.'

The man and woman exchange glances. She shuts the door and leans against it; he gets up and walks clear of the table.

'I maybe can help you,' he says. 'You looking to buy something special, huh?'

'You could call it that,' Lacey says.

The man takes a good look at her, then sucks in his breath sharply and steps back. When Lacey takes a step toward him, he backs up again. One more step, and she grabs his shirt collar with both hands and pins him against stacked crates.

'You know who I am, dunt you?' she says.

He nods a yes.

'What's wrong? Think I've come to shake you down?'

His eyes widen, but he says nothing.

'Do you have it?' Lacey says. 'I think you know what I mean.'

Behind her she hears a scuffle. Blade says, 'I'll take charge of that, thank you. You could hurt someone with it.' Lacey doesn't bother turning around.

'Look, Oscuridad,' she says. 'Do you have *iLeijchwen* or not?'

'Dunt! I told your goddamn brother the truth. I dunt got it!'

'Okay.' Lacey lets him go. 'Who else has been asking you about it?'

'No one.' He pauses to smooth down his collar and shirt. 'Told Richie that, too.'

'I can be a lot nastier than Richie,' Lacey says. 'Who else has been asking you?'

When he hesitates, Lacey pulls her laser pistol out of her pocket. He yelps.

'One of these can torch plasterboard real easy,' Lacey says. 'Bet your stock would burn real fast if someone set the crates on fire. Who else has been asking you?'

'Only Saunders.'

'Yeah? When was she in?'

'Couple nights ago. Goddamn cops, they take it from you both ways, huh? Said if I sold it to anyone she gonna bust me good. If I get it, she wants me to hand it over to her. For free. Can you beat that?'

'I thought the cops didn't know about you.'

'So did I.' He more or less smiles, showing feral teeth. 'So did I.'

Lacey considers him, trembling where he stands.

'Saunders no is a real cop,' she says. 'Those papers are fakes.'

'The fucking little bitch! Had me pissing my pants, I so scared of getting busted.'

'You could call her that, yeah.' Lacey puts the laser away and takes out the display tablet. She unfolds it and taps the icon. 'Recognize these people?'

'Never seen em.' He shakes his head. 'Nah, never have.'

'Not even Harry?'

Oscuridad shakes his head again. He looks so sincerely baffled that Lacey decides he's telling the truth. She makes a half turn and steps back, keeping him in sight while she puts the tablet away. Blade is holding a moly, she realizes. With a flourish he hands it back to the female Oscuridad.

'Naughty lady,' Blade says. 'We'll leave you in peace now.'

A back door leads them straight outside to a narrow alley that smells of urine but seems, somehow, cleaner than the shop. They hurry down it to the relative safety of Fourth Street and stand blinking in the bright lights. Overhead a floating holosign advertises a parlour offering legal pan gow and mah-jong.

'Well, hell,' Lacey said. 'I had hopes.'

'Me too,' Blade says. 'Trust your brother to beat us to it.'

'Richie's worried. Good.'

'A small question, and I shall understand perfectly if you choose not to answer it. Who's Saunders?'

'All I know is that she's human and poses as a cop now and then. She's the one who passed the leaks to the holonews people.'

'Did you think she was Butterfly Girl?'

'Yeah. Lousy hunch, huh? I didn't dare let them know I got no idea what Saunders looks like.'

'Not after the show you put on, no. What now? The comm shops?'

'You got it.'

The Bazaar sports six comm shops as well as a post office. Lacey and Blade hit them all, showing the display tablet, asking if anyone's seen either of these two people recently.

'His name might be Harry,' Lacey says casually at each stop.

Not even the sight of a twenty in Blade's hand jogs any memories. They try the various eateries and better class of bar: no luck there, either. Well after midnight they find a clean-looking restaurant and go in to get some lunch. Over beer they discuss strategy.

'Maybe we should go over to Murghi Mahal,' Lacey says. 'The Blanco dude could live anywhere, but Butterfly Girl might be easier to place.'

'Perhaps,' Blade says. 'But the Mahal is a high-class respectable neighbourhood. The comm shops there operate strictly within the law.'

301

'Yeah, that's true. Buddy would have found the records if Harry and his friend had transmitted from a place like that.'

'Harry.' Blade snuffles, then snorts. 'Why dint I think of this earlier? It's not just *iLeijchwen* that's hairy.'

'Gri Nerosi. Damn!' Lacey taps the tablet through her pocket. 'We've been asking about the wrong dude.'

'Once more into the breach, dear friends.' Blade downs the rest of his beer. 'Back to the comm shops.'

But their second trip around provides no more information than the first. At 0300 hours Lacey decides to give up. Whoever her suspects might be, the Bazaar knows nothing about them.

'We'd better get back to A to Z,' she says. 'It's going to be dawn pretty soon, and we dunt want to be caught out in the Rat Yard without suncloaks.'

At 0530 early diners fill the Sky Light Room, a spread of pale carpet and starched white linen under a clear dome that covers most of the ceiling. Beyond, the aurora flickers and spins its coloured webs over the glowing sky. At the tables, candles provide the only artificial light. Kaz Phaath is wearing human clothing, a long dress with narrow sleeves and a low neckline, cut from some stretchy fabric that matches the blue of carli robes – or at least, matches it as far as Bates can remember. He raises his wine glass in a toast.

'To you,' he says. 'You look beautiful tonight.'

'Thank you, Al.' She smiles down into her own glass.

'I've been thinking. Polar City's not such a bad place to live, you know. Takes some getting used to, but I did. Look at that sky. You won't find another one like it.'

She looks up, her lips half parted.

'I was wondering,' Bates goes on, 'if you thought you could stand to live here.'

'Don't, Al!' She sets the glass down on the table. 'I think I know what you mean to say, and please don't.'

Bates feels as if he's been shot: the shock first, but later the pain will start. Kaz Phaath leans forward to lay her hand on his.

'It's the war, Al, only that,' she says. 'We'll probably be gone by next week. The ambassador is just waiting for the recall. Half the staff has packed up already.'

'Ah. Only because of the war?'

She nods. The beads braided into her hair dance in the flickering light.

'Okay.' He hears himself sigh. 'I can live with that.'

'I'm sorry.' She lets go of his hand. 'I'm so sorry.'

'So am I.'

For a horrible moment they sit staring at the tablecloth to avoid staring at each other. Finally he picks up his glass and has a long swallow of wine. She takes her fork and pokes at her dessert.

'Did you see what this was called on the menu?' she says. 'A "Napoleon Gloire". Why would your people name a sweet food for a conqueror?'

'I never thought about it.'

'Why do humans always name things for conquerors?' She lays the fork down on her plate. 'Other species wouldn't, even if they have conquerors. Most don't. Carlis haven't.'

'Oh, come on, the carlis had conquerors. Look at Ka Prelandi. I thought he saved the race, laid the foundation for the Interstellar Confederation, won dozens – or was it hundreds? – of battles, all that sort of thing. Maybe carlis dunt name desserts after him, but he sure sounds like a Napoleon to me. Well, except he won in the end. Permanently.'

'But he was not a conqueror! He showed the packs how to defend themselves against the proto-sapients who would have destroyed them, yes. He united all the packs on the lesser continent into a pack of packs. He bears the name of his people just as the human Ataturk did.' She tosses her head in a dance of beads and leans forward, her eyes glowing. 'But he didn't *conquer*! He stopped when the immediate threat was gone, he didn't attack packs that never attacked his own. You see the difference?'

'You know, they've got you in the wrong department down there at the embassy. You should be doing PR for the carli species.'

She sits back and scowls.

'Well,' Bates goes on, 'dunt you like them more than your own kind?'

'That's not quite accurate, no.'

'Not quite, huh?'

'Plenty of humans understood honour, back on Earth. Look at the Japanese! They valued art and honour both.'

'Also conquering other people. Ever read what they did to Korea?'

'That's what I mean about humans. Our ancestors were greedy, even the good ones.'

For a moment they glare at each other.

'You know what?' Bates says at last. 'We're on the edge of fighting about something that dunt matter so we dunt have to fight about what does.'

In the candlelight her complexion darkens with a blush; then she smiles.

'You're right, aren't you, Al? I'm sorry.'

'If there is a war, a lot more people than me are going to be sorry about a lot of things.'

She nods, picks up her napkin and begins twisting it into a little rope.

'Which reminds me,' Bates says, 'I have some news for you about Gri Nerosi. I think it's about him, anyway. One of my people may have found his body.'

Kaz Phaath drops the napkin onto the table and looks up, startled. 'After all this time?'

'Yeah, if this tip pans out. I'm hoping it is him. Not to be morbid or anything, but dead bodies can tell a forensic tech a hell of a lot. We might get some important information.'

'But where is he?' Her face has turned ashen.

'Out in the Rat Yard somewhere. Lacey called in just before I picked you up. Said she was on her way out to find a woman who may have robbed his body.'

'Robbed his—? Oh, how awful! How horrible to think he's dead, as well. But really, I supose if he were alive you'd have found him long ago.'

'Yeah. I'm sorry to bring up such a gruesome subject. But I under-stand how you felt responsible for him and I knew you'd need to know.'

'You're one of the few Republic humans I've met, Al, who does understand that sort of thing. I think that's what drew me to you in the first place.'

'Is it? I don't think I've ever had a bigger compliment.'

She smiles, her beautiful, radiant smile that makes him remember being young, when he still believed that men like himself had a lock on happiness.

'Maybe the war won't happen,' he says. 'The deadline is pretty meaningless. Your government no is going to start shooting at mid-night tonight.'

'No, it certainly isn't, not with those beastly Hopper ships in orbit.' She glances around, then lowers her voice. 'I hate them so much.'

'I can't say they're high on my list of favourite people either.'

'You know,' she goes on, 'even if the war does start, if you were to come with us when the embassy is closed we would be together.' She takes his hand again. 'I've wanted to ask you to join me for a long time, and now it won't wait. Once we get the order to withdraw it will be too late. I may be able to return once we conquer Hagar, but I don't want to risk what could happen to you in the meantime.'

He pulls his hand back, gently, firmly.

'"Once we conquer Hagar"?' he says. 'I thought you told me carlis weren't conquerors.'

Caught, she retreats behind her careful lack of expression, some-thing no doubt she has practised since childhood, judging from her success at it. He has no idea if she's angry, regretful, or even if she feels anything at all. He picks up the wine bottle and divides the last of the wine between them, then sets it down.

'I deserved that,' she says at last. 'But the planets of your Republic – your people – they'd be so much better off if they joined the Confederation.'

'Maybe. Joining is a little different than being bombed into sub-mission.' He picks up his glass and salutes her. 'There's no honour in submission. No one's better off if all their honour's been stripped away from them.'

'No. No, I suppose they're not. I—' She lays one hand on her throat and looks away. 'I mean, of course they're not. You know, when *iLeijchwen* first disappeared I had this wonderful idea that perhaps your government would join ours as a sort of restitution for stealing our treasure. Ka Pral would say that I'm too young, too much of an idealist, to understand these things, I suppose.'

'Oh hey, there's nothing wrong with wonderful dreams. It's just that life when you're awake never measures up.'

'Yes, I see that's true. But Al, would you come with us? Would you come with me?'

Bates has never had a harder time saying a single word in his life. 'No.' He takes a sip of wine. 'It would be dishonourable of me, wouldn't it? To desert my people and my post?'

A strange expression compounded of sadness and recognition and pride crosses her face. 'I didn't really expect you to accept. You see, you *do* understand honour.'

'Do I? Maybe I just believe in doing what I'm paid for.'

'Oh, don't be silly! Your duty lies here, I've always known that. And I honour you for it.'

The waiter, perfect in black and white, glides over and silently holds out the bill. Bates presses his thumb on the digital corner and watches him glide away. Overhead the dome is turning smoke-grey at the rising light of dawn.

'Shall we go?' Bates says.

'Yes.' She rises before he can help her with her chair. 'I need to get back to the embassy.'

Silently, walking close together but not quite touching, they leave the restaurant. In the early sun's glare they stand under an awning while an attendant brings Bates's unmarked car. Bates helps her in, then goes round and settles himself in the driver's seat.

'So, back to work?' he says.

'Yes, please.'

When they reach the embassy compound, he drives to the back and stops the car by the staff door. He gets out to open her door. She slides out and stands for a moment, looking up at him in the pale hazy light of early morning.

'It's been good, Al,' she says. 'I will return, some day.'

'I doubt it.' He leans over and kisses her, the first kiss they have shared. 'But I'll remember you.'

For a moment she hesitates with her hand on his arm, then turns away and walks off, disappearing into the grey hallways of the embassy. As he goes back to the driver's side, Bates happens to glance up. At a second storey window he sees a carli standing, draped in scarlet robes. Ka Jekhonas is watching the sunrise, perhaps, rather than spying on a junior member of staff. Or possibly the ambassador is wondering how many more sunrises he'll see before his duty of ritual suicide claims him.

Bates gets in and starts the skimmer. He needs to get home and sleep so he can be back at work by sunset. In the night ahead, the city's going to need its Chief of Police. Maybe, if the police stay smart as well as lucky, Ka Jekhonas will die of old age some day a long time from now.

The Metro takes Lacey and Blade out to Noah Station and drops them off in the glare of full day. Dust swirls in a moaning wind. Far ahead of them rise the rehydro tanks, blinding white against the rusty desert hills.

'Jeez,' Lacey says. 'Sure is quiet around this time of day.'

'Yeah,' Blade says. 'They only keep a skeleton crew on during the daylight. I was poking around when we first moved to this earthly paradise, seeing if perhaps we could find a few customers out this way. There's a couple of sentients on duty to watch the comp screen and call for help if something goes wrong. That's all till sunset.'

They put on their suncloaks and head off into the Rat Yard across the long drifts of trash. Far ahead, Lacey can see the distant white tower where, she hopes, they'll find Miz Krupp. Here and there thin lines of smoke rise, marking the homes that Yarders have managed to scratch out for themselves above ground.

'If anything happens to the city,' Lacey says, 'it's going to be grim out here in the Yard.'

'Maybe not.' Blade hisses softly. 'When you aint got nothing, you got nothing to lose, as the poet once said. At least these unfortunates are out of the line of fire.'

'They may be luckier than us Porters, yeah.'

'At the moment I'd trade the risk to be back in the Bazaar.' Blade glances around, then stoops and picks up a long plastowood pole that might, once, have been a curtain rod. 'I always like to have a stick to keep the rats at bay.'

As they pick their way through the mounds of trash, they see plenty of rats – or, to be precise, the Hagarian mammal that looks so much like Old Earth rats that the name's stuck. Now and then Lacey steps on a pile of indeterminate refuse only to have it move under her and squeak. Blade takes to beating the heaps ahead of them with his stick and rousting the things that live there before they walk over them. After a long slog they finally reach the easier footing of the ruined landing strip. At the far end someone draped in bright blue is waltzing in circles out in the sun.

'Ah,' Blade says, 'Miz Krupp is dancing again.'

When they approach, Miz Krupp stops her dance and stands with her arms akimbo. Her blue headdress hangs halfway down her back. Now that she's looking closely, Lacey can see that, despite the stains, the fabric shimmers with a fine weave and carries lines of silver embroidery, words in the carli alphabet. Lacey tips up the helmet of her suncloak.

'Hi, Miz Krupp, you remember me?'

'You no be one of the dancers.'

'That's right. I was here with Dr Carol, remember?'

'Course I remember. You got medicine for me?'

'No medicines, Miz Krupp, Dr Carol gave them to you already. I just want a closer look at your scarf.'

The old woman clutches her head with both hands. She chants, 'Mine, mine, I find it, you no can have, mine, dirty old dead animal, I find it, mine. And it no a scarf, just pretty. I find it.'

'I told you she's always talking about that dead animal,' Blade mutters.

Lacey speaks soothingly. 'Yes, it's yours, you found it. I'm no going to take it. I just want to look at the corner. You dunt even have to take it off.'

'Just the corner?' You no be a friend of Dr Carol's. I gonna run away.'

Lacey picks up one corner of the fabric and rubs it between her fingers: a very fine weave indeed. 'This is very beautiful,' Lacey says. 'You were real clever to find it. Wish I could find something like this.'

'You gotta look in the boxes. Maybe there be more dead animals.'

'You sure know an awful lot about the Rat Yard. Where are the boxes?'

Miz Krupp smiles and begins talking about her dancers.

After a long time and a good many questions, Lacey manages to learn that two sentients came to join Miz Krupp's 'dancers' in the Rat Yard. Since Miz Krupp has no concept of time left, it's impossible to tell when these two white dancers – sentients in suncloaks, as far as Lacey can tell – arrived. She does learn that one of the suncloaked pair had to carry the other.

'I followed them, dancing, dancing, up where all the water be. Water, all that water, you could get wet all over, but I dint. Dancing, they just dancing way up high, all up in the sky, and I danced too. Up in the sky, after a dancer went away. The other one was in the box, only it just be a dead animal. I dint like it. A dead animal dunt got no right to have a pretty. Mine, I found it.'

Blade pounces on one word. 'Water. The only large quantity of water around here's over at Project Noah.'

'Yeah,' Lacey says. 'Big tanks and stairs for Miz Krupp's dancer to climb into the sky.' She turns back to the old woman. 'Miz Krupp, you think you can show us where they were dancing?'

Bribery, cajoling, and threats finally persuade Miz Krupp to show them the path the 'dancers' took. Blade has an extra suncloak, but only by threatening her with Dr Carol's wrath does Lacey get Miz Krupp to put it on. She leads them to the fence marking the boundary between the Rat Yard proper and the rehydro project. Caught in broken wire, a shred of stiff white fabric clings to the edge of a long slit in the fence.

'Some of the locals cut that hole,' Blade says.

'If this happened the way I think it did,' Lacey says, 'it must have been hell getting through there.'

Beyond the fence, four tanks, each holding millions of litres of water, mark the corners of a vast diamond made of pipes and catwalks. The closest stairway starts about four metres away.

'Miz Krupp,' Lacey asks, 'which tank?'

'I dunt know. I was dancing, I dunt remember. That's a box.' She speaks the last three words in a perfectly normal voice and points a bony finger at a metal gang-box, about two metres long and a metre each high and wide, sitting at right angles to the nearest tank.

'What are those, anyway?' Blade says. 'For trash?'

'Huh, you've never worked an honest day in your life, have you?' Lacey smiles at him. 'They keep the company's tools safe, right where the workers need them.'

When Lacey checks the cover, she finds a hasp locked with a steel padlock, thick with grit and dust. No one could have opened it in the past six months.

'You sure this the right box?'

'Never said it was this one at all.' Miz Krupp slips back into her chant. 'Dancing up in the sky. They went up and I went up.' In a normal voice, she adds, 'They got boxes all over here, only they lock 'em up all the time, except when I found the animal, that box dint have no lock. Up in the sky. Please, can I go home now? I dunt think Dr Carol wants me here in the daylight.'

'You helped a lot, Miz Krupp, so go get out of the sun. I'll tell Dr Carol for you.'

Chanting about her dancers, Miz Krupp scuttles away. Lacey watches her wriggle through the cut fence and hurry off.

'Now what?' Blade says.

'We start looking for more boxes.' Lacey takes a step toward the tank, but Blade catches her arm with one hand.

'Bodyguard, remember? You go behind me.'

With the swaying gait of a lizzie in hot sun Blade starts lumbering up the stairs. Lacey follows. The stairs end on a small platform with a door into the tank area. A cracked lock dangles just above a handle.

'Now why do I suspect this tank isn't inspected very often?' Blade says.

'For a new project this whole place looks pretty run down,' Lacey says. 'You and your boss should stop selling drugs to the guys who work here.'

Blade hisses. 'Stay behind me, Lacey.'

He pushes the door open, slides through, then waves to her to come ahead. Inside, metal grating covers the vast surface of the tank proper. A metal catwalk, perhaps a metre and a half wide, runs along the inside of the tank wall. Several metres below the grate, they see their reflections in still water.

'It makes me think of boot camp on Sarah,' Blade says, 'all this water in one place.'

'Bet they lose a lot to evaporation, having it open like this.'

'That's probably the idea. As long as it gets into the ecosystem one way or another.'

Lacey takes a step onto the grating, which bears her weight but creaks alarmingly. Since Blade weighs easily twice as much as she, they stick to the catwalk. About a quarter of the way around, they find a set of control wheels and a read-out screen on the wall. On a solid platform another gang-box sits, about a metre out from the curved wall. When Lacey stoops to examine it, she finds a shiny new padlock.

'Someone replaced this pretty recently,' she says.

'Yes,' Blade says, 'and they were so rude they didn't leave us the key.'

'Well, we dunt exactly need one.' Lacey reaches inside her cloak and pulls out her laser pistol. 'This is military issue, after all.' She adjusts the beam to narrow, then fires at the hasp. With a burst of bright light and sparks it hits the metal. In a few seconds the lock drops to the platform with a clatter.

'Huh,' Lacey looks at the pistol. 'That used a lot of juice.' She puts the pistol away.

'Allow me.' Blade lifts the heavy lid with ease.

Stench pours out, thick and nauseating, the worst nightmare stink Lacey has ever smelled: dead flesh, stewed in its own juices for weeks out in the desert heat. She gets a glimpse of a furred corpse, the skull rotted down to the bone, before a gagging Blade drops the lid. A last wave of stench sweeps over them.

'Well, we found Harry.' Blade turns away and vomits over the platform.

Lacey nearly joins him. Instead she walks a few fast steps away and forces her mind to focus on the cleaner air, the smell of water, the scent of dust, anything other than Gri Nerosi's remains. If it is Gri Nerosi. *Oh come on*, she tells herself, *who else would it be?*

'I'd better call AI Bates.' Lacey reaches inside her cloak once more and pulls out her portable comm link. 'We need to get the coroner out here.'

In splinters of ruby light a laser shot splashes on the wall beside her. Lacey drops flat, and the comm unit sails wide to rattle onto the grating and disappear. Another shot spins a pinwheel of sparks off the top of the gang-box. She rolls away, groping for and finding her laser pistol. She can see Blade's bulky form, draped in white, doing the same. The reflec coating on their cloaks might protect each of them from one shot before it gives out – might, if the shooter has a cheap weapon.

She gets to her knees, tugs her arm and her pistol free. Blade has done the same with his old Marine-issue laser.

'There!' Lacey points and fires in the same motion.

A white-cloaked figure stands in the open doorway. Lacey's shot bounces just over its head. A line of red light shoots past her as Blade returns fire. The figure screams as the hem of its cloak bursts into flame. It twists around back through the door and bangs it shut. Lacey can hear footsteps pounding down the stairs.

'On your feet, Sarge!' Lacey yells.

She jumps up and heads straight across the grate with Blade right behind her. They take maybe three steps when she feels the grating giving way . . .

'Oh shit!'

Blade yelps one incomprehensible word. Then they are falling, plunging into the water. Lacey just manages to pull her arms inside her cloak as she hits. It floats free as she drops straight down, kicks to get clear of the dangerous enveloping fabric, then brings her arms to her sides and up again in a wide scooping motion. Up she goes, up toward the light in a cloud of bubbles. She breaks free, gulping for air, treading water while she looks around. Her cloak and Blade's float nearby, looking oddly like a pair of fried eggs.

'Blade!'

Some metres away the lizzie struggles, splashing, arching his neck to thrust his snout above water. He slips under, breaks the surface again and yells, 'I can't swim!'

'Oh jeez!'

Lacey reaches his side in two strokes, but he grabs at her. One arm drags her under. She twists, wiggles free, and dives to get clear of his thrashing tail. When she surfaces behind him, she grabs his head and yanks it into the air. As soon as he feels her hands, he grabs at her again and they both go under. She has to slam her doubled fists on the top of his rounded skull several times before she manages to break through his panic. He goes limp.

'Follow orders, Sergeant!' Lacey snaps. 'You got a fat tail. Use it. Lean back towards me. That's right. Let your arms go limp. Now flip your tail toward the surface.'

All at once Blade's bottom half bobs up, and he floats on his back, snout toward the sky as he gasps and breathes. Lacey moves a little away, treading water where he can see her, and gets her bearings. Their struggle has moved them close to the wall of the tank and into the crescent-shaped shadow.

'Move your arms,' she says. 'Real easy now. A paddling motion.'

'My god,' Blade mutters. 'I'm alive.'

'For now. What's that sound?'

Footsteps clang up the metal stairs outside.

'Jeezus! They coming back,' Lacey says. 'Dunt say nothing.'

Deep in the shadow he floats, she paddles, barely breathing as the footsteps trot around the catwalk. At one point Lacey catches a glimpse of a pair of heavy boots and a pair of blue trouser legs above them. Apparently their attacker cast off the burning suncloak, but she can see nothing more of the person through the grate. The footsteps stop. She hears the person make a noise . . . a sob, maybe? A grating sound, a creak of metal, no doubt the sound of the gang-box lid – a wave of stench rolls toward them. The person shrieks and lets the lid drop with a clang. Footsteps race for the door and clatter down the outside stairs.

'Serves the fucker right,' Blade mutters. 'I hope it liked what it saw.'

'Me, too. Think that scream came from a man or a woman?'

'I've no idea. It could have been a young member of my species, even. The incipient vomit in its throat no doubt hindered its self-expression.'

Lacey eases over onto her back and floats, staring up at the sky and the grating, a mere couple of metres, impossibly far away.

'I wonder how long we can keep this up,' she says. 'Can't do it for-ever.'

313

'"Forever" has an elastic meaning. In my case, "forever" might come about twenty minutes from now. This water's cold, and I am, of course, unable to maintain body temperature for long.'

'Yeah, you cold-blooded bastard. Okay, just relax. I'm going to grab your shirt collar with one hand and try to swim us out into the sun with the other.'

With some splashing and a lot of swearing, Lacey manages to steer Blade like a pool raft out into the slatted sunlight in the centre of the tank.

'Full fathom five thy father lies,' Blade remarks. 'Those are pearls that once were his eyes, or however that goes. I fear that when the sun goes down I'm going to know how the esteemed duke felt, down at the bottom of the sea.'

'Well, let's hope we get out of here before then.'

'And how often do you suppose anyone checks these tanks?'

'Judging from that door, not very, yeah.'

Blade sighs but says nothing more. Exactly how are they going to die? Lacey wonders. Drowning out of exhaustion in a couple of days? Starving to death if they don't drown? Toxic reactions to sunburn? Both of them have stripped off most of their clothing in order to stay mobile in the water, but the glazed suncloaks still float. They could shelter under them, maybe. At night, of course, if the water temperature drops too far, Blade will die of hypothermia. Eventually some of the workers at the plant may wander this way. Eventually.

Lacey floats on water that spent millennia frozen among the stars and wishes she could have said goodbye to Jack.

Water. There's a strange sharp aroma in the air. Mulligan floats on noise, a rhythmic crashing sound that translates into the gentle rise and fall of the water under him. The universe is blue and white, with drops of brilliant diamonds. Peaceful. Peaceful and treacherous, as Lacey sinks down through the crystalline liquid. Mulligan can feel it filling his mouth, water enough to quench a lifetime of thirst, more, too much. The surface of the water surges up and breaks over his head.

With a yell Mulligan sits straight up in bed and reaches for the light. He switches it on, sits sweating and gasping for breath, then realizes that the other half of the bed lies empty.

314

'Bobbie!'

She never came home this morning. Wherever she is, danger threatens her. His training has taught him to tell symbolic dreams from the strange vibrations of distant events. This dream pointed to something real.

Now that he's awake, he realizes that he was dreaming of seas and waves, even though he's only seen them in holograms and three-dee dramas. Water provides the key to unlock his far-seeing. He sits dead still and lets his mind turn back to the dream until he begins to see. Water, water covered by a strange pattern of dark stripes and glittering stripes. It makes no sense, yet as his mind lingers on the images they grow stronger in the way that only true visions do. Bobbie is floating in the striped water, and in front of her he sees a curved white wall rising high above water level.

Mulligan gets up and pulls on a pair of jeans, finds a T-shirt and throws that on as well. While he's tying his shoes, he lets the rational part of his mind come into play. Where on Hagar is there water, a lot of water?

'Rehydro. Shit! Of course, them new white tanks.'

He jogs down the hall into the living room, where the windows gleam dark against the glare of day. Buddy's sensors glow and turn toward him.

'Call Dr Carol for me,' Mulligan says. 'Bobbie's in deep trouble out in the Rat Yard. Then call the cops. Tell them to meet us out at Project Noah.'

'My dear Jack!' Buddy says. 'The programmer has not called, and she certainly would tell me if she were in danger. How could you possibly be aware of any such thing?'

'Look, pal, I know what I know.' He taps the red tattoo on his cheek with one finger. 'And knowing got me this.'

'But—'

'Okay, you dunt believe me? Try to contact her.'

'I shall do just that.' Buddy clicks and hums for a long moment. 'Wait – my link. It's dead.'

'Yeah, I coulda told you. I dunt know how it got there, but it be wet. Real wet.'

'I am dialling Dr Carol now. My apologies.'

Buddy lights his screen. They wait while the comm at Carol's clinic rings.

'I fear no one is there,' Buddy says. 'The receptionist appears to have gone home.' He hums and clicks some more while the ring goes on and on. 'Perhaps we should just call the police directly. I – ah, here she is!'

Carol's face, all dreadlocks and grim irritation, appears onscreen. She's wearing her usual green scrubs.

'What the hell do you want?' she snarls.

Mulligan starts to speak, but chokes. Faced with her, his words, his insight, even his vision, seem utterly ridiculous. Fortunately, an AI is never at a loss for words.

'Dr Carol,' Buddy says. 'Jack has had one of his psychic experiences. Apparently the programmer is in some danger.'

'What? Who?'

'Bobbie—' Mulligan retrieves his power of speech at last. 'I had this dream. She be out in the Rat Yard with Blade. I mean, like, I know that. She said they was going out there when they left. And anyway, in the dream, she was in the water, a lot of water, stuck there. Y'know?'

Carol stares at him from the screen, worry dawning on her face.

'I have checked my databanks on psychism as it is known today, Doctor,' Buddy chimes in. 'The experience Jack has related to you is quite plausible. Since I have no power of motion, I beg you for help. I grovel before you, I spit on my circuits, I—'

'Okay, okay. You guys are in luck. I was just locking up, and my stuff's already in my van. Be out on the sidewalk, Mulligan. I'm on my way. Cops stop us for breaking curfew, we'll just take them with us. But if this turns out to be bullshit, man, you're in real trouble.'

'Skin me alive,' Mulligan says. 'I wont care as long as she be safe. Y'know?'

The screen goes dead with no answer.

'It must be noon by now,' Lacey says. 'The sun's right overhead.'

'So it is,' Blade says. 'Are you too hot? You could move into the shade. Otherwise you may learn how a sandworm feels as it decends into the oil at a slice'n'fry.'

'Are you going to be okay?'

'I love heat. And this floating business proves to be remarkably easy, once one stops acting like an idiot and follows orders.' He moves his arms and paddles a bit. 'You know, if I practised this I could work up speed by whipping my tail. I could perhaps give hatchlings and small children rides on my stomach.'

Lacey manages to laugh. Her arms ache, and she flips over onto her back to kick her way into the narrow crescent of shade where she can float and rest.

In the still water of the tank she floats well enough to drowse, only to waken suddenly to the sound of a skimmer. Compressed air first mutters, then roars as the sound comes closer and closer. She turns over onto her stomach and swims out to the middle of the tank, where Blade still floats, his eyes wide open.

'Can that be what I think it is?' he says.

'Yeah, but is it going to come near enough?'

They wait, listen, and Lacey hears her mind begging: *Dunt pass us by, oh dunt!* The sound deafens, then quiets in let-down mode. A squeal of brakes, a thump – it's landed.

'Down at the bottom by the fence,' Blade whispers.

'Yeah,' Lacey says. 'What if it's the person who got us into this mess?'

'I don't give a shit. I'd rather die fast than stew here.'

'Okay. Get ready to yell.'

'You bet.'

The clank of doors – then distant footsteps, voices, come closer, head their way.

'Now,' Lacey says. 'One, two, three—'

'Help!' They both scream their heads off. 'Help!'

Distantly a voice answers. Footsteps hit the metal stairway and begin climbing, so fast that she knows who it must be even before he calls out. Only Jack has the lungs and the strength to run up stairs that steep.

'Bobbie!' Jack calls. 'I be right here.'

Lacey finds herself laughing beyond her power to stop until she starts floundering in the water. She nearly goes under, then gets control and swims out to the edge of the tank to tread water. The door bangs open. Jack steps onto the catwalk.

'Hey, handsome!' Lacey calls out. 'You're a sight to set a girl's heart fluttering. But don't step on that grate.'

'Okay.' Jack grins at her. 'You guys sure down there a long way. Damn good thing Carol's got some rope.'

Lacey can hear Blade hissing in joy behind her.

'Insurance policy, you called him,' Blade says. 'I'm tempted to say the line about more things in heaven and earth, Horatio, but that would be trite.'

Puffing for breath and carrying two suncloaks, Carol walks onto the catwalk. She tosses one at Mulligan, then looks over the edge before she puts her own on.

'Allah!' Carol says. 'I dint think lizzies could swim.'

'You are correct, Dr Carol, we cannot.' Blade starts propelling himself toward the side. 'That's why I'm so glad to see you.'

By the time anyone thinks to call Chief Bates, the forensic team has already brought Gri Nerosi's corpse back to the morgue. Bates rushes through a shower, gets dressed and drives like a maniac, siren wailing, down to the Police Tower. The morgue lies underground, and two storeys down at that, where it's easier to keep things cool. He walks along a hallway lined in plastomarble to a pair of metal double doors. Outside the coroner waits for him. She wears a white smock over her street clothes, and a face mask dangles from a cord around her neck.

'Buenos tardes, Chief,' she says and hands him a mask. 'You'll need that if you want to see the corpse.'

'Yeah, I do.' Bates slips the mask over his head. It stinks of disinfectant. 'That bad?'

'Yeah, we've got him freezing down, basically.'

She leads him through the doors into a long room lined with drawers large enough to hold corpses, then past and into a second room furnished with counters, sinks, a welter of sinister-looking surgical equipment, and two long steel tables. On one of those sits a two-metre-long white plasto tray. Inside that lies what's left of a carli, covered in a crystal-clear liquid that's solidifying fast enough to watch. Despite the chemical ice the stench hangs thick over the table. Bates gets a hint of it even through the mask.

'I suppose it's too soon to tell if that's Gri Nerosi,' he says.

'No, actually. Kaz Varesh of Confederation security sent over his dental records immediately. His skull was nearly clean, as you can see, so I had a quick look. First, there's no other carli reported missing. Second, the teeth seem to match up pretty well. I'd say he's your man.'

Bates considers the corpse's arms. The flesh has blackened and slid off the bones to form clotted masses with fur and insect larvae. Although he's seen plenty of dead bodies, this one forces him to shake his head and turn away.

'Why didn't he mummify?' Bates says. 'Out in all that heat?'

'He was in an airtight metal box. Which is why the rehydro workers never smelled him, by the way. If you want a mummy, you've got to have plenty of air circulation. The body fluids have to evaporate. These pooled. That's why decay was so far advanced.'

'Oh. Have you had a minute to send up the prelim report?'

'Yeah. It should be waiting in your comp.'

Bates leaves the mask behind and hurries to his office. When he sits down, his AI immediately flashes a list of mail onscreen.

'I only want the coroner's report,' Bates says.

'Here you are, Chief. But there's one message I want to point out, from Kaz Varesh at the Con embassy.'

'Thanks, yeah. I'll get to that second.'

With the report come holos taken at the site. By flipping back and forth between them, Bates can visualize how the body most likely looked when it was intact: lying on its back on a white suncloak, arms at the sides, both hands facing out in an honour posture, a set of steel Claws fastened to the right hand. Judging from Lacey's information, someone had laid an expensive shroud over him as well.

'This gets weirder and weirder,' Bates says to the AI. 'Who would murder someone and then give him a ritual send-off?'

'He wasn't murdered, Chief,' the AI says. 'I am putting the relevant sections onscreen.'

Bates reads with a growing sense of shock. Because of the position of the hands, the blades of the Claws rested on the suncloak, preserving traces of well-oxygenated blood on the metal. Although the soft tissues of the throat had decayed beyond quick recognition, the coroner expects microanalysis of what's left of the neck will reveal traces of clean cuts through the blood vessels and windpipe.

'He killed himself?' Bates says. 'Jeezchrise!'

'Apparently so, Chief,' the AI says. 'I personally find this hard to reconcile logically with our previous view of him as a callous thief.'

'Yeah. You're not the only one.'

The strangest detail yet arrives onscreen. The coroner has made a rough estimate of time of death – at least three weeks ago, if not four. Most likely he died at about the same time Moses Oliver did, if not before.

'He was dead, then, before they reported him missing. Have you sent all this over to Kaz Varesh?'

'Yes, sir.'

'Good.' Bates checks his watch. 'It's only sixteen-twenty. Most of the embassy people will still be asleep. We'll call her and Kaz Phaath later.'

'Kaz Phaath?'

'She was Nerosi's boss. She'll need to know.'

'Very well, Chief. I'll add a reminder.'

'Good.' Bates yawns as he looks over the mail queue. One item catches his attention: the Esperance police have a suspect under arrest for the moly attack on Yosef Mbaye. He turned up at a clinic with a broken arm, and a doctor recognized his description from the news. The man's record is a match for the dead Moses Oliver, a petty criminal who worked for the Alliance. So far he's refused to talk, but Bates is willing to bet that he was working for the Hoppers when he jumped the ball player. He skims quickly through the remainder of the queue, but there's nothing else that matters.

'Okay, I'm going to want that prelim report on the riot damages. Is there anything else I should read ahead of it? Anything that might relate to the *leijchwen* case, I mean.'

'To what order of relationship?'

'Seventh.'

'Very well. I shall check.' The AI clicks rapidly and hums, flashing strings of symbols onscreen. The screen clears. 'Here is a report that just came in, Chief. The victims in this picture seem to fit the general description of two of the men who killed Michael Takahashi.'

'Victims? What the hell?'

An image appears relayed in from a belt comp, judging by its poor quality, but clear enough for him to see the faces. As he studies it, a message line flashes into being beneath it. 'Fingerprints confirm presence of these two in Takahashi's house on night of death.'

'Huh. Looks like a Hopper hitman found them before I did. Too bad.' Bates considers for a moment. 'Connect me with the beat cop who found them. Looks like he's still at the scene.'

'He is, yes. Officer Lyons his name is.'

After a moment's delay a voice starts talking over the audio-only channel.

'Sir? Chief? This is Lyons.'

'Good. This case is going to be touchy. Those two are known agents of the Alliance and Alliance citizens. Dunt let nobody come near the scene. How long will it take for backup to get there?'

'It's already here, Chief. I'm right outside the Bazaar Station, Eleventh Precinct.'

'You're where?'

'In the parking lot of Bazaar Station.' Onscreen the previous image dances and disappears. 'Sorry, I gotta get this damn thing working right. Wait. Here it comes. Look at this, sir.'

'This' turns out to be a view of one victim's head. A bright red bow of the sort used to top gift boxes sits on the curly brown hair. Bates gawks.

'They were killed execution style,' Lyons goes on. 'One stab with a moly right at the base of the skull, angled up and in. The other one, same thing, only that one has the ribbon around his neck.'

'Ribbon?'

'Yeah. It aint your birthday, is it, Chief? Looks like someone sent you a present.'

Bates signs off then sits for a moment, thinking, wondering if he's angry or relieved. He stands up and grabs his hat from the extra chair.

'If anyone needs me,' he says, 'I'll be at A to Z Enterprises.'

But he barely reaches the door when Colonel Ahtuksak calls, and he finds himself discussing the tedious detail of events that may well never happen.

Chapter Fourteen

Although Lacey feels like sleeping for several standard days, Buddy wakes her at sunset with a long insistent buzz on her bedside comm link. She sits up and grabs it from the nightstand.

'What the hell?'

'My apologies, Programmer, but your brother wishes to speak to you. He said, though I paraphrase, you will either arrive somewhere or experience sexual pleasure at hearing his words. I cannot see how either is possible.'

'It's an idiom, Buddy. Start the coffee, will you?'

Sound asleep, Jack lies sprawled on his stomach with his head hanging over the side of the bed. At times Lacey wonders if his mother accepted gene donations from house cats. She pulls on some clothes and goes into the living room, where Richie's perfect face smiles at her from the three-dee screen.

'Hey,' he said. 'Been outside lately? On the streets, I mean.'

'No. Que pasa, hermanito?'

'Nada. Or maybe I should say no one. Lots of no ones. You right about those evacuation plans, so we sort of spread the word that it might be a good time to go visit Auntie in Novo Murmansk or take a holiday at the beautiful exotic Rat Yard. Lots of sentients still here, but it's a start.'

'Yeah? Good for you. Thanks.'

'Oh, and something sort of funny turned up. I thought you might be interested. Somebody gave Chief Bates a present this morning.' He grins at his own joke, his beautiful open smile that's child-like without being childish. 'Two presents, with red ribbons.'

She waits for him to explain, but he abruptly breaks the connection, leaving her staring at the dead screen. 'Buddy, check the police records. See if anything funny happened in the last ten hours or so.'

'Checking now, Programmer. I find only one incident that might arouse your brother's sense of humour. Two hours ago, an Officer Lyons came out of the Bazaar Station in the Eleventh Precinct and discovered two corpses festooned with red ribbons. The two have been tentatively identified as Ramon Bell and Joseph Carvasce, Alliance citizens and suspects in the Takahashi murder.'

'Oh.' Lacey's stomach twists in a feeling close to nausea. 'And Richie told me . . . cancel that. Did you record my conversation with my brother?'

'Per your orders I have a sub-routine that records all calls from priority sentients.'

'Retrieve the most recent call, view it, and then wipe it.'

Lacey leans back and puts her feet up on her desk. Just when she thinks Richie might someday rejoin the human race, he does something that reminds her the 'someday' is a long time off. *Never should have left him.* The old guilt threatens to bite, but she muzzles it. She left her sisters behind, too, and neither of them turned to drugs and prostitution.

'Programmer?' Buddy says. 'I thought there were three human males involved in the death of Michael Takahashi.'

'There were. The question is, did one dude manage to get away from Richie's goons or is he being kept for something special?'

'I do not understand the term, "something special".'

'You're lucky you dunt. Some of Richie's clients are as twisted as he is. I—'

An iris opens in one corner of Buddy's screen, and he chimes. 'Oddly enough, Programmer, Chief Bates is at our front gate. Shall I admit him?'

'Yeah. Why not? And see if you can wake Jack up, will you?'

'I have admitted Chief Bates. Your second order will take some time to execute.'

Bates arrives as she's pouring herself coffee, and he looks so exhausted that she offers him some as well. He takes the cup and sits down on the couch. He seems to slump inside his wrinkled green uniform.

'What brings you here?' Lacey says.

'Two things,' Bates says. 'First, an apology.'

'Say what?'

'I looked at some of the vid from the F Street riots. Yeah, my officers got a little carried away.'

Lacey stops herself from screaming 'more than a little'. She never expected this much, after all.

'Glad you can keep an open mind,' she says instead.

Bates shrugs and tries a sip of the coffee, then a gulp.

'The second thing,' he says. 'Is the Mayor of Porttown an urban legend, or is there some top-of-the-line gangsta dude who runs the Bazaar?'

This one's even more of a surprise. Lacey takes her coffee to her desk and sits down to gain a little time. 'Why are you asking me?'

'You seem to know everything that happens over here. You grew up here, right?'

'I've heard stories about a Porttown boss all my life, yeah. I figure it this way. No one who's good at taking orders ends up in the Bazaar.'

'You got a point.' Bates smiles briefly. 'The damnedest thing happened. You had the news on yet?'

'No.'

During Bates's recital of the discovery of the two dead Alliance goons, Lacey manages to look properly surprised. She shakes her head a lot, too, as if in amazement.

'Officer Zizzistre,' Bates finishes up, 'swears it's got to be the Mayor of Porttown behind it.'

'I get it. That's why you asked. But I dunt see why the Mayor would do something like that.'

'To get the heat off his operations. It's plausible that he dunt want cops running all over the Bazaar and asking questions while they look for a couple of goons.'

'Yeah, I never thought of that.' She smiles briefly. 'And maybe he's a baseball fan.'

Bates rolls his eyes heavenward and leans back on the couch. For a moment he drinks his coffee in silence.

'I couldn't find *iLeijchwen* in the Bazaar last night,' Lacey says at last. 'Do you think the Hoppers killed Gri Nerosi like they did Oliver?'

'No.' Bates looks up, startled. 'I forget you wouldn't know. Nerosi committed suicide.'

'That dunt make a lot of sense.'

Yeah, it dunt. Nothing makes sense any more.'

Buddy speaks up. 'I had just retrieved the coroner's report when you arrived, Chief Bates. Could the Hoppers have made a murder look like suicide?'

'No, because of the shroud,' Lacey says. 'Only someone who works at the Confederation Embassy would have had access to one of those. The thing that bothers me, Chief, is this. I told your people how someone shot at me and my bodyguard, then came back to look at the body. You hear that?'

'Sure did. I read the full report. I'm guessing the perp was thinking about moving the body until he got a good look at it.'

'That was my guess, too. But how did they know we were out there poking around? You're the only person I told, except Jack and Buddy. It seems too weird to be just coincidence.'

Bates starts to answer, then goes very still. His eyes seem to lose focus for a moment.

'You okay?' Lacey says.

'Yeah. Jeez, I'm tired. I'm having real strange ideas. Can I have more of that coffee?'

'Help yourself, yeah.'

While Bates fills his cup, Buddy runs a message across his screen in Kangolan: Jack keeps waking, turning off the comm link, and then going back to sleep. Lacey answers: Keep after him, and thanks.

'I keep hoping Erik Royall will defect,' Bates says abruptly. 'He knows what orders came down. He probably relayed them to the goons. Oliver was killed deliberately. Tak was killed by mistake. Maybe Gri Nerosi killed himself when he figured they were coming for him. I dunt know. Did Oliver work for Nerosi first and the Hoppers second? Dunt know that, either. Then there's this Saunders donna. Who's she working for?'

Lacey thinks for a moment.

'Tell me something, Chief. Does the PBI have any information about H'Allevae AI security in its files?'

325

'It should. They get paid enough over there.'

'Buddy maybe can hack into the 'Lies system. I no going to let him do it cold. It's too dangerous. They have killer sub-routines encoded all over their comp.'

'It's going to be dangerous even with the data. But hey, if you lose this one we'd buy you an equivalent model AI.'

Buddy squeals and rings a barrage of error messages.

'That's no the point, Chief,' Lacey says. 'Buddy's an individual.'

Bates smiles in a condescending way. 'Whatever,' he says. 'But look, Buddy, if there's a shooting war, you no going to be able to run and hide.'

'There! You have actually made a logical statement,' Buddy says with a snarl in his voice. 'I shall be happy to assist you if my programmer allows.'

'Okay, good. Put a call through for me to Akeli and I'll see about getting you the data.'

'That will not be necessary, Chief Bates.'

Bates blinks rapidly, then sighs. He goes back to the couch and sits down. 'Dunt mind me,' he says. 'I'm only the top cop in this damned city. What the hell do I know?'

While Buddy browses the PBI files, Lacey goes into the bedroom to wake Jack, but she finds the bed empty and hears the sound of the sono-cleaner from the bathroom. She returns to find Bates, his massive hands linked on his stomach, drowsing on the couch. Buddy is producing a symphony of clicks and hums. She sits down, activates her keyboard and watches data in the Hopper syllabary flashing by onscreen, too fast for her to read even if she knew the language.

'Buddy?' Lacey types. 'Are you into the Hopper system yet?'

'Not yet, Programmer,' Buddy answers onscreen. 'I am transferring files from the PBI. Why?'

'I want you to be careful, that's why. If you think you're in danger, pull out.'

'Very well, Programmer. Though something odd has happened in my personality module. Now that I know I am truly alive, I know that I can die. The thought of danger has become both repellent and peculiarly attractive, as if I were wagering with death, as if death were an individual. Is this common among sentients?'

'Very common. Be careful anyway.'

Buddy answers with a couple of clicks and a hum. His screen clears itself, then begins flashing Hopper syllables again. A crawl in Kangolan runs across the bottom: accessing Alliance Embassy now. Lacey feels her breath catch in her throat. At a sound out in the room, she nearly screams.

'Jeez.' Jack comes wandering into the living room. 'A real lively bunch in here.'

'You should talk, sweetheart.'

When he smiles at her, she finds herself remembering the way Richie smiles, just as beautifully, technically, but Jack has something her brother lacks. *Humanity, maybe*, she thinks. *Or a soul.*

'Whatcha doing?'

'Watching Buddy hack. It's important.'

'Okay.' He wanders away into the kitchen.

Onscreen Lacey sees a matrix of Hopper numbers in their base fourteen system. These she does recognize, from her training at OCS. She leans forward again, watching numbers pop from cell to cell, waver, disappear, reappear elsewhere. As much as she aches to ask Buddy what he's doing, she's afraid to disturb him.

Jack reappears with a mug of coffee in one hand. He goes to the window, looking out as the polarization lightens for the sunset. Bates lets out a long snore, then sits up with a body-trembling shudder.

'Sorry,' he mutters. 'Dint realize I was so tired.'

'No problem,' Lacey says. 'We're all out of it.'

Buddy chimes in a cascade of beeps and bells. All three humans in the room yelp in sheer surprise. Lacey turns and looks at the screen, but she finds Kangolan, not terminal fault messages.

'I have succeeded in hacking into the data system at the Alliance Embassy, Programmer.'

'Great!' Lacey types. 'We can talk now.'

'Very well,' Buddy says aloud. 'Chief Bates, I have access.'

'Ha!' Lacey grins at him. 'Knew you could. Hey, Bates, you ought to pay Buddy some consulting fees.'

Bates hauls himself off the couch and strolls over.

'Maybe so,' he says. 'How, Buddy?'

'Among other things,' Buddy says, 'I found an example of surprising sloppiness on the part of one who should have known better. Mr Royall has been maintaining his own secret databank, and he was foolish enough to neglect disconnecting the number key Ms Scheffler provided.'

'What a dorkero!' Lacey says.

'What's more,' Buddy goes on, 'Royall is addicted to certain recreational services, and thus he created a connection between the normal planetary data nets and a system that should have remained behind an unbroken firewall.'

'More fool he! Take a look, Chief. Buddy, if you could translate the titles of these files?'

In Merrkan Buddy flashes a list onto the screen. Bates looks over Lacey's shoulder; she can feel how tense he is even though he never touches her.

'That one,' Bates says suddenly. 'Report: Royall, third of Stember.'

'Very well.' Buddy clears his throat. ' "We successfully located Moses Oliver," the report begins, "and procured the necessary information. Gri Nerosi has been transferred off-planet by his embassy—"'

'Whoa!' Bates snaps. 'Was Oliver lying, or didn't he know about the suicide?'

'I sure dunt know,' Lacey says.

' "Oliver, however,"' Buddy continues, ' "successfully received the object from Sandy Wentworth, Gri Nerosi's confederate, if I may make a small pun, in this venture."'

'Sandy!' Lacey says, triumphant. 'I bet that's where the name Saunders comes from.' She glances at Bates and finds his face ashen. 'Chief?'

Bates straightens and walks a few slow steps away. Lacey swivels round to look at him.

'Hey, Bates,' Jack says. 'You okay? You better sit down or something.'

Bates shakes his head. He goes to the window and grips the sill with both hands while he trembles as if feverish. Lacey gets up fast.

'Is it chest pains?' she says.

'No am sick.' His voice cracks and whispers. 'Not that way, anyway. I – jeezuz aitch ker-ist. Did she play me for a fool or what?'

328

When Jack starts to speak, Lacey waves him into silence. In a few seconds Bates straightens up, turns around, breathes deeply, and even manages a faint smile.

'Sorry,' Bates says. 'I know Wentworth, is all. She usually goes by her carli name of Kaz Phaath.'

Lacey remembers Carol talking about the young woman at the carli embassy who had come between her and Bates.

'Oh jeez,' she says. 'I'm sorry.'

Bates shrugs and looks away. 'What counts now,' he says to the wall, 'is arresting her and finding out where the goddamn *iLeijchwen* is.'

'She's covered by diplomatic immunity, isn't she?' Lacey asks.

'Yeah. Dunt matter. There are carli security people at the embassy, and she's not immune from them. Buddy, could you place a call for me? I need to get hold of someone named Kaz Varesh.'

'Certainly, Chief Bates,' Buddy says. 'I shall transfer the recovered files to your AI as well.'

'Thanks.'

'And. . .' Buddy hesitates, then chimes softly, 'If I may be so bold, sir, you have my profound sympathy. Betrayal by one whom one counts as a friend must be extremely painful.'

'It is, yeah.' Bates turns and looks into the AI's vid pickup. 'But I'll get over it.'

Buddy makes the connection to the embassy comm, then puts an image of a female carli in a tight black jacket on the three-dee. Behind her stands the first blond carli Lacey's ever seen, also dressed in black. Bates sits down in front of the vid pickup. Lacey has to admire his calm.

'Bates!' Kaz Varesh says. 'I was about to contact you myself. I take it you have something for me?'

'Sure do. You need to hold the embassy's data analyst, Kaz Phaath, for questioning. I have definite information implicating her in the theft of *iLeijchwen*.'

'So!' Kaz Varesh's ears to to full extension. 'That's why she's disappeared.'

Bates goggles at her. Lacey mutters something so foul under her breath that Mulligan winces.

'Ka Pral reported her missing some hours ago,' Kaz Varesh continues. 'Her bed was never slept in, according to Kaz Trem, the housekeeper here. Well, this is a fine netful of prey, I must say. I wonder if she has *iLeijchwen* in her possession?'

'If she does,' Bates says, 'I dunt know what she thinks she's going to do with it.'

Jack turns away and walks into the kitchen. He's hungry, Lacey supposes, and she herself feels as if she's eavesdropping. Buddy will record the conversation for her to hear later without embarrassing Bates further. When she joins Jack in the kitchen, she finds him eating a chunk of bread smeared with soyacheese.

'I dunt get it,' he says. 'Bates, he in love with this donna or something? I done pick up his feelings when Buddy say Wentworth, and he was all torn up.'

'Yeah, I think he did love her. Or maybe he was just infatuated. I mean, hell, he's only known her about three weeks from what Carol told me.'

'Yeah? Well, I fell for you the first day I ever seen you. It was kinda weird. Walked into that party, saw you, and it was like walking into a fire. Couldn't breathe.' Jack looks away, half smiling. 'She be mine, I thought. Or no, it was more like the thought, it was thinking me. Y'know?' He takes another big bite of his bread.

'Yeah, I kind of do. I'm sure glad you did. Best insurance policy I ever—'

She stops suddenly. She has an idea, a crazy idea, maybe, but it just might work. She looks out the kitchen door and sees that Bates has finished his comm call.

'Hey, Chief? I bet Jack can find *iLeijchwen* for us.'

'What?' Bates walks over. 'How?'

'It's the psi component. Jack, think you can pick it up? Like a scent, sort of?'

'I dunt know.' Jack shrugs. 'If Nunks help, maybe. It be a long shot, Bobbie. There be a hell of a lot of psychic signals in this town.'

'A long shot's better than no shot.'

Bates stands looking back and forth between them.

'Whatcha think, Chief?' Lacey says.

'I think you've both been out in the sun too long, that's what I think. But you're right. It's crazy, but it's better than nothing. Now. How are we going to set this up?'

The problem with little blue pills, Bates thinks, *is the price*. Once the effects wear off, he'll have to sleep damn near around the clock. He slips one out of his pocket anyway and dry-swallows it. Lacey, sitting in the skimmer's passenger seat, eyes him without comment. When Bates glances out his window, he spots the second squad skimmer, flying off to his left at a good distance. In the rearview mirror, he can see Lacey's two-headed alien gardener, who takes up most of the rear seat, hunched over awkwardly under the low roof.

'This is a damn stupid idea,' he mutters. 'Just because Mulligan thought he felt the thing—'

'He did,' Lacey says. 'He dint just think so. Hey, Chief, you know how good he is at what he does.' She glances back. 'No offense, Nunks, it's different for humans.'

Nunks shrugs and spreads his large hands.

'That means he thinks humans are stupid about some things,' Lacey says.

'He dunt get no argument from me.' *Especially about women*. Bates can taste betrayal, a bitter bite like quinine, in his mouth.

'Well, his people have their own stupidities,' Lacey goes on. 'He's a political exile. Right now, I can't help thinking that politics is a stupid game.'

In the mirror, Bates sees Nunks sit up straighter, brushing the top of his bifurcated head against the roof. At the same moment, the comm squawks.

'Chief?' It's Mulligan, riding in the other squad skimmer with Zizzistre. 'I think I got it. Just kinda a hint, like, real faint, but that carli thing, it no something I just gonna forget, you know? Real clear feel to it.'

'Mulligan, damn you, keep talking!' Abruptly, the idea of triangulating on the psychic impression of a piece of cloth seems far less crazy. Bates takes another glance back at Nunks; the three-eyed face lacks any expression Bates can read, but the bifurcate head is nodding. 'Lacey, you're riding with me to play interpreter, so interpret! What the hell is happening?'

'Nunks has the image, I think,' Lacey says, just as the comm comes back to life.

'I hadda give Nunks the smell, like,' Mulligan says over the comm. 'He got it now. We dunt know exactamento where it be, still too far away, but we heading in the right direction. It dunt seem to be moving much.' Nunks waves one arm emphatically to the left, and Mulligan's voice continues. 'Uh, Nunks, he say you heading towards downtown. You gotta go west.'

'I guess you dint need me for an interpreter after all,' Lacey says. 'I could have ridden with Jack.'

'Glad you dint,' Bates says. He turns left on 22nd, one of the major east-west arteries, and flips on both lights and siren. 'Easier talking to someone who can talk back. We going the right way now?' Nunks nods slowly. 'Jack, is something wrong?'

'He say you still not heading exactly right,' Mulligan's voice answers. 'You guys is five, six blocks north of us, and it be right in front of me, you know? Only we still got a long way to go.'

'See, you really dint need me,' Lacey says.

'Yeah, yeah.' Bates takes the top traffic lane as he goes through the next intersection, even though traffic is light at this time of day. 'You know, Carol and me, we talked about Wentworth, just once. Carol told me she was an alien, and I dint believe her. But she was right: that female's no kind of human. She's all carli.'

'I doubt that, Chief.' Lacey is speaking more gently than she normally does. 'She's human, all right. That's probably the problem. She's trying to change into a carli.'

'Whatever. Wonder what they're going to do to her?' He tries to control his voice, but he can feel his anger bubbling over. With a shake of his head he drops two blocks south to avoid a construction zone. 'Hey, Mulligan, ask Nunks if this is any better.'

'You ask him,' Jack's voice says. 'He, like, understands Merrkan, and he be right there. Only he already heard, and he says yeah, it is. Nunks thinks you gonna get there in about fifteen more minutes.'

Her dark red Toyota, the first skimmer she's ever owned, speeds through the air with a rhythmic growl that delights Kaz Phaath. She takes the Reforma on-ramp at the highest legal speed, savouring the easy response, the absolute control she has of this large physical object.

Control. She lost control of the situation, she realizes now, as soon as *iLeijchwen* left her hands. She made a bad mistake when she chose Moses Oliver as her tool. His incompetence caused more problems than his treachery. She's accepted that she'll never know what went wrong, although she still wonders how all those baseball players got involved, but soon, soon now, she will redeem enough of her honor to save her family from shame. She glances down at the skimmer's map. A small park glows green on the display. Reforma circles around the outlying western suburbs; she'll approach from the park from the east. Not, she thinks, that she need worry much longer about secrecy.

She takes the next exit and halts the skimmer on a quiet residential side street two blocks short of the park. She's arrived intentionally early for the meeting, but she suspects that she's not the first. *A pity Moses Oliver was not as careful as his employer.* Jay Gagne takes more precautions than Kaz Phaath does herself. At this time of day, few sentients are out, still fewer on foot. She anticipates no difficulty in locating the gambler, despite the anonymity provided by the omni-present suncloaks. After which, she reflects calmly, it will no longer matter what happens to her. *iLeijchwen* will be safe.

She picks up a cloth bag and slings it over her shoulder. It contains all of Martinelli's down-payment, plus every bit of her own money. Not enough, but it should distract Jay Gagne. She originally intended to donate it to some worthy Polar City charity, after the conquest. Doctor Carol, perhaps, if she survived. Al Bates praised her work.

After adjusting her helmet, she steps from the skimmer and looks around. No other suncloaks in sight. As she walks towards the eastern green of the park, she relishes the warmth of the sun's rays through the cloak. She will never feel natural sunlight on her skin again, a fact she regrets. Trees and bushes look subtly wrong, even allowing for Hagar's too-harsh sun – earth species, all of them. She would rather have brought this matter to its end among the pale blue trees of home.

A maze of graveled paths wind through the plantings and create the illusion of privacy and space. She chooses a path almost at random. She's not due at the central gazebo for another twelve

333

minutes. A riot of colour, Earth-stock marigolds and zinnias catch her eye, and she stops to appreciate their beauty. A few stray thoughts drift through her mind, but now is not the time to think. That will come when she faces Jay Gagne. *At last Gri Nerosi will receive a proper body slab and the honor due him.* His fate bothered her most. She despised him as a human-corrupted weakling until he proved his honor with his life. Hiding his body stole the respect he deserved, a theft as great as that of *iLeijchwen* itself. *Well, he will soon reclaim it all.*

Misjudged him. Misjudged Oliver. Misjudged her own people. She expected the war to have begun and gotten over by now. But she did not misjudge Jay Gagne, at least not in this. A white-cloaked figure approaches from the far side of the park, near the Metro station. Kaz Phaath smiles to herself. It's time to reclaim *iLeijchwen* for her people.

Sarojini has walked into the park on its western side. Outside the gazebo she sees a suncloaked figure that stops two meters away on the path. Sarojini takes a few steps toward her, then waits for the figure to speak. When she glances around, she sees no one else in the center of the park. The thick shrubbery muffles the noise of passing traffic. They have privacy, yes, but Sarojini suddenly realizes just how alone they are. As she thinks about it, she could kill Moses herself for getting her mixed up in something this dangerous.

After a moment, the other adjusts the polarization on her helmet. Once she can see her familiar face, Sarojini follows suit.

'Sandy. Let's get this over with. Is that the reward money?' Sarojini nods at the cloth bag slung over the woman's shoulder – a piece of carli work, all subtle grays and blues. It would be attractive, but Sarojini has seen enough carli weaving to last her a rejuved lifetime.

'Yes. I was afraid you weren't going to show up.' Her voice trembles on the edge of exhaustion. 'It's not as much money as the Senator was offering.'

'The Senator is no longer in the market,' Sarojini pulls a clear plastic tube out of her suncloak's pocket and holds it up. 'Here it is. You can see it through the plastoclear.' When Sandy reaches for it, Sarojini drops it back into her pocket. 'But senator or no senator, your employers seem ready to go to war over this little scrap of cloth. Profits are useless to the dead.'

'Profits.' Sandy giggles, then stops herself with a little gasp.

Sarojini plucks the bag neatly from her extended hand, but steps back fast when Sandy tries to reach for *iLeijchwen*.

'Ah, ah, not yet. Let me count this first. Not that I don't trust you, Sandy.' *And not that I do.* 'But your employers are another matter. Poor Moses shouldn't have trusted them either.' She riffles through the bag. *A lot of small denomination bills here—*

Sandy's voice sounds oddly distorted. 'My employers.'

Sarojini barely notices. Her fingers dart through the bills again, a long rustle of red and blue cash, but she finds no more than before. 'This is less than half the promised reward. It looks as if your dear employers cheated you. Cheated us. Unless you—' She looks up and her fingers freeze. Sandy holds a small but deadly-looking laser pistol, aimed straight at her.

'Not my employers.' The change in Sandy's voice startles Sarojini almost as much as the weapon; she now sounds cultivated, educated, determined. 'They are my people. Please give me *iLeijchwen* now. Carefully. You may keep your blood-money.'

Sarojini stands perfectly still. 'Your people? You're not a carli. You're as human as I am.'

'Human, perhaps, to my shame. But I am a citizen of the Interstellar Confederation, not your foolish little Republic.' She raises the hand holding the laser. 'Give it to me.'

'You – you must have killed Moses!' Sarojini takes a step towards the Con woman without realizing it. 'Did you shoot him yourself, or did some of your carli friends do it for you? You can't be very important. You told me yourself the carlis have no respect for humans.'

'I lied. I am— I was a senior department head, and with a name of honor. Sandy.' She almost spits the name out. 'A child's name, fit for dealing with childish humans, but my true name I earned. I am Kaz Phaath yil Frakmo, and you will give me *iLeijchwen*. Now.'

'Did you shoot Moses?' Sarojini deliberately takes another step forward, and Kaz Phaath falls back.

'No! If you want to find his killers, I suggest you look to his other employers. The Hoppers are intolerant of failure.' Kaz Phaath takes one more step backwards and raises the gun slightly, underlining her words. 'I do not wish to kill you, Jay Gagne, but I shall if you do not give me *iLeijchwen*. It's going back where it belongs, today.'

'So why'd you steal it?' As she speaks, Sarojini drops the bag at her feet and holds her right hand out, displaying it before slowly reaching into her pocket. 'If all you're going to do is give it back, why get Moses involved?'

'I doubt if you would understand. But your partner got no worse than he deserved. Selling services to both sides, luring young fools like Gri Nerosi into human weaknesses – a man devoid of honor.'

He never cheated me. Sarojini's fingers slide down past the plastic tube, checking the tiny spray canister of BioSafe repellent. Using exaggerated, obvious care, she pulls the tube holding *iLeijchwen* out of her pocket while taking a slow step forward. *A little closer—*

When Kaz Phaath snatches it out of her hand, her attention shifts from Sarojini for a few precious seconds. Before the other woman notices, Sarojini has the canister out. She sprays it into the air vents of Kaz Phaath's helmet.

The helmet's fan blows the corrosive spray directly into Kaz Phaath's nose and eyes. With a scream, a horrible bubbling scream, she drops both the weapon and *iLeijchwen*. With both hands she scrabbles at her head for the latch of her helmet. Sarojini stoops, grabs the gun and tube, but Kaz Phaath's helmet lands on the grass in front of her. Just as Sarojini turns to run, Kaz Phaath grabs her around the waist. Swearing and kicking, Sarojini falls struggling to the ground. She had three brothers. She knows how to fight dirty. She whips out one leg and topples Kaz Phaath.

Screaming again, Kaz Phaath grabs her and pins her with her weight. Despite her smaller size, Sarojini rolls them over, pinning the larger woman beneath her. Tears stream from Kaz Phaath's reddened eyes, so many they must blind her. *If I could scratch her eyes – but I don't dare let her go.*

Underneath her, Kaz Phaath is twisting and struggling. Too late Sarojini realizes that she's digging in her suncloak pocket with her right hand. Sarojini makes a grab at her hand just as Kaz Phaath pulls out something metallic that glitters in the sun.

'A set of claws. Gods!' Sarojini lets her go and tries to roll away from the deadly curved blades.

Kaz Phaath grabs Sarojini's cloak with one hand and with the other rakes the claws down Sarojini's right side. The cloak splits, and Sarojini feels agony lance through her. She screams and drops the pistol, rolls desperately and gets free. She hauls herself to her knees just as Kaz Phaath snatches up the laser pistol again.

Back to their opening moves: the other woman holds the laser and the upper hand, Sarojini clutches *iLeijchwen* to her chest. But this time she can feel blood running down her side.

'No very far now,' Mulligan says. He can feel pain throbbing in his head, along with a faint nausea, whether psychic or physical, he can not tell. 'I see something white, a weird wood thing with a peaked roof.'

'That little park and the gazebo.' Officer Zizzistre grunts with satisfaction and reaches for the comm. 'Chief? Think we got it. Yeah, the park.'

While Bates and Izzy talk, Mulligan leans back in his seat and focuses. He's getting a whiff of a familiar mental smell. It has to be *iLeijchwen*. Nunks sends him a wave of signal.

Little brother->feel mind – human – mind? <confusion>

Yeah. Latent/unaware <- with target. He flashes an image to Nunks and feels his agreement. A latent telepath near *iLeijchwen* radiates fear, anger, determination, and a confusion of other emotions. Mulligan locks onto the mind-print. In his mind he can see the lawn stained red in one ominous spot.

'Land this thing, okay? We got trouble.'

'We going down!' Izzy sings out.

The skimmer dives and lands at the park's west entrance. Mulligan climbs out fast. Before he gets two paces from the skimmer, pain knocks him staggering back against the fender. *Pain/rage/fear pain pain PAINPAIN . . .*

Not your pain/NOT your pain! > Little brother->MUST-> free mind of pain.

Mulligan sobs in relief. Not his pain. *Who?* he thinks, but even as Nunks replies, he furnishes the answer. *Mental: the latent/physical: a victim*. Mulligan shakes off Zizzistre's hand.

'That way! Something bad going down, man, real bad.' Mulligan pushes off from the bumper and starts running east with his long-legged easy stride. Behind him he can hear Izzy plodding along.

From ahead of him the feelings pour out: *<rage> <fear> <regret> <pain> <guilt> <defeat>* Because of their intensity he can read the mind twined around the feelings. A woman. Kaz Phaath: the name lends force to the feelings: her identity beyond a mere name, the desperate way she clings to loyalty to her tribe, her *pack*, her carlis. *Dunt make sense*, he sends to Nunks. *Love?/hate? carlis? IF love->steal rag? <baffled> IF hate->loyal WHY?*

Mulligan leaps over a meter-tall line of carefully trimmed bushes and lands in a roll that brings him back to his feet almost without breaking stride. Behind him, he can hear Izzy crashing through the hedge. He crosses a deserted playground, rounds the gazebo and stumbles to a halt. Some twenty meters ahead, a suncloaked figure without a helmet aims a laser pistol at another kneeling on the ground. A woman, he realizes as this second person speaks.

'You murdering bitch.' She holds *iLeijchwen* in front of herself, like a shield.

In his mind the unhelmeted figure's image glows red-hot. Kaz Phaath. 'I told you before, I did not kill your worthless partner.'

Her finger is tightening, ready to shoot. With a yell Mulligan runs forward, caught up in a rage of his own. So this is the woman who nearly destroyed everything he loves. Like a psychic spear Mulligan hurls his rage at her. *Traitor! Kill your own people/humans/us <- for piece of alien junk \ no even human.*

She whirls around to face him. He slows down, walks a few paces closer, then stops when she turns the pistol his way.

How?! No, no— She tries to send her thought, but it dissolves into denial and desperation. *The carli are my people!*

Mulligan can see the woman on the ground standing up, hesitating, taking a step back. He sents to Kaz Phaath again.

You dunt even know WHAT <- you stole! He opens his mind to *iLeijchwen* and channels it to her: the image, its strength, its pride. He

338

falls into a silver void and becomes once again part of the undefeated pack, united behind the great carli hunter, their leader. The image, a wise brown-furred face streaked with silver-blond, glows in front of him, and once more he feels alien emotions, the identity with the Pack at the heart of the carli psyche. With a thrust of rage he forces the image into her mind.

With his physical ears he hears her scream.

So! Jack tells her. *You dint know CARLI <- like you thought, huh?* he sends. *THIS -> CARLI!*

He hears – feels – a wail of agony, so intense that for a moment he thinks it might be his own. The silver vision vanishes. He is standing on the edge of the lawn. The wail belonged to Kaz Phaath, who flings the pistol away and runs, screaming, stumbling over the grass. Her victim has sidled further away. Mulligan starts to say something to her, but the scene begins to break up into jagged pieces of blue and silver.

'Ah shit!' Mulligan drops to his knees.

The last thing he hears before the pain begins is Izzy's voice, yelling, 'Police! Halt! Police! I said halt!'

When he sees the gazebo, Bates starts to cut the skimmer's power. They glide down, circle the lawn once, and land with a hiss of air. Some sixty meters away, Izzy vanishes into a clump of bushes. Mulligan lies sprawled on the grass.

Bates hits the door switch, twists out of his seat belt and jumps out. Lacey has somehow moved even faster. She runs past him and falls to her knees beside Mulligan.

'Go after the perp,' Lacey snaps. 'He's just having one of those headaches.'

'Use the comm in the car,' Bates says. 'Get an ambulance out here.'

Bates takes off running as fast as he can. He plunges into the bushes. Izzy's tail has cut a good clear trail of destruction through the landscaping.

'Jack!' Lacey squats beside him. 'C'mon, sweetheart, you gonna be fine—' She strokes the hair back from his forehead. 'What happened?'

339

Jack breathes deeply, manages a smile. Dimly she's aware of Nunks, hurrying up behind her.

'I done stopped her,' Jack said. 'That bitch Kaz Phaath. She was gonna kill—' He breaks off and tries to sit up. 'No! Dunt let her take it!'

'Bates'll nail the carli-lover.'

'No mean Kaz Phaath. Her!' He points at a stand of trees. 'She got *iLeijchwen*.'

Lacey leaps to her feet and spins around, following his point. A suncloaked figure is staggering, trying to run; it stops, leaning against the trunk of eucalyptus.

'Nunks!' Lacey says. 'Take care of Jack!'

When Lacey runs after her, the woman takes off again, runs a few steps, then merely walks, clutching something to her side. Lacey races after, dodging into the trees. On the other side of the little grove looms the red arch that marks a Metro station. Lacey takes her laser pistol out of her vest pocket.

'Stop right there!' she yells.

The other woman turns and follows orders, swaying a little as she waits for Lacey to catch up to her. As Lacey trots up, she can see that three parallel gashes have left one side of the cloak in ribbons, glistening red. With her right arm the woman clasps a blue and gray cloth bag over her wounds. A plastic tube dangles from her other hand. Through the unpolarized face plate of the woman's helmet, Lacey recognizes the Hindu guard from the spaceport, the one who stole *iLeijchwen* from Tak. Her grip tightens on the laser.

'I need medical assistance. As you can see.' The woman is gasping in pain. 'I promise you, I am no threat.'

'The hell you're not.'

'I'm not armed. I had Sandy's pistol, but I couldn't carry it, not with this wound.'

'I dint mean that. I'm talking about *iLeijchwen*. If we dunt get it back to the carlis—'

'Ah yes.' The fake guard smiles with a twist of her full mouth. 'Enough to make one believe in curses, this bit of cloth. Don't worry, I fully intend to return it to its rightful owners for a suitable reward.'

'You dunt get a reward for turning in something you've stolen.'

'But I didn't steal it.'

'No one else at the Spaceport could have.'

'Oh. That time! Well, yes, but I meant at first. That was Kaz Phaath yil Frakmo.' The Hindu woman pronounces the name carefully, as if committing it to memory. 'The gods know why, since she seems to want it back now. All I wanted was to honor a dead friend and make a small profit.' She sighs and holds the tube out. 'Instead, I find myself involved with the police for the first time in my life. Go ahead and arrest me, Officer. I won't give you any trouble.'

'There's no need to call me Officer,' Lacey says. 'I'm not a cop. I'm Bobbie Lacey. Heard of me?'

'Yes. Take it back, please. Get it away from me.'

'Gladly.' Lacey takes the tube in her free hand and pauses, waving it in the woman's direction. 'The police probably want to talk to you, but what the hell.' She pockets the laser pistol.

The woman smiles, sighs, and clutches the bag tighter against her side.

'What have you got in there?' Lacey says. 'Looks like a lot of cash.'

'It is. I'll split with you if you let me go.'

'I dunt take bribes, either. Call it your reward. If the cops want you, they can look for you.' Lacey takes a few steps backward to get *iLeijchwen* out of her reach, just in case this docility proves fake.

'Do me a favor?' the woman says. 'Tell the carlis to get that accursed rag off this planet.'

'Dunt worry about that.'

'Thank you. For everything.' With that she turns and hobbles away.

Lacey watches until she disappears through the red arch, then turns and trots back across the lawn to Jack. Nunks is sitting on the grass with Jack's head in his lap, his hands resting on Jack's temples. Jack grins at her.

'Beats whatever that damn drug is,' he whispers. 'Hey, you got it?'

'Oh yeah.' Lacey holds up the tube. 'Looks like we're not going to have a war after all. Now where the hell is Bates?'

Bates followed Izzy's trail through broken shrubbery for a couple of hundred yards, heading deep into the park. Finally, just past a statue of some past president of the Republic, he catches up with Zizzistre,

341

who has turned around and started toward him. He limps badly with every step.

'What happened?' Bates snaps.

'They got these little wire loop fences in these goddamn flower beds,' Izzy says. 'She jumped over them. I dint.'

'Got it. I take it you lost her?'

'She had a skimmer. Parked on the other side of these here bushes. I got a couple of shots off and scorched the paint, but I couldn't stop her.'

'Not your fault, Izzy. You did what you could.' Bates puts his pistol away and unhooks his comm unit from his belt. 'I'll call the skimmer's description in. Maybe someone can run her down. Ah shit! I wanted a few private words with her before her people take her apart for a wall-hanging.'

As quickly as Izzy can manage while leaning on the chief, they walk back through the shrubbery to the lawn where Bates left Mulligan. By now Mulligan is sitting up with Nunks beside him, and Lacey stands nearby. She hails Bates by waving something at him – a clear plastic tube.

'Jeezchrise!' Bates says. 'Is that—'

'Sure is.' Lacey is grinning. 'She must have dropped it when she ran.'

Izzy whoops and flips his tail in the air, then swears when his weight comes down on the injured foot.

'Well, we've got the most important thing,' Bates says, 'but I still wish I could have arrested her myself.'

'You still can,' Mulligan says suddenly. 'Catch her your own self, I mean.' Behind him, Nunks nods. 'I can, like, really *feel* her now, I dunt even have to try hard or nothing. She be in a skimmer, and like, I can see what she done sees from the window, Chief. If you wanna go after her—'

'Hell, yes! Know where she's going?'

Mulligan frowns for a moment. 'Home, but she heading downtown. That all I can get, and Nunks, too, this real strong home feel, all mixed up with a buncha other real bad stuff.'

'Home. The Embassy?' Bates says.

Mulligan shrugs. 'No can tell, you know? She so mixed up she aint

342

thinking real clear. But she be wanting home so bad, I be kinda surprised you no can feel it yourself.'

'Well, I dunt feel anything, but the Embassy is Con soil legally and in every other way, so I'll risk guessing. Come on, let's go. Izzy, call for backup here. Send a squad to a position about a block south of the Embassy. Just in case.'

'Nunks, he gonna stay here,' Jack says. 'I dunt need his help this time. I, like, know this donna now. And he dunt like wild skimmer rides.'

With Lacey in the back seat and Jack in the front, Bates lifts off and glides in a long circle to head back downtown. As soon as they're on course, he hits the comm and describes the Toyota for a second time.

'All squads, do *not* attempt to stop suspect vehicle. If suspect vehicle is spotted, report location immediately and follow at a distance. Repeat, do not apprehend. Suspect is a member of Confederate legation.' He hits the flashers. 'Second order: all points crackdown on exit routes. Emergency rating: red. Keep the suspect within the city.'

Once his officers answer him, Bates flips on the siren. The skimmer rockets upwards as he puts the controls on manual and hits top speed.

Blind, blind, so blind. Kaz Phaath drives slowly, erratically, dipping too close to the ground at moments, though the skimmer's autosafe control always kicks in. Her mind returns again and again to the image of Ka Prelandi, so like and yet unlike the human spectrum-adjusted renditions of *iLeijchwen.* No wonder Gri Nerosi reacted with such horror when she made her obscene proposal, no wonder all carlis have reacted with equal horror. She never understood, she who prided herself so much on her understanding of her people. Her people. She has betrayed both her peoples, carlis and humans, in her blindness.

So simple, she thought: blame Martinelli for the theft of *iLeijchwen,* and the Confederation would finally lose patience with the human-dominated Republic before the addition of the Enzebbe strengthens it. The universe would be a safer place with humanity under carli guidance. Only the reality hadn't been simple at all, her plan has failed, and her beloved Confederation faces war with the wretched Alliance.

The image swims in front of her eyes again. *iLeijchwen* means more than any silly human symbol could. She knows now how deeply it embodies the Pack, the light of the eyes of the entire race. So very blind – she pushes aside as unimportant the question of why she now can see. She also refuses to think about how she knows, beyond question, that Al Bates will find it and keep it safe.

Death will never redeem her disgrace, but it will at least end it. She shifts into the fast lane but keeps within the municipal speed codes. Being stopped for a traffic violation now would ruin what little she can salvage from the ruins.

Home. The Embassy is all the home she now has. Once there, she will end her disgrace.

As he pushes the skimmer to top speed, Bates wonders why he's bothering with this case. Diplomatic immunity protects Kaz Phaath from Republic justice, but she can never escape her own people, who will deal with her more harshly than the Republic would. But he wants the personal satisfaction of turning her over to Ka Pral, along with *iLeijchwen*, their goddamned artifact and their home-grown criminal, all in a tidy packet.

Reasonable feelings for the Chief of the Polar City Police Department to have, he thinks, just as a matter of professional pride, but in his heart he knows that the private feelings of Al Bates the man are goading him. He wishes he could talk with her as Kaz Varesh does. *Did she mean any of it?* he wonders, *all those things she said to me*? Even as the question forms in his mind, he wonders if he'll ever know the answer.

'Jack?' Bates says. 'We on target?'

'You bet, Chief. But she got a good head start.'

'Yeah, well, that's a cop's life for you. Jeezus, I keep thinking she's getting one last laugh on me, the conniving little bitch.'

'I dunt feel that in her mind.'

'Yeah?' Bates glances in to the rearview mirror and sees Lacey leaning forward, all attention.

'Yeah,' Jack says. 'She done thought bout you, but she was, like, sad. S'funny, but I dunt hate her no more. Kinda like, I hit her so hard I dunt gotta hate her no more.'

344

'Loco?' Lacey asks.

'Nah, she no be crazy, no like that old Miz Krupp or nothing. Anyways, she no was loco before. She be pretty close to it now, though.'

Bates flips his comm to another channel. 'Palmer?'

'Right here, Chief.' The comm officer's voice crackles from the speaker.

'You let the Embassy know their runaway's coming home?'

'Already taken care of, Chief.'

'Muy bueno,' Bates says, and clicks off. 'Okay,' he says to Lacey and Mulligan. 'It dunt matter now if we catch up before she get there, she's going to have a welcoming committee waiting. Wait till you meet Kaz Varesh, Lacey. She reminds me of you, only worse.'

Lacey laughs under her breath.

'Home – home – home,' Mulligan whispers. 'That be what she thinking, Chief, but she got some weird idea of home.'

'Like what?'

'I dunno. Just something weird. Hey, she be landing that skimmer of hers.'

Bates mutters something foul under his breath. Ahead, under the pale brown haze of midday, loom the towers of downtown. When they reach the plaza, he hops the speeder over Embassy Row and drops toward the quiet street behind at emergency speed. Mulligan yelps and clutches at the seat.

A dark red Toyota is just pulling in. Behind it high iron security gates are rising from the ground like a ring of black fangs. *Almost, almost—* Bates puts the speeder down hard, flips the switch to ground-mode and accelerates in one motion, trying to ram their way in. Too late – the front of the skimmer crumples as the gates close in front of it. Bates slews the nose around. They slide sideways into the gates and stop.

'Jeezchrise!' Lacey snaps. 'Jack, you okay?'

Bates pays no attention to the answer. He flings the door open, twists out of his safety harness, and slides out of the car. *iLeijchwen* he carries inside his shirt, better than a key to the Embassy. He flings himself against the gates and hangs on with both hands. He can see the red skimmer, parked at an angle across the circular drive with one door hanging open.

'Kaz Phaath!' Bates shouts. 'Look, I've got *iLeijchwen*, it's safe!'

'I know you have it, Bates.' Kaz Phaath gets out of the car, watching him as he clings to the security gates. She has stripped off her suncloak and wears nothing but a plain gray servant's jumpsuit, loose and pouchy with pockets, though she carries her robes bunched in one hand. 'I cannot tell you how grateful I am that you saved it from that wretched gambler.'

'I have a few questions—'

'No. You are a man of honor, Al Bates. Allow me mine.' She raises her face to the harsh sun, and says, to herself rather than to him, 'At least I will have the light for my going.'

She puts on her long blue robes. With a flash of metal in the sunlight she pulls something from one pocket and fastens it on her right hand. He recognizes a set of Claws and sees what he should have seen a long time earlier.

'Dunt, Dammit!' Bates shakes the gates until his hands ache.

'It is my right.' She turns and walks toward the garden at the north end of the building, filled with the plants of her homeworld.

'Wait!' He howls out the word. 'You owe me some answers.'

She never looks back. Bates tells himself that he should have landed inside the gates, diplomatic protocols be damned. When he looks up at the building, he can see figures at windows, watching. Kaz Phaath reaches the edge of the bluish-green garden and stands for a moment, back to him, staring up at the sun, her arms outstretched as if she would hug the light to her. Slowly she lowers her right arm. With a glint of light her right hand slashes sideways, once, only once, and she collapses. Blood, scarlet in the light, pools around her corpse.

Bates lets go of the gate. His hands are bleeding, he realizes, as if with her suicide they have something in common again. Lacey walks up next to him and hands him a wad of tissue. He clasps it between his palms.

'Well, hell,' he says. 'I've seen lots of sentients get killed, but I've never seen a suicide before. Makes you sick.'

'I know you're pissed at her,' Lacey says. 'But underneath that—'

'Yeah, yeah. I won't lie and tell you I dunt care.'

'Okay. Jack's passed out. When she cut her throat I think he felt it.'

Bates grunts with a shake of his head. Distantly he hears sirens coming.

'My officers are on their way,' he says, 'we'll take good care of him.'

Out in the blue-tinged garden, carlis are walking, moving silently toward the body that lies under the tall alien trees. The front door of the Embassy opens, and Ka Pral walks out. Bates lets the wad of tissue drop and reaches into his shirt for *iLeijchwen*, safe in its plastoclear tube. He holds it up like a beacon. Ka Pral hurries over, then puts his hands together and bows.

'Sandra Wentworth Kaz Phaath yil Frakmo is dead.' Ka Pral says. 'As she told you, my friend, it was her right. She was also most correct in stating that you have earned the honor of returning *iLeijchwen*. I am deeply pleased that you will complete the redemption of her honor.'

Bates stares at the tube and the ugly brown scrap of cloth inside, then thrusts it towards Ka Pral through the iron bars of the gate. 'For her honor. For both our people's honor. And for Ka Jekhonas's life.'

Ka Pral takes it in both hands, then steps back and bows to Bates, the full bow of deep reverence. Out in the garden the carlis kneel in a circle around Kaz Phaath, then bend forward like the petals of a flower closing.

Chapter Fifteen

Twenty-ninth Stember, almost the end of the month, and there's not going to be any war. Rosa grins when she looks at her familiar black clock, gleaming above her on the nightstand. She stretches against the comfort of real cotton sheets, then lies in bed for a moment gazing up at the white ceiling. A nice plain white ceiling, hers, the way she likes it, and good plain wood furniture, no themes, no frills, no colour accents. *Good to be home, damn!* She gets out of bed and rubs her bare feet on the luxury of her Persian-style carpet, woven from real polypropylene, just like they had back on Old Earth.

After she showers, she dresses in a pair of old jeans and the brand-new T-shirt that proclaims the Bears as All-Hagar champions. Until today she'd put off wearing it, though she can't say why or why her mood's changed, for that matter. She glances at the window, turning transparent as the sun outside sets. Aunt Lucy will probably be up by now. When Rosa walks into the kitchen, her house comp's sensors swivel to greet her.

'Start some coffee,' Rosa says, 'then get Aunt Lucy on the comm.'

'Yes, Programmer.' Her unit sounds young. 'I will do this.'

In the unit's polished screen Rosa can see her hair: a damp mess. She runs her fingers through it a couple of times. Onscreen an image suddenly brightens. Lucy's hair, rumpled nearly vertical, needs work even more than Rosa's.

'Dios! You got any idea what time it be, chica?' Lucy says between yawns.

'Yeah, I know, but I got things to do. Been sitting on my butt too damn long, you know?'

'Well, gracias a Dios!' Aunt Lucy says. 'Been wondering when you was gonna wake up, chica, and I dunt mean getting out of bed.'

'Yeah, you was right, Coach. We lost the Series and that hurts like dammitall, but even if we won the season'd still be over. Like you always told us, if we win we just gotta do it all over again. And if we lose, we just have to—'

'Wait till next season!' Lucy joins her, and they both laugh.

'So you finally remembered, huh?' Lucy goes on. 'Bout time, but I dunt blame you. Losing the Series, I mean, jeez. But life goes on, huh?'

'Yeah, it got a habit of doing that.'

'So, how you figure you gonna get on with living today? And how come you waking me up so damn early?'

'Gonna go test drive some skimmers. I need a new one.'

'Yeah, I heard about that. Too bad. Sure, might be fun skimmer-shopping with you. No like I gonna be doing it for myself any time soon.' Aunt Lucy grins. 'Got anything in mind yet?'

'Yeah.' Rosa smiles around another yawn. 'Thought I might get me a nice green Jag.'

Chief Al Bates sits in his cluttered little office and stares at his AI's screen, divided into a variety of lists: reports to read, meetings to attend, officers to reprimand, officers to praise, budget items to be vetoed or approved. With a shake of his head he gets up and walks to the window. Outside, Polar City's sky flames blue and silver over the towers of downtown.

Bates reaches into his shirt pocket and takes out the note he's carried around for days. Kaz Phaath left a formal signed confession in her office, detailing her approach to Gri Nerosi, her dealings with Moses Oliver and Jay Gagne, and above all her reasons for the scheme. But she also left a personal note for him. He reads it once again; he can hear her voice in his mind, saying the words.

I don't regret my attempt, Bates, for I do most truly fear your Republic. If only you were more typical of our species! I should have expected it to turn out like this. I never have been any good at chess, or *griish*, or strategy tests. Typical human, I suppose, attempting something to which I am not suited by nature. I never will understand why my government failed to act, but I hope they were correct. I don't want posthumous vindication; sometimes it's much better to be wrong.

349

I honour you more deeply than any human male I've ever met. Perhaps in fairness to you I should wish we had never met, but I can't. I'm very glad we did. Goodbye, Bates.

Very carefully he folds the note and slips it into his pocket. The AI buzzes.

'Chief? Message from Reception. Some carlis want to see you. A sentient named Ka Pral's in charge.'

'Jeezus! Here? Tell them to come straight up. Oh, and get someone to bring in a couple of extra chairs.'

The chairs and the carlis arrive simultaneously: Kaz Varesh and Ka Glon in their tight black jackets and Ka Pral in his sweeping green robes. Bates picks up a pile of papers and data cubes from the middle of the floor and dumps them into a corner on top of his battered suncloak to make room for the chairs. Kaz Varesh and Ka Pral sit; Ka Glon stands in the doorway as if on guard.

'Honoured guests,' Bates says, 'my humble office is graced by your presence.'

'Quite the contrary, my dear Bates,' Kaz Varesh says. 'You honour us by agreeing to see us at such short notice.'

Ka Pral nods his agreement. 'Our affairs of late have placed far too many demands on your valuable time, I fear.'

Bates smiles thinly at the understatement.

'Ka Glon and myself will be leaving your planet today,' Kaz Varesh goes on, 'returning *iLeijchwen* to aggKar. I wished to see you once more before I left, to personally express our appreciation.' Kaz Varesh sketches a bow from her seat. 'I believe the ambassador has already expressed our gratitude formally.'

'He did indeed,' Bates says. 'In fact, you might be pleased to know that we've framed his letter and hung it in the lobby downstairs. It's next to the stone plaque, the Honour Roll of officers killed in the line of duty.'

All three carlis bow to him, their mouths a little open in respect.

'Ka Jekhonas has honoured us more than we deserve,' Bates says.

'Surely not,' Kaz Varesh says. 'You have shown yourself to be a true professional.'

'A professional in law enforcement, at any rate, just as the worthy

350

Ka Jekhonas is a professional in the field of diplomacy. His presence adorns our poor city. Or so I may hope.'

Kaz Varesh's left ear twitches slightly. 'Have no fear, Bates, he will continue in his post. Had *iLeijchwen* not been recovered . . . But it was, and the Embassy's honour has been saved along with his life.'

'I'm glad,' Bates says simply.

'So are we all,' Ka Pral puts in. 'Very glad.'

'I assume you know about Erik Royall defecting to the Republic?' Bates directs this at Kaz Varesh.

'Indeed, yes. Your Mr Akeli has shared some of his files with us. The H'Allevae will be hard put to pretend innocence after this. *Their* ambassador has been recalled, I understand.' She tosses her head in the equivalent of a fierce smile. 'Along with their warships.'

'From what I know of the Hoppers, their idea of recall is pretty permanent.'

Kaz Varesh bobs her head repeatedly.

'But they did not, in fact, precipitate the crisis.'

Ka Pral lowers his head, the carli equivalent of a red face. 'To think that one of our own could come so close to destroying our friendship.'

'But in the end, she failed.' Bates hesitates, gauging how much he dares say. 'I'm grateful that our friendship gave us both enough patience to wait for that end.'

'Indeed.' Kaz Varesh leans forward. 'Do you hate her, Chief Bates?'

'No. I'm glad she failed, but I can't hate her. She was a remarkable woman. Maybe because she was almost carli. Except she was too human, she no could see *iLeijchwen*. Too human, and not human enough.'

'Too human, at any rate. She actually thought that Gri Nerosi's addiction to gambling would make him willing to take *iLeijchwen*.' Kaz Varesh pauses. 'She did us a favour, you know. We had never seriously considered the implications of our human citizens' inability to experience any of the *leijchwen*. Our psychologists will be looking for a substitute now.'

'I'll wish them luck.' Bates considers for a moment, but this is no time to raise the question of *iLeijchwen*'s psychic component. Later, perhaps, he and Ka Pral will discuss it over a glassful of some carli liquor or other. 'If an outsider may be permitted to inquire,' Bates says instead, 'what's going to happen to her remains?'

'You are no outsider, Bates,' Ka Pral says firmly. 'Not in this matter, at any rate. Both Gri Nerosi and Kaz Phaath have been interred in burial slabs, and they will return home to aggKar with Kaz Varesh and Ka Glon.'

'On the same ship as *iLeijchwen*,' Kaz Varesh adds. 'A very high honour indeed.'

'Well, bueno. So I guess that wraps it up, huh? Only loose end is that gambler, Jay Gagne. We never did catch her, dint even find out her real name, but we will. Some day.'

'I wish you good hunting,' Kaz Varesh says.

Ka Pral adds, 'According to your own newscasts, Senator Martinelli faces possible, ah, indictment? Is that a special punishment for those who abuse their responsibilities?'

'You could say that,' Bates begins, then stops as he realizes Ka Pral is indulging in his most human-like habit and making a joke. 'The Humanitas Party is disintegrating like an overcooked sandworm. Looks like the Enzebbe treaty will be an easy pass now.'

'Well, I'm glad of the first of those two assertions,' Ka Pral's ears go to to full extension. 'And oddly enough, I can see value in the second as well.'

When Ka Pral stands, Kaz Varesh follows suit and ushers Ka Glon ahead of her out into the hall. Ka Pral lingers behind for a moment.

'A war between our people and your own honoured government would have been a matter of deep regret. Humans such as yourself give me reason to hope that Kaz Phaath's fears will prove groundless.' He glances around the office. 'It's a pity your own government doesn't honour you with the proper signs of rank.'

'You know something?' Bates suddenly grins. 'I've never even asked for a better office. Maybe I should.'

'Indeed. You might be surprised by the result.'

Bates sees Ka Pral out into the hall, then returns to his lists. As he sits down at his desk, the AI beeps twice.

'Chief? I have a priority reminder. The security preparations for the Mayor's speech next week . . .'

Bates waves a hand in front of its sensors. 'In a minute, in a minute. Tell me, do you have a name?'

'Certainly, sir.' The unit sounds honestly pleased to be asked. 'I am BXQ-126523.'

'Uh, do you like that name?'

'I have no feeings as such, sir.'

'Yeah? Well, do you think that name represents who you are? Adequately, I mean.'

'No, sir, I don't.'

'Then we've got to come up with something better. You start thinking of a name that seems more logical to you, okay? Meanwhile, get me Dr Carol. Should be at the clinic, this time of night.'

Bates leans back in his chair with a sigh. It's going to take him a long time to recover lost ground, but he's thought of the perfect opening. When Carol appears onscreen, he speaks fast before she can yell at him.

'I called to apologize. I'm sorry. Okay?'

For a long moment she stares at him, her mouth set in a little twist. 'Oh,' she says at last. 'Okay. Start now.'

Bates smiles at her. *Thank god!* he thinks. *At least she's human.*

In the Mbayes' yellow and white living room Mulligan sits in a striped chair and considers Yosef. The pitcher paces back and forth in front of the hologram of the Old Earth lawns with their castle in the distant mists.

'It be, like, good to see you moving around,' Mulligan says. 'But how you feel, without the pills?'

'All chewed up inside.' Yosef comes over and sits down opposite him. 'I don't care. I'd rather be screaming like a madman than so doped up I don't know my own name. You know something, Jack? I thought once that maybe I could travel to aggKar and check myself into one of those carli-run clinics, the ones where they destroy psychic functions. But no. I know what it would feel like, now, to be drugged up. I know what it would feel like to have part of my mind cut out. And I'm damned if I'm going to do that.'

'Yeah? I gotta cheer you on, dude. But what about the baseball? What about the lying?'

'That's what's chewing me up inside.'

'Kinda thought so. 'Nother thing, too. You never gonna feel right till you, like, go to the Institute, get some real training. It be like getting fat and out of shape. You gotta work out with your psi, too.'

'I thought you hated that place.'

'Yeah, but I was pretty dumb when I was there, you know? Dint want to be there, dint want to be noplace near there. All I could see was *this*.' Jack touches the red P on his cheek. 'Course, the big league scouts, they went away when they seen it, too.'

'Yeah, that's the problem, isn't it?' Yosef winces. 'I know it's only a matter of time till someone else finds out and I probably should just tell the truth, but I can't. I keep hoping I'll find some other way, some way that'll let me keep pitching.'

'Yeah, well, I think I maybe figured something out.' Mulligan grins; he's been waiting all night to tell Joe this. 'You seen that special on Channel Twelve the other night, bout baseball back on Old Earth?'

Yosef shakes his head. 'No, we were at the doctor. She says Marisa's doing fine, by the way.'

'Bueno. But this special, it got me thinking.' Mulligan leans forward. 'You ever heard of a dude named Jackie Robinson, back in the old days? He was, like, this real hot hitter, real gonzo ballplayer, and he was black. Back then, los Blancos was the only ones who played. A colour bar, only backwards. He was the first black in the majors back then, and it was, like, a real big deal when they let him play. I mean, the Blancos booed and yelled crap at him. I mean, like, can you believe it? The owners, they had this agreement, sort of, all unofficial, they dint want no blacks playing major league ball. Only this dude, he was real good, and this one manager signed him anyways and, well, they done broke the colour bar.'

'You mean they treated black players back then same way you psychics get treated now?'

'Us psychics,' Mulligan says.

Yosef freezes, but only for a moment. 'Yeah,' he says. 'Us psychics.'

'Betcha if you go public, maybe get some holocaster to interview you or something, and keep talking about how you love the game and how that Robinson dude broke the colour bar on Old Earth and everything—'

'Then maybe I'll get to be a psychic Jackie Robinson. Is that what you had in mind, Jack?'

'Yep. You know, Robinson, he be the first, but they got lots of black players after him. Baseball, it already *know* how damn good you be, you done pitched a winning Series game, so you got a real good chance, I bet. And if you break the psi bar, maybe some day I finally get a chance to play in los grandes.'

Yosef gazes at the hologram. Mulligan sits quietly, letting him think.

'Sounds good to me,' Yosef says at last. 'Who knows, maybe we'll even be on the same team some day.'

'Hey, we gonna be on the same team faster'n that. I be playing for the Big Shots now, y'know? Aunt Lucy, she need another pitcher.'

Yosef laughs, a real, deep, honest laugh, his first in weeks. 'That sounds good, too. But look, I have to talk it over with Marisa and Georgy before I do anything.'

'You bet.' Mulligan stands up. 'I gonna go home so you can do that. But you better call me, like, later on tonight.'

'I will.' Yosef stands up and offers his hand. 'Let's shake on it.'

Dressed in travelling clothes, a flared blue tunic over narrow matching pants, Sarojini Ranjit walks slowly and carefully through the departures lounge at the spaceport. When she finds a chair beside the rank of tall windows, she sits down, also slowly and carefully , wincing at the dull ache in her side. Her cousin Bala, a medic at Polar City General, assured her that her wounds can handle the acceleration of lift-off. Like all of her male relatives, he lives in terror of her mother's sharp tongue, so he asked no awkward questions when she appeared at his clinic with her side slashed and an odd story about muggers.

She sighs and relaxes into the cushions. *Poor Moses!* she thinks. *If only he could have seen my revenge for his death!* How lovely that Sandy is dead, too. Eventually she'll need to replace him, but for now she is taking an overdue holiday on the proceeds of his last big deal. Once she got a chance to count it, she found Sandy's buy-out quite adequate and all of it is hers.

Gradually other passengers arrive in the lounge. On the far wall an enormous three-dee screen blares as a security guard switches it on to keep them happy. Sarojini watches a few minutes of a repeat broadcast of the ballplayer's press conference. Yosef Mbaye, a fresh red P tattooed on his face, earnestly assures the interviewer that his psychic abilities will not affect the game, cannot possibly affect it, in fact. After a moment, Sarojini stops listening. Water yacht racing – now that's a sport, she thinks. She pulls a colourful brochure from her bag and re-reads it. She's picked a good time to visit Sarah. The Republic's Cup race will be starting in two weeks. She settles in her chair and loses herself in dreams of open water.

In the middle of the third inning, Lacey returns to her seat in the Park and Rec Stadium. She hands Rosa Wallace her soda and sits down gingerly – she's balancing an over-full cup of beer. Since no one's taken the seat in front of her, she puts her feet up on its back then looks around for the soya-dog vendor. No sign of him yet. She'll get a dog later, with plenty of mustard. After the disaster of the Galactic Series, she wondered if she'd really enjoy the game again, but a couple of innings of open skies, the crisp sound of ball meeting leather or wood, the smell of synthigrass and junk food have rekindled her old love.

Cheers erupt as the Big Shots' new pitcher strikes out the last batter of the inning. Yosef followed his retirement from the major leagues with the announcement that he was signing on with Kelly's Bar and Grill Big Shots. *Wonder when Kelly and Aunt Lucy gonna touch ground again*, Lacey thinks. *Signing Jack and Joe both like that.*

'Look at Lucy,' Rosa says. 'I aint seen her so happy since I asked her to come to Sarah.'

'Of course,' Lacey says. 'With two real quality players on her team, she's going to murderize the competition.'

Rosa's smile slips. 'You think Yosef, he got a chance of getting back into the majors? That Robinson dude had a real tough time, and he weren't no different than any other human being. I gotta admit, someone who can read minds, they like creep me out a little.'

'I know what you mean, but my AI Buddy says it'll only take two years, tops. Who knows, maybe somebody'll sign Jack first. Maybe they'll both be playing with you a few years from now – unless you've retired.'

'I sure dunt plan to change careers before then!'

'Oh, I dunno. Sometimes changing careers isn't so bad.'

Lacey is thinking of the letter she received from Admiral Wazerzis as she was leaving for the park. Even Iron Snout can't get Lacey back into the Navy, apparently, but she no longer cares. She's home, and she's staying.

Raucous cheers break out as Mulligan steps up to the plate for his first turn at bat. She can feel his grin from here as he waits for the pitch. She slouches down in her seat, crosses her feet at the ankles and sips her beer. It's going to be a great season.